SIXTY-THREE CLOSURE

Anthony Frewin

SIXTY-THREE CLOSURE

President Kennedy's assassination was the
work of magicians. It was a stage trick,
complete with accessories and false
mirrors, and when the curtain fell
the actors, and even the scenery,
disappeared.

– James Hepburn *Farewell America* (1968)

NO EXIT PRESS

First published in Great Britain by No Exit Press, 1998.

This edition published in 1998 by No Exit Press,
18 Coleswood Road, Harpenden, Herts, AL5 1EQ.

http://www.noexitpress.demon.co.uk

A CIP catalogue record for this book is available from the British Library.

ISBN 1 901982-04-1 Sixty-Three Closure

1 3 5 7 9 10 8 6 4 2

Typography by the author.
Composed in Palatino by Koinonia, Manchester
Printed and bound in Great Britain by
Caledonian International Book Manufacturing Ltd, Glasgow

FOR RUBY JEAN FREWIN

However imperfect and unfinished it may be, it is my contribution
to that final record of fully ascertained fact which, as Bacon observed,
is a work to be done 'by many and not by one, and in the succession of
ages, though not in the hour-glass of one man's life'.

– Reginald L. Hine *The History of Hitchin* (1929)

SIXTY-THREE CLOSURE

ARE YOU BEING REAL?

YOU PICKED UP THE NEWSPAPERS yesterday and read about me, didn't *you*?

Disregard that stuff. It was all lies. All of it. The 'quotes' attributed to me in the tabloids were invented and the speculations in the 'quality' papers that I'd salted away a fortune in Holland and Switzerland were fantasy.

So, if we know where it ends or, rather, where it has got to now, then the next inevitable questions are – why and how did it begin?

I'll say it began with three photographs …

The three photographs.

The three photographs.

That's when it really began.

But before that there was the telephone call, and before that there was the green paint. That's the true beginning for me, the real genesis, as those were the last moments of my *un*-knowing.

The green paint.

I could hear it peeling off the walls.

The whole room was covered in this light green paint, including a bulwark of a radiator, probably dating from the early 1930s, situated under the window. The sole window.

All green. Bilious green.

It must have been the Party's Paint of the Month some time way back when there was a Party. Even the floor was green – some ersatz linoleum: chill and reflective and unforgiving.

The hotel room was like a cell in a mental institution … and, indeed, it was a mental asylum before it became the Hotel Pauli, or so the girl in the cigarette kiosk downstairs said in her fractured English. And she should know, being the daughter of some highly placed but now disgraced Party flunkey.

The window overlooks a tram wrecking yard that is encircled by drab commercial office buildings put up in the 1960s. Beyond these I can just make out the twin spires of the cathedral of SS Peter and Paul.

The Hotel Pauli. Brno's worst hotel, I'd guess. The production company back in London had said they'd booked me into a 'pretty good place'. In fact, a shit heap of a place. The Czech Republic's second largest city couldn't do much worse.

January here … very cold … but plenty of cheap vodka. A bottle a day is dead easy. At weekends I can double that, almost.

I don't piss around any more. No glasses or paper cups. I take it straight from the bottle, whenever I'm alone that is, or if nobody is looking.

I've spent the last two months out here scouting locations for an American-financed feature film with the title *Blue Lou*. We'll do the interiors back at Pinewood Studios and the exteriors here. All I need is the OK on the last lot of photos I sent back and I'm out of here … but until then, I'll drink myself insensible. There isn't a lot else to do. And it's so fucking cold. And there's another reason too – I'm holding a one-man wake for Dizzy Gillespie who died last week.

I take another hit from the bottle.

There's a knock on the door. A hard crack, like a Sid Catlett snare drum rimshot. Insistent.

'Yeah?'

The door creaks open. It's Ernie, the floor porter. Ernie

isn't his name, I just call him that. He's Jiri or something. He's in his mid-sixties and looks on a good day like someone who has spent the last week sleeping rough. On a bad day he looks like one of the mummified monks in the Capuchin tombs downtown.

Ernie stares at me from the doorway, then glances down at the vodka bottle. He knows I drink and I know he drinks.

He takes two steps forward, removes a cigarette from his lips with his thumb and forefinger, coughs and says *Tele-fon, tele-fon*! And continues to stand there transfixed, like a shop front mannikin.

Díky, I say to Ernie. Then I take a swig of vodka and follow him out and down the corridor. An interminable corridor with grubby carpet running the whole length and framed photographic portraits of long-forgotten Czech notables on the wall. And, like the rest of the hotel, it always smells of cabbage.

We arrive at Ernie's under-the-stairs sort of office.

The heavy black handset of the phone is on the desk. Ernie points to it and says again, *Tele-fon*. I get the message.

This is the call that puts me back on the plane to London, thank God. Out of here and gone.

'Harry?' I say.

'Christopher?'

'Uh-huh. Harry?'

'No, Christopher. It's Dick.'

'Dick?'

'It's me, yes.'

Dick? My mate in Hitchin? My mate I grew up with? 'What are you doing calling me out here?'

'I needed to talk to you … something has happened.'

'What? Barbara OK? You OK?'

'No, everything's fine that way. I need your help … on something.'

'And what's that, dear boy?'

'When are you back here?'

[3]

'Soon, I hope. I'm waiting for a call. Next few days. Why?'

'I'm being followed.'

'What?'

Is Dick having a mid-life breakdown or what? I call Ernie who is sitting the other side of the desk making roll-up cigarettes for his little tin case and point to his bottle of vodka on the filing cabinet. He obligingly hands it to me. I need a drink.

'Followed, huh?'

I take a big swig that gives a burning feeling to my lips and throat. Strong spirit this.

'That's right, I'm being *followed*.'

'You been giving it to somebody else's wife, huh?'

'No. This is serious.'

What? My old friend Dick North who still lives in the town we grew up in, who is a headteacher and an active member of the local antiquarian society, who married the boring Barbara Bradley back in the early 1970s and who hasn't fucked another woman since (save perhaps Rachel Green, Laura's friend, a couple of years ago at a party in Letchworth), who is just about to complete volume one of *An Ichonography of Hitchin*.

He is being followed?

'Tell me something, Dick – *who* is following you?'

I wave the bottle at Ernie who raises his tumbler full of vodka. Cheers to both of us!

'They've got something to do with … they're serious.'

Who is following him? Dwarfs, or little green men from Mars, or the Illuminati, or the Freemasons, or Nazis from South America, or the CIA or KGB (whatever remains of them), or even agents of the Knights Templar?

'Dick, is this some kind of put-on or what?'

'No, it isn't.'

'You need, Dick, a damn good drink. Know that?'

'Listen, I've found something out. Things aren't what they appear to be. There's something strange going on.'

'Are you being real?' I said.

There was a lengthy silence the other end of the phone and then I heard a *Yes*, a long sigh, and the line went dead.

I took another mouthful of Ernie's vodka. This time I noticed it was flavoured. Similar to but not cherry.

'Good stuff, Ernie, good stuff,' I say, pointing at the bottle.

Ernie gave me one of his rare toothless smiles and nodded his head and said, 'Eh, gooood stoufff.'

'Very good stuff, yeah.'

'Gooood stoufff.'

Ernie waved me to sit down and then produced a small glass from his desk. I handed him the bottle and he filled this glass and his to the brim. I gave him a Marlboro and took one myself.

'Cheers!'

'Chhh-earrrs!'

I downed the glass in one and then saw something on the wall behind the desk that I hadn't noticed before. An old photograph, cut out of a magazine and taped to the wall, of Premier Khrushchev and President Kennedy shaking hands, way back in the good old Manichaean days of the Cold War.

'Chhh-earrrs!' said Ernie.

[2]

I got the call from Harry. The photographs were fine and I was free to return to London. I flew back but I can remember nothing of the flight. I can't even remember leaving the hotel. I was in an alcoholic daze the whole time. Totally out of it.

I started to come to in a taxi cab on the Westway some-where, but even then the rain and the greyness conspired to make me think I was still somewhere in the Czech Republic, rather than in London. I looked down at my lap expecting to find a Nikon cradled in my hands and instead

I found an empty bottle of vodka. Nothing else. *Sic transit*.

As soon as I got back to the flat in Tufnell Park I headed for the bathroom and began throwing up – gallons of vodka and bile and God knows what else. I was retching my guts up. I then passed out and remained unconscious until the next day when I awoke to find myself floating in a sea of vomit. It stank. I stank. The whole place stank.

I put the percolator on and began tidying the place up. Then I have a strong coffee and stumble back to the bedroom and fall on the bed and pretty soon I'm asleep.

[3]

The telephone.

It continues ringing and while I know I've got to answer it I cannot move my arms just yet. Give me time.

Somehow I manage to pick it up. 'Hello?'

'Christopher?'

'Yes.'

'It's Laura. You're back. I thought you would have called me.'

'I was going to.'

'When did you arrive?'

'Soon.' What do I mean, soon? I can't even talk straight.

'Soon? What does that mean?'

'I don't mean that … I mean I just got back … you know?'

'Don't you ever listen to your answering machine?'

'I was going to … I –'

'You didn't get my message then?'

'I guess not … yet.'

'Uh-huh.'

'How are you then, Laura?'

'It's about Dick.'

'What about him?'

'He's dead.'

'Dead? Dick? He can't be.'

[6]

'He is. He was found on the tracks near the station. A train had hit him. Last Friday. It's in the papers. Looks like suicide.'

'What happened? How come? I mean ... I can't believe this.'

'He's dead.'

'But why?'

'You tell me. He's dead ... and the funeral is on Monday.'

'I'll come up ... on Saturday. If that's OK with you.'

'Please do.'

'Can I call you back later? I've got to take this on board.'

'Sure.'

I sat there sobbing. Dick North – dead. A friend I'd grown up with and known for forty years. Gone. Just like that.

There's an irritating little itch in the back of my consciousness. Something about Dick and something recent at that. But what? Something in Brno.

My head's caving in with this news. I need a drink. A big drink, but there's fuck all here. I'll call the cab company down the road and ask them to pick up a bottle of Smirnoff for me. They're helpful that way, yeah.

[4]

There was still a pile of mail on the floor in the hall. I gathered it up and glanced through the envelopes. There was nothing that looked interesting. I dumped it all on the kitchen table. It'll have to wait. Screw it.

Then it came to me.

An epiphany over the sink as I filled the kettle. Dick had phoned me while I was in Brno. That was it, wasn't it? He called me and said ... he needed my advice or something. Yeah, he called me while I was waiting to come home, in that poxy little hotel. And he said he was being ... *followed*. I'm sure he did. Yeah. Being followed. I don't remember it clearly, but I remember that. He was being followed by people who had something to do with, what? He didn't say.

Followed though?

I need to speak to Laura.

No, I'll wait. I'll talk to her tomorrow when I see her. Approach it obliquely like. It'll wait. Better to talk to her when we're together. Yeah.

I feel like someone's just stomped on my brain.

CHAPTER ONE

LIKE A WHISPER, A SUSURRUS

145.689MHz is a radio transmission channel reserved for the British security and intelligence services. The channel is continually 'open', broadcasting white 'carrier' noise in which messages are embedded. Other agencies, as remote from the security services as they are from the public, 'hitch' the wavelength for their own use. These hitchers have never been identified.

On Friday, 22 January 1993, at 1640 Zulu the following encrypted transmission was hitched:

'Identify.'

'Bellerophon ... 666B.'

'Location?'

'North Hertfordshire.'

'Proceed.'

'Still active on LANCER grail. Second WAYSIDE passed without incident. Further avenues now open.'

I ARRIVED AT KING'S CROSS station ten minutes before the train was scheduled to leave. I would have driven up but Dennis the Greek down in Camden Town still hadn't put a new clutch in the old Merc even though he'd had it for over two months. Dennis'll do it cheap, but you've got to be patient.

It was a cold Saturday. A penetrating wind. Intermittent rain. A sky full of vast grey and black clouds dramatically changing shape and heaving towards a storm. It reminded me of Prague.

I walked the length of the platform down to the first carriage. It was empty and I got a forward-facing seat on the left side. I took a half bottle of Smirnoff out of my shoulder bag, had a quick glance about to see that I was alone, and had a big hit. The first one of today … aside from a couple of quick nips at breakfast.

Laura thinks I've got a drink problem, but then she thinks anyone who has more than two glasses of white wine a week has a drink problem. I might have a problem and if I do … if I were to have one … as it were, she is not to know that. The thing is I've only got a drink problem if I think I have *and* if I mention it to someone else.

I picked up a copy of *The Independent* back in Tufnell Park. I'll have a quick rifle through it and see if I'm missing anything.

Right, what's in this section? A few book reviews of books you'd never read by reviewers you've never heard of, acres of 'life-style' features and columns, and not much else.

The train pulls out as the storm breaks. Thunderous rain crashes athwart the roof and cascades down the windows.

Squinting out I see through the downpour a high retaining wall built of dark blue engineering bricks. There are whitewashed letters some three metres high arcing down to the right:

MARK THATCHER – WE'LL GET YOU!

I light a cigarette.

There's a piece in the paper here about Bosnia. Skip that. Bill Clinton has only been in the White House three days and they're already evaluating his performance (!). John Major is wittering on about some trade deal. This drug dealer says he is totally innocent and was fitted up by the security services because he knew about some corrupt overseas aid deal involving Thatcher's government that he was going to expose (probably true, but who'd believe a drug dealer?), and now there's a big piece about the health service. Should read that. I read and re-read the opening paragraph and though I recognise the words, the separate individual words, I cannot take in the meaning. There are things dancing about the periphery of my mind now, preoccupying me, making me distracted. Well, not things, but a thing, and not a thing – a person. Dick.

A further couple of hits of vodka disperse some of the unfocused anxiety that seems to be dogging me, but Dick remains.

He phones me up and he obviously needs help. I'm pissed out of my mind and just ass about. I don't take him seriously. The next thing I know he is dead. I should have done something ... but what? Could I have done anything? Could I have brought him back from the brink? I'm never going to know, am I? This is one of those big questions that will dangle there for ever. Unanswerable. Absolutely fucking unanswerable.

There's the stark surprise of it all too. I could tell you fifty people I'd think more likely to commit suicide than Dick. Fifty. Perhaps more. But Dick?

The rain is abating. Through the windows, the drenched fag-ends of London's northerly suburbs. Soon it'll be New Barnet station and then after that the interrupted greenery of Hertfordshire. Only twenty minutes or so and I'll be in Hitchin.

Hitchin.

I remembered now.

Reginald Hine. The historian who had lived in and written a monumental history of the town. Reginald Hine – he committed suicide at Hitchin station too. Back in the late 1940s. He threw himself under a train and that was that. About the year I was born, 1947, the same year Dick was born. Or was it a year or two later? Hine had been a lawyer in the town all his life. He'd written half a dozen or so books including the monumental *History of Hitchin* in two volumes. Then, hey presto, he went and did himself in at the station. They had a big funeral for him in the town and even opened a little park in his memory.

But nobody ever talks about the suicide in the town. That's all been blanked out. You never find any reference to it. A no-go area. I could never find out why he did it.

I wonder if there's some connection between Hine and Dick? Dick had all his books and knew them inside out. Dick was working on his *Ichonography* of the town, treading in the footsteps of Hine, coming into contact with him daily as it were. When Dick was at the end of his tether, did he then decide to emulate Hine's last exit?

As Thomas Nashe might have written, have you to Hitchin station and end it all?

We'll be there in a few minutes. I have a final taster of vodka and pack my stuff back into the bag. Outside there's an enveloping wintry gloom.

I'm coming back to Hitchin at the end of January and I'm here because my best friend committed suicide.

[2]

I'm the only person to get off at Hitchin. I stand there motionless as the train pulls out. The station is deserted apart from a couple of young kids huddled together sharing a cigarette on a seat over on the down platform. The sound of the train dies away.

Behind that fence there, more than thirty years ago, you would have found Dick and me trainspotting. We'd be at it all day Saturday and Sunday, evenings whenever we could make it, and certainly throughout the day during the school holidays.

Those were the days of steam trains, about 1959/60. They've gone now … but memories … even the aristocratic A4 class 4-6-2 'Pacifics' designed by Sir Nigel Gresley with the sloping fronts and streamlined sides that would hurtle up to Scotland with a rake of fourteen or more passenger carriages … gone, like Dick himself now.

Those days, I thought, would last for ever, I really did. Adult life was a million light-years away. We'd be having fun for ever. There was an eternity of trainspotting in front of us. There'd always be steam trains, there'd always be that old guy whose name I can't even remember in his dark blue railway uniform and his black shiny peaked cap to show us around the sidings, there'd always be your mum and dad back home. There'd always be those perpetual Sundays with the smell of Sunday dinner and Ted Heath on the radio endlessly playing that jazz standard, *Opus One*. But now it's all history.

This passage of time makes my heart skip a beat and gives me that existential shiver I used to get when I closed my eyes and tried to imagine the immensity of the universe.

Three decades! God almighty – I never thought it would go so quickly. Never.

The station forecourt is deserted apart from a couple of taxi cabs parked up over by the station master's house. No sign of Laura. She did say it was doubtful that she would get back in time from Cambridge. Just as well, I could do with the walk anyway. It'll only take ten minutes or so. I'll soon warm up.

On the wall up from the booking hall I can just make out the faintest tracery of the HANDS OFF CUBA! slogan Dick and I daubed here in whitewash back in 1962. The letters are about a metre high and slope down to the right. You might not notice it if you didn't know what you were looking for, but I can see it clearly at an angle.

Dick and I painted it in the early hours of a Sunday morning. About 2 a.m. As soon as we'd completed it a police car arrived and we were carted off to the police station. We were charged with defacing railway property and found ourselves in the magistrates' court a week or two later where we were both fined £3, a hefty sum in those days.

One of the arresting officers said in court that Dick had in his pocket *War Upon the World*, an 'inflammatory anarchist tract' that 'advocated the violent overthrow of society'. This was a bit of irrelevant information tossed into court to make sure the magistrate got the message about us two highly subversive individuals, and he did, as the fine demonstrated.

Dick and I laughed about the alleged anarchist tract afterwards because there was no such thing. What Dick did have in his pocket was a copy of the orange-coloured Penguin paperback edition of H. G. Wells' *The War of the Worlds*. Hardly the same thing.

About a week after that Dick pulled me aside at a Campaign for Nuclear Disarmament meeting that was being held in a church hall on the Walsworth Road. He had that smirky bright-eyed look that overcame him whenever he knew something you didn't.

'Christopher, don't you think there was something odd about that copper saying I had an anarchist tract?'

He always said your name at the beginning of a loaded question or statement. Hearing your name let you know that what followed was of some import.

'Well, beyond telling a lie, no.' I really hadn't given it much thought since it happened. The copper had lied and that was that.

'Nothing odd?'

'Odd?'

What was he playing at? What could be odd about it? Everyone knows coppers tell lies. But odd? Dick wasn't silly enough to think there was something odd about a policeman telling a fib, was he?

'Think what the copper said in court,' Dick continued. 'He said it was an … inflammatory … anarchist … tract. Look at those three words.'

'Yeah?' I said, puzzled.

'Where do you suppose one of our local country-bumpkin coppers gets those three words?'

'I'm still not with you, Dick.'

'Look – did that cop strike you as any sort of intellectual? Do you think he reads the *New Statesman* or is even a member of the local library?'

'No … just local … average.'

'Right. Yet he uses those three words. Now you might allow him to use the word *anarchist*. He thinks an anarchist is just someone who wants to blow everything up, nothing more. He wouldn't know about utopian anarchism or Kropotkin or different kinds, would he?'

'No.'

'But *inflammatory*? He wouldn't use that word. Inflammatory to him is something like a blanket that goes up in flames. And *tract*? No. It wouldn't be a tract to him. It would be something else to him. Not a tract. He'd call it a booklet or something. Perhaps a leaflet.'

'So what are you saying, Dick? I don't follow.'

'He got those words from somewhere. Somebody put them into his mouth. That's what I'm saying.'

What's he talking about? Did the copper have a drama coach or what? Who put them into his mouth?

I must have continued to look puzzled because Dick started smiling at me and saying nothing, just waiting for the penny to drop. Which it didn't. He realised he'd have to come to the rescue.

'Think about our political connections,' said Dick as he lit up a Consulate menthol cigarette.

'Just this – the Campaign for Nuclear Disarmament. If you can call that a political connection.'

'*They* would call it a political connection.'

'They?' Who are *they*, I wondered?

'What did we do that Saturday a couple of weeks before we got arrested?'

'What, when we went to London?'

'Yes.'

I thought back. We caught a train early up to town, went to Dobell's jazz shop on Charing Cross Road, looked in a couple of bookshops, went down to the King's Road and wandered up and down, had a drink and something to eat, and walked down to the anarchist bookshop in Fulham, in Maxwell Road. *That* was it. The anarchist connection: 'The anarchist bookshop? The little place we went to down in Fulham?'

'Yes,' said Dick, 'we went there, and we'd phoned them up earlier in the week to find out when they were open, didn't we?'

'Yes. But how many people know that?'

'Look, the place is under surveillance and their phone is probably tapped and we were identified going there. Somebody, somewhere is keeping a file on all of this. They made the connection when we got arrested for polit-slogging and they briefed the copper who went into the witness box. They are the people who think of political tracts being inflammatory. They know about anarchists. But they aren't clever enough to realise when their own toes are showing.'

'Couldn't it have been a coincidence?' I wondered.

'There aren't any coincidences in this neck of the woods,' Dick stated flatly.

I thought then as I do now that this was pretty unassailable reasoning. It was just too fantastic for the copper to use the term anarchism, particularly a Hitchin copper in the early 1960s, *and* bookended by inflammatory and tract.

Back in those days we were aware of mail interceptions and telephone tapping and other things that Special Branch or the intelligence services secretly got up to, but we weren't aware of the extent or the enormity of their activities. These were the innocent days of our youth before the murky Profumo Affair, before the assassination of President Kennedy and the strange death of Lee Harvey Oswald, before Bobby Kennedy's assassination and Martin Luther King's too, before Watergate, before the 'Spycatcher' Peter what's-his-name told us that he and MI5 were careening through London trying to destabilise Harold Wilson's democratically elected government. Back in 1962 not even the most paranoid of us could ever have imagined the half of it.

HANDS OFF CUBA! The white tracings still there on

the brickwork. A palimpsest of the past. I reach forward and my fingertips touch the C of CUBA. I can feel the brickwork as my fingertips move from side to side over the pitted surface. It's like I'm touching the past. Reaching out to thirty years ago merely with a flex of an arm.

I can see myself standing there in the dark with a brush and pot daubing the letters in eager strokes. I'm dressed in a pair of cheap blue baggy jeans (these were pre-designer days), a dark roll-neck sweater, and a black shiny rubber-ised mac. Dick is similarly dressed but with a donkey-jacket. We're fifteen or sixteen and we're what the local police see as the last word in political subversion, an undoubted threat to civilisation (and maidenheads too, I suppose). Big deal. We didn't even have the price of a cup of coffee between us. And neither of us had yet taken a maidenhead.

'Pretty exciting, eh, Christopher?'

'Yeah. We'll cover the whole town in slogans!'

'The whole fucking town! Our slogans everywhere!'

We never quite got around to painting the whole town, but we did succeed in getting a good number of BAN THE BOMBs up hither and thither, including one on the post office and one on a wall right by the police station. We also daubed a few of a slogan that Dick thought up in a puckish moment: HANDS OFF ARMS! The local Labour Party and CND too thought we were taking the piss out of them. We were. Anyway, we'd soon realised that you'd never get anywhere listening to *them*. Their idea of action was writing a letter to your local Member of Parliament, no less. (Enough letters would eventually usher in utopia. A firm article of faith this.)

In those couple of years after Cuba Dick and I were a two-man anarchist cell. We'd put up stickers and slogans all over the place:

VOTE NOW, PAY LATER!

PROPERTY IS THEFT!

[17]

And some were even original, such as the following:

KROPOTKIN LIVES!

THE RED AND THE BLACK FOR EVER!

SURRENDER TO MAD LOVE!

This last showing the influence of surrealism, the other big -ism we were then into.

Of course, for all the effect these had on the citizens of Hitchin they might just as well have been written in Mayan script. How many people in the town had ever heard of Prince Peter Kropotkin and his idea of mutual aid? About as many as knew that red and black were the anarchist colours. What did we care anyway? The act of doing it was the important thing.

We even travelled up to London and went to a couple of London Federation of Anarchist meetings at the Lamb and Flag pub in Covent Garden. All the anarchists there seemed to be about sixty-five years old, though I dare say they were probably younger than I am now. It wasn't for us. And they were so dull. They knitted their own sweaters (we assumed) and only ever seemed to drink fruit juice. We were the only anarchists we knew who were also boppers, real cool individuals, that is.

Anarchism shone brightly in Hitchin through Dick and me for a couple of years and then it was extinguished as quickly as it had ignited when I started work down at the old MGM film studios in Boreham Wood and Dick began preparing for university. Our street fighting (!) days were over, even if the libertarian mind-set never entirely left either of us.

'What's it like being a headmaster now, Dick?'

'Intellectual pimping for the middle classes!'

My fingers were still tracing the letter C when a movement in my peripheral vision compelled me to stop. A woman in her thirties, slim and well-dressed, was staring at me from over towards the booking hall, trying to puzzle out what I was doing. I looked at her and she turned her head sharply and disappeared into the station.

I walked down past the station buildings and into the car park that parallels the track. This wasn't always a car park, it used to be sidings right up until the what, the late 1960s?

Here you can appreciate the siting of the station. Some distance from the tracks on either side are the chalk walls of the grand cutting through which the railway sweeps. And here is an old chalk pit with sheer walls of white rising up some twenty metres or more upon which trees and bushes balance precariously at the top. We used to find deadly nightshade growing in abundance here and even the deep red wild sainfoin, a great rarity in these parts. You'd probably be lucky to find either of them now.

On the floor of the pit nestles a miniature industrial estate of frame buildings and sheds. A builders' merchants, a car firm, even a snooker club, and something called MUSCLEMANIA which may or may not be a health club/gym.

A rumour widespread in Hitchin when we were kids was of a secret cave somewhere in the chalk pit, its entrance hidden behind the greenery or disguised with a fake front. Dick and I spent hours searching and never found anything. Our continued failure to find it made its existence stronger. It was there somewhere and we merely had to look harder. Great rewards, we sensed, wouldn't come easily.

I turn and look up towards the station. Somewhere there on the track Dick decided to terminate his life, as Hine did before him. Did Dick simply lie down on the track and wait for a passing train or did he lurk in the shadows and then rush out and throw himself in the path of an oncoming express? Morbid thoughts, but the mechanics of this act of self-immolation fascinate me more than they should. It's as though knowing this will give me an insight into what Dick was thinking and feeling when he did it.

But that's an illusion, isn't it? How am I ever going to know what was in his mind?

It is getting darker now and colder. There are little pockets of mist and fog appearing. There's an eerie feel to this isolation.

[3]

Here on the corner of the entrance to the station and the Walsworth Road I notice two differences right away. The old Talisman pub has been demolished and a lacklustre piece of modern office building shite has gone up in its place called, funnily enough, Talisman House.

The Talisman was the first pub Dick and I ever went into and ordered a drink, only it wasn't called the Talisman then but, I think, the Railway (or the Railway Inn or Hotel. I can't remember), the newer name wasn't bestowed on it until a few years later.

I was about fifteen then. A group of us had just returned from a CND march in London. Dick and I were the youngest and when all the rest went in we followed them nonchalantly and ordered rum-and-cokes. That was about the time of the Cuban Crisis. I stood there cradling the glass in my hand feeling about ten feet tall. What a milestone in our lives! We'd soon be able to get in the cinema and see X-rated sex films. Wow!

Over there in the elbow between the Walsworth Road and Nightingale Road was an old malthouse or mill. It was one or the other. Built of blue brick, I think. Bowman's Mill. That's gone too and what do we have now to replace it? Nothing less than a B&Q do-it-yourself megastore for the shell-suited working classes in Ford Sierras and their middle-class equivalents in personalised number-plated Range Rovers ('So useful for going over the traffic humps in the Waitrose car park, dear').

Who now remembers the Bowmans, whoever they were?

'The cunts of consumerism,' whispered Dick in between

puffs on his black Sobranie cigarette, 'who say to themselves, I spend, therefore I am.'

God knows why the mill was pulled down. The brick
was designed to last a thousand years and longer. Couldn't
the council have found some other use for the building?
Why pull it down? But it's gone now. Just like the Talisman
and all those other things that now exist only as history.
The Hitchin we've lost. The Lost Town of Hitchin. But we
know it existed because we lived in it, because we were
part of it.

There's another item from Lost Hitchin that existed over
there where Dacre Road starts. A little family-run café that
did simple fried breakfasts and sandwiches and teas and
where the radio always seemed to be playing Nat King
Cole records. There was a pinball machine too, about the
only one in the town, where Dick and I would spend hours
playing each other for small bets. It was a Gottlieb all right,
but not Shipmates. It may have been Criss Cross.

It's dark now and there's a wet wind blowing. I can hear
a ghostly rustle in the trees about the Dells.

The Dells.

This is where Dick and I used to play when we were
small. The two of us and Dick's dog, Laddie. He was a
medium-sized long-haired mongrel who went everywhere
with us. Whatever we did he would do too.

The Dells is the scooped-out half of Windmill Hill which
looms above the town. If whoever was excavating it a
hundred-odd years ago or more hadn't been stopped the
whole hill would have disappeared. What's left has building
encroachments on the east and south but there's still a clear
run of sward to the summit (and the old water tower). The
grass is cut regularly and the area is generally neat and
tidy.

But not the main dell. Here there is the wilderness
screened off from the ordered parkland. The dell has
almost sheer sides with trees and bushes growing out at
odd angles. The undergrowth is thick and impenetrable.

[21]

It's untamed – and only spitting distance from the town centre. This was all we needed for adventure-packed summer holidays … in those summers that would last for ever.

'Let's explore the top of the cliff.'

'We've never been up there before. Not all the way.'

'It's ever so high.'

'And don't the savages live up there who eat people?'

'And dogs. They eat dogs too!'

Savages indeed! That was the all-purpose term in those days for … tribesmen and natives. Guys who had spears and hadn't yet invented the TV chat show. Hunters. Jungle dwellers. But you don't hear the term 'savage' too much these days.

The whole point of savages was, of course, that they were *savage*. They were bloodthirsty jungle psychos with but two purposes in life – savagery and mayhem. God rest their souls. And their habitat has disappeared too. There isn't any jungle any more, just rain forests.

There's the theatre named after the Queen Mum through the trees and there's the Woodside Hall which I'm sure still has that sign on it saying HITCHIN THESPIANS (despite a thousand music-hall jokes about this Greek word for the acting profession).

It was just across the road from the Dells that the three of us grew up – Dick, Laura and me. In Whinbush Road.

Shall I walk down it for old times' sake? I always ask myself this when I'm in the town and I always reply with a firm *No*. The Whinbush Road I know, I *knew*, exists now only as a memory.

I cross the road up by Portmill Lane and walk through St Mary's Square as this glorified car park is somewhat grandly called. This used to be where all the town's slums were but they were swept away in the 1920s and the view to St Mary's Church was opened up with the River Hiz dammed and widened to the fore for effect. This was only a part of some grand civic scheme that soon ran out of money. The shops and flats that were supposed to front the square were never built and now, sixty years later, the square still looks unfinished and incomplete. Just as well perhaps.

St Mary's is as fine a parish church as can be found anywhere in Hertfordshire, indeed, anywhere in England. It's big, almost like a small cathedral. Dick says it was largely financed by the rich wool merchants of the town who wanted to display their wealth and announce their importance in an edifice that would stand down the ages to the Day of Judgement. It's now been here for six hundred years or more so I figure they've partly achieved what they wanted.

I descend the steps towards the river and then turn around to see if the lettering is still there on the brick risers. It is:

> THESE WORKS WERE EXECUTED BY THE
> HITCHIN URBAN DISTRICT COUNCIL AD 1930.
> ON THE ADJACENT AREA FORMERLY STOOD
> 74 COTTAGES WHICH WERE DEMOLISHED
> UNDER SLUM CLEARANCE SCHEMES AND
> THE OCCUPANTS 137 IN NUMBER HOUSED
> ELSEWHERE AD 1925-1929.

I continue along, past the pigeons and ducks, over the bridge and up Churchyard Walk. When I'm by Halsey's shop I stop and look towards the church – the lights are on inside and I see a couple of people coming out through the south porch.

'A beautiful church, don't you think?'

Who said that? The voice is near and the question is aimed at me.

'What mean ye by these stones?'

The same voice.

I turn and standing close to me and looking at me is this vast Orson Welles-ish figure, a visitation.

He's about six feet tall and overweight. He has long flowing dark hair and a neatly trimmed Vandyke beard.

He's elderly but ageless. After his size it's his dress that strikes me the most. A black corduroy suit, three-piece, with a matching cape lined with what looks to be red silk and a billowy black felt hat. There's something rakishly aristocratic about him. Totally out of place for hereabouts.

'Very beautiful,' he says as he waves a silver-tipped cane in the direction of St Mary's.

He has very small eyes that dart about as though they have a life of their own. Tiny, piercing eyes that look like they belong to someone else.

He introduces himself as Georges something-or-other. I don't catch the second name and I'm ill-inclined to ask him to repeat it. The voice is a resonant baritone with, possibly, the faintest background trace of an east coast American accent (Boston, perhaps?).

What does Georges want with me? What indeed is a figure like this doing in Hitchin on a Saturday night?

He's staring at me now, probably waiting for me to introduce myself. I don't.

He breaks the silence: 'You are?'

'I'm Christopher.'

'Just Christopher?'

'No. Christopher Cornwell.'

'Good.'

Georges waves his cane in the direction of the church again. 'He who looks upon an image of St Christopher will suffer no harm that day. That's why murals of him were so popular in churches.'

'I didn't know that.' Which was true, but I didn't add that I didn't care I didn't know that. I continued, 'It didn't do him much good himself though, did it?'

'No, it didn't. A martyr for his beliefs.'

That seems as good a way as any of describing a saint being put to death (but was he a saint when he died? Or did beatitude come later?).

'Not many people are prepared to die for their beliefs these days, are they?' says Georges.

He then wraps the cloak around his chest with a theatrical gesture and motions thither with the cane.

'Are we going in the same direction?'

Why's he asking me this?

'I don't know. Where are you going?' I reply.

'I'm going in the direction of the station,' he replied, straightening his hat.

I was curious about this guy. 'What are you doing in Hitchin? Do you live here?'

He looked me up and down before replying in a conspiratorial whisper. 'I've been coming and going ... recently.'

I nodded.

Then he added, 'It was a great pleasure meeting you ... I'm *sure* we will run into each other again.'

'You think so?'

'I'm sure we will. Goodnight, Mr Cornwell.' And he touched his hat.

'Goodnight.'

He strode off down towards the river in agile strides that belied his weight.

What was all that about?

I head off down Churchyard Walk and into Market Square which, aside from a stretch of development on the east side put up a few years ago, is unchanged since I was a kid.

The adjoining and nearby streets – Sun Street, Bucklersbury, Tilehouse Street (where Laura lives), and Bridge Street have also changed little and would be instantly recognisable to some mid-Victorian time traveller. Hitchin has been lucky. It has preserved what Reginald Hine called its 'antique grace'.

There's an off-licence open in the corner of the square and as I've travelled up empty-handed I should really pick up something for Laura.

I get her a couple of bottles of Cordon Negro and some fresh orange juice, myself a bottle of Blue Label Smirnoff, and for the girls some cans of Coke.

SIXTY-THREE CLOSURE

As I walk down the narrow and gently winding Bucklersbury I remember that this was where Dick and I always did our serious drinking. There isn't a pub here that didn't ban us at some time or another. We've been totally and irredeemably pissed in all of them. It was in Bucklersbury that we smoked our first joint.

There was a guy called Stephen Maliphant. He was a couple of years older than us and he lived down on Bancroft somewhere. His parents were pretty rich. Stephen was our hero for a time in the early 1960s because he was doing what we only dreamt about doing.

First off, he had long hair. It was right down to his shoulders, and at that time you just never saw anyone in England with long hair. You saw photographs of beatniks in the States with long hair but nobody in England had it past their ears.

Stephen was the first 'beat' we ever knew (beats came after beatniks). He only read beat writers and beat-approved writers. He used to lend us stuff by Ginsberg, Kerouac, Ferlinghetti, John Clellon Holmes and all those other poets and writers associated with the movement, including Sartre and assorted existentialists and Zen Masters and not forgetting the divine Marquis de Sade. His big favourite was, however, Henry Miller and he turned us on to him. Miller's books were banned in England at the time so getting your hands on those Olympia Press editions in the green covers smuggled in from Paris was quite something.

One sunny Sunday afternoon Dick and I went down to the churchyard after visiting Stephen. We sat down on the bench and both started reading books Stephen had lent us. I began *Tropic of Cancer* and Dick began *The Naked Lunch*. And there we were for the rest of the day, reading and smoking our French cigarettes. We were super-hip and cool. And *très* existential.

If you could get high by reading books about the drug experience then Dick and I were well-established dope

fiends. There wasn't a drug that we hadn't experienced –
vicariously. Pot, grass, cocaine, heroin, LSD, peyote, and
even ether and amyl nitrate and Benzedrine (which, it was
rumoured, could be obtained from breaking open one of
those plastic sniffer things you stuck up your nose to clear
your sinuses). You name it – we'd been there reading about it.

On a cold December night shortly before Christmas of, I
think, 1964, Dick, Laura and me were in the Red Hart on
Bucklersbury when Stephen swanned in dressed like a
Californian biker. He'd just got back from a *satori* in Paris.
He arrived at our table with a large gin and tonic and a fat
herbal cigarette he had rolled himself.

'I thought you smoked Gauloises?' said Laura.

'Why roll-ups?' asked Dick.

Stephen smiled seraphically as was his wont (to steal a
phrase from Jonathan Miller in *Beyond the Fringe*) and
inhaled deeply on his herbal cigarette. He held the smoke
down for several seconds and then exhaled a billowing
cloud of blue. The smell was acrid yet sweet.

The roll-up cigarette was actually more a cigar than a
cigarette, and a big cigar at that. It looked as though
Stephen had used about four or five papers to make it.

But why was supercool and hip Stephen smoking a
herbal cigarette?

He was emitting more billowy clouds of smoke and
waving the cigarette about. He started to say something
but whatever it was became strangled in his throat by
giggles that went on and on and on.

Dick said to no one in particular, 'Is he all right?'

Laura and I looked at each other and shrugged our
shoulders. We didn't know what was going on.

Somewhere in the background I heard the booming
voice of the landlord say, 'Put that bloody herbal cigarette
out or leave the premises. No herbal cigarettes in *here*!'

As Stephen showed no inclination to stub out the roll-up
we said to him we'd better leave. He didn't hear us. He
was smiling and giggling to himself and right out of it still.

Dick and I supported him under his arms and gently marched him out to the street where the cold air seemed to sober him up.

'This,' said Stephen, waving the cigarette in the air, 'is another first for Hitchin!'

Had he completely flipped or what?

'This night,' he continued, 'will go down in history as the night I, Stephen Maliphant, brought the first joint to Hitchin!'

A joint? A reefer? A dope cigarette? No, this couldn't possibly be true. Who'd ever heard of a joint in Hitchin?

Dick said, 'You're having us on … aren't you?'

'No, he isn't,' cried Laura.

'I'm not having you on … and to prove it here's another joint I rolled not half an hour ago.'

That was the first time Dick, Laura and me turned on (to use a phrase from the then current drug argot).

I remember very little of the rest of that night. Laura said we all went back to Stephen's (his parents were away) and smoked more dope and listened to Mose Allison and ate ravenously and continuously. It's all a blur to me, though I do remember asking Stephen why his LPs had such enormous gaps between the tracks (temporal gaps, that is, not spatial). One track would end and it would be *years* before the next one started.

It's often said that the first few times you smoke the stuff it has no effect, but it certainly worked for me and Dick. In fact it had to, we'd read and thought about the stuff so much it couldn't but work. We'd culturally conditioned ourselves to such an extent that even if it had been a Heath & Heather herbal cigarette we'd still have got high. Laura, however, said it made her feel a bit sick initially.

Dick and I became regular smokers whenever Stephen had some stuff. It later became more widely available but the quality wasn't always that good. We never got into LSD or anything like that. We figured these substances were mindfuckers and we didn't want anything to do with them, but reading about them was OK, so we tripped at one remove as it were.

And what became of Stephen? Choose any one of the following fates:

1] He is incarcerated in a mental asylum for the criminally insane on the outskirts of Paris.
2] He is a monk in a Tibetan monastery.
3] He died of a drug overdose in Katmandu.
4] He went to New York and:
    A. Teaches a writing course at NYU
    B. Was mugged to death in Battery Park
    C. Works in a black poverty program
    D. Is a junk-bond dealer on Wall Street
5] He is an antique dealer in Suffolk.
6] He disappeared in the Bermuda Triangle.

I've heard all of these over the years and each time it was told to me as absolute, incontrovertible truth. If I had to choose one I think I'd go for 5], though Dick always favoured 3].

And as to Stephen's joint being the first in Hitchin? Well, that was true up to a point. Many years later I discovered that William Ransom & Son Ltd, the local Quaker herbal chemists, used to grow their own dope in the fields hereabouts and produce Tincture of Cannabis. This was being done as late as the 1950s, when doctors could still prescribe it as a painkiller and relaxant. So, Stephen may have made the first joint, but the stuff itself had been around Hitchin a lot longer.

It begins to rain again as I turn out of Bucklersbury into old Tilehouse Street and there ahead of me is Laura's house. And the lights are on.

[4]

'Christopher!'

Laura put her arms around me, gave me a big kiss on my lips and pulled me into the house.

'It's so good to see you!'

'Good to see you too, Laura. You look terrific!'

She did. I was telling the truth. She always looked terrific. She wasn't blessed with great beauty but she was attractive. Very attractive. Something more solid than beauty that was rooted in her personality. She had pale skin like a rare marble and a few freckles. Her eyes were big and brown and her lips full. Her hair was straight and naturally very dark and she still had it long.

When we were teenagers we were always on the verge of going to bed together. It was a foregone conclusion. There was plenty of time to do it. We had such an understanding of each other that we wouldn't rush it (which seems strange looking back on it, although at the time it didn't). It was not a matter of if, but when? We could do it any time and we would. Well, we didn't ever quite get around to doing it and now it is too late. Us going to bed would be like a brother and sister doing it.

'Put your bag down and come on through.'

Cathie and Lucy put their heads around at the top of the stairs and shouted Hi! and then scampered back to their rooms.

'The boyfriends have just come by,' confided Laura.

Laura asked me about this and that and I asked her about this and that and we ran around each other with small talk trying to avoid the inevitable – the subject of Dick. We were both thinking about him. He was the third person sitting at the kitchen table.

Laura asked me if I had seen Charlotte lately. Charlotte was my ex-wife.

'I haven't seen her for about two years. We speak on the phone about twice a year, that's all.'

'Do you miss her?'

'No.'

'How's your son?'

'Rupert? He's fine. He's backpacking around the world with a friend. I got a postcard from him a month or two ago. He was in India.'

There was a silence and then I reciprocated by asking Laura about Andrew, her ex-husband.

'He married his secretary … still lives in Paris. He never writes or anything. I don't mind that, but I think it's hard for the girls … or *was* hard for the girls. They're used to it by now … I suppose. They still have his name, but I've gone back to my maiden name. They're Clifford, I'm Sayer again.'

'Were you a maiden once?'

'Yes, but I can scarcely remember it.'

Another silence. Laura poured us both some more coffee.

'Would you like something to eat, Christopher?'

'Not right now. Can we eat later?'

'Fine.'

Another silence.

'I was just coming down Bucklersbury and I thought of Stephen and remembered that evening he turned up with those joints.'

'I remember that. We were in the George.'

'No. We were in the Red Hart.'

'No – the George!' Laura declared.

'Are you absolutely sure?'

'Sure I'm sure,' said Laura. 'No doubt about it.'

'I could have sworn it was the Red Hart.' I said.

'No.'

There was a pause as we looked at each other.

I then started thinking about Stephen and what became of him. 'Do you know what happened to Stephen. What became of him?'

Laura was clasping the mug of coffee in her two hands on the table and staring at it, not moving. I saw a tear roll down from her left eye. A big wet tear that rolled all the way down to her upper lip. Another followed it. Laura quickly took a coloured handkerchief from the sleeve of her sweater and wiped her face. She stifled a sob and said, 'I'm so silly.'

'Let's go out for a drink. How about that?' I said this in my best bright and perky let's-change-the-subject voice.

Laura peeked out from behind the handkerchief and said, 'The George or the Red Hart?'

I'd often wondered whether she had had a fling with Stephen. Now I knew.

[5]

It was early so we had the Red Hart largely to ourselves. I got myself a large vodka and Laura had a Martini. We found a seat in the corner at the round table in the Snuggery as it was known. We sat in silence for a while sipping our drinks. A high wall-mounted TV was tuned to some rock music channel.

Dick was still with us, a mute presence.

Laura lit one of her More cigarettes and said quietly into her glass, 'I'm so glad you could come. I couldn't face it by myself.'

There was no doubt what the 'it' was.

She continued, 'For some funny reason I've got almost resentful since Dick died. Resentful of Barbara ... I don't know why. He may have been Barbara's husband, but he was *our* friend. We knew him before she did, and we knew him better.'

'I feel the same way. It's strange, isn't it?'

Barbara was prissy, unimaginative, homey and, for want of no better word, *boring*. She was, in actual fact, just the sort of woman Dick had spent his whole life avoiding. Why Dick married her God alone knows. I could never ever see anything they had in common. When he was single he went out with some wild girls and some zippy educated ones too, but how he ended up with Barbara, who was neither, I just do not know. She was one big wet blanket. We all thought that.

'When did you last see him?' I asked.

'He called around just two days before … *it* happened. Turned up about 9.30 one evening. He said he'd had a couple of drinks here in the Red Hart. He was going to walk home.'

This was the last time we had contact with the living Dick (*in persona*). The very last time. I was curious. I wanted to know more. I had to know more. I wanted to see if there was some clue in his speech or behaviour that could unlock the mystery of his suicide, some tell-tale sign that would deliver answers.

'Tell me everything that happened.'

'Well, there's really not much to tell. He turned up and I invited him in for a cup of coffee. I usually saw him about once a week for an hour or so. He'd just pop in at odd times.

'Of course Barbara never knew about the visits, not that there was anything to hide. But she wouldn't have understood that. She would have thought there was something going on.

'We'd talk about old times or last night's television or whatever entered our minds. Nothing specific.'

I was wondering if Laura was forgetting or overlooking something. 'There was nothing special or noticeable about that last time?'

'Nothing, and God knows I've turned it over in my mind and thought about it enough,' continued Laura. 'He seemed in good spirits, if a little tired. There's nothing that sticks out. Nothing at all. That's why it came as such a great shock to me … you know? That last meeting was, you know, almost … *banal*.'

It was the Wednesday that Dick called around to Laura. The next day he phoned me. And on the Friday he was dead. Three days. One, two, three. What had happened on the Thursday that resulted in him phoning me in Brno? Why hadn't he seen Laura instead or as well? I couldn't make sense of that. Why leave her out of anything?

'Was he in good spirits that Wednesday evening?'

'Reasonably good. Average for him. He was all right,' replied Laura.

'How was he over the last few months generally?'

'You know Dick as well as I do. He has the odd mood swings, but he keeps on a pretty even keel.' Laura was talking of him in the present tense.

'Nothing of note? Out of the ordinary?'

'No. His life had remained the same for several years. Headmastering during the week, counselling at the hospice a couple of weekday nights, researching his book ... and a spot of gardening. That was it. Nothing much else.'

'You don't suppose the hospice counselling was getting him down?'

'No,' said Laura, 'he'd been doing that for too long. He'd made the necessary adjustments ... like a doctor.'

There didn't appear to be any clues to his suicide that Laura was aware of ... but there was the Brno phone call.

I got another couple of drinks and decided now was as good a time as any to tell Laura about the call.

'You saw him on Wednesday. Right? The next day he phoned me.'

'But you were out of the country!' Laura said, startled.

'I know. He called me in Brno.'

'Where did he get the number from?'

'That wouldn't have been difficult – either the production office in town or Pinewood Studios.'

'What did he say?'

'He said he needed my help ...'

'And?'

'That he was being followed.'

'Followed?'

'That's all he said – *followed*. I got the impression from the way he said it that he was, you know, talking more *surveillance* than … uh … being followed by stray dogs. *That* sort of followed.'

'Who was following him?'

'I don't know. He started to say something about them and that they were serious and that was it. I was a bit pissed and I think he knew I wasn't in too good a state.'

Laura fixed me with a stare and in her best solicitor's voice said, 'A bit pissed?'

'Well, pretty pissed.'

'I bet.'

'Listen, I know I let him down, but I'm going out of my mind in this boring fucking Czech town and there's nothing else to do but get pissed, believe me. How did I know he was going to call?'

'You're too touchy. I wasn't having a go at you in regard to how you behaved with Dick. I was having a go at you for being out of your mind … understand?'

I guess I am a bit touchy.

'Did he ever mention to you anything about being followed?'

'Certainly not,' said Laura, 'and I'd remember something like that all right.'

'Can you think of any reason why anyone would want to follow him?'

'You say that like you think he was being followed!'

'Laura, he *said* he was being followed. Either it was some put-on aimed at me, for what reason I do not know, or he was being followed, or he was going insane and imagined it. It's as simple as that. There's nothing else.'

Laura shot back at me with, 'Yes, there is!'

What on earth could that be? I scratched my head and tried to puzzle it out but I couldn't. I admitted defeat to Laura and asked her to tell me what it could be.

'There's actually two further possibilities.'

Two? I can't even come up with one.

'Yes. You could either have *imagined* him saying *followed* or you *misheard* what he did say.'

Those possibilities had never occurred to me. It takes a lawyer's brain to come up with something like that.

Was it possible that I'd got it wrong? Could it be? I remember the call so vividly now. Ernie. The office. Me thinking it was Harry, the flavoured vodka, the modulations of Dick's voice.

Followed. That was what he said. Followed. It was said with some agitation and fearfulness, I think. Followed was the word he used.

'I didn't imagine it and I didn't mishear him. He said *followed*.'

'That's what you believe he said, but could you be wrong?'

I suppose I could. It's always possible that one can get something wrong. But I didn't feel that I had got this wrong. This was too real to me. Even when I'm totally stoned I can sort fact out from fiction. Dick's call and the word followed were fact. Hard fact.

'I don't think I am wrong ... I'm not wrong.'

'In that case, then, why would someone be following Dick?'

'I've about as much idea as you.'

I finished the vodka and took a More from Laura. I lit it myself. I gazed at Laura as she inspected her fingernails. She wasn't aware that I was looking at her. There were tremors on her lips. Then she pursed them and ran her tongue across them. They were dry before but now they glistened. She then looked up and saw that I was staring at her. She giggled and her eyes dropped down like a shy schoolgirl.

'I wonder if Dick was going a bit loopy?' I said.

Laura snorted and said very firmly, 'No, he wasn't.'

'Just an idea ... only an idea. But what happened between Dick seeing you and the phone call to me on Thursday? Something happened.'

'He was at school all day. That's what they said at the inquest.'

'Were you at the inquest?'

'Only for a little while.'

'What did the coroner say?'

'He returned a verdict of suicide.'

'Based on what?'

'Not much. There was no evidence of foul play, therefore Dick committed suicide, therefore his mind was disturbed. That was about it. There were no doctors or shrinks to say they'd been treating him for depression or anything. He drank a fair bit – not as much as you – but there was no alcohol in his bloodstream ... and no toxic substances either.'

'Don't coroners investigate something like this in any depth?'

Laura was used to explaining legal procedures to Joe Six-pack and she did so patiently: 'Yes, they do. But there were no *suspicious* circumstances. Somebody saw Dick hanging around the booking hall having a cigarette. Somebody else found his body on the track. Nobody saw him being thrown under a train. He was not a villain but a well-respected member of the community. He didn't deal in drugs and didn't have any enemies. And he wasn't in hock to organised crime. An autopsy takes place. Nothing is found. No witnesses come forward to suggest anything odd had happened. Family and colleagues are questioned. That's it. What more can a coroner do?'

'If I'd been back from Brno I would have gone to the inquest and told them about the call. In fact, shouldn't I tell the police about it now?'

'Christopher, I don't think that would have made any difference at the inquest. Your *following* is a dead-end. It leads nowhere, and I'm sure if the coroner had started asking you questions about your state at the time of the call and your drinking habits generally you would have ended up with an egg facial, as they say.'

'You think I invented it. Don't you?'

'I don't know. Perhaps you just got something wrong.'

[37]

'Should I go to the police?'

'You can if you want. They'll take a statement and file it away. You've got no hard evidence to give them. The case is now closed.'

I looked up from my empty glass. The pub was now full. It was 10.30 p.m. according to the large clock over the bar.

There were plenty of faces at the bar but nobody I knew.

Laura stood up and said, 'We should go.'

'Right.' I tottered to my feet.

'I'm running the girls into Bedford in the morning. I won't bother to wake you.'

'I'll sleep in … if you don't mind.'

'I don't mind.'

And out of the Red Hart we walked, arm in arm, into the cold and the bright moonlight.

[6]

My eyes opened slowly and through the windows I could see a blue and cloud-free sky. There was a thick frost on the roofs of the houses opposite. I could hear isolated footsteps in the street below and then the peals of the church bells. Sunday in Hitchin.

I look at the bedside clock: 10.30 a.m. The house is silent. Not a sound. Everybody must be asleep … no, they're out. Gone. Laura and the girls must have left already. She said they were going somewhere.

Pushkin the cat is startled by my entrance into the kitchen and flies out of the cat flap. I look around and realise what I like about this house. It is cluttered and untidy.

There's some cold toast on the table. I take a slice and spread it thickly with butter and Vintage Oxford marmalade and wolf it down while gazing out over the garden. I make a mug of decaff instant coffee and take one of Laura's More cigarettes from a packet left on top of today's as yet unread *Observer* over by the old kitchen sink.

The last time I saw Dick was here in this kitchen. Last autumn. He was standing over there, leaning against the red Aga, forking cubes of feta cheese from a jar. Laura was sitting on the floor combing Pushkin. Lucy, or was it Cathie?, was in the sitting room with her boyfriend listening to some heavy metal band at full blast.

That was the last time I saw him. Standing there, eating feta. I'd never see him again. That was it. It is all the past now. Another memory.

He was wearing that old herringbone jacket of his, worn jeans and white trainers. Lazily leaning against the cooker. I was sitting at this table drinking a neat vodka.

There was a sad sun low in the sky.

'The thing about the sixties,' declaimed Dick, 'is that they now need to be rescued from the Thatcherite revisionists. Right, Christopher?'

'Yeah, sure,' I said on auto pilot, figuring I usually agreed with what Dick said so I might as well agree with this too. I was a bit out of it anyway.

Dick took a sip of my drink and said, 'Got to be rushing. Got to get a haircut and pick up a new toaster.' And he was gone. That was the last time I'd see him alive.

Got to get a haircut and pick up a new toaster. Dick's last words to me in person some four months ago.

I'll have a shower and walk up to the paper shop, get a bit of exercise and some fresh air.

[7]

I stepped out on to Tilehouse Street and looked up and down. The street was deserted. Nobody. No sounds either. I pulled the front door shut behind me. It closed with a deep assured thud.

I walk up Bucklersbury and across the square and into the paper shop. I pick up a pack of Marlboros, *The Sunday Telegraph* and a large box of chocolates for Laura. I realise I don't have any cash on me so instead I pay with the old plastic.

I leave the shop and turn right and as I'm passing the old Corn Exchange I hear someone behind me calling my name. I look around and see a figure waving his arms and walking towards me. It's Briscoe, all 5 feet 6 inches and sixteen stone of him. I wait for him to join me. He's got a baggy pair of track-suit pants on, a zippered jacket with some American football design on it, worn trainers, and a baseball hat. He looks the archetypal mini-cab driver. And he's got *The News of the World* under his arm (I can't see its title, but it's the only paper he ever reads).

He ambles up and throws his arms around me.

'How you doing, Chris? It must be a couple of years since we had a drink, eh? You do look very prosperous. Makin' a living then?'

'Just about. And you?'

'OK, yeah. Still cabbying. Another kid on the way.'

Briscoe has a moon-shaped face and a look of oat-fed innocence that hides his native shrewdness. He has prominent bright red cheeks and a dimpled chin. If anyone were ever to remake the film of *Moby Dick* Briscoe would be perfect as the ship's carpenter. He has a face you could never get from the Film Artistes' Association.

Briscoe isn't his real name. His name is actually Leonard. Leonard Draper. But nobody has called him that for thirty years because when Dick and I were getting into Jelly Roll Morton we came across a trumpeter on some obscure Morton recording date called Briscoe Draper. We both looked at each other and thought the same thing: Leonard is really a Briscoe, not that we were sure what Briscoe conjured up, but it seemed tremendously apt. And the name stuck. Briscoe ever since.

'Come round and have a drink some time. Come round for a meal. Gloria would love to see you.'

Briscoe's Gloria. Gloria Denford. Little Gloria Denford. She had a chubby little face and bright red cheeks like a

Mabel Lucy Attwell drawing. Briscoe and Gloria used to go around holding hands when they were thirteen. They were destined for each other from the moment they met.

'Do give her my love.'

'Sure will.'

'Where you living now?'

'Still in King's Road, Chris. I'll never have the dosh to move out of there, but I'm trying to do it up, a bit at a time.'

There was a momentary silence.

'You come up for the funeral?' asked Briscoe, matter of factly.

'Yes. I'm staying with Laura. I'm going with her. You going?'

'No. I didn't get an invite.'

When did Briscoe last see Dick?

'Just a couple of days before –' He was searching for the right word or phrase. ' – before they found him up at the station, as it happens. He was standing outside of Halsey's down in the churchyard with some shopping. Seemed cheerful enough. Couldn't understand it when I'd heard what happened.'

'Any idea what made him do it?'

'You tell me. A mystery. But then suicides usually are, aren't they? Unless, of course, they leave a suicide note. And he didn't, did he?'

I asked him how often he saw Dick.

'Once a week on average, I'd say. I'd bump into him in the street, or in a pub, or I'd take him up to the hospice and back if Barbara had the car. We saw each other pretty regularly.'

'He phoned me just before it happened and said he was being … followed.' I'm not sure why I mentioned this to Briscoe. It just came out. A shot in the dark.

'Followed?' Briscoe craned his neck as he said this, like a puppy not understanding a word of command. '*Followed*?'

'Followed, that's right.'

He scratched his chin and thought for a moment. 'Odd. Very odd you should say that.'

'Why? Did he ever mention that to you?'

'No, he didn't mention that. He didn't say that. But there was this evening when I was driving him back from the hospice when he kept telling me to pull over and stop. It was like he was being followed, only he didn't say that. I just thought to myself – Dick, you're acting like you're being followed. He'd be sitting there staring back like he was expecting somebody to appear. He was a bit agitated. Odd.'

'When was this?'

'A few weeks ago.'

'Did you say anything to Dick? Ask him about it?'

'I didn't like to, you know?'

'And Dick never said anything?'

'No. Nothing.'

I wondered if this was corroborative evidence that Dick was being followed. It depended so heavily on Briscoe's interpretation as to melt away in terms of tangible evidence. Just an odd coincidence perhaps, nothing more.

'A few weeks ago?' I asked.

'Yeah, just before Mr Drax died.'

'Mr Drax?' An odd name.

'Old man out at the hospice. Lived up Shadwell, before they sent him to the hospice, I think.'

Briscoe then craned his neck again. 'Got to get some shopping and then get over to Stevenage, Chris. Call round soon, won't you?'

'I will.'

'Be seeing you!'

'Yeah, all the best, Briscoe.'

Briscoe hurried down towards the newsagent's and I turned and continued along into Bucklersbury.

Rain began falling.

Briscoe … Jelly Roll Morton. It's years since I've listened to Jelly Roll Morton. Dick and I used to be crazy about him.

We listened to New Orleans jazz then, *real* New Orleans jazz.

Morton, we decided at an early stage, was the first hipster. One hip dude. And Stephen agreed with us too, and there wasn't any better imprimatur than that.

I even remember Dick once saying to me that when he died he wanted a Morton piano solo, 'Creepy Feeling', played at his funeral. It's a slow tango (if it isn't actually a tango, then it's something similar) with several themes or figures, or whatever you call them in musical terms, repeated over and over again throughout the composition. Very haunting. It's still dancing about in my head and I haven't heard it for thirty years. I can recall it note for note … almost.

Perhaps I'll tell Barbara that Dick wanted 'Creepy Feeling' played at the funeral? See how that idea would go down.

I'll zip through the Sunday papers before Laura gets back, then take her out to lunch before we go to Barbara's this afternoon. Should be enough time.

And when we're at Barbara's do I mention the phone call to her? Do I ask her if she knows anything about Dick being followed?

And what about Briscoe's little recollection?

Creepy feeling all right.

CHAPTER TWO

SEE HOW YOU GOT ME SPINNING!

'Identify.'
  'Bellerophon … 666B.'
  'Location?'
  'Capital.'
  'Proceed.'
  'Little progress. This isn't going to be over quickly.'
  'You were advised.'

'THE PASTA HERE IS PRETTY GOOD,' Laura enthused, 'and you can eat as much as you like for the basic price.'

We're sitting at a window seat in a little pasta place on Sun Street, Fatso's. I'm looking out diagonally across the street to the Conservative Club, as elegant an example of a three-storeyed Georgian house as you'll find anywhere in Hertfordshire. The members drift out of it in twos and threes after a boozy lunchtime session and melt into the rain.

'Have the decency to get a hip flask or something … rather than just swigging from a bottle. Even tramps keep it wrapped in a paper bag.'

Laura's admonishment sinks in slowly. I'd taken the bottle out of my coat pocket without thinking.

Do tramps keep their drink in paper bags? I was momentarily deflected by Laura's statement. I've never seen any tramps over here clutching paper bags. Does she know something I don't? The only tramps (or rather, winos) I've ever seen with bottles in a bag have been in the pages of *The New Yorker*.

'We're the only people here, aren't we?' I say in my own defence. 'And, anyway, it's my first drink of the day.' Which was a lie all right. I knew it and Laura knew it.

'So? Does that make any difference? If you want a drink, order one.'

'I will. Would you like one?'

'I'll have a Shirley Temple.'

I ordered two drinks and we puzzled over the menu. Laura ordered the tagliatelle verdi with mushroom. I went for the conchiglie with ham. The two dishes seemed to arrive in no time at all.

'Don't put so much black pepper on it. You'll ruin it,' said Laura.

'Is this bash Christopher day or something?'

Laura ignored my question and continued eating. Then she said, 'I'm getting nervous about this afternoon.'

'Yeah, me too. Did Barbara invite you around there or did you offer to go … or what?'

'It was Barbara's mother's idea, I think. A few people, friends and colleagues are going around.'

'Like a before wake rather than an after wake?' I suggested.

'Something like that.'

We continued eating in silence. I noticed there was a Van Morrison song playing in the background, 'Moondance'. Dick was quite fond of his music and had many of his records.

'I went up to get the papers this morning and bumped into Briscoe.'

'How's he?' inquired Laura as she sprinkled more parmesan over her pasta.

'Fine. Got another kid on the way.'

'That must be his sixth or seventh. Is he Catholic or something?'

'No. I just think his wife is one of those women who likes to have a baby every couple of years. It gives her

[45]

something to think about.'

Laura looked up, stared me in the eyes and said, 'What a patronising remark!'

'I was just being facetious.'

'Uh-huh.' But Laura didn't sound convinced.

I finished the pasta and pushed the plate away from me. Laura was still eating.

'Are you happy, Christopher?'

I raised my eyes to Laura. What a strange question. It startled me. Laura was looking right at me.

'This minute am I happy? Or generally?'

'Generally.'

'A strange question to ask a friend.'

'It would be stranger *not* to ask a friend.'

After a pause I said, 'I'm not even sure I know what happy is any more.' A glib response that I hoped would defuse this line of questioning, but one that had some truth in it. When I was younger I wanted to be happy, now I'm content with merely surviving.

'What about you, Laura?'

'I asked first.'

'I guess if I really think about it – no. I'm going nowhere professionally ... intellectually ... emotionally. I'm just holding on. But ask me again tomorrow and you'll get an entirely different reply. I don't know. I don't know much any more.'

'That's a pretty positive answer,' said Laura.

'I guess it is – for me.'

We both laughed and then I cadged one of Laura's cigarettes. She gave me a light.

'When I was talking to Briscoe this morning he said he thought Dick was acting like he was being followed one evening when he picked him up from the hospice.'

'Did he?' said Laura.

'Yes.'

'You didn't lead Briscoe into saying that, did you?'

'No. I told him about the call and Dick saying he was

being followed and Briscoe said he thought Dick was being followed that evening from the way he behaved. Briscoe thought it at the time, back then. I didn't put the idea in his head.'

'That's odd,' said Laura quietly.

'It is.'

We finished our cigarettes in silence and then Laura said, 'Let's settle up. We should be getting moving.'

[2]

There was still rain in the air as we walked through Market Square and past the church. I thought of the encounter last night with the velvet-clad Georges on the corner here. I wonder if Laura knows who he is. She knows everyone in Hitchin.

'Do you know a guy who goes around the town dressed in a black velvet suit with a matching cape and a big, floppy hat?'

Laura chuckled, then responded with, 'And answers to the name of Mephistopheles? Or even Old Nick?'

'I'm serious.'

'And smells of sulphur?'

'No, I'm really serious. I'm not joking,' I protested.

'In a word – No. Why?'

'Because,' I patiently explain, 'he stopped me here last night and said, "What mean ye by these stones?" pointing at the church, that's why.'

'What an odd thing to say.'

'It's a quotation, isn't it?'

Laura looked at me quizzically and said, 'Why did he ask you that?'

'I haven't got the faintest fucking idea. Have *you*?'

Laura shook her head as we continued down, across the river and the car park to the foot of Windmill Hill.

'We can walk up and over,' I said as I pointed up the steep path that led straight to the top of the hill. 'If you want.'

Laura nodded towards the dell: 'Easier through here.'

We got to Highbury Road and turned up the hill and crossed the road to Dick's house which looked out over the the Dells, all three floors of it.

Laura rang the doorbell and took a bottle of sherry from her canvas shoulder bag. 'This is all they drink here.'

'If Dick's mother is here,' I added, 'she'd want a decent drink. Some Scotch or a strong lager.'

We waited. Laura rang the bell again.

'Anyone in, Laura?'

'Yes, someone's coming.'

The door opened and there was Mrs Bradley, Barbara's mother, dressed up to the nines as though she was going off to the Conservatives' annual conference. Not a hair out of place. Wrapped up in some dark green shiny number with folds and bows. Her thin lips pursed before she said in that anally-retentive nasally voice of hers, 'I'm *so* glad you could find the time.'

She ushered us down the corridor and into the back sitting room that overlooked the garden. There were about thirty people there: Dick's mum who waved to me, Barbara's two sisters and their suited husbands, some others who I vaguely recalled as teachers from Dick's school, several quiet children, and others in the background I didn't know. I didn't see any of Dick's three sisters. Most people had a schooner of sherry in one hand and a watercress sandwich in the other. I nodded and smiled at those I knew, as did Laura.

Where was Barbara?

Mrs Bradley jumped in with an explanation before I had a chance to ask her.

'Barbara will be down shortly. She's exhausted by everything, and we had the police here again this morning.'

I flashed a look at Laura. The police?

'There was a burglary, but luckily nothing was taken. They were disturbed.'

'Nothing taken?'

'Nothing, thank goodness. And the only damage was the window they prised open.'

Laura wanted to know when this happened.

'The day after Paul … was found.'

Not even Dick's mum ever called him Paul, even though that was his christened name. But Mrs Bradley always found *Dick* too common.

Schooners of sherry were placed in our hands and Mrs B. wafted off to see Barbara.

'You should try to be a little more friendly to her, Christopher,' chided Laura.

'I was.'

'You're not very good at camouflaging your feelings.'

'Was it that obvious?'

Across the room I see Mrs North walk out towards the kitchen. I ask Laura to excuse me for a moment and manœuvre my way across the room and after Mrs North. I arrive in the kitchen as she is pouring herself a Scotch. I give her a hug and kiss.

'I'm very glad you're here, Chris.'

'Nice to see you.'

She knocks back the whole glass in one and wipes her lips with her forefinger.

'I needed that,' she sighs, and then turns to me. 'How are you then? And how's your mum?'

'I'm fine and Mum's fine too. She's still living with her sister down in Torquay.'

'That's good to hear. We always exchange cards at Christmas. I've been meaning to write her a letter ever since, but somehow you don't get around to it, do you? Always something else to do.'

'Laura said you've moved.'

'Yes, got a nice little maisonette now in sheltered accommodation. The council were very good about it. Just up the road.'

'That's good.'

Mrs North nods. I look at her face and see the lines

[49]

running out from her eyes. Big watery blue eyes tinged with sadness. She's a capable and intelligent woman who has always reminded me of my grandmother, so I wasn't at all hesitant in telling her about Dick's call to me in Brno. She listened carefully, nodding and taking it in. Unlike Laura, she didn't doubt for a moment what I was saying.

She was turning over in her mind what I had told her. Then she said, 'Dick wasn't given to romancing … so either he was being followed or he got the wrong end of the stick and thought he was … I don't know what to make of it.'

'Nor do I. It puzzled me. Then earlier today Briscoe said he picked Dick up from the hospice a little while back and Dick kept getting him to stop. Dick was acting like he was being followed.'

'Mmmm,' she murmured as she poured herself another drink.

'Do you suppose the work at the hospice upset him?'

'No, Chris, he'd been doing his counselling too long for that. Though, come to think of it, something about Mr Drax's death seemed to make him a bit, you know, *agitated*.'

'Who was Mr Drax?'

'Old fellow who used to live up Shadwell Lane. Stinking rich, he was. But you can't take that with you, eh?'

'I guess not.'

Mrs Bradley then breezed in with 'And what are you two conspiring at? More sherry? Another sandwich?'

We both shook our heads.

'I'm going up to Dick's study for a while.' That was a statement aimed full frontal at Mrs B. She stared at me blankly. I kissed Mrs North on the cheek.

The study was at the front of the house, at the very top, up some four flights of steps. As I ascended through the house the chatter and bustle below me faded away and I felt increasingly alone. Right at the top there was not a sound. I stood in front of the door, frightened to proceed, transfixed by the thought that Dick would no longer ever be in there. Never again would I hear him say – *Come in, old boy*. I turned the handle and pushed. The door creaked almost imperceptibly as it swung open and there was the study, quiet and chill under its burden of absence.

I stood on the threshold not knowing whether to go in or to return downstairs. Going in without Dick being here seemed like an impertinence at the very least, perhaps even some violation of Dick's privacy. But then I realised these were just excuses I was manufacturing in order to avoid confronting the inevitable. Going in would force upon me the irreversibility of what had happened, the awesome finality of it. Dick was no longer here. Dick was dead.

Then it was as if the chill atmosphere lifted. The study beckoned me in. Dick was waiting for me. This would be the last time we would be together. We'd share a few moments and talk about old times. *Come in, I've been expecting you*. I could feel his presence in the room. He was here and all about me, but he could not stay long.

I walked across to the desk and sat down in Dick's swivel chair and not the wicker chair to the side that I usually sat in. The desk was in front of the window and I could see out down Highfield Road and across to the Dells. I reached forward and took one of Dick's cheroots from the carved wooden box under the desk lamp. I rolled the cheroot between my fingers before lighting it and then inhaled deeply.

There were folio folders in front of me thick with photographs, engravings and maps. These were chapters of Dick's book that would not now be completed. He had titled it *The Ichonography of Hitchin*, borrowing the antiquated spelling of iconography from Sir Henry Chauncey who wrote the first history of Hertfordshire back in the 1600s. The *Ichonography* would reproduce every print, drawing, map and photograph of Hitchin up until 1900 that Dick could trace, together with his accompanying notes and commentary. He reckoned it would run to a quartet of large volumes. Now none of them would see the presses, and the half-completed work would probably end up in the local museum gathering dust.

'This'll take you for ever to complete, Dick.'

'I know, but someone's got to do it.'

Someone's got to do it. *Got* to do it.

He would be philosophical about not completing it. The important thing with him was that you had to try. You had to start. If it was completed that was a bonus. Just get out there and have a go and keep at it.

One side of the study is bookshelves, floor to ceiling, while on the opposite side, the long wall, are nothing but framed engravings and prints of Hitchin and several county maps. There are also photographs of Dick with his mother and father, and one of Dick, me and Laura taken on the Aldermaston March. White lettering in the corner says that it is Easter 1963. We're standing under a banner that loudly proclaims HITCHIN CAMPAIGN FOR NUCLEAR DISARMAMENT. We're all gazing into the camera and smiling, full of hope, optimism and idealism. Three kids from a county town at the beginning of their adult lives.

But there's something missing from the wall. An area about a metre square is empty. I can see the square of fresh unnicotined paint where something hung. What was it? I should know, I've been in this study enough times. Dick never changed this wall. He liked it exactly as it was. What was it? It frustrates me that I cannot recall what has gone, but perhaps it'll come to me later.

I sit down at the desk again and flick some ash from the cheroot into the ashtray. The desk is cluttered with papers, pens, stationery, books and imponderabilia. Vestiges of Dick.

The word 'Kennedy' catches my eye on a pile of books to the left of the Anglepoise. *Who Killed Kennedy?* Underneath this is a paperback entitled *Legend: The Secret World of Lee Harvey Oswald*. I look through the books. There are about ten titles altogether, all about the John F. Kennedy assassination. Each volume has several markers and Post-It notes interleaved and sticking out. Dick must have been studying them closely.

Dick always wrote his name and the year of purchase in any book he acquired, in soft pencil at the front. I see Dick's name – Paul North – and the year 1992 in the two books at the top of the pile.

I wonder why he got all these? Kennedy's assassination? It wasn't the type of thing I would have thought he would now have become interested in. Years ago, perhaps, but not now.

Kennedy was assassinated in 1963, the same year as the Aldermaston photograph on the wall. Three decades ago. I remember coming home from the library on that Friday and my mother saying Kennedy had been shot. I said, what do you mean, *shot*? She said he was dead. I couldn't believe it, I thought it was some joke and then I saw it on TV in the news.

I rushed around to Dick's. He couldn't believe it either. We just sat there watching TV and wondering what would happen next.

Soon after the assassination the police in Dallas had grabbed this guy, Lee Harvey Oswald, who they said was responsible for the Crime of the Century. He was a Communist, they said, and had defected to Russia and then returned home to the States. He was as guilty as fuck. No doubt about that. Bang to rights this little Commie bastard.

Dick and I looked at each other and prayed this wasn't the beginning of the Third World War. Was Khrushchev getting his revenge after the Cuban Crisis? Or was this down to Fidel Castro and his compatriots?

It was soon announced that Oswald was a lone mad nut. He didn't have any accomplices and he wasn't part of a conspiracy. It began and ended with him. He was just disaffected and a lunatic. But before anyone had a chance to question him in any depth he was shot on the Sunday morning by a Dallas night-club owner, Jack Ruby. And that was the end of it. Finis. All nice and neatly concluded.

Or, rather, it should have been.

And so, as the years rolled by, the question as to who assassinated JFK became our generation's contribution to those historical mysteries that will probably never be satisfactorily answered, mysteries like who murdered the princes in the Tower and who was the Man in the Iron Mask?

I stubbed the remains of the cheroot out in the ashtray and got up from the chair. I looked out of the window and saw something that startled me. Totally fucking startled me. Just down the road a little was the figure of Georges whatever-his-name-was. The fat guy in black I met last night. He's standing by the entrance to the youth club place, the Caldecott Centre, and looking up towards me, or rather towards the house. No, towards *me*. Standing there staring, doing nothing else. Motionless. Staring up.

I pull back and turn the lamp off. The lack of light may prevent him from seeing me. I feel my heart beating faster and I'm overcome with a wave of unease I cannot explain. It's crazy I feel like this. I take a few deep breaths and edge forward to peer around the side of the window casement. He's still there and he's still staring up. What's he doing? Why is he *here*?

I walk across the study and take one last look around from the door. It is time to say goodbye, but there is no spirit of Dick here now to say goodbye to. The room is empty. Dick is elsewhere.

As I reach the bottom of the stairs I see Laura coming out of the kitchen with a glass in her hand.

'Come and see this,' I say, pointing towards the front door. 'It's that strange guy I was telling you about.'

'What strange guy?' she asks, not remembering what I had told her.

'The strange guy who stopped me by the church last night.'

'Oh, really?'

[54]

I beckoned her to follow me as I went down the corridor to the front door. I opened it a couple of inches and peered through the gap. The street was empty, there was no Georges. No one anywhere.

'Where is he? Let me see,' Laura said as she pulled the door open wider.

'He's gone.'

'Gone?'

'Yes, gone,' I replied. But where had he gone? He wasn't walking up the street or down it, he'd still be in sight. He had vanished. Swallowed up in the gloom of a winter's Sunday afternoon in Hitchin.

'What's so important about this man?'

'Nothing is important about him … just odd, that's all.'

I leant against the door as it closed. My heart was still racing.

'I was up in Dick's study and I looked out of the window and he was standing across the street staring up at the house. Up at the study actually.'

'Where you were?'

'Yes, exactly.'

Laura sipped her drink and looked at me suspiciously. She then said, 'Why was he doing that?'

'Why was he looking up at the house?'

'Yes.'

'That's a dumb question. How would I know why he's looking up at the house? Ask *him*.'

'You need a drink. Coming here in these circumstances is all too much for you, I think.'

'That's a patronising remark, Laura. Really patronising.'

'You need another drink.'

'Yeah, a really large one.'

I walked back down the corridor leaving Laura at the front door. She had opened it again and was peering out, perhaps waiting to see if Georges would reappear.

There was no one in the kitchen so I poured myself a very large vodka and topped it up with fresh orange juice from the fridge. Laura appeared and looked disapprovingly at the drink.

'I bet that's more vodka than orange.'

'Correct,' I answered as I took another hit.

'Do you think we should go?'

'I haven't seen Barbara yet.'

Laura motioned with her eyes towards the ceiling and whispered, 'I don't think she'll be coming down today.'

'Like that, huh?'

'Right.'

Laura followed me into the sitting room and I looked around for Mrs Bradley. There were still about a dozen people sitting around but she was nowhere to be seen. Mrs North was standing by the far door putting her coat on. We walked over to her.

'Hello, Christopher, Laura. I'm off now.'

'So are we,' Laura responded.

Mrs North smiled faintly and confided to us, 'It won't do just standing around here and getting maudlin. And anyway I've got to get back and feed Barney.' Barney was her old mongrel dog.

The three of us waved and said goodbye to the others as we slipped out of the room. In the corridor we were greeted by Mrs Bradley.

'All off, are we?' she inquired in that sharp voice that could cut through a block of hardened cheddar.

'Yes, we should be going,' I said in a tone that was more an apology than a statement, though I hadn't intended it to be.

'It was so nice of you all coming here,' Mrs Bradley declared, as though we'd turned up for an afternoon of croquet or whist.

Laura and Mrs North thanked her as she waved us out the front door and down the steps. 'See you tomorrow!' she boomed as the front door slammed shut.

'Come on, Mrs North, we'll walk you home,' and as I said that I took her arm and held her close to me.

'No, you won't. It's very nice of you to offer but I'll be

walking home by myself. I don't want you troubling yourself.'

I knew better than to argue with her. She kissed us both goodbye, turned and took little old lady steps down the road into the misty darkness.

Laura and I just looked at each other and then we walked in silence up Highfield Road and took a right down the footpath that leads to the summit of Windmill Hill where, suddenly, the ground falls away steeply to reveal the town nestling below around St Mary's Church. Lights were flickering in the darkness and patches of mist hung above the river and around the open spaces. There was a quiet, inviting silence.

I put my arms around Laura and pulled her towards me. A rich leathery smell from her suede coat mingled with traces of a subtle perfume borne on the smell of her skin.

There was nobody else about. We had the town to ourselves.

[3]

Laura and I were the last ones to arrive at St Mary's. The funeral service was just about to begin. There were some fifty or so people there but hardly anyone I could recognise from behind, aside from Mrs North, and Barbara and her mother at the front, and a few assorted relatives.

The service began and I closed my eyes. In the darkness I could just make out an abyss in front of me. A deep chasm yawning into infinity, its depths beckoning me. I began falling forward into it, space rushing past me. My speed accelerated and a feeling of nausea swept over me. I was going ever faster, hurtling through some space-time continuum. And then I came into contact with something hard and unforgiving and a piercing pain shot across my forehead. There was silence. I wondered what would come next and waited. I opened my eyes slowly and saw three figures looking down upon me. One was Laura, the other two were elderly men I did not recognise. The figures reached down to me and took my arms. I realised then that having a half-bottle of vodka for breakfast was not a prudent decision.

'I must have fainted. I'm OK, thanks,' I said lamely. I could tell by the look in Laura's eyes that she knew I'd been hitting the sauce.

The service continued in the background.

'I've got to get some fresh air,' I whispered to Laura.

'Do you want me to come with you?'

'No, I'm all right. Stay here.'

I walked down the aisle steadying myself against the chairs and then managed to make my way across to the south porch unaided by taking small hesitant steps.

The fresh air brought me to my senses somewhat. I stood there leaning against the porch taking deep breaths, trying to get my head straight. Trying to understand how Hitchin could continue going about its business as if nothing had happened while my friend Dick lay dead within the church.

But that's the way it is.

When I am being buried the local video shop will continue hiring out films while the Chinese take-aways will be piling cartons of noodles in carrier bags ...

Chinese take-aways ...

There used to be a little Chinese take-away on Brand Street (it might even be there still) ...

I remember coming back from London late one night with Dick, it must have been around 1970, and we chanced upon this little place but we only had the money between us for a couple of spring rolls, and they were the finest spring rolls I've ever tasted. We walked down and through Market Square eating them. They really did taste good and even now I can close my eyes and conjure them up, their taste and their texture.

'These are benchmark spring rolls, all right,' spluttered Dick as he munched his way through one.

'Out of sight,' I added.

'Yeah. And look, that Chinese guy put a fortune cookie in my bag as well.'

I looked in my bag. No cookie. 'I didn't get one.'

'He must have run out. You can share this one but the motto thing is mine,' said Dick in consolation.

'You got a deal.'

We shared the cookie here in front of the south porch of the church, where I'm now standing. It tasted of ginger and spice.

As I finished my bit of the cookie I could see Dick unfurling the tiny roll of paper that was contained inside it.

'What's it say?'

Dick held it in the moonlight and announced, 'Confucius say, "Man conceived out of wedlock on back seat of car grow up to be shiftless bastard".'

'No it doesn't!' I objected.

Dick smiled and read from the small strip of paper: THE FULL MOON DOES NOT FACE THE SUN.

'What does that mean then?'

'Search me,' replied Dick, 'is it from the I Ching or something?'

He handed me the piece of paper and I scrutinised the text, as though looking at it closely and intently would somehow fill in the meaning. I shook my head. 'Think it's got anything to do with astronomy?'

'No, I'll tell you what I think it means,' replied Dick, 'and it is quite simple. It means you shouldn't shine too brightly in the presence of a superior. The sun is the Chinese emperor, you know?'

'I thought fortune cookies were supposed to tell you your fortune?'

'Perhaps this is an advice cookie?' offered Dick in explanation.

We both laughed.

A penetratingly cold wind rushes up the side of the church and I'm suddenly brought back to the present. I take a couple of steps back into the porch. The service seems to be continuing inside.

From the pocket of my coat I take out the hide wallet I've had for some thirty years and extract my driving licence. Nestling within the licence is that little piece of paper from the fortune cookie: THE FULL MOON DOES NOT FACE THE SUN. It is perfectly preserved, the cheap red print still bright and readable. On the reverse of the slip, written in black ink with a 0.25 Rapidograph pen (I've never used anything else since the mid-1960s), is the date – Saturday, 9 May 1970.

I fold the fortune cookie 'motto' neatly and return it whence it had come.

There is movement within the church, the service must be coming to an end. I take out the vodka and have a couple of quick hits to see me through to the cemetery. I'm not dreading that so much, it was this service that was getting to me.

'How are you feeling now?'

I turn and it's Laura. She glances down as I put the bottle back into my pocket and says nothing. She just looks at me. 'How you feeling?'

'I'm fine, I think. Just fine.'

She takes my arm and propels me out of the porch to the churchyard. We stand to one side as the coffin is carried out and into the waiting hearse. The mourners shuffle out in file behind it and then I find myself sitting in a limo with Laura and several people I don't know.

As the car pulls out of the churchyard I see Briscoe standing alone by the gate, huddled in the cold. He's holding his baseball cap in his hands and his head is bowed.

There's some movement in my peripheral vision that takes my attention. Laura is doing something. I shoot a sly glance at her. She's wiping tears from her cheeks. I squeeze her hand and she squeezes mine back.

Hitchin seems quiet and empty as we go down Sun Street and into Bridge Street. There is a big sad sun in the sky, and this is just another day in the history of the world. I feel like I'm living in the past already. This too will soon all be a memory.

We drive up the hill and turn a couple of times and here we are. This is Dick's final resting place. This is what his life culminated in – led up to.

I'm still holding Laura's hand as we walk from the car into the cemetery. I can see Mrs North ahead of us and her daughters, Mrs Bradley in a black suit, Barbara in some designer black costume with veils that look totally inappropriate for the occasion, Dick's colleagues, people I half know, people I've never seen before.

We're all gathered around the grave and Dick is lowered in. This is it, old pal. This is where we say goodbye. This is the end of it all.

Several crows alight on a nearby grave and begin arguing amongst themselves. A black cloud engulfs the sun and chill winds appear from nowhere. I look around at the cemetery, at the old and overgrown graves, monuments to the living-who-are-now-dead, and think how this final fate overshadows us all. The knowledge of death is that icy companion who never leaves our side.

Here it is, the city of the dead. The necropolis.

I take my wallet out and find the fortune cookie slip of paper and then bend down for a handful of earth and I throw it all into the grave. I look at the white slip as it hits Dick's coffin and as I gaze at it more earth falls and then it is gone …

Mrs North was wiping her eyes and gently sobbing as she stared at the grave. I put my arm around her and she turned and looked into my eyes.

'At least there were no children,' she whispered. 'That would have made it worse.'

'That's true.'

'I'll see Dick again one day.'

'You will … we all will,' I replied and as I said that I really believed it for that instant.

Mrs North walked slowly back to the cars supported

and surrounded by her daughters. I turned and looked for Laura. She was talking to Barbara. Behind them, over by a row of mausoleums, something caught my eye. There was a parked stretch limo with its engine running. It was black and its windows were smoked, preventing you from seeing inside. The vehicle looked brand new, a Mercedes possibly, I couldn't tell from this angle. It wasn't with us and I'm sure it wasn't local. The funeral directors around here had only old Austins and Fords. This was out of town. Another funeral perhaps? But no, it appeared to be alone. A rear window opened halfway. I couldn't see who was inside but I did see a large camera lens poke out and move from side to side, presumably taking photographs. Whoever this was it certainly wasn't the local newspaper. The lens withdrew and the window went up. Then silently the limo pulled forward, accelerated quite rapidly and shot through the cemetery gates. I stared after it. Something about it unsettled me.

'Thank you for coming, Christopher.'

It was a broken female voice, Barbara's. She was standing in front of me.

'I'm so sorry about this,' I said, not knowing what else to say.

'Yes,' replied Barbara, 'and he was your friend too.'

She said this in a sort of professional-widow-coping-under-the-strain voice that mixed self-pity with the patronising. But before I had an opportunity to say anything further she was gone, whisked off by her mother and relatives. There was just Laura standing in front of me now shrugging her shoulders and attempting a smile as if to say, 'Oh, well. That's how it is.' I took her hand and we followed the others back to the shiny black cars of the funeral convoy where Mrs Bradley was busily fussing about dividing the party into those who were returning to the centre of town (and, presumably, work and prior appointments) and the remainder of us who were returning to the house for drinks.

Laura and me found ourselves alone in a big old Austin Princess being driven by an elderly guy in a dark suit and peaked hat from the funeral director's. We were the last car to leave.

Laura snuggled up to me and I put my arm around her. I don't know whether she was so close to me for comfort or to keep warm. It was cold and there appeared to be no heating in the car.

'I hope they get Dick a simple headstone. Elegant and simple. Nothing silly,' said Laura.

I told Laura I hoped so too.

'Of course, they'll take the words from a catalogue.'

'What catalogue? The *Whole Earth Catalogue of Headstones*?'

'Masons, funeral directors – they have catalogues. You choose the style of the headstone, and they have sample verses and words too. I can see you've never done this.'

It's true, I hadn't. There'd always been someone else to take over from me. I'd always managed to avoid it.

'How long is it before someone starts rotting in a coffin?'

'What a gruesome question, Christopher!'

'It isn't. I'm just curious. Weeks? Months? Years?'

'I don't know. Ask the driver.'

I looked up at the driver sitting in the front with his straight back to us. He probably had us down as weirdos anyway, certainly me from the glance he gave me as we got in the car, so perhaps it's best I don't quiz him on the subject. A legitimate question, nonetheless, and certainly one Dick would have posed had it been me in the coffin back there.

'I'd hate people to get sorry and depressed when I die. I hope they'll go out and have a good time. Get really pissed. That's what Dick thinks too,' I said.

'You got a head start on everyone else,' stated Laura.

'What's that mean?'

'You know exactly what that means and ...' but her voice trailed away.

I knew exactly what she meant and I decided silence

[63]

was the best policy. Don't pick quarrels with men who buy ink by the barrel, said Benjamin Franklin. And don't pick quarrels with women who manifestly have right on their side, I codiciled.

There was now a gentle rain.

We arrived at Highbury Road and climbed out.

'Do we tip the driver?' I asked Laura in a whisper.

'No, but why don't you try thanking him?'

'Yeah.'

Laura went ahead. She still has a beautiful glide as she walks, moving from the hips down only. She'd look good on a catwalk.

I turned to the driver. 'Thanks for the ride.'

He smiled and nodded. He looked a lot more simpatico than he seemed from the back.

I feel an arm around my waist. A comforting and soothing arm. And then a kiss on my cheek. It's Laura. She's giving me one of those comforting smiles of hers where she doesn't part her lips and where all those attractive lines suddenly appear in the outer corners of her two doleful eyes.

'What would you like, Christopher?'

I always loved the way she said Christopher. Tenderly, soothingly.

'The past, I guess.'

'Well, I can't get you that ... but come inside.'

We walked up the steps together into the house. In fact Laura walked, I just stumbled. She led me through into the sitting room and guided me to an armchair.

'I'll get you a drink. Would you like something to eat as well?'

'No, just a drink.'

There were knots of people standing around, chatting, drinking. There was even some quiet laughter somewhere over the back by the French windows. Mrs Bradley was being terribly effusive with two young guys I didn't recognise in double-breasted suits who may have been colleagues of Dick's from school, and Barbara was showing off her porcelain figurines to an elderly middle-class couple who looked like they had just stepped off a pension plan leaflet put out by one of the high street banks. I couldn't see Mrs North anywhere, nor Dick's sisters.

Laura was now kneeling in front of me, offering me a tumbler full of a dark plum-coloured liquid.

'What on earth's that?' I asked her.

'Fresh grape juice.'

'I hope there's some vodka in it.'

'There is.'

I took the tumbler and sipped it slowly. The grape juice was very cold and left a trail down my throat that was then stung by the spirit.

Holding the glass in front of me I said, 'You know what this mix is called, don't you?'

'I do. A Purple Jesus. You used to drink it years ago when you affected those ridiculous black Russian cigarettes.'

And so I did. Carousing around at parties with this drink in one hand and a Russian cigarette in the other. Only they weren't ridiculous, they were expensive Balkan Sobranie cigarettes. Dick smoked them too.

Laura said she was going over to see Barbara and I said I'd sit there for a moment and gather my thoughts (finish the drink, that is), which I promptly did. I then remembered that Dick used to keep a little bit of dope in a secret compartment in his desk. He never told Barbara about it though we did from time to time smoke it under her nose, and she just assumed like the other innocents that it was just some herbal tobacco and nothing else.

I pushed myself up out of the armchair and wobbled misty-eyed over to Laura and Barbara. I tried my damnedest to stand up straight and still but I was helplessly listing from side to side, like those toy clown figures with a round bottom. Laura ignored my waverings but Barbara kept shooting me anxious glances. I had difficulty focusing on what they were talking about, so I steered myself in the direction of the kitchen.

I was staring up at an old framed map of Hitchin above the Aga when Laura came in with an empty glass. She seemed surprised to see me: 'I thought you'd gone upstairs for a snooze.'

'No. I'm fine.'

'Uh-huh.'

'Fancy some fun, Laura?'

'What sort of fun?'

'A smoke.'

'You got something on you?'

'No, but I think I know where there is some.'

'Here?'

'Follow me.'

We left the kitchen and went into the hall. There was nobody about so I took Laura's hand and led her up the stairs to the top of the house, to the door of Dick's study.

'We often used to smoke it here together. He had a little stash.'

Laura seemed bemused. I became bemused.

This was like being young again and doing something naughty or illicit. We went into the study and I closed the door behind us. Laura sat on the desk while I opened the top left drawer and felt around inside for the secret compartment. I pulled out some grass and a packet of large liquorice cigarette papers in a polythene bag.

'There's enough here for one of my three-paper Hitchin Torpedoes!'

'Oh, goodie!' laughed Laura as she wiggled about on the desk.

I broke a couple of my Marlboros and mixed the grass with the tobacco. Then I joined three cigarette papers together and rolled the joint, putting a small spiral of cardboard in as a tip at one end and twisting the other.

Laura was rubbing her hands together in anticipation. 'Do you remember those joints we used to make with menthol filter tips?' she said.

I did. I often used to smoke Consulate fags in those

[66]

days. A menthol cigarette. Those joints were cool, literally.

'Dick,' I said, holding the joint in the air, 'this little one is for you!'

'It's for you, Dick,' Laura echoed.

In silence I handed the fat reefer to Laura. She put it between her lips and I leant over with my Zippo. She looked straight at me as if to say, hurry up and light it. I held the flame just short of the joint and teased her.

'Light it, damn you,' she whispered, and I did.

Laura closed her eyes and inhaled deeply. She kept the smoke down for several beats and then slowly exhaled through her nose. She repeated this and then gradually opened her eyes before handing it to me.

'Is the spirit reaching you, sister?'

Laura didn't reply, she was staring ahead, eyes wide open. Going with it.

I take a couple of hits and watch the lazy smoke curling upwards and away. I turn very slowly to Laura and hold out my hand. She reaches out and our hands meet in a clasp.

'This is so funny!'

I agree with her.

'Here we are at the top of the house,' confides Laura, 'smoking an illicit drug.'

'A very illicit drug! And what if Barbara discovers us?'

'But not as illicit as it used to be ...' and my voice trails off. I was going to say something else but I couldn't, *didn't* want to formulate it. I was thinking along the lines of when I was young getting a feel of a girl's breast was pretty exciting, whereas now ... whereas now ... I wanted to reach out and touch Laura's thighs. That would be more exciting than a blow-job from any other woman.

And we laugh again.

I see Dick's record player deck and the two speakers on the floor over by the door. Through the transparent cover of the player I can see a 12" LP sitting on the turntable. That must have been the last record Dick played.

'That must have been the last record Dick played,' I said.

'What?' Laura turns her head to one side.

'The record over there. Must have been the last one he played.' I waved towards the door.

'I wonder what it was?'

'I'll go and see.'

I let go of Laura's hand and spent ages getting out of the chair. I steadied myself against the desk.

'I'm going over there now, Laura,' I said, motioning towards the player.

Laura turned and looked, very slowly. Then turned back and looked straight at me: 'Do you want me to come?'

'No. Stay here!'

We giggled and I crossed the room. I knelt down and lifted the cover. The centre of the LP was upside down so I rotated it. The label said *King Pleasure*. I remember King Pleasure. There were not many vocalists, jazz or otherwise, I ever much cared for but he ain't too bad. In fact, he's pretty good. I got turned on to him because there used to be (maybe there still is) a track of his on the jukebox at Joe Allen's in Covent Garden.

'It's King Pleasure.'

'Who?'

'Just listen.'

'King *Pleasure*?'

'Right. *Him*.'

I pressed the amp mains on and lifted the pick-up arm and placed it, somewhat clumsily, on what was supposed to be the beginning of the LP but ended up a third of the way in. The stylus bumped and jumped a couple of times and there was a screeching sound through the speakers before the track started.

The music billowed out of the speakers and enveloped me and Laura and filled the room. I closed my eyes and I was *there*.

I took a couple more hits and watched Laura do the same. Wow!

SEE HOW YOU GOT ME SPINNING!

Red Top!
My little Red Top,
See how you got me spinning.
Going round and round
And don't know how to stop.
You've got me so if I don't go around
I'm sure gonna drop, gonna drop, gonna drop.
So, Red Top
You just go right on spinning!

I started shuffling about the floor in time with the music. Laura came and put her arms around me and we moved to and fro, sharing the joint in our own reverie. This was our private wake for Dick.

We were still moving after the music had stopped and after we'd finished the joint.

'We better go back downstairs,' I suggested.

'Uh-huh,' said Laura as she straightened her hair.

I went over to the desk and put the remains of the joint in the ashtray. I casually looked out of the window in front of me and my eyes involuntarily focused on a car parked on the other side of the road, down a bit, by the Caldecott Centre. It was half up on the pavement. A big black Mercedes. New and shiny it seemed. I realised then that it was the limo that I'd seen at the funeral. It was parked exactly where Georges had been standing on Sunday. Was there a connection?

I grabbed Laura's hand and pulled her after me out of the room and down the stairs.

'Where are we going?'

'I'll show you.'

We turned at the bottom of the stairs and raced to the front door. I opened it and there was the car still. Its engine running.

I let go of Laura and bounded down the steps and out on to the street. Laura was following me.

The car was big, much bigger than I thought. I was

approaching it now but I couldn't see who was inside because of the dark glass. But there must be someone inside, the engine was running.

From somewhere behind me I heard Laura say, 'What's this all about?' But I didn't bother to reply, I was now reaching for the driver's door handle. I clasped it and attempted to open it, but it was locked. I started banging on the window with my fist, pummelling it with as much might as I could muster and shouting, 'Open this fucking door!'

'Christopher!' cried Laura.

'Open this fucking door!'

'Christopher!'

My hand was aching from hitting the window, but it seemed the hand belonged to someone else. The pain didn't seem to connect.

The car juddered as it was put into gear and then slowly edged forward. It rapidly gained speed and I had to release my grip on the door. I continued hitting the window until it pulled away and I managed to kick the rear wing as it fled.

'Fuck you!' I shouted after it.

'Christopher?' said a quiet voice behind me.

'That was the limo at the funeral,' I said.

'The what?' asked Laura.

'It was hanging about at the funeral!'

'So?'

I was too uptight to explain.

[4]

I awoke to a long enveloping silence.

The clock said 10.45 on TUESDAY, but the face failed to reveal what actual day of the month or what year, but given enough time I'd remember.

Silence.

TUESDAY. Uh-huh.

When I got down to the kitchen after a shower there was

silence too and a scribbled note in black caps on the table:

EAT SOMETHING SENSIBLE BEFORE YOU GO!
Love – L.

I couldn't face anything to eat, but a drink? Yes. A little old vodka and coffee would do nicely.

It was time I was moving. Get back to London, sort out the flat, get the photographs together, go out to the studios and try and get some decisions on this bloody film. Reimmerse myself in work and all that.

Dick's now buried and it's all over. Over. It really is now. Me sitting here on a wet Tuesday morning by myself. This is how it finally ends.

I put the mug in the sink, made sure everything was switched off and let myself out.

The drizzle was increasing as I turned into Bucklersbury from Tilehouse Street. Perhaps I should have got a cab? No, only another expense. I headed through the Market Square and straight on down the High Street.

I take a right into Portmill Lane, past the solicitors' where Reginald Hine used to work (a beautiful Georgian house), and then along at the end into Walsworth Road.

I take a cigarette out of my bag halfway along the road and pause to light it. The rain is trickling down my face and my fingers are numb.

As I'm crossing the station approach a car speeds by me at about 30 m.p.h. and very nearly knocks me over. Muddy water from a puddle arcs up and drenches my legs. The tops of my socks are soaking and I can feel the damp incrementally seeping into my shoes.

I look up and see the back of the car as it gradually comes to a halt by the ticket office, and as it turns and stops I realise that this is the big black Mercedes I saw at Dick's funeral and outside the house last night. I stand there in the rain staring. A chauffeur climbs out and walks around to open the nearside rear door. The chauffeur leans down

[71]

to help someone out. I can only see the figure's back but then as it turns I realise it is that Georges guy in his black corduroy suit and cape. He enters the booking office, but not until after he stares at me, and for a beat too long for it to have been without intent.

I'm striding across to the station now with a singularity of purpose when some mass enters the corner of my eye and stops in front of me.

'You got a light, mate?'

It's a guy in his late twenties or early thirties dressed in a green insulated army jacket. He's got short ginger hair and a moustache and he's holding an unlighted cigarette in my direction, staring at me. His eyes are small and twitchy. There's something shifty about him but I can't quite put my finger on it.

I hold out the cigarette and say, 'Can you take it off this?'

He steadies my hand and leans forward with his cigarette between his lips until it touches the lighted end of my cigarette But he's not focused on this, his eyes are darting about.

Come on! I think to myself. Come on! Take the fucking light.

I'm waiting impatiently for the guy to get the light and wondering what Georges is doing in the station when I feel something glance off the right side of my head. A searing feeling starts to radiate from the point of impact, tunnelling through my consciousness in paroxysms of pain. My mouth opens and I stumble forward towards the guy with ginger hair.

What's happening?

He doesn't have any answers.

A voice behind me says, '*Where* are they?'

I feel hands tearing at me, pulling me apart … dismantling me. A thin liquid runs down my face and covers my eyes. Other rivulets score a course down my neck and on to my chest. My hands are dripping with this bright red liquid. It's everywhere. I can even taste it upon my lips. Blood.

Where are they?

And now I'm horizontal and cold water covers my face. Signals are still coming in from the far parts of my body, damage here, pain there, something else there, but the signals are having difficulty getting through as the last pockets of consciousness are extinguished by an engulfing black nothingness.

He's only got colour!

'I've come to take your temperature.'

A long silence.

'She's come to take your temperature.'

A second voice.

Another silence.

'Christopher, the nurse wants to take your temperature.'

A third voice.

I hesitatingly open my left eye. Laura. Seated.

I focus and see Briscoe standing behind her, grinning still and drumming on a pack of cigarettes.

A nurse steps forward and sticks a thermometer under my tongue. Laura reaches forward and takes my hand.

'A couple of cans of Special Brew and you'll be all right,' declares Briscoe.

Oh, yeah?

The thermometer is whisked from my mouth and the nurse vanishes, literally.

And now I'm out of it once more.

I come to again and now I'm completely conscious. The ache in my head has subsided but it still makes turning my head difficult. Laura and Briscoe are sitting either side of the bed.

'How long have I been here?'

'Two days,' says Laura.

Two whole days!

'Where am I?'

'In hospital,' Laura replies.

Why? How come?

I don't understand this two whole days in the hospital.

Briscoe whispers something to Laura. She looks up at him, thinks, and then whispers a reply to him. Briscoe shakes his head.

Briscoe now draws closer to me. 'You got mugged, at the station.'

Somewhere on the far side of my memory was a picture of me walking across the forecourt at the station. But it seemed countless years ago, an incident lapping on the shores of memory, a half-recollected dream. An incident dissolved by time.

'I was dropping off a fare and I pulled in and I saw this geezer on the ground taking it from these two blokes.'

'Then what happened?' This was exciting, I thought.

'Well, I waded in and let them both have it. I think I broke one of them's nose. And I bent down and the poor geezer on the floor was you. Quite a surprise, I tell you. I thought you were a gonna, covered in blood and that and not conscious. So I radioed back to base from the car and they got an ambulance. And here you are, old mate.'

'I was mugged?'

'You were mugged all right.'

There was a picture in my mind of a man's face. He was leaning forward to take a light from my cigarette. In his late twenties, early thirties he was. Eyes flitting about.

'How old were these two guys?'

Briscoe scratched his chin and thought it over. 'Not sure really. Didn't pay too much attention. It was all over so quickly.'

'They weren't kids?' I asked.

'No, definitely not kids. No.'

And they mugged me.

'I don't think they took anything,' volunteered Briscoe. 'Not least your wallet, cash and credit cards and that.'

'Briscoe, you are a real pal.'

Big Briscoe went coy and didn't know where to look.

'You had a mild concussion but no fractures, thank God,'

said Laura. 'They are going to discharge you tomorrow. You can spend a few days with me.'

'I'd love to, Laura, but I've got to get back to town. I really have.'

'I'll run you home then.'

And I sank into a slumber before the reply of OK could form in my throat.

The policeman sitting at the side of the bed looked like he could be one of my son's friends. He was young, blond and slim and had an easy-going manner. He apologised that this had happened in Hitchin and assured me that mugging in this town was a very rare occurrence. He took down all the details and expressed little hope of the culprits being brought to justice unless, of course, they decided to turn themselves in.

The officer continued writing.

Something else came back to me: this Georges figure getting out of his big black Merc at the station. This fat freak staring at me across the station forecourt immediately before I got done over. Should I mention this to the copper? And if I do, what do I say?

The policeman continued scribbling away.

'Have you been stationed here long?' I asked.

'Three years almost,' he replies without looking up.

Uh-huh. He must know the town pretty well then.

'So you know most of the faces in the town?'

'Some of them.'

'Do you know a big guy, I guess in his early sixties, with long hair who goes about in an expensive black suit with a hat and cape, and a cane, who drives a big new Merc … with a chauffeur?'

The copper looks up, sucks the end of his pen, thinks a moment and looks bemused. 'That's not an individual who readily comes to mind, sir. Why do you ask? A friend of yours?'

'No, no. Not at all.'

[75]

'There's no relevance to this incident is there?'

'No, none. None whatsoever.' And I'd better get him off that line of inquiry. 'Just somebody I bumped into the other day – that's all.'

I gathered my stuff together and waited outside the hospital. It was damp and cold but I needed to get out and get some fresh air.

There was still an ache down the side of my head but I could cope with it. The bruising on my body, particularly around my shoulders and hips, didn't cause me any discomfort except when I moved, so my movements were slow and considered. The walking stick helped greatly.

I soon felt very tired and I needed to sit down. I hobbled across to a bench and waited. Laura was ten minutes late. She'd said she'd be there at noon.

The next thing I remember is a voice saying 'Wake up!' I opened my eyes and there was Laura standing over me and shaking me.

'Sorry, I must have nodded off.'

'Come on, let's get you moving!'

I felt stiff and fatigued and without Laura helping me I doubt I could have made it across to her old and battered Volvo estate.

'That's a fair black eye you've got,' said Laura.

I reached for the rear-view mirror and turned it to get a look at myself. My right eye, in the daylight, certainly looked a lot worse than it did in the uniform bright lighting of the hospital – an artist's palette of blues, purples and blacks radiating out. That and the large plaster across the bridge of my nose made me look like some street-fighting guy, albeit an unsuccessful one.

'Why not get an eye patch for maximum effect? You'd look really dashing then,' suggested Laura.

'Yeah, and a duelling scar too, eh?'

Laura crashed the gears several times before we pulled out.

'I need a new gearbox.'

Yes, I thought, and what was it Dick used to say? If you can't find 'em, grind 'em!

'Can we call by an off-licence?' I asked.

Laura shot a stern rebuking glance at me.

'No, it's not for me. I wanted to pick up a bottle for Briscoe. To thank him, you know?'

Laura's facial muscles relaxed and she nodded a smile. But come to think of it, I could do with a drink too. That would certainly take the edge off me.

'Are you taking any medicine … tablets?' Laura asked.

'No. They gave me some painkillers, but I don't really like taking that stuff. Not unless I have to.'

'So you're suffering … stoically?'

'Yeah.' Well, I'll suffer stoically until I'm back at the flat – and then a couple of hits of vodka. I know what works for me. I know how to treat myself.

Laura pulled up outside the big off-licence in Hermitage Road and turned to me and said, 'I'll go in for you. What do you want?'

'No, I need the exercise. I'll go in. You want anything?'

'See if they've got some decent chocolate.'

'Right.'

I pushed myself out of the car and a searing pain shot down my right leg, emanating from my hip. I quickly straightened up and the pain dissolved. I steadied myself against the car and got my breath back. I was shaking. Laura leant across and asked me if I could manage. Sure, I said.

Leaning against the walking stick I made it in small steps across the pavement and into the shop. What do I get Briscoe? He's a beer drinker by and large, but on high days and holidays he likes Scotch. A bottle of Bell's? No, I'll get him a decent Scotch, a straight malt. There were about twenty different malts on the shelf and I settled on Glenfiddich which most people seem to like. I should also get Laura something. She likes claret. There's a good selection here and I choose a couple of bottles of a medium-priced

Château I've never heard of. I also buy a half bottle of vodka and … some strong cough sweets. And also a box of Belgian chocolates for Laura.

While the guy behind the counter was doing the VISA card business I unscrewed the cap of the vodka bottle and took a couple of big hits. The guy eyed me suspiciously. I must have looked odd to say the least – black eye, nose plaster, hitting the juice here in his shop.

I took a couple more hits and then stuck a cough sweet in my mouth to take away the smell of the spirit (vodka does have an odour to it). I secreted the bottle away in my pocket.

The vodka descended to my stomach and then seemed to leach out to the rest of my body. It was like calming fingers massaging and soothing me from the inside. A warmish glow that eased and dissolved the pain. The walk back to the car was a hell of a lot easier than the walk from it.

'Here you go, Laura. Thanks.' And I leant across and kissed her.

'What's in here?' she said as she took the bag.

'Just a couple of bottles and some chocolate.'

She kissed me and thanked me and then said, after a pause, 'Where does Briscoe live now?'

'King's Road.'

'King's Road?'

'By Ransom's Park.'

'Uh-huh, I know. Where the Indians live.'

I nodded (but I think they're mostly Pakistanis, actually).

Laura took a left at the top of Hermitage Road and then down Whinbush Road where we all grew up. We were both thinking *that*, but neither of us said anything. I looked across at her. She was concentrating on driving but her tongue was lubricating her lips, tripping back and forth and depositing a glistening patina of saliva.

Whinbush Road. Then we were three – now we are two.

'Whereabouts?'

'Briscoe's just up here on the right,' I said indicating

midway along the straight terrace of late nineteenth-century artisans' houses.

I took the bottle of Scotch and climbed out of the car sans pain. The house looked quiet. I pushed the gate open and went up to the front door. The paint was peeling and the push for the doorbell buzzer hung loose on a length of bellwire. I banged the knocker a couple of times and waited. Nothing. There was nobody in. Somewhere inside a dog barked. I put the bottle in a rack meant for milk bottles and wrote a little note on a sheet drawn from my pocket notebook.

'I hope it ain't stolen,' I said as I climbed back in the car.

'Not in?'

'No.'

Laura executed a six-point turn and we were on our way again. The sun was lamely peering out from behind the clouds and it looked as though we were in for some heavy rain later.

We drove back through town and up Park Street with its high overhanging embowering trees that still, in summer, manage to meet high above the road.

Coming down Park Street, with its high banks and the trees, is still the best approach into town: the descent into Hitchin.

And here is the hill, Hitchin Hill, Hitchin's 'left-hand' as George Chapman calls it in the introduction to his translation of the *Odyssey*.

I wondered which way Laura was going to drive to London and I asked her.

'Straight down to the A1.'

'Why don't you go down the old London Road? We can pick the A1 up at Welwyn.'

'Why?'

'I haven't been down that way for ages, that's all.'

'If you want.'

Leaving Hitchin now seemed in a way the very final act in Dick's death. There's a presence people have even at their funeral, but when even the funeral is in the past, they are in the past.

I felt my eyes begin watering. I wanted the reassurance of Laura so I reached out and put my hand on her thigh. She put her hand on top of mine and held it firmly. I felt my sadness and anxiety dissolving away. I put my head back and closed my eyes and floated off into slumber.

I came to as we were descending the Archway Road in north London. My hand was still on Laura's thigh. I gently squeezed it.

'You're awake then?'

I mumbled agreement.

There was a phrase echoing around in my head, in fact a sentence. I was only aware of it obliquely to begin with. It was unfocused and distant, then it came into sharp view. I wondered where it came from? First it was just words, then a voice was added: Where are they?

Where are they?

I know that, I thought. I know that, but from where?

I turned to Laura, 'Where are they?'

'What?' she said, startled.

'Where are they?'

'What are you talking about?'

'Where are they? That's what this guy was saying when I was being done over! Where are they?'

'So? What does that mean?'

'I'll tell you what it means,' I said anxiously. 'It means they were looking for something.'

'Muggers … robbers, they're always looking for something. That's why they rob people, you know?'

Laura's cold logic wasn't going to rob me of a theory, or was it? 'They were looking for something specific.'

'Specific?' asked Laura.

'If you're robbing someone, you don't say, "Where are they?" You say, "What's he got?" Right?' This was unassailable.

'They could have been looking for your credit cards.

[80]

Nobody seems to carry much cash around with them any more, do they? So, they're going to say – Where are they?'

I suppose I had to concede that, but I didn't let on to her. They could have been looking for credit cards, say, but I had this feeling they weren't, and anyway, they hadn't taken them. Was this because Briscoe had suddenly appeared or what? It was also the way the guy said it. The mere words themselves don't convey what he said. It was the tenor of his voice, the intonation. *That* conveyed the meaning. They were looking for something specific … I think.

'Anyway, what have you got that they wanted?'

I could not answer the question.

'I've dealt with hundreds of people who've been robbed. You cannot but help take it personally. Everyone does. It's victim syndrome.' There was a matter-of-fact authority in Laura's voice that upset me.

A victim, huh? I'd never thought of myself as a victim. Somebody who's been robbed, yes. But not a victim. That really makes you feel … uh … powerless … and insignificant. A victim. What an awful word. Passive in the face of events.

'OK, but there was something else about it that was a bit odd.'

'What?'

'Just before they set on me this big Mercedes drove up to the station and that fancy guy Georges got out. And he looked across at me!'

'What's that got to do with it?'

'It was the same car that was at the funeral and he is the same guy who came up to me by the church on Saturday night *and* who was outside Dick's place. Isn't that odd? I mean we're not talking footling coincidence here, we're talking design and intent.'

Laura laughed and said, 'He *looked* at you?'

'Right. Yes.'

'Perhaps he finds you irresistible, Christopher?'

'Perhaps it's actually a bit freaky? Perhaps there's

something going on we don't know about? Eh?'

'Apparently there is, for you. Are you saying there is some connection between him being there and you being mugged?'

'No, not necessarily.'

'Why mention it then?'

'Because there might be,' I replied. 'Might be.'

'And what would that connection be?'

'I don't know,' I whispered.

Laura giggled.

'Jesus! I'm trying to be serious about this. You just think it's a joke!'

Laura tutted under her breath and put on her magistrates' court voice. 'It is sometimes very difficult to accept accident or coincidence for what they are. We tend to look for a design or a pattern in events. You're thinking like many victims think.'

'Don't call me a victim, please.'

We continued on and were soon in Tufnell Park. Then, past the Victorian splendour of the Boston pub on the right, down a bit and we were there. There was a parking space right in front of the flat. Laura took my bag and got out. As I eased myself up I had that pain down my thigh again, but not as piercing as it had been earlier.

Laura went ahead of me down the steps to the basement. I had to take it easy down the steps, just one at a time. I felt some drops of rain on my face. We'd got back just in time.

'You left the front door open.' Laura's voice managed to convey alarm, accusation and exasperation all seamlessly bundled together.

You left the front door open? What does she mean? I've got two hefty locks on it and I'm obsessive about locking it and checking it before I leave, even when I'm totally pissed. Last Saturday when I left for King's Cross I checked the locks. I always do.

Down one step. And now another.

'Christopher!'

Laura was standing just inside the doorway.

The door had sprung open and there down the left hand side of it were black marks, splinters, and two gaps where the locks had been. Some mighty crowbar had prised it open.

I followed Laura in and gazed around – Jesus fucking Christ!

'God almighty!' echoed Laura.

The flat looked like it had been taken apart piece by piece. Nothing was where it had been when I left nearly a week ago. Everything had been moved. Every drawer had been taken out and emptied. Every cupboard opened. Every book had been pulled from the shelves and flung to the floor. The sound system had been taken from the stacking cabinet and now formed angled masses peeking out of cushions and upturned chairs. All the pictures had been removed from the walls and flung in the centre of the room, upon the Sony TV that was face down.

'Christopher! Oh, my God!'

I pushed the door shut and then saw on the floor a week's mail, several dozen envelopes of varying shapes and sizes – all torn open, the contents resting where they had fallen.

I up-ended a chair and told Laura to sit down.

The bedroom was the same, but luckily they had fallen short of hacking the duvet and mattress with a knife (things could always be worse). The bathroom was a disaster too. The two wall cabinets had been emptied and the contents were heaped on a bath mat, oozing unguents, emollients and preparations. And the same in the kitchen – everything emptied, including the fridge and the freezer, but with one extenuation – the only extenuation – the fridge and the freezer had thus both finally been defrosted. Even the plants had been emptied from the flower pots.

I took a bottle of orange squash from off the floor by the cooker and poured some into a mug. I added the vodka from the bottle in my pocket, took a couple of hits, and slumped to the floor. I wanted to go to sleep and wake up to find this was all a dream or, failing that, wake up to find the place clean and tidy.

Well, there was nothing really valuable here they could have taken that I can't replace easily enough – a couple of cameras and lenses, a video recorder and so on would be about it. The books all over the floor upset me more than anything. I hoped not too many of them were damaged. They were about the only thing I really valued.

But the tidying up … and the insurance, or rather lack of. Christ – what a bore!

I drained the last vodka from the bottle into the now empty mug and downed it. Fuck this!

Laura appeared in front of me and shrugged her shoulders. She sat down and put her arms around me. I closed my eyes in despair.

'Let's make a start,' said Laura.

'Leave it … some other time,' I said groggily.

'We'll start now. Won't take too long.'

'Do we really have to?' I asked.

'Yes. I'll start in here and while I'm doing this you can phone the police.'

'They'll come around and help us, will they?'

'You've got to report it.'

The two police officers arrived just after 8 p.m.

We'd managed to get most of the place back in shape, or rather Laura had. I'd just done the light stuff – putting the books back (only a few bent pages and one broken spine), straightening things, sorting out papers and so on.

Laura said it could have been a lot worse – they could have pissed and shit all over the gaff, a common enough way for vandals to register their presence. Perhaps I got off lightly?

'I'm Harry and this is Alan.'

I invited the two uniformed officers in. They were both in their late twenties.

'You been in an accident?' asked Harry as he looked at my face.

'I got mugged in Hitchin.'

The two officers exchanged glances.

They both seemed a little surprised when they saw Laura, as though she shouldn't be here. Laura got up from the sofa and introduced herself.

They both nodded at her and said nothing and it fell upon me to introduce them by name.

They asked me to show them around the flat.

'We've managed to do most of the tidying up as you can see, but when we got back the place was totally chaotic, everything had been taken apart, and was everywhere.'

'Uh-huh,' said Harry, 'and how did they gain access?'

'Through the front door here,' I said as I showed them where the locks used to be.

'Did any of your neighbours hear anything?' asked Harry with his hands in his pockets.

'Mrs Winter, the old lady upstairs, didn't hear anything, she's partially deaf anyway, and the people in the top flat have been away for several months.'

'Uh-huh,' nodded Harry as Alan scribbled away in his notebook.

'What's missing?'

'Nothing,' I said.

'Are you sure?'

'Yeah. Pretty sure,' I replied. 'I've checked everything.'

'Nothing? Bit of an odd break-in, huh? Perhaps they were professionals who reckoned you had something special?' said Alan.

'What about breakages?' asked Harry as he gazed over the spines on the bookshelves.

'Just odds and sods, really. Apart from the TV.'

'Uh-huh. When did all this happen?'

'I'm not sure. I left here last Saturday afternoon and went up to Hitchin. We got back here a few hours ago. Some time this week, I guess.'

'Some time this week,' echoed Harry. 'That narrows the time frame down a little. Eh, Alan?'

'I'm sorry,' I said, 'I can't be any more specific than that.'

Laura, uncharacteristically, was saying nothing. She was just sitting on the sofa looking at us intently and taking it all in.

'Well, Mr Cornwell, to be quite frank, I don't think there is much we can do for you. We get break-ins like this all the time around here. Most of them we don't solve.'

'I'd figured that.'

'But you never know your luck.'

'I can't think of anything else to ask Mr Cornwell, can you, Alan?'

Alan said no and folded his notebook up.

'We'll be in touch then, should anything happen,' said Harry as he turned to me.

They both said goodbye to Laura. She merely smiled demurely at them. A transient nodding smile.

I thanked them and showed them to the door.

Harry pointed to the locks and said, 'You'll need to get all this fixed.'

'I know,' I replied, 'I've got a carpenter coming tomorrow.'

'Good.'

And they were gone. I closed the door and put the chain latch up to prevent it from being blown open by the wind.

'Laura, fancy going down the pub?'

'Not really. I'm too tired. I'm also too tired to drive back tonight. Do you mind if I stay over?'

'Not at all. Of course.'

I was in bed first so I could watch Laura undress. She always undressed unselfconsciously, matter-of-factly, right down to her knickers, which tonight were cream and satin-looking with lace trims. She rooted around in my wardrobe and found an old sweat-shirt that she pulled on over her head. She climbed in beside me and I closed my eyes and took draughts of her smell – partly her and partly some subdued lemony perfume. She put the light out and backed into me for warmth.

'Wake me early,' she said.

'Sure.'

We always slept together when she stayed over, but nothing had ever happened. I sometimes wanted something to happen but I could never be the one to make the first move.

It was a bright starlit night. And, for this neighbourhood, surprisingly quiet. I couldn't hear any traffic or Irish drunks.

Nothing has ever happened to me, and then in the same week I get mugged and my place gets broken into. Jesus!

Every time I closed my eyes I was confronted with a picture of the flat as it was when we walked in – the contents strewn everywhere, the sheer chaos of it. I couldn't sleep. And the thought kept recurring: what were they looking for?

This place, I realised, had been professionally turned over. These weren't kids. Whoever had done it had methodically, systematically taken everything apart, item by item, piece by piece.

What were they looking for? What could they have been looking for?

And what about the burglary at Dick's place? I'd forgotten about that. Only two burglaries in my whole life and both within such a short space of time.

Coincidence … or me being paranoid?

CHAPTER THREE

SOME BIZARRE, OCCULT SIGNIFICANCE?

'Identify.'
   'Bellerophon … 666B.'
   'Location?'
   'Capital.'
   'Proceed.'
   'LANCER grail has dropped from sight. Further leads to be developed.'
   'Stand by for Collateral Intercepts.'

I ARRIVED AT PINEWOOD (STUDIOS) late on the Friday, a little after 10.30 a.m. The last week had been pretty hectic (and chaotic) and I hadn't been getting away much before 10 p.m. each day.

I got to the studios too late to grab my usual parking place outside the stage where the art department offices are so I had to go over to the car park at the front of the Mansion and dump the old Merc there.

As I was strolling down the house corridor en route I heard someone call my name. I turned. It was Rachel, the production secretary.

'Christopher, we've got an awful lot of mail for you, sweetie. I keep forgetting to tell you.'

'You have?'

'Yes, it's been mounting up since you went over to

Czech land. Do you want me to drop it over?'

'No, it's OK. I'll pick it up at lunchtime.'

I left the Mansion by the side entrance and hot-footed it across the road and down corridors lined with stills from *Carry On* films and portraits of half-remembered J. Arthur Rank 'stars' of the 1950s and 1960s.

I opened the office, put the blow heaters on, and rinsed the percolator out and filled it with fresh coffee. In front of me were several thousand photographs taken out in the Czech Republic that I still had to sort and group. I'd been on this a week and I reckoned I had a further week to do. The time-consuming part of the job was joining the 360° multi-picture panoramas together with 3M Magic Mending tape and then mounting them on card.

While waiting for the coffee I pour myself a small nip of vodka in a glass of orange and continue with the pictures. Photo. Tape. Photo. Tape. Photo. Tape. Photo. Tape. Then with every fourth group I mount them on the boards with Cow Gum and add underneath in spirit marker the actual locale and the scene number.

And so it goes on.

A little after 1 p.m. during my third coffee and third vodka (I like to observe parity in my liquid intake) the phone rings. It startles me.

'Cornwell. Hello?'

'Hi, sexy!'

'Who's that?'

'Laura. Who'd you think it was?'

'Sorry. I didn't recognise you!'

'How you doing?'

'Not too bad. Working away here and pissing about and not much else. What about you?'

'Fine. A heavy caseload this week. But fine,' said Laura.

'I phoned you at the beginning of the week but you were out.'

'Working late.'

'Uh-huh,' I replied.

'How's your head? Your face?'

'My head's still a bit sore. My eye's gone down but I've still got the plaster on my nose. I'm managing. What's it the French say – to be beautiful one must suffer?'

'Yes. Courage, Camille.'

'That's me,' I replied. 'By the way, are you in town over the weekend?'

'No. I told you. I'm off skiing with the girls for two weeks, with the school. We're leaving tomorrow.'

'Oh, yeah. I forgot. Shit, it would have been nice to see you.'

'A pity. Still, I'll send you a postcard.'

'Right.'

'I found out something yesterday that may be a little odd, Chris. I was talking to Barbara.'

'How is she?' I asked.

'She's fine, all things considered, but I think she's still on the Valium,' said Laura.

'I hope she doesn't get addicted,' I said with as much concern as I could muster.

'Barbara was telling me that she can't sleep alone in the house, particularly since the burglary. Her mother goes round.'

'Uh-huh.'

'Well, the burglary doesn't quite seem … *kosher*. I thought it was just a normal break-in – TV and video-recorder taken. You know?'

'Wasn't it, then?'

'No. It doesn't appear to be. Barbara said the burglars started at the top of the house, but they were disturbed, and fled. And it came out that the only room that was touched was Dick's study. Something might have been taken from Dick's room, but nothing was taken from the house. Do you see?'

'I think so,' I replied, though I wasn't sure I did.

'This idea that nothing was taken because the burglars were disturbed is Barbara's invention. It's her reasoning to

[90]

explain why only one room was touched. She comes back, finds a back window smashed, finds only one room in a bit of a state, and concludes that they were going to turn the whole house over but they were disturbed. Do you see? It didn't and doesn't occur to her that they might have only been interested in that one room. Dick's room.'

'Did she disturb them?' I was beginning to see what Laura was getting at.

'No, she didn't. She was with her mother that day. Nobody disturbed them as far as I can see.'

'Who discovered the burglary then?' I asked.

'You know that elderly couple next door? The Pynchons?'

'Yes.' I could always remember them because of their rare name. The same as the American novelist and the same as the lady proprietor in *Lou Grant* on TV.

Laura continued, 'They saw a couple of shifty characters leaving the back door about lunchtime and they phoned the police. The police turned up and found the window smashed, and then Barbara arrived. Nobody *disturbed* the burglars as far as I can see. They were already leaving when they were first seen.'

'Are we talking one, two, three or what?'

'Two according to Mr Pynchon,' answered Laura.

The complexion of this burglary was decidedly changing. But what to make of it? What does Laura make of it? Perhaps they stole that missing picture or map from the wall? Big deal. There was nothing of any real financial value there, save some books, but they all still seemed to be there as best as I can remember.

'I don't know. It's just strange.'

'What do the police make of it?' I asked.

'Just another breaking and entering, that's all.'

Was I making connections where there were none? My mind was racing, but I was purposely ignoring the break-in at my place.

'Did the Pynchons get a look at the burglars?'

'It was Mr Pynchon only. He was burning leaves in the

back garden. About ten yards away. I think he gave a good description.'

'What are we going to do about this, Laura?'

'You tell me.'

'I don't know either.'

'Listen, Chris, perhaps we'll speak before I leave?'

'Yeah, let's try to.'

'Good. Lots of love.'

'The same to you.'

I hung up, poured myself a small vodka and lit a cigarette. The two burglars. Mr Pynchon saw them. What did they look like?

What *did* they look like?

I looked at the photographs in front of me. I'll concentrate on this to stop my mind racing.

Photo. Tape.

Photo. Tape.

And on I continued undisturbed for an hour or so.

At around 2.30 p.m. I decided that I needed to speak to Mr Pynchon. Had to speak to him. I'd convinced myself that the two burglars were the same two guys who did me over in the station car park and the only way I'd know for sure was to speak to him and get a full description. I dialled Directory Enquiries and got the Pynchons' number which I carefully wrote on the A3 drawing pad. I stared at it. I needed to plan what I say to him.

Phoning isn't a good idea. No. He'll probably remember me, but he may not be sure it is me … but even so, I could be someone else. He might think I'm something to do with the burglars and I don't want to freak him out. He'd get in a panic – his wife certainly would.

Phoning isn't a good idea.

I finished pasting up the Prague neighbourhood I'd been working on, had a small shot of vodka, turned the lights off, locked the office up, and skidooed down the corridor.

I bumped into Rachel who handed me a wodge of mail secured with several rubber bands.

'Your mail,' she said.

My heart sank. Boy, it mounts up.

'Thanks, Rachel.'

'Any time.'

I continued down the corridor and out to the car park. It was now coming up to 3 p.m. The traffic was always pretty horrendous on a Friday but I thought I should make it up to Hitchin in not much more than an hour.

The Pynchons' front lawn was immaculately kept. The borders were neat and symmetrical and the total effect was a garden run by obsessives. Even the fencing looked like it was dusted and polished each day.

I stepped into the porch and pushed the button. Deep in the house I heard two chimes. The front door was bright and sparkling and looked as though it had been painted within the past week.

The house seemed unnaturally quiet. Then I heard footsteps coming towards the door.

The footsteps stopped at the door. Then there was silence. I could hear nothing. Then I noticed, just above the button, the convex lens, about 5mm in diameter, of a spy-hole. Whoever is in there is taking a good long look at me.

Three door locks were opened rapidly in regular succession and the door then opened about three inches. It was on a chain.

'Yesssss?' said Mr Pynchon as he peeked around the door, his nose leading. 'Yesssss?'

'Mr Pynchon, I'm Christopher Cornwell. You may remember me?'

He continued staring at me down his long curved nose.

'A friend of Dick North's? Next door?' I added.

Still nothing.

'You don't remember me, Mr Pynchon?'

He relaxed his vigilant face.

'Yesssss ... I think I do.'

'Good.'

'And what can I do for you, Mr Cornwell?'

This question was asked in that upper middle-class way that combines a frosty politeness with the perplexity of a patrician wondering what on earth someone like *me* could possibly want from *him*.

'I wanted to ask you a couple of questions about the burglary … the burglary next door … at the North house.'

Pynchon's eyebrows shot up, his nose flared. 'I'm most terribly sorry, but that is something I'm not prepared to discuss. Not under any circumstances.'

'All I want to know is what these two burglars looked like.'

'I do not want to discuss this.'

He started closing the door and when I realised what was happening I stuck my shoe against it firmly. Pynchon looked up at me.

'I just want you to tell me what they looked like.'

'Both my wife and myself are not discussing the matter.'

I hear someone else within the house. Pynchon disappears and there is some whispering going on behind the door. Then Mrs Pynchon appears through the gap in full outraged mode. She stares at me like you might stare at a dog turd on your shoe. 'Did my husband not make this clear? We simply do not want to discuss it any more. Do you understand?'

'Why?'

'I'm not saying anything more. Is that clear?'

I removed my foot from the door. 'I'm sorry to have bothered you and Mr Pynchon. Thank you.'

The door slammed shut.

I walked around to Dick's house and rang the bell. There was no reply. I rang it a couple of times more. Still no reply. I used the knocker several times. Still no reply. The lights are on but nobody's in.

I looked at my watch. Laura doesn't usually get back until after 7 p.m. and I don't really fancy hanging around in Hitchin for a couple of hours. I'll drive back to town. Back home. It shouldn't be too horrendous, I'm driving against the traffic.

[2]

I got back to Tufnell Park just before 6.30 p.m. I was knackered. I slumped down on the sofa and fell asleep.

I wake up.

And before I can reach for the vodka bottle, the phone rings. I stretch over and grab the portable.

'Hello?'

'Chris, it's Laura.'

'Hi! I must tell you I've just had the most awful dream sitting here.'

'What was it?'

'I dreamt I was in Dealey Plaza when Kennedy got shot. He was just about to say something when his head was blown off.'

'How gruesome.'

'Yeah, and the Pynchons were in it too.'

'The Pynchons?' said Laura.

'Yeah.'

Laura giggled and said, 'Why the Pynchons for goodness sake?'

'Well, easy. Because I went up to see them this afternoon,' I explained. 'That's why.'

'Why'd you do that?' asked Laura.

'I'll tell you in a minute. But first, how are you? I'm just rabbiting on about this dream, sorry.'

'I'm OK,' said Laura, 'but the girls are out tonight and I just felt a ... I thought I'd just call you and speak before we take off.'

'You poor thing. I should have stayed up there and waited for you. Shouldn't I?'

'Don't mock me!'

'You can always get tea, sympathy and an ego massage here.'

'I'll remember that. Now tell me, why'd you go and see the Pynchons?'

'I just got this thing, sitting in the office there by myself, that perhaps the burglars were the same guys who duffed me up at the station.'

'What made you think that?'

What did make me think that? Reason? Paranoia? Fantasy? The idle connection of disparate events? Well, it was certainly that. But was it anything else?

'Intuition,' I said. 'Just a funny feeling.'

'And was your intuition proven correct?'

'I don't know. I couldn't get anything out of the Pynchons. They just clammed up, which I thought was odd.'

'And why was it odd, Chris?'

'I don't know. Just odd.'

'Perhaps they weren't sure who you really were? You could have been some confederate of the burglars.'

'No. They knew who I was.'

'They just didn't want to speak about it. They're an odd couple anyway,' said Laura.

'Why don't you pop around and ask them? Get a description of the burglars. Eh, Laura?'

'Then they'd really start feeling got at. I know what they're like.'

'You're right. But we're left with only Dick's study being turned over.'

'I know,' said Laura, 'but we don't know the full story there either, do we? That's certainly a bit odd.'

You can drive yourself batty speculating about the unknown and end up down some paranoid cul-de-sac with the crazies. You need facts to go on and there were really none of these about.

'I'm off to bed now. I'll call you when I get back,' said Laura.

'Right. And have a safe flight and a good time.'
'I will.'
Then I poured myself a half-mug of decaffeinated percolator coffee, filled the remainder with vodka to make Russian coffee, drank it in three gulps and went to bed.

[3]

Saturday. I didn't get up until midday. The postman woke me up. I went to the hall and found a picture postcard. A sandy beach in Australia. On the back:

> *Old Man!*
> *Having a mega time in Perth.*
> *Great girls and dope.*
> *Speak to you soon.*
> *Y'r devoted son – Rupert*
> *XXXXXX*

Good for him. I wonder where he is now? He usually phones me reverse charges every few weeks or so. Hope he's all right. I'll call Charlotte and see when she last heard from him.

I put the postcard on the mantelpiece.

I had a shower and got myself organised. I went down to Camden to do the weekly shop.

I caught the bus back with my three bags of shopping and got home just before 3 p.m. I put the shopping away, made myself some Russian coffee again, loaded the washing machine and was all prepared to get on with joining and mounting the photos when I realised I had something else to do. It's that old NASA maxim – Before you can do what you want to do, you've got to do something else. The something else was the stack of mail Rachel had handed me yesterday.

I sat down at the desk, removed the rubber bands from the bundle and started wading through it.

Letter from young art student wanting to work in films. A boy. Upper middle-class name. Snotty pretentious letter. Bin it.

Leaflets about new Canon colour copiers. File for reference.

Brochure about Coral Draw. Bin it.

Some income tax form or statement. Send to Harry the accountant.

And so on and so on.

And then – a letter in an envelope from which three smallish black and white photographs fall as I open it. An A4 sheet of torn-down computer paper, white, and dot-matrix printed. It was signed Mikhail Bakounine.

I knew who it was from.

I glanced at the photos. Small and printed on a flimsy paper. A couple of guys somewhere, then the two of them somewhere else, then a close-up of one of them. All taken in the open, and a good few years ago.

I returned to the letter.

13 January, 1993

Dear Chris,
Keep these SAFE – in a locked filing cabinet or
safe deposit, you'll know – but SAFE!
I'll explain when you get back here.
Don't talk about them.
Silence saves lives!
Ever
Mikhail Bakounine

There was nothing else on the sheet and nothing on the other side either. Just those few lines. *Keep these SAFE.* Safe written in large block caps – both times. *I'll explain when you get back here. Don't talk about them. Silence saves lives.*

And *Mikhail Bakounine* written in that elegant italic hand

of Dick's. He often signed his letters and notes in the name
of some character we used to go a bomb on. The Russian
anarchist Bakounine (or Bakunin) one time, André Breton
the next. Dick's way of reminding me of who we were.

This note and the photos were in a sealed white DL
envelope with CHRISTOPHER written on it. This in turn
was inside a – here it is – an A4 manilla envelope, stiff-
backed, that reads:

      Christopher Cornwell Esq
      Art Director
      c/o Xanthe Productions Ltd
      Pinewood Studios
      Pinewood Road
      Iver Heath
      Bucks
      SLO ONH

This is written with a bold black spirit-marker in large
and small caps and dominates the front of the envelope.
The words PERSONAL & PRIVATE are written above it, to
the left. And above that is a post office sticker showing the
envelope went by registered delivery. There is no return
address shown.

There's nothing else inside the manilla envelope.
Nothing I've overlooked.

I take the three photographs and look at them. Two are
landscape format and one is portrait. They're original
prints, probably about thirty years old. Brittle. Worn and
scratched in places. I carefully lay them next to each other
on my jotter and bring the Anglepoise above them so they
are brightly illuminated.

They each measure about 15 cm x 10 cm overall with a 5
mm white border within. They aren't crisp black and
white, but rather soft muted greys. Probably taken with
some cheap camera that had a plastic lens.

SIXTY-THREE CLOSURE

PHOTOGRAPH ONE

A bright sunny day in a street in front of a building. A fattish guy in a suit in his, what, fifties? While to his left, a young guy in his early twenties dressed casually. Both staring into the camera in medium shot. The fat guy is holding something.

I know this street all right. It's Hermitage Road in Hitchin, looking east towards Windmill Hill. The two figures are standing in front of the old cinema that used to be there – the Hermitage. It was demolished back in the 1960s. I recognise the entrance and the columned arches above it with HERMITAGE in illuminated lettering at the top curving around.

You can make out Windmill Hill in the background. A few people on the pavement in the middle distance. Only a couple of cars parked along by the pavement.

The fat guy is wearing a dark suit that looks a size too small for him. He's moonfaced with a beaming smile. White shirt. Dark tie. Dark suit. Highly polished shoes. His hands are joined together in front of him – holding something. I can't make out what it is. I take a linen tester out of the drawer and bring the Anglepoise down to see if I can make out what it is he's got, but I can't.

The young guy isn't so much smiling into the camera but just staring matter-of-factly. He's medium height and of slight build. His dark hair is shortish and receding on his left. He's wearing a light-coloured bowling (?) shirt and baggy lightweight slacks. They may be loafers or plimsolls on his feet.

He's not good-looking, but he isn't plain either. Something about him suggests that he may not be British.

His left hand is in a trouser pocket and his right is at his side holding what I think is one of those airline hand-bags you used to see about in the 1960s. The ones you stuffed under the seat.

Who is he?

Or, indeed, who *was* he?

SOME BIZARRE, OCCULT SIGNIFICANCE?

PHOTOGRAPH TWO

The same two figures again standing to the fore of what I immediately recognise as the south porch of St Mary's Church in Hitchin. The fat guy on the left as before. More a medium long shot.

They are both dressed as they were before, so one can reasonably assume this picture was taken on the same day as the previous shot.

The fat man still has his hands together in front of himself holding something, but from this distance it is impossible to say what.

The young guy now has both hands in his pockets, so what became of his bag, or, indeed, where did it come from? Which question is the right question depends on the sequence of the photos.

PHOTOGRAPH THREE

An exterior close-up of the young guy, waist up. He wears the same noncommittal but somehow knowing expression. He has a squarish chin with a slightly jutting lower lip. There's stubble where he hasn't shaved for a day or so. And there's something vaguely familiar about him, but I can't place it.

So there we have it. Three photographs taken with a cheap camera in Hitchin some time in the late 1950s or early 1960s.

What do they add up to?

Precious little, I'd guess. But why did Dick send them to me? Was this some joke or part of some madness? Was he putting me on or what? Are these pics some artefacts of insanity? Some bizarre or occult significance known only to Dick? I don't know. We'll never know, I dare say.

I looked at each photograph again. The fat guy I certainly didn't know. The young guy I might have known. There was something distantly familiar about him. I didn't think I knew him but he might remind me of someone I do know. That must be it. But who? Was he someone Dick knew?

I reach for the phone to call Laura and then remember she's left for Switzerland. That may be as well, on reflection. She'd think Dick was really wacky if I told her about these pictures. Or would she? I'll let her see them when she gets back, perhaps.

The letter is dated 13 January 1993. 13 January? I reach down and take the diary out of my shoulder bag. Uh-huh. 13 January was the day before Dick called me out in Brno. It was the Wednesday, the day he called around to Laura's for the last time. Does that mean anything?

Yes, dated the day before he phoned me. And he says in the letter he'll explain when I get back. But he was dead by then …

What can I do?

These pictures might have some personal significance to Dick.

I can show them to Mrs North and to Barbara, but I needn't tell them about the covering letter. That could disturb them. I'll just say Dick gave them to me – no, I'll just say they were in some book Dick gave me. No, I won't mention Dick. I'll just say I came across them. Do they know anything about them? It can't hurt, just asking them that.

[4]

I left for Hitchin just after 6 p.m. Any earlier and I'd get snarled up in the shopping traffic, any later and it would be a bit too late to make unannounced social calls, particularly on Mrs North.

I drove up through Archway and Barnet and got on to the A1(M) at the old Bignell's Corner. I was in Hitchin by 7 p.m. I decided it would be best to see Mrs North first. She lived not too far from the station. I pulled up outside and then realised I had come empty-handed. That wouldn't do. So what could I get her at this time of night? She likes a drink.

SOME BIZARRE, OCCULT SIGNIFICANCE?

I drove back to the off-licence on Hermitage Road. She always liked her whisky, particularly Johnnie Walker, but that's been taken off the market. What is it she drinks now? Bell's? I'll get her a bottle of that. I looked for it on the shelf behind the counter – there were dozens of different whiskys, including Bell's. But no, I'll get her something really decent. A straight malt. Glenfiddich? No, that's too common. Something really good. Laphroaig? No, she might not like its smoky taste. I'll get the … uh … Smith Brothers Glenlivet (which George Saintsbury reckoned was the very best Scotch of all). That'll do her. And a box of chocolates. And I'll take this claret for Barbara.

I paid for it all with my VISA and the young guy put it in a bag.

As I came out of the shop I stopped and stared ahead. Just over there, of course, was where the Hermitage Cinema was. Right there. That's where it stood for thirty-odd years until it was demolished at, I think, about the time of the Cuban Crisis.

It was there that the photograph was taken all those years ago. Right there on that spot. Perhaps Mrs North will be able to shed some light on the pictures? She's certainly more likely to than Barbara … if, indeed, there is any significance. I wonder.

But there must be someone in this town now who knows who the two figures are. Someone. And then what would that tell me?

I drove back around to Mrs North's.

The door of the block was locked. I could see an illuminated hall through the security glass. There was a box to the left with about thirty buttons and the number of each flat to the side. At the top there was a bigger buzzer for THE WARDEN.

I pressed the bell for No.18.

Mrs North's voice came out of the speaker grille. A cautious 'Hello?'

'Mrs North?'

'Yes.'

'Hi, it's Chris Cornwell.'

'Oh, Christopher! Come in, I'm on the first floor, at the front.'

'Thanks.'

A sharp buzzer sounded and the door swung open. I walked into the hall. Neat and clean, if a little antiseptic, with potted plants in the corners. There was a lift but I thought it quicker to take the stairs.

Mrs North's flat faced me on the first floor. I could hear her little dog barking or, rather, yapping. The door opened.

'How nice to see you, Christopher!'

I walked towards her and she embraced me. I kissed her on the cheek.

'How are you keeping, Christopher? And you can stop your barking! Barney's not used to visitors. You must forgive him. Come through. He's a friend – so no more barking!' said Mrs North, addressing both me and her little dog in the same breath.

I followed her through and she shut the door behind me while ushering me into the sitting room.

'What have you done to your face?'

'Uh – I got into an argument … of sorts.'

Mrs North looked at me disapprovingly. 'At your age?'

I nodded. She shook her head slowly from side to side and sighed.

'Now sit down there and I'll put the kettle on.'

I sat down on one of those big bulbous armchairs you don't see much any more. The type you want to fall asleep in the moment you sink down in them.

Barney started sniffing me and wondering who I was. I patted him.

The sitting room was immaculately tidy and clean. All those little knick-knacks and ornaments and things on the shelves were highly polished and sparkling. There wasn't a speck of dust in the place. It was warm and inviting.

'It'll be ready in a jiff, Christopher,' announced Mrs

North as she reappeared in the room. 'And can I get you something to eat?'

'No, I'm OK. But I wouldn't mind a biscuit.'

'I've got an unopened pack of custard creams.'

'Great.'

Mrs North sat on the edge of the sofa facing me. 'You haven't been to my little place before, have you?'

'No, it's really nice.'

'It is. The council are very good to us OAPs. There's this room and the bedroom over there, and a nice little bathroom and kitchen. I couldn't ask for anything more. And they provide the central heating as well.'

'I hope I end up living in somewhere as nice as this, Mrs North.' Immediately I said this I regretted it. End up? Hardly the right phrasing, but Mrs North just smiled.

'How long have you been here now?' I asked.

'Since Edward died. Three years this September.'

Eddie North, Dick's dad. Three years ago!

'So what are you doing in Hitchin, Christopher? Have you come to see Laura?'

'No, she's gone skiing.' But what do I say about being up here? A white lie. 'I was just driving down and I thought I'd pop in.'

'I'm so glad you did, dear. I can hear the kettle.'

Mrs North went back into the kitchen. Barney was asleep at my feet. I looked around the room. Every shelf and flat area had some little statuette or curio on it. There were dozens of framed photographs in free-standing frames as well. All polished. All gleaming. And plants everywhere too. It must have taken her most of the morning just to water them.

Looking slightly incongruous was the large matt black Sony Trinitron TV Dick had bought his mum a year or two ago. I remember her telling me what a relief it was not to have to get up to change channels. She said she loved just sitting back in the armchair channel-hopping with the remote control.

She came back in with a tray upon which were two cups of tea, a sugar bowl, a milk jug and a plate of biscuits. The crockery was from a set, some delicate bone china (from which tea never tasted better). Mrs North put the tray on the low table, asked me how much milk and I told her when.

'Help yourself to the biscuits.'

Mrs North retired to the sofa with her cup and I dunked a couple of custard creams.

'How is your mum, Christopher?'

'She's OK. I spoke to her the other day.'

'Do give her my love when you speak to her again. I've just started a letter to her, telling her all the bits and pieces. It's so important to keep in touch.'

'Yes, it is. How are the girls?' The girls being Dick's three sisters.

'Well, Janet and Terry have sold their house and bought a new one in Baldock, because Terry's been promoted. Susan's started a new job with a computer company in Stevenage, and Marion is expecting again. It'll be her fourth.'

'Gosh.'

'That's what I said,' and she gave me one of those knowing nods that meant the news didn't entirely meet with her approval.

'All the grandchildren are OK too?'

'Yes, and little Matthew has just started nursery school, bless him.'

Mrs North delicately sipped her tea. I had another custard cream. Barney was now pawing my leg and letting out little cries. He wanted a biscuit.

'Is it OK if I give Barney a bit of my biscuit?'

'He's a real mumper, he is. Yes.'

I broke off a piece and handed it to him. He swallowed it in one gulp.

I opened my notebook and took out the three photographs. 'Can you have a look at these and tell me if you know anything about them?'

I leant across and handed the pictures to Mrs North.

'Let me just find my reading glasses.' She sorted through a *Radio Times*, a jar of boiled sweets and a pile of knitting that was on the sofa and extricated her glasses. She put them on and scrutinised the photos.

'That's the old Hermitage Cinema.'

'Uh-huh.'

'This one was ... taken at St Mary's and ... who's this fellow? Oh, yes. He's in the others too.'

'Have you ever seen these before, Mrs North?'

'No.'

'Do you recognise either of the two people?'

'No. Don't know who they are. I'm sorry.'

'That's OK.'

She handed the pictures back to me and I put them away.

'Where did they come from, Christopher?'

I had to lie about this. 'I just came across them in an old book I had. I wondered who they were.'

She looked at me and I could tell she didn't believe a word I had said, but she was too polite to say anything. She stared at me for two beats and then said, 'The weatherman on the TV says that we are going to have a very fine spring this year.'

'I hope so.'

God, she's seen right through me. I can bullshit some of the best bullshit artistes at Pinewood Studios but I come up against Mrs North and she detects it right away. Jeez!

'I nearly forgot. I brought you a little something,' I said.

'What have you got there?'

I take the Scotch and the box of chocolates out of the bag and hand them across to her. She's terribly pleased.

'Don't dilute the Scotch. Drink it neat. It's pretty good stuff.' But, I thought to myself, you go up to Scotland and you see them drinking the best malts mixed with lemonade, Tizer, Irn Bru and whatever else they can get their hands on. It's only down here we have this reverence for the single malts. So, I added, 'But it's a pretty good mixer too if you want.'

'Oh, you really shouldn't have, Christopher. *And* a box of chocolates. You really mustn't go spending your money like this. You'll never get rich.'

I told Mrs North that I had to be rushing and we exchanged pleasantries as she showed me out. I said I'd give her a call in the coming week. She told me I must pop in to see her whenever I am in Hitchin, and if she ever found out that I was here and didn't, she'd be most put out.

As I started the car outside I realised that we had not mentioned Dick once …

I drove back down Walsworth Road and up to Barbara's, parked opposite and walked across. Just as I was about to enter the gate and walk up the garden the front door opened and Barbara and Mrs Bradley came out. Both were dressed to the nines.

'Hi!' I shouted.

'Hello, Chris,' said a subdued Barbara.

'Christopher,' said a dour Mrs B. 'We're just off to see *The Gondoliers* in Letchworth.'

'Not to worry,' I said. 'I was just passing on the off-chance.'

I went up to the front of the house and took out the photographs. 'Just have a quick look at these before you go.'

'What are they?' demanded Mrs B, holding them to the porch light.

'They were taken a few years ago in Hitchin. A good few years ago. Have either of you ever seen them before?'

Mrs Bradley looked quickly at them over the tops of her glasses and then passed them to Barbara. 'I've never seen them before.'

Barbara stared at each one and handed them back to me apologetically, shaking her head.

'Neither of you recognise the two figures?'

'I don't,' said Mrs B. 'And how is your nose?'

'My nose?'

'Yes, your nose. The incident?'

The incident? Mrs B obviously knows about the little bit of business up at the station.

'Oh, that.'

'Yes, *that*.'

'It's fine. A little sore, that's all.'

Barbara shook her head again. She didn't know anything about the photos.

'Right. Well, enjoy *The Gondoliers*. Have a good evening.'

'Thank you,' Mrs B declared. And Barbara nodded her head.

I opened the gate for them and waited as they passed. Mrs B unlocked the two front doors of her brand spanking new BMW.

'See you soon,' I shouted.

'Bye!' said Barbara.

They drove off and I sauntered across the road into my old but classy Merc (well, I think it's classy). I switched the ignition on and decided I could do with a drink before I headed back to town. I drove down to St Mary's Square and parked up there. On the seat beside me was the claret I'd forgotten to give Barbara

St Mary's looks splendid at night illuminated by the sod lamps. Small groups of ducks and pigeons huddled together near the river in the cold.

I walked up past the church, across the square and down to the Red Hart. There was a rock band testing the PA out back and the sound could be heard at the top of Bucklersbury.

There were about six people in the front bar. I ordered a large vodka with ice and added some Malvern water to it. The round table in the corner was free so I took my drink over there and lit a cigarette.

So, Mrs North doesn't know about the photos, and neither do Barbara or Mrs B. Therefore we can conclude with reasonable certainty that Dick wasn't flashing them around at his mother or at home.

What else can we reasonably conclude at this stage?

He wasn't using them in his *Ichonography*, that's for sure. The pictures are too late.

So what are we left with?

Fuck all, I guess.

Where did they come from?

Dunno.

What could they mean?

Dunno.

What significance could they have for Dick?

That's a secret he's taken to his grave, unless he's left some expositional document somewhere explaining it all, and there's a fat chance of that.

I looked at each of the pictures again, spreading them out on the table: elderly fat guy and slim young guy outside the Hermitage, elderly fat guy and slim young guy outside the church porch, portrait of slim young guy.

All presumably taken the same day in Hitchin ... in the late 1950s or early 1960s. Right.

Someone in this town must know who these two are, but then what would that tell me? If I found out the fat guy was – let's invent some details, some biography – say, Syd Harris of ... Henlow, and the young guy was ... Dave ... Wilkins of ... the Bedford Road, Syd's nephew say, then what do we get? I go to see them and they say, 'Yeah, that's us all right!' then where do we go?

Perhaps one or both of them knew Dick?

The more I run it over and back and forth in my mind the more I realise that the only person who could shed some light on the pictures is Dick, and he's dead. Either he sent them to me as some put-on or joke, or they're evidence of pre-suicidal weirdness.

I stub my cigarette out and look up. The pub is half full now. The door in the corner is pushed open and two guys in their late teens fall into the pub laughing loudly and back-slapping each other. They approach two girls sitting at the bar. That was me and Dick thirty years ago ...

'We've got some dope!' says Dick.

Laura and Christine looked at us incredulously.

'We have, really. Enough for two joints or so,' I explain.

'Come down to the churchyard with us in a minute and we'll smoke it down there,' says Dick.

'Where did you two get it then?' Laura asks.

I smile and say, 'It's a secret!'

Dick puts his arm around me and says to the girls with an air of hip nonchalance, 'Never ask a gentleman who his dealer is.'

The girls start laughing and Christine says, 'There aren't any dealers in Hitchin! And it's probably herbal mixture anyway!'

Christine was right of course. This was 1963 and there weren't any dope dealers in Hitchin. The only 'dealers' around here dealt in scrap metal or horses. We'd scored from Stephen who we had just bumped into down on Bancroft. He'd just got back from Paris again.

Dick leant towards Christine. 'This, madam, is finest Yucatan Gold. The genuine thing. A couple of drags of this and you'll be pushing yourself off the ceiling! The effects of this shit are guaranteed.'

'Let's see it then,' demanded Laura.

'Later,' I said.

'Yes, later,' Dick echoed.

'Have you got some cigarette papers?' Christine wanted to know.

'Of course,' said Dick. 'We always come prepared.'

We went down after closing to St Mary's and got stoned out of our minds for only the second time in our life. Dick, Laura and me did, but for some reason the stuff had little or no effect on Christine. We staggered around by the river laughing and falling over and talking nonsense, and the couple of people we chanced upon who knew us shook their heads and said we were drunk. We knew it was dope and in those days that was something pretty special.

What an evening!

But something else happened that evening now that I think about it. Back in the pub, before we went down to the church.

We ordered a couple of half-pints of light ale and Dick told the girls we'd be back in a minute as we had some 'business' to talk about. Dick led me out to the back of the pub where we sat in the corner.

'I've got something really interesting to show you,' said Dick *sotto voce*, his eyes darting about to see that nobody was looking at us or taking an interest.

'What's that?'

'This.'

He produced from the pocket of his jacket a tightly folded map that he laid out on the table. It was a large scale Ordnance Survey map of the Hitchin region. Hitchin was in the centre and the map's coverage extended out in a radius of five miles or thereabouts. Here and there across the mapped topography were coloured dots and crosses, some isolated, some in wavy lines, some clustered. There appeared to be no pattern to their incidence.

'Look at it,' said Dick.

'Yeah. What about it?' I asked, not knowing what I was supposed to be looking at. 'What is it? What are these dots and things?'

'You know Mr Sells?'

'Yeah.'

'He was an air raid warden during the war and he put this map together based on official reports and eyewitnesses and things. It shows all the bombs that were dropped around here by the Germans during the war.'

'That's interesting,' I yawned.

'Well, it is actually. It's *very* interesting,' Dick enthused.

I mean it was interesting. Marginally interesting if you had nothing better to be occupied with, but not that interesting I wouldn't have thought.

'Now the fascinating thing about this is the concentration of bombs here. Look at that.' Dick pointed to the Shadwell

Lane area south of the station. 'Just take a look at that. See?'

True, there seemed a high concentration of bombs in the area, and overshoots to the north, south, east and west. Amazingly, the station itself didn't seem to have been hit. But I wasn't sure what it or Dick meant.

'There was nothing of real interest, military interest, to the Germans around here during the war. Well, there was the RAF airfield at Henlow but if you look that seems to have been ignored largely. There was nothing for them here, was there? All these are random bombings or planes dumping bombs on the way back to Germany.'

'And?'

'But you come to up here, around here, south of the station, and you've got this high concentration.'

I was beginning to see what Dick was getting at. 'So you're saying they were going after something there? They had a target *here*?' I pointed at the area on the map.

'Right.'

'What?'

'I'm fucked if I know.'

'Hold on a minute, Dick. This could just be where they happened to dump bombs on their way back.'

Dick shook his head and smiled. 'Wrong on two counts. First, when they dump bombs you get a straight line of them. They're falling from a moving plane, you know? And they're usually all the same type. Here there's all different types – incendiaries, high-explosive, oil bombs – and they are concentrated. Look.'

'OK, yeah. But perhaps this was just like some accidental thing, coincidence. Either that or they got their navigation wrong. They were after something else.'

'No. Bombing was, you know, almost an exact science. It wasn't an approximate thing.'

I could see Dick's argument now. 'What were they after then?'

'All that was up there then were some big houses.'

'Do you think one of them could have been requisitioned

during the war? Used by some special government department or something?' I asked.

'Something must have been up there, but nobody I've spoken to knows. You'd need to do some real digging around. Somebody must know.'

We'd got interested in the secret preparations of the secret state after the 'Spies for Peace' pamphlet was given out on the Aldermaston March. The 'Spies for Peace' had uncovered these top secret government bunkers, the Regional Seats of Government, that were littered about the country. These were bomb-proof underground bunkers in the event of nuclear war. Nobody had any idea they existed. And that was only part of it.

Hitchin wasn't the most promising place to start investigating the government's secret contingency plans in the event of nuclear war or civil unrest, but we were surprised by what we discovered: strange mounds and concrete emplacements out at RAF Henlow; small fallout shelters for the Royal Observer Corps at Wilbury Hill, near Charlton and a suspected one near Tingley Wood that we never could find (the ROC would be plotting anything that moved through the sky and measuring radioactivity); a secret underground communications centre in the grounds of a large house at St Ippollitts; a suspicious 'reservoir' at Jack's Hill, and so on. We suspected that part of Windmill Hill might have been hollowed out as a bunker and that this was somehow connected with the odd aerials on the water tower at the top of the hill. We seriously noted rumours that the TA Centre out on the Bedford Road was really a store for radiation- and chemical-proof suits for the government (but not for us, the populace); and there were innumerable other will-o'-the-wisps that we tenaciously hunted down as best we could. This sleuthing soon led us beyond the 'World War Three' stuff as we liked to call it, into World War Two. For instance, the rumours that Rudolf Hess had been kept at the Priory for several months and that Churchill himself had visited him there engaged us for several months. We never came up with anything conclusive but it got us wondering about Hess and what was really going on at that level during the war.

Our greatest success in nosing about was, however, something that made the national newspapers. Fortunately we were not identified.

The Buffer Depots.

Just beyond the railway bridge on the left as you're going towards Letchworth was a half-decayed industrial site. Originally it had been the Herts Ironworks site years ago but the company had closed and the premises were divided up and leased out to other concerns. Here was a heavily secured warehouse that looked like it dated back to the 1930s. It was a long, low building, black its entire length, with bars over the windows. Surrounding it was a high chainlink fence with dannert wire curling along the top.

It looked as though nobody ever came or went and our inquiries showed this to be true. The building's very anonymity was precisely what attracted us to it.

At the front of the fence were strong double gates that led on to a concrete apron to the fore of a loading bay at the front of the warehouse itself. These gates had a sign mounted on them above a metal letterbox:

BUFFER DEPOT
No. 98

That's all. Nothing else. No name of a company, no names of any individuals to be contacted. Nothing.

We used to check the letterbox regularly to see if any mail had been delivered. None ever came. The box was just rusting away.

Some guys who worked nearby told us that they thought the place had something to do with the government, but they weren't sure what. We continued making discreet inquiries and got nowhere, so one night we cut through the fence with bolt-cutters and broke in. This was surprisingly easy. We covered an entire window with wide adhesive cloth tape then started tapping it firmly with a hammer. The tape muffled the sound of the breaking glass and prevented it from falling inside. The bars were then easily prised away from the fast-rotting window casement.

Right. We were now in.

And what did we find?

We found nothing but enormous wooden packing cases. Row upon row of them piled from the floor to the ceiling. Letters and numbers were stencilled all over them and the word ARGENTINA was prominent on every last one.

Dick was ahead of me with his torch deciphering some lettering. He turned, smiled and said, 'All these cases are nothing but fucking corned beef … from fucking Argentina!'

'Corned beef?'

'Yup.'

'*All* of them?'

'Sure enough.'

What was a whole warehouse of corned beef doing in Hitchin? And, moreover, from the dates on the cases, doing here since 1944? Then Dick and I clicked it at the same time.

'I got it,' I said.

'Me too, snap!' shot back Dick.

This corned beef Buffer Depot was one of the secret foodstores the government had up and down the country in the event of nuclear or other war, insurrection, or what have you. We'd read about them. Some researchers knew they existed but nobody had any details. We'd discovered one.

We continued our search, but found nothing else of interest. We sneaked off the premises and hotfooted it home in the dark and shadows of the sleeping town.

I forgot all about the Buffer Depots until Dick turned up at our house one Saturday morning about three months later with a copy of *The Guardian*.

'You seen this!' exclaimed Dick pointing at a headline in the paper.

The headline said: GOVERNMENT TO INQUIRE INTO SOURCE OF CONTAMINATED CORNED BEEF.

'Yeah, it's been on the TV too,' I added.

'It's been everywhere, this story. All the papers are running it.'

'So?'

'Listen,' said Dick patiently, 'all this old corned beef starts turning up in shops up and down the country. Most of it is *eatable*, but a lot of it is pretty bad. The tins are rusted or they've got these microscopic holes in them that germs have got in and the stuff ends up contaminated. Right? There's a big outcry and the government says they're going to look into it and see where it all came from, and at the same time they put out this thing that they believe some private company imported all these tins, thousands and thousands of them during the last war – millions of them, in fact – and then this company *forgot* they had them until now. Now, does that make any sense to you? Eh?'

'I can't believe some company imports them and then forgets them.'

'Exactly. That's all horse-shit. There is no company. This is the government rotating the stuff they've got in the Buffer Depots. That's what's happening. Only they won't admit it. They're trying to hide it. You see?'

'Yeah, I do see. They want fresh stuff in the depots so they sell off all the old stuff. The fuckers!'

'Pre-*cisely*,' says Dick. 'That's their little game. The corned beef isn't good enough for them, but it's good enough for us!'

'What are we going to do then?'

'We're going to phone up the guy who wrote the piece in *The Guardian* and spill the beans to him.'

'Spill the beef, you mean.'

And we did.

We had no real evidence, of course, to prove our supposition at the time. But we knew we were right. It was a pretty good hunch, and it was a hunch that was proven right in the end. *The Guardian* ran the story and there was a big stink and the government was highly embarrassed. They came up with all this guff that selling the stuff to the public was a departmental oversight and that it should have been sold to animal foodstuff manufacturers instead. Some poor clerk in Whitehall who was in charge of wastepaper baskets or whatever took the can and that was that. Search for the guilty. Punishment for the innocent.

That was all a long time ago.

I finished the vodka and took the glass back to the bar. The pub was now crowded, and I realised I was the oldest person there. There's nothing like that thought to sober you up.

Nick Melville, a friend who lived over Henlow way, once said to me that the transition from dynamic young whizz-kid to boring old fart is instantaneous. I feel the transition from being a teenager to being middle-aged is the same.

As I crossed Market Square I started thinking about Dick's map and the bomb plots again. I didn't know if Dick had ever found out what the Germans thought they were bombing out there, and if he had, he hadn't ever shared the 'intelligence' with me, but I did remember the map was on the wall to the right of the desk in his study for years.

But it isn't there now.

That's what was missing.

I got back to Tufnell Park and went straight to bed. I tried to put Dick's photos and Hitchin from my mind, but there was a phrase of Reginald Hine's that popped into my consciousness from some deep memory: 'the colour of Reason'. Not the colour of money, the colour of Reason. I kept associating it with the photographs. What is the colour of their reason?

I was soon asleep.

And then I was awake again. I was dog-tired but I was wide awake. I got up and went into the kitchen and made some decaffeinated coffee. I took it back to the front room and sat on the sofa. The three photographs were on the low table in front of me where I had left them when I came in.

I sipped the coffee and looked at the three pictures. I was thinking that perhaps there was something so glaringly obvious about them that I was overlooking it. But what could it be?

There's the picture of the two of them outside the cinema, the picture of the two of them by St Mary's, and the single portrait.

The two of them outside the cinema. The old Hermitage Cinema on Hermitage Road. That was demolished some time in the mid-1960s, wasn't it? Some time then. But when? I've got something here that may answer that.

The wall of bookshelves here was never in a highly tuned order that a librarian would approve of but there was a rough grouping by subject matter. After the break-in I just threw the books back and I still haven't got around to sorting them out. I'm looking for a paperback collection of Hitchin photographs I bought some time back in the early 1980s. I can't remember the title but I know it's got a cream cover. There were several pictures of the Hermitage Cinema and I think it said something about when it was demolished.

And here it is on the top shelf, the little book I was looking for – *Fifty Years of Change in Hitchin*.

I go back to the sofa and flick through the pages. Here's the section on the Hermitage. There's a photograph looking down Hermitage Road towards Windmill Hill with the cinema on the right taken in 1963, and below it the reproduction of an early advertisement:

North Hertfordshire's Acknowledged
Centre of Entertainment

The HERMITAGE
Cinema and Café

HITCHIN
Phone 525

SIXTY-THREE CLOSURE

The Luxury Cinema
With Perfect Sound

It says here the cinema opened in February 1932, with a British film, *Michael and Mary*, starring Herbert Marshall. I think I once saw this at the National Film Theatre years ago in some season devoted to Gainsborough pictures. It was directed by Victor Saville, if I'm not mistaken, the British director who subsequently went off to Hollywood and directed *Goodbye Mr Chips.*

The last film to be shown was *Heavens Above!* with Peter Sellers in September 1963 and then 'this great institution' was demolished in 1964. So, the last film was shown in September 1963 and the cinema was demolished the following year. Therefore these three pictures were taken no later than September 1963 because it looks like there's still a film playing – there's a poster behind the two guys. But what does that tell us?

CHAPTER FOUR

AM I PARANOID ENOUGH?

'Identify.'
  'Bellerophon ... 666B.'
  'Location?'
  'Capital.'
  'Proceed.'
  'The LANCER grail may have been destroyed. Investigations continue.'
  'Stand by.'

JANUARY HAD MERGED insensibly into February and February became March without me noticing and then, soon after, it was suddenly April. The grief and shock arising from Dick's death I had not so much confronted as shunted away into a little-frequented mental siding where it sat awaiting attention. I thought of Dick continually. In fact I don't think a day went by without me thinking of him, but it was the living Dick of the 1950s and 1960s that I remembered, the Dick that enabled me to draw back the curtain and peer at my own youth. The dying and dead Dick figured not at all. This was the Dick that was disturbing and unresolved and worrying.

In May *Blue Lou* collapsed and I found myself out of work. I then spent a week down on the south coast visiting my mother, a couple of weeks redecorating the flat, and a week staying with some friends in Deal before I got a call for six or so weeks' work on a picture at Ardmore Studios in Dublin for Martin Liebling, the ex-Warner Bros producer who came over from LA to London in the late 1970s and never went back.

The picture Martin was doing was from his own original story and screenplay and was entitled *Prize Fighters*, the story of an eighteenth-century Irish bare-knuckled prize fighter called Joseph O'Connor.

It was an easy and pleasant enough job and it didn't hurt any spending some serious drinking time in Dublin again. I temporarily switched horses and moved from Smirnoff Blue Label vodka over to Bushmills whiskey.

By late August I was finished. I drove down to Dun Laoghaire and caught the ferry back over to Holyhead. As I was driving across the Menai bridge I felt an acute and momentary strike of pain in a tooth somewhere at the back of my left lower jaw. It was like an icepick striking at the core of the tooth. I prayed that it would not return, but it did, somewhere near Chester, and for keeps.

Pain collapses the universe. Everything shrinks to the singularity of the pain. Nothing else exists. This was the worst toothache I'd ever had and the intensity of it approached the pain I had when I had some trouble a couple of years back with kidney stones.

I got back to Tufnell Park and crashed out. I was exhausted.

The next day I got up early, had a shower and phoned the dentist. Be down at 10.30, said the receptionist.

I was there on time.

The current receptionist was another Australian stunner. They always were. She had this straight blond hair pulled back and tied in a bow and a suntanned complexion that needed no make-up. She was wearing a tight white T-shirt tucked into figure-hugging jeans and she moved like Dame Margot on Librium. Her eyes were green and enormous and inviting. She took me by the arm and led me into the waiting room: 'Dennis will be with you in a few moments.'

Dennis was Dennis O'Malley, an Australian dentist on the make. An antipodean tooth fixer who not only fixed your teeth but also offered up a lifestyle for you to emulate. The receptionists and assistants were always from God's favourite country and always beautiful – drop-dead beautiful.

The surgery and the waiting room were designed by the sort of interior decorator you read about in *Casa Vogue* and a visit here was as much a fashion statement as a dire necessity.

I sit down in a designer armchair and lean back. I'm counting the seconds until I'm delivered from this agony.

The long low table in front of me that looks like it is made from curved laminated wood and is supported on precision-engineered engine pistons is awash with glossy magazines. I need to get my mind off the pain by reading something.

Here's something – *Axis*. Only here would you find a copy of this Japanese design magazine. I flick through it. Pages and pages of impossible designer stuff. A feature on chairs you could never sit in and another on telephones that look like they've been sculpted from foam. I heave *Axis* back and take a copy of something else. And what's this? I know that face. A photograph of someone I recognise. It's a picture of a young guy in a helmet. A close-up. He's looking into the camera and smiling. Big eyes. A tentative smile.

There's a hand on my arm.

'Dennis is ready for you now, Christopher.'

The receptionist leads me into the surgery where Dennis is scrubbing up. He's dressed in something that looks like a Japanese kimono (no white overalls here!).

'Sit down, Christopher. Good to see you again. How's the film industry these days?'

'Fine.' I point to my mouth and shake my head.

'This is Suzie, my new assistant,' continues Dennis.

Suzie is another Aussie stunner like the receptionist. She too is dressed in a kimono-style wrap-around. She beams a 1000-watt smile at me.

'It's at the back here, Dennis. At the bottom.'

Dennis is now delving around in my mouth, prodding and poking and examining. The assistant is handing him different tools and devices. My eyes are closed and I'm just praying that the pain soon ends as I'm really at the end of my tether. The pain has exhausted me.

'I'm going to give you a little injection now. Open wide.'

Then there's drilling and rinsing and drilling and rinsing.

Then there's the photograph in front of me. The photograph I was looking at in the waiting room some indeterminate length of time ago. The photo pops up in front of me like a pop-up target on a rifle range. The young guy in the helmet with the shy smile. He looked familiar. I can place him. He is familiar, but I don't know him. He's the lad in the photographs – those photographs, the weirdo photographs – that Dick sent me. That's where I know him from. That's where he is.

But what's he doing here?

In a dentist's surgery?

At Dennis' place?

I mean it must be him.

'Final rinse.'

I obey.

'Will the pain go away now?'

'Yeah, you should be as right as can be now.'

'What was wrong?'

'Partial collapse of a filling – and *not* one of mine – that took a piece of tooth with it. Plus a possible infection. I've given you a new filling and I'll give you a script for some antibiotics.'

'Thanks, Dennis.'

'Any time, sport.' Dennis always pronounces *sport* in an exaggerated Aussie manner.

Suzie guides me through to the waiting room. Dennis

[124]

takes his Mont Blanc pen out and psyches himself up for the undemanding and profitable task of composing a prescription.

The photo pops up in my head again. It was that guy in Dick's photographs, wasn't it? In a magazine on the table here.

I put it down here, right just here, and here it still is. I pick it up and the guy in the photograph not only looks like the guy in Dick's photos, but it is him. Must be. And there are a couple of other pictures of him in this mag too. Who is he? Where's the caption?

Oswald's two years as a Marine were the happiest of his short life. At the Marine-CIA base at Atsugi, Japan (*left*), he learnt Russian and studied Marxism. At 19 (*above*) he returned to the US, then left the service.

His name is Oswald, or rather was Oswald. He's dead now. An American, apparently. Served in the US Marine Corps and learnt Russian and studied Marxism. That's him on the left in fatigues at the camp in Japan. A fuzzy photograph but I can still see the resemblance.

And here's another picture. He's standing with a woman to the fore of some temple, some classical-looking building. What's it say here?

After a brief romance in Minsk (*left*), Oswald and Marina were married. Oswald did factory work for high wages and spoke good Russian. But he tried to speak well of the US to his Russian friends.

Oswald? I know who this is.
What's the magazine?
I fold it back to the front cover.
Murder Casebook.
There's a photograph of John F. Kennedy surrounded by solid black. The type is white reversed out.
The Kennedy Assassination.
Dallas: 22nd Nov '63.
'SEVEN SECONDS THAT SHOOK THE WORLD.'

This is uncanny. Seriously uncanny.

The Kennedy assassination?

I turn back to the spread of photographs. The three photographs. Of Oswald.

Lee Harvey Oswald. *That* Oswald.

The supposed assassin of John F. Kennedy.

There's some crossed wire here. This can't be right.

Is it really the same guy?

If it isn't, then Oswald and the guy in the photograph look dead ringers. But it can't be. When did I last see those pictures that Dick sent? Back at the end of January or thereabouts? That's when? Six, seven months ago? How well do I remember them? Pretty well. But can I be sure? They certainly look similar … I think.

I took the magazine with me and waved it at the receptionist asking her to tell Dennis I was borrowing it and would let him have it back some day. She smiled and instructed me to have a nice day.

I walked quickly back along the road and turned down Parkway. It was now a beautifully sunny afternoon and all the girls were out in their summer frocks showing off plenty of leg, arms and chest. But I haven't got time for that. I've got to check these photos against the ones Dick sent me.

But first, the chemist there. I'll pick up the prescription. No, I'll have a drink first down by the tube station in that pub on the corner the name of which I can never remember. The big pub. That one or the Spread Eagle? No, the one down by the tube.

The place was empty and I got a large vodka with orange and retreated to a corner seat. I gulped down half the glass and spread the magazine in front of me.

There's the photo of the nineteen-year-old Oswald taken in the US just before he left the Marines. What year would that be? It doesn't say here. No. It must be the same guy. The eyes, the nose, the mouth, the shape of his face. There can't be any mistake.

AM I PARANOID ENOUGH?

What other pictures are there here?

Marina photographed Lee (*right*) with his guns and socialist newspapers in March 1963. Many experts believed this was faked.

He's standing in front of a fence with a folded newspaper in one hand and a rifle in the other, staring expressionless into the camera's lens. That exact same look you'd recognise in Dick's pictures. Just blank. Staring. Giving nothing away.

Why do experts think it was faked?

Other pictures of him, as a child, laughing with a friend in 1957, and with his Russian wife, Marina. Another one of him here in 1963 giving out leaflets in New Orleans, but very blurred. And opposite – yes. I nearly forgot: the moment when Jack Ruby shot him in the basement of the police department in Dallas. And two more pictures on the following pages taken in the basement just moments later.

I finished the drink and sat there staring at the pictures.

This was high weirdness.

I left the pub and picked up the prescription from Boots on the High Street and then caught a cab back home, my mind whirring with questions.

First off, where did I put the photos?

They should be in a thick file of Dick's letters that I kept in the filing cabinet. They weren't, of course, so I decided I must have misfiled them. Slowly and laboriously I started going through all the other folders looking for them. And they weren't there either.

I spent the whole afternoon looking for them without success. Then I remembered where they might be. One last chance at finding them.

Over to the bookshelves here. Where was it? I thought it was on the top shelf. No. Second shelf down. No, not there either. It's got a cream-coloured spine.

There it is – *Fifty Years of Change in Hitchin*. I stare at it on the shelf. Its small thin spine buttressed between *Dark City:*

The Film Noir and *The Englishman's Flora*. I stare at it afraid to reach out and take it down. If the pictures aren't there then I really have lost them.

Please God they're there.

I finish the tumbler of vodka and place it carefully on the mantelpiece.

Back in January, the last time I looked at the pictures, I had this book open with them. I was looking at the old photographs of the Hermitage Cinema and comparing them with the shot of the same building in Dick's photograph. I had the three pictures and this book on the table there. I put Dick's note and the three pictures in the book and closed it, figuring they would be safer there than adrift in the filing cabinet.

Well, I think I did that. I certainly did have them all together, but …

There's no hesitating now. Either the pictures are here or they've gone. It's that simple.

I reach forward and withdraw the limp-bound book. It falls open in the palms of my hands and there is the note from Dick wrapped around the three photos.

I give a triumphant yell. Wow!

On my desk I lay the three photos out in a line below the magazine and switch the Anglepoise on.

Three pictures from Dick and three in the magazine spread.

I jump from one photo to another comparing them.

If this guy standing outside the Hermitage Cinema and St Mary's Church and in the portrait isn't Lee Harvey Oswald then I'm Emma Thompson's favourite panty liners. If it isn't, and these are two different guys, then they must be twins.

This is spooky whatever way you look at it.

I was looking at these photographs as a wave of unease swept over me. It was as though this was some terrible secret I'd been burdened with, and one I shouldn't know.

I poured myself another drink and returned to the desk.

I reread Dick's note:

AM I PARANOID ENOUGH?

13 January, 1993

Dear Chris,
Keep these SAFE – in a locked filing cabinet or
safe deposit, you'll know – but SAFE!
I'll explain when you get back here.
Don't talk about them.
Silence saves lives!
Ever
Mikhail Bakounine

What did he mean?
I looked at the pictures again.
Lee Harvey Oswald in Hitchin?
Does this mean something, or anything, or what?
Now what do I know about Oswald? Fuck all really. He was supposed to have shot Kennedy according to the government inquiry, but since then there's been a lot of doubt as to whether he did. He may or may not have pulled the trigger, and there may have been, probably were, others involved in the assassination, but we don't know. After he shot Kennedy he shot a police officer (well, they said he did, but there's doubts about that too) who was trying to arrest him and then he was arrested a little later and taken to the police headquarters where he was shot himself by some night-club owner who said he wanted to save Jackie Kennedy the pain of testifying at the trial.

And what else?

He defected to Russia for a while and got a Russian wife.

That's about it.

I didn't know he was in England though.

But, presumably, those who investigated him know that he was? And what was he doing here, if, indeed, it was him? Is this news or ancient history?

I look at the three pictures again and this time my eye is

drawn to Oswald's companion, the fat guy in the suit with the moonface and the broad smile. He certainly looks local, local to Hitchin. Someone must know who he is and where he is, but who? If I could find him I could confirm the identification, but how do I do that?

When I was in Dick's study just before the funeral what did I see on his desk? A pile of books on the JFK assassination. I remembered wondering what he was doing with them – and now I know. He had made the identification too. He must have done. It would be just too coincidental for him to have sent me these pictures and got interested in the subject, independently as it were.

I reread the letter.

Somewhere SAFE. These pictures must be important.

So what do I do?

I've got to get my head straight and work out a course of action.

The pictures have been safe here for six months so another night isn't going to put them in the shadow of jeopardy, I wouldn't have thought. I'll put them back where they were. Have an early night and sort this out tomorrow. Tomorrow's Friday. I'll get organised then. Take it considered and coolly.

But first I'd better phone Laura.

I dialled her number and it rang.

'Hello?'

'Laura, it's Chris.'

'Hi, Chris. How are you?'

'Fine. Now listen. I need to see you. It's important.'

'What about?'

'Are you in town tomorrow? At the office?'

'Yes.'

'What time will you be leaving?'

'About four-ish. I want to get away early.'

'Uh-huh. OK. Let me pick you up then. You've got nothing on this weekend, have you?'

'Not really. Why?'

'I'll travel back with you. I'll explain then.'
'Is everything all right with you?'
'Everything's fine with me. We'll talk tomorrow, Laura.'
'OK. I'll see you then.'
'Right.'
I went out and got some cigarettes.

I had an eerie feeling as I walked back to the flat. People in the street could be keeping me under surveillance and I'd never know it. What was ordinary this morning could now be extraordinary. Plain old everyday Tufnell Park could now be harbouring a thousand threats. The world had changed in a mere twelve hours. It had been stood on its head merely because of a few photographs.

Another drink and I'm to bed. A big drink.

[2]

I put the percolator on and checked the photos are still inside *Fifty Years of Change*. They are.

After making a large mug of Russian coffee I arrange Dick's three photos on the table in front of the sofa and look at them. I reread Dick's letter.

I run through what happened at the beginning of the year. There's Dick's call to me in Brno. He's being followed. It's the last time I speak to him, and then he's dead. Suicide, it seems. I go up for the funeral and learn nothing beyond Briscoe telling me that Dick acted one night as though he was being followed, but that's Briscoe's subjective interpretation. An interpretation, however, that would be consistent with what Dick said on the phone. That, of course, leaves aside whether he really was being followed, but it is independent virtual corroboration of Dick believing that he *was* being followed. That's something.

OK, so we don't know whether he was being followed or not, but we do know that he thought he was being followed.

So where are we now?

He sends these photographs to me without explaining what their significance is. He tells me to keep them safe, but not why. I chance upon some pictures of Lee Harvey Oswald and satisfy myself that it is the same guy. I conclude that Dick had made the same identification because of the presence of several books on the JFK assassination on his desk, a subject I did not previously know that he was interested in.

Am I correct in all this deduction?

Dick had a wide-ranging interest in politics. He'd read catholically in that area and in current affairs too. But a dozen or so books on the JFK assassination surely demonstrates a deep interest. Presumably those books were illustrated? Yes, they must have been. Dick would have seen the pictures of Oswald and made the identification. Right. It's more inconceivable that he didn't make the identification than that he did, and that's the importance of them.

So why did he mail them to me?

For safe-keeping presumably. Dick felt they would be safer with me than with him.

Why? Was someone after them?

The people who were following Dick … the people who broke into his house?

Hold on just a second. I'm getting frightened going down this avenue, very frightened. I start shaking and take a long draught of the coffee.

Let me get all this straight again.

Dick thinks he's being followed and he's worried about the safety of the photographs. He sends them to me. The people who were following him then break into his house but the pictures are gone. So what do they do then?

Didn't I think at one time that the two burglars at Dick's house might have been the two guys who duffed me over at the station? That puts a different complexion on things. If that were the case would they also be the guys who broke into the flat here?

This is getting sinister ... and I haven't even mentioned Mr X yet. The onetime ubiquitous big fat Georges. That fat presence who approached me in the churchyard, appeared at the funeral, outside Dick's house and at the station when I was being done over. Where's he fit into this scheme of things?

Jesus fucking Christ.

There's something going on here all right.

But what?

Is this all coincidence, misinterpretation, paranoia, or is it something more?

And what about Dick's suicide if, indeed, it was suicide? I can't think about that. It's just too mind-fucking.

Do I go to the police with all this or contact the newspapers or just keep my mouth shut or what?

First I owe it to Dick to keep these pictures safe, and then I'd better go and see Laura and discuss everything with her. I need some sound counsel.

I left the house mid-morning. I walked up the steps and stared up and down Fortess Road before continuing. I don't know what I was looking for but I felt I had to be on my guard. I had an uneasiness about everything. That parked van there could contain someone keeping an eye on me. Those women at the bus stop could be employed by Georges. The whole street could be something very different from what it appeared to be. I was getting more paranoid by the minute.

As I walked up to Tufnell Park station I kept throwing glances over my shoulder to see if I was being followed, to see if there was something out of the ordinary that gave them away, whoever they were.

My mind was racing and my heart was beating nineteen to the dozen. I was hot and cold and perspiring and clammy. My hands were soaking wet. Then something erupted in my mind that made the anxiety about being followed almost evaporate. I was reliving the mugging at Hitchin station when I remembered what one of the guys said.

He said, 'He's only got colour.'

Only got colour.

I now realised the significance of that statement. They were looking for the Lee Harvey Oswald photographs which were black and white, and the only photos they found on me were colour shots taken in the Czech Republic that I'd brought up to show Laura.

He's only got colour.

That's what they meant.

They were looking for Dick's pictures. They must have been! The whole story is coming together now. The pieces are falling into place.

Boy, I could do with a drink.

I got off at Tottenham Court Road, walked up the escalator, then down the corridor and emerged under Centre Point on the Charing Cross Road. I need a drink all right but it'll have to wait. I'll go to Don's first.

I've known Don for years. He produces finished artwork for the West End film distributors, everything from comp slips and letterheads to video wraps and posters.

I crossed the road, ducked down the alley to Soho Square and continued on to the little turning off Dean Street where Don has his studio on the second floor.

Don was out but his partner, Lew, told me to help myself to the photocopiers.

I walked down the other corridor to the room where the copiers were. There's the big Canon CLC300 colour mother, the black and white Sharp, and there in the far corner is a young guy working on the Grant projector. He won't see what I'm doing. Good.

I checked the paper in the Canon. The A4 and A3 was just regular photocopying paper so I went over to the cupboard and found the Mellotex. This stock has more of a finish and reproduces copies better. I loaded the cassettes with it.

By switching to the black only mode on this colour machine you can get copies of black-and-white original photos that are 99% as good as the result you'd get by re-reneging. It's that good.

I placed Dick's three photos face down on the glass plate one after the other, selected the A3 cassette, and ran off four copies same size. I then made 200%, 300% and 400% enlargements of each picture by itself, doing again four copies of each.

I took a stiff-backed 10 x 8 envelope from the stationery cupboard and put the three original photos in it. I then sealed the envelope on every seam with 3M Magic Mending Tape and pressed it down firmly. Over each run of tape I signed my signature in spirit marker. On the front I wrote:

> Christopher Cornwell
> LEGAL TRUST DOCUMENTS/August 1993

I measured Oswald's face width on the 400% enlargements and then reduced and enlarged the pictures of him in the magazine so these were the same size. Some of them didn't come out terribly well, but they would aid in the comparisons.

I put all of these copies in a folder that I placed in my shoulder bag which I then locked. I was out of there.

Out in the street I stopped a cab and asked him to drop me off at the St James' end of Pall Mall. This place was the answer. There'd be nothing to connect me with it. It's as safe as houses.

The highly-polished three-dimensional brass letters read CENTAUR SECURITY. They were affixed to the brickwork to the right of a massive door that just exuded security. This was where ******** *********, the actor, kept his wacky-dust when he was working at Pinewood. A private security box was the only answer.

I walked in and a woman stood up behind a desk and asked if she could help me. There was thick carpeting on the floor and expensively framed pictures on the wall and a few plants. I explained that I wanted to open a box and she nodded and took me through to see Mr Pettrolli, the general manager.

Pettrolli showed me the various sizes of drawer and box that were available – samples of each were on display to the right of his desk for prospective customers. I chose the smallest size, just a little bigger than a ream of A3 paper, and he told me that this was £15 a week, and the minimum period was three months, payable in advance.

I paid the advance with my VISA card and was then required to sign an order for my bank to direct debit Centaur Security the monthly fee in advance thereafter until further notice.

Pettrolli took details of my name and address and so on and got me to sign a form saying that I would not keep perishable goods in the drawer, nor dangerous, illegal or inflammatory substances, and further I acknowledged that Centaur Security could not be held responsible for any loss or damage to whatsoever I stored there. Simple enough.

Once the paperwork was in order I was taken out and introduced to a blue-uniformed security guard, Mr Costello, who issued me with and got me to sign for two keys that would open my box. He asked me to enter sample sign-tures into two leather-bound ledger books and then sat me in a chair opposite a permanently rigged-up Polaroid that produced two pictures of me.

'Before you're allowed in you have to give a signature that matches, then we check you against the Polaroid just to be sure.' It sounded secure enough.

Costello asked me to follow him through a safe door that was about a foot thick. The next door couldn't be opened until the one we had just come through had been closed. It was impressive. Further guards were stationed at about every corner. I was shown through to a room that was about sixty feet long and only about six feet wide. On the left and right and from the floor to the high ceiling (reached by sliding ladders) were nothing but drawers the size I had chosen, thousands of them. Each vertical column of drawers was marked with a number and letter – A1, A2 and so on. Costello looked at my keys which were identified as A82/42, and explained that I was down there on the far left, at A82, and I was box number 42, some height up and requiring the ladder-on-castors. He explained that he would now leave me alone and wait outside. The door closed with a dull metallic thud and I was by myself.

The room looked like a cross between a James Bond set and that opening credit sequence shot in *The Prisoner* when Patrick McGoohan's file is dumped in a filing cabinet.

And it was silent here. So silent.

I walked down to A82, the sound of my footsteps echoing and reverberating the whole length of the room at an exaggerated level. Box 1 was just a few inches above the ground while Box 42 was some nine or ten feet above it. I slid the nearest angled ladder along and snapped the locking mechanism shut with my foot.

I took the envelope out of my bag and ascended the steps to Box 42. I unlocked it and put the envelope in. I pushed it shut and the lock snapped into position with a loud click. The pictures would be safe in there.

I owed this to Dick.

Mr Costello led me out through the safe rooms to the front office. He said they were open twenty-four hours a day, 365 or 366 days a year. And they'd never had a complaint yet, in twenty-five years of business. They were totally discreet. Totally. I thanked him and headed east along Pall Mall.

I stopped for a moment and looked at the two keys secured on a plastic ring I was carrying in my hand. They were Ingersoll-type keys with nothing beyond CENTAUR A82/42 engraved on each. Anyone seeing them would immediately realise these weren't keys for a garden shed or a bicycle lock, but for something a little more serious.

I joined the keys to the ring with my house and car keys and stuffed them away in an inside pocket.

I continued along and up Haymarket and Shaftesbury Avenue. I had some time to kill before I went over to Laura's so I decided to arc by the French pub and have a couple of drinks for old times' sake.

In fact I had a good few drinks more than a couple. Then I left.

I stopped a cab and asked him to take me over to Finsbury Square.

I had a couple of hits of vodka in the cab and lay back in the seat. I'm not going to tell Laura anything today, I'm too whacked and strung out to do that. I'll explain to her tomorrow when my head's a lot clearer.

The cab dropped me right outside Laura's building and I sauntered up and through the lobby to the lifts. Her firm was on the fifth floor. In fact her firm *was* the fifth floor, there was nobody else.

The receptionist said Laura was with a client. I sat down in one of the enormous armchairs and I was soon asleep …

'Christopher?'

What was that?

Laura's voice? Yes.

I open my eyes. Laura is leaning towards me in a denim-like blue dress. I can see the tops of her breasts. She's wearing a black bra.

'Christopher?'

'Sorry, I nodded off. You ready?'

'Let's go.'

'Yeah.'

I grabbed my bag and followed Laura out. She wished the receptionist a good weekend and I thanked her for her trouble.

We walked down through the lobby and on to the street.

'Let's get a cab,' I suggested.

'Save your money. We'll go the way I always go.'

'How's that?'

'Walk down to Moorgate station and get the underground up. Change at King's Cross.'

[138]

'But it's so hot and stuffy!' I protested.

'And cheaper.'

There was no arguing with Laura so I obediently followed her.

'Why do you need to talk to me then, Chris? You sounded at the end of your tether last night.'

'I'll explain it all to you tomorrow when I'm more relaxed. I need to lay it all out before you.'

'Lay what?'

'This and that. It's difficult and involved, complicated.'

'Are you in trouble or something?'

'No. It all arises from those photos Dick sent me.'

'Photos. What photos?'

Shit – I'd never told Laura about them.

'Boy, I thought I had told you.'

'No, you haven't. Photos? What sort of photos? Pornographic photos?'

'Heavens no! Why did you say that?'

'I'm just trying to come up with some reason as to why you kept them secret.'

'I didn't keep them secret. I just forgot to tell you about them. I was going to tell you about them but you were going on your winter hols or you'd gone or something! I can't remember. I didn't want to discuss them on the phone there and then. At that time I just thought they might have reflected badly on Dick. You'd think he really was some secret total weirdo or something. Then I forgot about them. That's all.'

'Uh-huh. So now you do want to talk about them? What occasioned this?'

'Something I discovered … quite by chance.'

'Which was?'

'Let me explain it all tomorrow. I'll feel better doing it then.'

'God, you are a tease!'

'I'm not. I just want to be able to explain it properly, correctly. You know?'

'OK.'

'But we must never talk about this on the telephone. Right?'

'You are not only a tease, you're also a *paranoid* tease.'

'Listen, this isn't some joke. We're talking serious stuff here. Heavy serious stuff. You understand? And I got very paranoid today.'

We travelled in silence on the underground up to King's Cross. There we changed and walked up to the mainline station. Our train was due to leave in ten minutes. We went to the front of the train and found a near-empty carriage.

'You know,' Laura said, 'it must be over twenty years since we last travelled up from town together on a train.'

Over twenty years? Yeah, easily. Before either of us were married. Nearer twenty-five I'd say.

'Over twenty years,' Laura said again as she looked out of the window and ran her tongue over her lips.

The carriage started to fill up with commuters and I began to feel drowsy. 'Wake me up when we get to Hitchin.'

'A fine travelling partner you are.'

'I've had a busy day, dear heart,' I said.

Laura tutted and opened some legal journal she'd taken from her shoulder bag.

The train pulled out and I was asleep even before we got to the Copenhagen tunnel, I think. Occasionally I would almost come to and out of a half-open eye I'd see a station rush by or the backs of houses or Laura with her glasses on deep into *All England Law Reports* or whatever it's called.

We walked all the way back from the station to Tilehouse Street and collaborated on making a chef's salad. Laura left to do some late night shopping and see her mother and I watched *Alien* on the video before going to bed around 10 p.m.

Tomorrow I'd explain all, and perhaps Laura could come up with some answers or, at the very least, offer some sage advice.

And I haven't had a drink for about seven hours. Maybe a personal best.

Right now I'm done for.

[3]

It was a bright warm Saturday morning so we decided to take our coffees out into the garden. Laura put a large blanket on the grass and I sorted through my photo file.

Laura lit a More and said, 'Talk to me. Tell me.'

'OK. Now I got these three photos from Dick by registered delivery. There was a covering note dated 13 January, the day before he phoned me, two days before he committed suicide, died. And he said to keep them safe. He'd explain it all to me when I got back from the Czech Republic. He didn't send them to the flat, he sent them to me at the production office at Pinewood Studios. And that's where they sat for a while. Now, saying that he would explain them to me precludes him thinking of suicide, doesn't it?'

'It precludes him having suicide on his mind while he was writing the letter.'

'Yeah, but what's going to happen in a couple of days?'

'A lot,' said Laura.

'OK, but we know Dick and we can be pretty sure that it didn't, can't we?'

'No, we can't,' Laura replied.

'He was our friend!'

'So?'

'Listen, don't be that antagonistic to what I'm saying, Laura.'

'I'm not. I'm just trying to approach what you're saying as it would be approached in a court. That's all. Like you asked. And anyway, it's true.'

'Well, let's forget about that for the time being.'

'Carry on.'

'I've forgotten where I got to.'

'Dick sent the photos to Pinewood. He said he would explain when you got back.'

'Right. Anyway, I don't get the letter until after the funeral and I look at the photos and don't know what to make of them.'

'Can I see them?'

'Not the originals, but here's copies enlarged 200%.'

I lay the three A3 sheets in front of Laura. She crouches over them and her eyes dart from one to another and back again.

'What do you see?' I ask.

Laura sucks on her cigarette and exhales. 'Three pictures taken in Hitchin twenty-five or more years ago. Two certainly taken in Hitchin, but we can only assume the third was, the portrait of this young fellow. This one was taken outside the old Hermitage Cinema and this by the church. A sunny day, hardly any shadows. Taken in summer some time.'

'What else can you say?'

'Not much at all. This portly chap looks local but I'm not sure why I'm saying that. This young fellow looks interesting. He's a dead ringer for Lee Harvey Oswald.'

'Who?'

'Lee Harvey Oswald. Kennedy's assass – '

'I know,' I say interrupting Laura. 'It *is* Lee Harvey Oswald.'

Laura bursts into laughter. 'How ridiculous!'

'I'm telling you. It is Lee Harvey Oswald. Look at these.'

I take from the folder the other pictures of Oswald that I'd copied from the magazine and lay them out in front of her. Laura checks them against Dick's pictures.

'He certainly looks similar … very similar … but I doubt you'd convince some sceptic.'

'I'm not trying to convince some sceptic. I'm satisfied it's Oswald. And anyway, Dick believed it was Oswald.'

'How do you know?'

'Because that's why he sent them to me and told me to look after them. He didn't feel they were safe up here and

[142]

after that burglary we know they wouldn't have been.'

'That's a lot of supposition.'

'But it's not all. Dick had a dozen or so books on the JFK assassination on his desk. They would have been illustrated. He knew who this was. And, besides, even you thought it was Oswald!'

Laura looked at me and said, 'I didn't say it was Oswald. I said it was a dead ringer.'

'That's all you can say. Nobody can say that it is Oswald for a fact, not even me. But it couldn't be anyone else.'

Laura stared more closely at the pictures. 'Do we know if Oswald ever came to England?'

'I don't know anything about him much. He defected to Russia for a while.'

'Wasn't he in the Marines?'

'Yes. Why?'

'Perhaps he was stationed over here for a time?'

'Possible. I've got to check all this out.'

Laura sighed and said, 'But what was he doing here? In Hitchin?'

I shook my head.

'Where did Dick get these pictures from?' Laura asked.

'No idea. If we had the answer to that we'd be home and dry.'

I fold the copies up and put them away in the folder. 'Now let's move on to the next stage.'

'Which is?'

'The burglary at Dick's house. They were only in Dick's study. These pictures were what they were looking for, but they didn't find them.'

'Uh-huh,' said Laura.

'The next thing is I get mugged and before I pass out one of the muggers says "He's only got colour." They were looking for these pictures which are black and white but all they could find was the colour stuff I'd shot on location.'

'I get your drift, but I think you'd have a tough time convincing anyone else.'

'The next thing they do is break into my flat because they think the pictures might be there. See?'

'That could have been a coincidence.'

'Can't you see, Laura, there's something going on here? Something weird and actually a bit frightening.'

'I don't know what to make of it. Who are we dealing with here?'

'Georges could answer that question.'

'Who's Georges?'

'He's that odd bohemian guy who stopped me in the churchyard when I was coming here for Dick's funeral. The guy in the Merc at the funeral, the guy standing outside Dick's house, the guy who was at the station just before I got mugged.'

'Georges.'

'Yes, Georges.'

'Who is he?'

'You tell me. I've no idea. He appears and disappears like a magician.'

'Perhaps he is?' Laura lit another More. 'So what do we do now?'

'If we can find the other guy in the pictures he'd be able to fill us in on the story.'

'He might be dead.'

'But we've got to look for him. If I give you copies of the photographs can you show them around up here? If he's local someone might recognise him. See if your mum or any of her friends know. That would be a good start.'

'OK. You know there's another person who could tell us all about these photographs?'

Another person? 'Who's that for God's sake? I can't think of anyone.'

Laura mimed holding a camera to her eye and pressing the shutter. 'The happy snapper.'

'Who's that?'

'The man who took the photographs!'

The man who took the photographs, yes. I'd forgotten

all about him. 'Right. The third man. I'd overlooked him. Unfortunately he didn't put his signature on them.'

'More's the pity,' said Laura.

'Anyway, if you can show the picture around and identify the fat guy he could lead us to him.'

'Is that all we can do?'

I thought for a moment. 'Do you want to come around with me to Barbara's this afternoon?'

'Why?'

'I want to ask her a couple of questions, discreetly of course. And also see if she's still got Dick's books on the assassination. They'd be valuable to have.'

'I'll phone her. She shares the house now with her sister who got a divorce.'

'Good.'

CHAPTER FIVE

WHO SPEAKS FOR DRAX?

'Identify.'
  'Bellerophon ... 666B.'
  'Location?'
  'Capital.'
  'Proceed.'
  'Further auxiliaries have been employed.'

BARBARA WELCOMED US IN and directed us down to the kitchen. Her skin seemed to have aged, particularly her cheeks, and bereft of make-up she looked a lot older than she was.

'Angela has gone to Stevenage to choose a new bed. She'll be back later,' said Barbara.

Angela was Barbara's divorced sister.

Barbara had a scarf around her head and a pair of secateurs in her hand. She'd been doing something in the garden, one of her 'main interests' now.

Laura chatted with Barbara about her mother and sisters while she made a pot of tea. I sat by the table gazing out into the garden and thinking how only a year ago Dick and I were sitting there quietly getting smashed on tequila while reading aloud jokes from Gersh Legman's *Rationale of the Dirty Joke*. A whole year ago. It seemed like yesterday. It seemed like an eternity ago.

Barbara handed me a mug of tea and she and Laura sat

down opposite. There was a plate of those small white German biscuits, the ones with the gingerbread taste, and I started helping myself to them. I ate about six before Laura noticed and chided me for being so greedy.

'Now, Christopher, what are you up to? Are you working?'

Barbara asked this in a little girl voice with a fragile smile on her face. I sensed she found it awkward talking to me.

'I've just finished on a picture out in Ireland. Easy money. A doddle.'

'But did you *enjoy* it?'

'I don't know if enjoy is ever the right word ... these days. It was tolerable. Wasn't too bad, you know?'

'And what are you going to do next?'

'There's a couple of pictures on the horizon, but nothing definite. One of them's going to be shot out in Africa. It would be nice to get that, but I doubt I will.'

'Oh, what a pity.'

'Yes.'

Barbara had run out of questions. She gazed into her mug of tea. Laura was eating a biscuit and staring out into the garden. Aside from the birds singing there was silence. I'll jump in now. I cleared my throat and said, 'I wanted to ask you something, a favour actually.'

Barbara looked up from the tea slowly. 'A favour?'

'Yes. I wanted to borrow a few of Dick's books.'

'I can't lend you any of the Hertfordshire books because we've already given all of them to the museum. That's what Dick always wanted, you know.'

'Yes, I know. It wasn't any of the local books in fact, but those books on the John F. Kennedy assassination that were in his study when I was last here.'

'If they were in the study when you were last here, they'll still be there. I've only taken out the Hertfordshire books, as Dick wanted. Do please borrow them.'

'Right. Thanks.'

[147]

After a short pause, almost as an afterthought, Barbara said, 'I didn't know Dick had any books on that subject.'

Didn't she ever look around when she went into Dick's study? Didn't she notice things? Obviously not.

Laura gave me a glance and turned to Barbara. 'Was Dick very interested in Kennedy's assassination then?'

Barbara sipped her tea and thought for a moment and looked up at the ceiling as though that would jog her memory. 'I wouldn't say he was very interested, no.'

Why did he have the books then? He'd obviously been reading them as markers and Post-It notes were stuck in them. 'But he was interested, wasn't he? Barbara?' I asked.

'I suppose so. Yes.'

I continued. 'He'd been reading those books. It was more than just an idle passing interest.'

'Yes, you could say that.'

It's hard work getting information from Barbara. She just reacts to the specific question and nothing else. She doesn't appreciate your drift and volunteer information. Each item of information has to be separately mined. And there's something about her eyes, that otherworldliness and unfocused look. I wouldn't mind betting she was still on tranquillisers.

'When did he first become interested in Kennedy?'

'Oh, I think it must have been about this time last year, or a little later.'

'It wasn't a long time before he … passed away?'

'No, it wasn't.'

'What did he ever say to you about it?'

'It? What?'

'Kennedy. The Kennedy assassination?'

'I can't really remember, Christopher.'

'He must have said something about it to you.'

'I don't remember. He may have mentioned it.'

'Such as? Mentioned what?'

Barbara gazed at the ceiling again. She was having a tough time remembering anything.

Laura put her hand on Barbara's arm and said, 'Dick had so many interests, didn't he?'

Barbara smiled. 'Yes, that's true. He was interested in all sorts of things … he was.'

'Was there something,' Laura continued, 'that started his interest in the Kennedy murder?'

'Mmmm, just talking, you know. Conversation.'

'With you?'

'Heavens, no! With people.'

'People?'

Laura was having as hard a time as I was but she persevered.

'Yes. People.'

'Lots of people?' asked Laura.

'I don't think it was lots of people, just one person.'

Laura looked at me to see if the reply had registered. It had. Just one person.

'Who was that, Barbara? Can you remember?'

'I never met him, you see. Dick knew him quite well. Would you both like another cup of tea?'

'I'm fine,' I said.

Laura ignored the question and continued. 'You never met him, I see. But who was he?'

'He was retired.'

'From what?'

'I can't remember.'

'What was his name? Can you remember that?'

Barbara started staring at the ceiling again and after a few beats said, 'Yes, I can. Drax. It was Mr Drax. And I can remember that because it was where my father was born … in Drax, West Yorkshire.'

'Who was Mr Drax, Barbara?'

'He died of cancer of the face. He suffered for a long time, Dick said.'

'So,' Laura said, 'he was at the hospice? He was one of the people Dick counselled there?'

A sharp deduction of Laura's. I'd missed it. I was still

trying to figure out where exactly Drax was and why I'd never heard of it.

'Yes, Dick counselled him … until the very end.'

'And it was Mr Drax who got Dick interested in the Kennedy assassination?'

'I believe so, yes.'

'Why was Mr Drax interested in it?'

'I don't know. But Dick listened to him a lot.'

'Listened? You mean talked with him a lot?'

'Yes.'

'Can you remember when Mr Drax died?'

'It was just before Christmas last year.'

'Do you know when Dick first met him?'

'It was at the hospice.'

'Yes, but when?'

'I don't think Dick knew him for very long. All the people who go into the hospice don't have very long to live.'

'So,' said Laura summing up, 'Mr Drax died just before Christmas and it was he who got Dick interested in the Kennedy business?'

Barbara nodded.

'And Dick didn't know him for very long?' asked Laura.

Barbara nodded again.

Laura looked at me as if to say – you won't get anything more and then said, 'Why don't you get the books while Barbara is making us another cup of tea, Christopher?'

'Yes, I will. Thanks, Barbara.'

'You know where they are,' replied Barbara.

I left the kitchen and climbed the stairs to the top. I didn't want to spend any more time than I had to in Dick's study in case memories started tumbling back so I walked straight in and took the Kennedy books from the desk, from the exact position they were in when last I saw them. All of Dick's Hitchin and Hertfordshire books had gone and most of the framed maps and engravings from the opposite wall too.

I returned to the kitchen and thanked Barbara for the second cup of tea. I drank it in silence while Laura and Barbara chatted about some mutual friend who was a local teacher.

The Kennedy books were in a pile in front of me. My eye ran down the horizontal spines: *The Final Assassination Report*, *Rush to Judgement*, *Oswald in New Orleans*, *Legend: The Secret World of Lee Harvey Oswald* and others, including a fat volume entitled *The Official Warren Commission Report on the Assassination of President John F. Kennedy*. The official report, huh? I had a fair bit of reading to do and I was anxious to find out what Oswald was doing in England.

Laura stood up and said, 'Thank you for the tea, Barbara. But I'm afraid we really should be going now.'

I stood up too.

Barbara said, 'We must have tea again,' and stood up. 'I'll see you out.'

We followed her out and down the passage to the front door. I kissed her goodbye and said I'd call her. Laura did too.

Barbara stood at the front door waving to us until we got into Laura's car. In fact she was still waving to us as we drove off down Highbury Road.

Laura turned left into Walsworth Road and I said, 'The hospice is out on the Pirton Road, isn't it?'

'Yes, why?'

'You fancy driving out there? It's a gorgeous day.'

'What for?'

'I just want to ask a few questions. See what we can find out … about Mr Drax, and anything else.'

'If you want. Yes.'

I took out a fresh half bottle of Smirnoff from my bag and unscrewed the cap. The noise of the seal breaking alerted Laura and she shot me a disapproving glance and said, rhetorically, 'You're not going to drink that in the car, are you?'

'I don't smoke in your car,' I replied.

'I'm not stopping you smoking.'

'Well, I just need a quick drink.' Which was true. I needed something to fortify me against the hospice. I'd never been to a hospice before and I felt more than a little anxious about going there. I wasn't sure how I'd react. I was thinking of all those people who knew they were going to die. Dying doesn't, I think, frighten me – as long as it's instantaneous, as long as I'm not aware it's going to happen to me, but that foreknowledge does. Knowing you are going to die, I couldn't handle that. This is one of the reasons I don't like flying. Imagine you are up in a plane and something goes wrong and it starts to plummet down. Those last few minutes of consciousness when you know what your fate is going to be. Even thinking about it frightens me. The Lockerbie explosion was a dreadful tragedy, but at least it was instantaneous. The passengers didn't know what was going to happen to them. Bang, and it was over.

'You've been to the hospice, haven't you?' I asked Laura.

Laura nodded and said, 'Couple of times … with Dick. My mother knows one of the matrons there, Miss Oxnard.'

'Is this a council or health authority place or what?'

'Dick told me it was run by a private charity. It has quite a good reputation.'

We drove through town and then along Upper Tilehouse Street to the Pirton Road. The houses thinned out and ahead of us was the rolling open chalkland where the Chiltern Hills gradually peter out. Over there is where the Oughton River rises and where Dick and me spent timeless summers fishing, tadpoling and building camps on the wetlands.

We turned into a drive on the left. Sorrel House. This was the hospice. It was a large mid-nineteenth-century country house with flanking ranges added to it by subsequent generations. At the back of it I caught a glimpse of a long single-storeyed conservatory-style extension that curved around on the lawn. There was a friendly air to the place, not at all off-putting and antiseptic like most convalescent homes and private clinics.

What knocked me out right away was the age of the patients. I'd just taken it as read that they would all be old and very nearly infirm. They weren't. There were people here in their thirties and even twenties shuffling along the gravel drive and sitting in the garden chairs. That really shocked me.

The Angel of Death had his hands full here.

I followed Laura through the large main door that had been propped open with a pile of telephone directories. This opened on to a vestibule that led to the main hall of the house: large and high and panelled in a dark wood. Staircases swept up on the left and the right to a minstrels' gallery on the first floor from which dark corridors radiated.

Laura pressed a bell set within the wood that had a notice underneath it saying RING IF YOU WANT SOMEONE! I liked that, particularly the exclamation mark.

A woman in a dressing gown in, I guess, her early forties was slowly walking across the hall with the aid of a Zimmer. A dressing or bandage covered half of her face. Her progress was painfully deliberate and slow. An old man in a wheelchair stared at her, transfixed, oblivious to anything else.

I said to Laura that it really surprised me, the age of the people here.

Laura wasn't listening, she was looking at two middle-aged men over to the right sitting at a table playing Monopoly. They were dressed in slacks and shirts, and they had the look. The look of the institutionalised.

A young nurse appeared in a green uniform. She couldn't have been more than eighteen or nineteen. She was blonde and buxom and had an endearing smile and an unaffected manner. She said, 'Can I help you? Are you visitors?'

Laura replied, 'Is Miss Oxnard on duty today?'

'No, it's her day off today. But Miss Cottle is here. Would you like to see her?'

'We would,' continued Laura, 'if she's not too busy.'

'I'll just go and see,' said the nurse. 'You can sit down there if you like.'

'Thank you,' said Laura.

We sat down and had only waited a minute or two when a tall bustling woman in her early sixties strode across the hall to us. She was wearing a green uniform too and a scarf-hat. Her manner was purposeful and determined. This must be Miss Cottle.

'Good day, I'm Miss Cottle.'

Laura and I stood up. Miss Cottle's eyes belied her body language, they were soft and seemed understanding, and were a deep green.

'I'm Laura Sayer,' said Laura as she extended her hand.

'Laura Sayer? Oh, yes. Jean Sayer's daughter?'

'Yes, I am.'

'Daphne, Miss Oxnard, that is, is a friend of your mother's.'

'She is.'

There was a moment's silence before Miss Cottle said, 'Can we be of any help to you?' The we, I take it, referring to Sorrel House generally.

Laura said, 'This is Christopher Cornwell.'

'Nice to meet you, Mr Cornwell,' said Miss Cottle as she extended her hand.

We shook hands and I said, 'The same.'

Laura continued, 'Christopher and I are very old friends of Dick North's. We all grew up together.'

Miss Cottle held her hands together and looked to the heavens. 'We all miss Dick so much. He was the most reliable and regular visitor. We were heart-broken when we heard what had happened. Heart-broken. It was so very sad.'

'It was,' said Laura very quietly.

'We'd like to ask you a few questions if we may, about Dick and about Mr Drax,' I whispered. There were a couple of patients walking by and I didn't want them to hear me.

'We'll go to my office,' stated Miss Cottle.

Laura and I followed her down a corridor to a high-ceilinged room that overlooked the front lawn. The office was pure 1940s. I couldn't have designed and built a better example with an unlimited budget at the studios. Right down to the filing cabinet, the carpet and the fans – all authentic 1940s. The only concessions to the present were a coffee-and-cream push-button telephone and a current calendar put out by a drug company who made 'Oblivimex' which, unmistakably, sounded like something you gave the terminally ill.

Miss Cottle sat down in a wooden swivel chair behind a deep desk and we sat facing her on the other side in wooden chairs with curved arms.

'How can I help you then?' asked Miss Cottle. She had a pleasing direct manner.

I thought I would start from the top. 'How long did you know Dick?'

'I began here in 1970 and Dick first came in 1980 as a visiting counsellor. So, it must be some thirteen years. Yes.'

'Did you know him well?'

'I wasn't an intimate friend, but I knew him reasonably well. A counsellor cannot fake qualities he or she does not have. Dick took his work here seriously.'

'Did you know that before he died he thought he was being followed?'

Miss Cottle seemed surprised. 'Followed?'

'Yes.'

'Who on earth would want to follow Dick?'

'I don't know. Now, did you notice anything odd in his behaviour in, say, the last six months of his life? Anything that would, in retrospect, point towards suicide?'

Miss Cottle thought for a moment and considered what she was going to say.

'I worked for many years as a psychiatric nurse ... and while this gives you certain insights into people's behaviour ... it also handicaps you. You develop what I have always called a textbook mentality. You interpret behaviour in terms of the textbook. He does this, it means that. In other words, you simplify things.'

She was then silent. I wasn't sure what she had said. Would she volunteer something more or did I need to ask her? As it was, Laura filled the void with another question.

'In other words, you didn't see anything that would indicate suicide?'

'You are correct. I didn't. What I was trying to say in a roundabout way was that it would be easy with the benefit of hindsight to say that I did, but I didn't, to be perfectly honest. It was a very great surprise to us all. I could not believe it.'

'Neither could we,' I added.

'Was Dick very close to Mr Drax?' asked Laura.

'You are always close to those you counsel,' replied Miss Cottle. 'Mr Drax was a withdrawn man and Dick was the only counsellor he would talk to. They seemed to get on very well together. Mr Drax gave up on the other counsellors and he didn't mix at all well with our other guests.'

I wanted to know more about Drax. 'Who was he? Where did he come from?'

'I don't know an awful lot about him. As I said, he kept very much to himself. He was well-read and most intelligent, but he was very shy when it came to talking about himself. Birds were his hobby. He knew all there was to know about birds. He was very good at identifying them.'

'Where did he come from?'

'I don't know where he came from originally, but he lived locally for very many years. He'd lived a long time … in Hitchin. We may have something on record.'

'Did his relatives come and see him?'

'No. He had no relatives, or friends. No visitors at all as far as I'm aware, though you can check with Daphne, Miss Oxnard.'

Drax was turning into a zero.

'Do you know what he did, Miss Cottle?'

'I know that he travelled a lot. There wasn't a country he hadn't been to. I think he was involved with some private charity or foundation.'

'What did he die of?'

'Facial carcinomas. He was very disturbed towards the end and he suffered greatly. It was down all one side of his face. On the other side he had a scar diagonally across the eye. It looked like a *duelling* scar. I once asked him about it and he said it was an accident, but I doubted *that* very much.'

'I see.' I was running out of questions.

'Why are you asking questions about Mr Drax?' Miss Cottle asked.

I started to say something but Laura interrupted me. She knew exactly how to pitch the response.

'Because, Miss Cottle, Dick appeared to be close to Mr Drax and Mr Drax may have been a factor in what happened. If we know more about Mr Drax we may know more about Dick.'

'I see,' Miss Cottle said as she pondered what Laura said and fiddled with a pencil. Then she stood up and said, 'Let me get the records. I'll be right back.'

After she left the room Laura looked at me and said, 'She seems quite co-operative.'

'There's no reason why she shouldn't be,' I replied. The picture I was getting of Drax didn't square with what Barbara had told us so far. Had Barbara got it wrong? Was it someone other than Drax who had turned Dick on to the Kennedy assassination? Was this a dead-end or, worse, a wild goose chase?

Miss Cottle returned holding two folders. She opened one on her desk and looked surprised. 'Goodness, most of Mr Drax's records appear to be missing!'

Great! Not only does nobody know much about him but now his records have gone walkies.

'We must have misfiled them. It does happen.'

Fabulous! I looked at Laura in resignation.

Miss Cottle was looking through what remained of the records. 'Tyler Michael Drax. Born New York, uh-huh. 10 September 1910.'

I hurriedly took out my Rapidograph and a small notebook I always carry with me and asked Miss Cottle to repeat Drax's details. She did. I wrote them down. New York, eh? Perhaps Barbara was right after all?

'Mr Drax was admitted here on 26 May 1992. He had been undergoing treatment at the London Clinic prior to that. He died on Saturday, 19 December 1992, here.'

1910 to 1992. Eighty-two years old. And the London Clinic? He must have had some money. Not short of a bob or two.

'You said that he had no relatives, but isn't there something there about anyone who should be informed when he dies? Anyone?'

'No, there isn't. But a firm of solicitors who represented his estate was in touch with us ... here it is ... Greenwood, Ware and Scott, Temple House, Tottenham Court Road, London. They also took away his possessions from here after he died.'

That's a dead-end for sure, I thought. You hardly ever get anything out of solicitors.

What else can I ask her? 'Do you know where he was buried?'

'London, I believe. We released the body to the solicitors.'

Laura touched me on the arm and said to Miss Cottle, 'Do you have his address?' I'd forgotten about that too.

'Yes. It's here somewhere ... he'd lived there for many years. The Leys, Shadwell Lane, Hitchin.'

I wrote that down too. I knew Shadwell Lane quite well, but I couldn't place The Leys. Shadwell Lane, funnily enough, led off at an angle from the Walsworth Road at the spot where Dick's road, Highbury Road, joined it.

I wondered if Dick knew Drax prior to Sorrel House? If he did he never mentioned Drax to me, but it was worth asking. 'Do you know if Dick knew Mr Drax before he was admitted here?'

'No, he didn't. I assigned Dick to Mr Drax and introduced them. They had never met before. In fact I don't think Mr Drax knew anyone. He was almost a hermit at home, so I gathered.'

Laura said, 'Do you know anything about Mr Drax's interest in the John F. Kennedy assassination? Did he ever talk about it to you?'

Miss Cottle thought for a moment and then said, 'I didn't know he was interested in that.'

I guess Dick was the only person he talked to.

'I've got a folder here,' Miss Cottle said, 'that I've been meaning to return to Mrs North.' She looked at Laura. 'You see her from time to time?'

Laura nodded.

'Well, let me give it to you. It has Dick's name on it. We found it in Mr Drax's room. Dick must have loaned it to him. There are pictures and maps of Hitchin. Nothing very valuable, I wouldn't have thought.'

Laura got up and took it from Miss Cottle.

'Thanks, Miss Cottle. You've been terribly helpful,' I said.

'Yes, you have,' echoed Laura.

'I hope I have,' Miss Cottle said as she showed us out of the office. 'And I'll leave you to find your own way out if you don't mind. I have a staff meeting. Just straight on and left. Bye!'

'Bye!' Laura and I said in unison.

We walked off in silence and got into the car. There were many more patients now sitting and strolling on the lawn at the front. The sun was blazing down and the sky was blue and cloudless. In the midst of life indeed.

A little way down the Pirton Road Laura said, 'How far has this advanced us then?'

'Well, we know a little bit more about Drax, but there seem to be precious few leads on him to follow up. No

[159]

relatives, no wife, nothing. We need someone who knew him, and there isn't someone.'

'Try the solicitors.'

'We can, but they probably won't say much, if anything.'

'Probably.'

'I'll tell you what though,' I said, 'I think Drax might be the guy who took the photographs and if he was he was certainly the guy who gave them to Dick. That's my hunch.'

'We'll see,' said Laura as she concentrated on the driving.

I had to be right about Drax giving them to Dick. He introduced Dick to the JFK business and the photographs were somehow linked with Drax's interest. The alternative is … is what? That Dick somehow came across the pictures, identified Oswald and got talking to Drax about the subject. I suppose that is possible, yeah. But this now comes back to what Barbara said. Was it Drax who turned Dick on to JFK? Barbara had no reason to lie, though she could have got it wrong. We really need some independent corroboration of Drax's interest in the subject … and where's that going to come from?

We were soon back at the house.

Cathie was in the kitchen with her boyfriend, Matt, a nineteen-year-old with long hair and a black leather jacket which had a demon (?) airbrushed on the back with the word SEPULTURA underneath. They were cooking a curry together and the smell from it had engulfed the whole house. There were pots and pans and plates and things everywhere and the kitchen looked like the kitchen in *Withnail and I*. Laura closed the door on the mess and we went into the front room for a drink. Lucy was there doing her homework. She looked up at us and scowled. 'Every time I start this someone comes in and *disturbs* me!'

Laura said firmly, 'If you were to do it in your room nobody would disturb you.'

'I like working down here!'

'Other people live in this house too.'

Lucy closed her books in a huff, sighed, and stormed out of the room, slamming the door behind her.

'You hungry, Laura?'

'Yes, I am.'

'Let's go and get something to eat.'

It was 6 p.m. and we'd had nothing to eat all day. I picked up the folder Miss Cottle had given us and we walked around to Fatso's in Sun Street.

There were only about a dozen or so people eating there and, luckily, the window table in the corner by itself was free. We each ordered a lasagne and I got a bottle of house red. Van Morrison's 'Moondance' was playing again on the restaurant's sound system: *Can I just have one more Moondance with you?*

Laura nodded at Dick's folder on the table. 'That's an American legal folder. Very expensive. You don't often see them over here.'

'I've got some. Perhaps this was a present from Drax?'

The folder was foolscap in size and made out of strong brownish card or board. The bright red gussets down the side were made of cloth. There was a greyish-blue ribbon tied in a bow to keep it closed.

'Let's see what's in it,' I said.

I undid the bow, opened the flap and pulled out a dozen or so photographs and postcards and a number of maps.

I looked through the pictures and handed each one to Laura as I finished with it. Most of the photographs were originals and dated back to, I would guess, just before the First World War. They were all of Hitchin and despite their age they were mostly identifiable:

— The north side of St Mary's taken from the bank of the River Hiz. Summer.

— A view of the town from the top of Windmill Hill.

— The Triangle, or Bull Corner as it was sometimes known, where Bridge Street runs into Queen and Park Streets. Several children stand in the middle of the photograph staring into the camera. Others in the background look away.

— The Priory, taken from Tilehouse Street.

— A shot looking up Tilehouse Street from Bucklersbury.

'There's my house on the left!' said Laura.

— A photograph taken at the station.

— An old woman weaving straw plait sitting on the doorstep of a narrow terraced house. Presumably taken in one of the slum 'yards' that were subsequently demolished. Straw plaiting was supplied to the hat trade in Luton and a lot of the poorer people in Hitchin depended upon it.

— Another view of the station. A steam train pulling out.

— A view of Market Square.

— The Sun and the Angel Vaults Inn in Sun Street.

'You remember the Angel Vaults in Sun Street?' I said.

'No.'

'Yes you do. We all went up there to watch it being demolished. Dick came too. Next to the Sun.'

'When was that?'

'Mid-fifties, was it?'

'I don't remember.'

— A view down Bucklersbury taken from Market Square.

— A large Victorian house I didn't recognise.

— A further shot of the station.

— A view looking northwards up Bancroft.

There were half a dozen postcards of St Mary's, the Priory, the old town hall, Hitchin market, the Corn Exchange. They were all black and white except for the one of the town hall which was awash with garish printed colours, obviously some now forgotten tinting process. Several of the postcards were sent to local addresses. All had simple messages, for example: 'Dear Em, I'll pop over on Tuesday. I hope Ernest is well now. Love, Dot.'

I handed them to Laura. 'I guess Drax was interested in local Hitchin history too.'

'Mmmmm. What about those maps?'

'They're mainly photocopies of early 6-inch and 25-inch Ordnance Survey maps of the town.'

This one was unlike the others, it wasn't a photocopy,

but a large folded original, linen-backed. I unfolded as much of it as I could and I immediately recognised it.

'Jesus. This was the map Dick used to have on his study wall!'

'What is it?'

'He got it years ago. It shows all the bombs and stuff the Germans dropped around here during the last war.'

'Oh.'

I folded the map back up. Its whereabouts were no longer a mystery.

'You know what this is of?' Laura was holding up the photograph of the Victorian house I didn't recognise.

'No.'

I looked at the picture more closely. A substantial Gothic Victorian pile rising to three storeys. A large lawn to the fore of it with a drive curving around to the front of the house. About a dozen servants and maids were arrayed on the drive, all looking into camera.

'Have a guess,' said Laura.

'Absolutely no idea at all.'

'On the back here it says "The Leys, built 1872." In ink.'

'The Leys?'

Laura frowned at me and said, 'Have you forgotten already?'

'What?'

'The Leys. The Leys! That's where Drax lived. This is where he lived.'

'Oh, yeah.' I took the photograph from Laura and looked at it and then looked at the writing on the back. 'Do you suppose Drax wrote this on the back?'

'He may have done. It looks freshish, not ancient. And the writing's very spidery.'

'Spidery?'

'He was old and ill, wasn't he?'

'I guess so.'

I continued looking at the photograph. I didn't recognise the house and I couldn't place it on Shadwell Lane. And then it came to me: it could only be that house surrounded by a high brick wall that years ago Dick and I thought was somehow connected with the underground passages in the town. That must be it. This was the first time I'd seen the house itself.

We had a good meal and afterwards we wandered around to the video shop on Hermitage Road to see if there was anything worth getting out. Laura wanted to see *Hannah and Her Sisters* and I was all for Oliver Stone's *JFK*. As a compromise we got something out that neither of us was terribly enthusiastic about – Michael Powell's *A Canterbury Tale* (filed under Foreign Films, no less). In fact we both enjoyed it, even if we felt that we were as unsure about the story-line as the director. A wonderful film nonetheless.

Laura went to bed just after 11 p.m. and I stayed up another hour finishing off the half bottle of Smirnoff and channel hopping on the TV and mentally fencing with all the possibilities thrown up by Drax.

[2]

I didn't wake until just after noon the next day. The house was empty and there was a note on the kitchen table saying, 'Gone to Cambridge with the girls. Back about six-ish. See you then? Love Laura.' I wrote underneath it, 'Gotta rush. I'll phone you in the week. Thanks. Love – Chris.'

The kitchen was still the most dreadful mess but I managed to find the electric toaster and I made myself two slices to which I added lashings of butter with healthy dollops of Vintage Oxford marmalade.

After a quick shower I gathered my stuff together and took Dick's folder from the hall table and then I walked up to the paper shop in Market Square. It was closed. Damn!

It was much cooler today and the skies were greying over. Perhaps it was going to rain.

I arced by the Indian newsagent's on Nightingale Road

and got the Sunday papers there. I didn't want to get back home to Tufnell Park and find that everybody had sold out. I picked up *The Observer* and *The Sunday Telegraph* and then walked down Radcliffe Road to the foot of Shadwell Lane. I thought I'd check out The Leys before I caught the train back.

Originally Shadwell Lane was a narrow trackway (in fact, it's still narrow, even where paved) that originally continued over to the Wymondley Road. A spur was taken off it when the railway was built that led over a brick bridge to Purwell Mill. This was the old bridge that was demolished in the mid-1970s.

Here at the beginning of the lane on either side are modest narrow Victorian terraced houses. Ahead, it rises rapidly. There had been some very big houses further up but most of them had been torn down and more modest dwellings put up in their place, including some God-awful 'town houses'.

Where was The Leys then? Up on the left I think.

The road was deserted so I couldn't ask anyone. I continued on. Then I remembered I had Dick's bombing map in his folder in my shoulder bag. I took the large and unwieldy map out and unfolded it a section at a time until I found the Shadwell area.

There's the railway and there's Shadwell Lane to the south. Right. There's the beginning of the lane and the terraced houses. It wasn't easy reading the map as the whole area here was covered with different coloured circles. It was heavily bombed all right. There's the Fairfield estate on the south, there's Benslow House in its grounds on the north (that's all gone now), and here's The Leys, between the Lane and the railway, its grounds extending to the chalk pit in the railway cutting. I was right.

I continued up the lane and crossed the road diagonally towards The Leys. It was quiet and deserted.

The property was protected and hidden from the road by a brick wall some eight feet high built of blue engineering bricks. Along the top of the wall I could see metal spikes, some bent and every one rusted, that would deter all but the most determined of trespassers, and beyond were the tops of fir trees and stag-headed oaks. Sections of the wall had obviously been damaged at some time or another and repaired with a similar but not quite matching blue brick.

I could see from where the frontage ended on Shadwell Lane that the wall then took a right-angled turn and headed towards the railway.

Whoever built this certainly liked their privacy, though in 1872 I wouldn't have thought the rich would have had much to fear from the intrusions of the working classes up here.

I found the house, the estate, as forbidding now as when Dick and I were kids. Anything could go on behind those high walls and you'd never know. Sinister almost. Didn't Dick and I think years ago that Baron Frankenstein lived there? And that he used the underground passages for his nightly body-snatching forays? It would have suited him perfectly.

In the middle of the wall frontage and slightly set back from the road by curves in the wall either side were the double entrance gates. They were made of heavy decorated wrought iron with floriated curls and leaves that at one time had been covered in gold paint. Now only small specks of the colouring remained. Aside from the peeling paint they seemed solid and in good working order.

To the left of the gates was a stone, lozenge in shape, let into the wall that declared monumentally in caps: THE LEYS. Moss or lichen partly obscured the lower parts of the letters.

I looked through the gates. There was a Gothic-looking lodge on the right with a veranda at the front. It looked in good condition but unlived in. The gravel drive curved around to the left and a solid wall of Irish yews obscured the house itself though I could see a mansard roof and chimney pots rising above the evergreen barrier.

I wasn't getting good vibes peering into this place. There was something about it that made me nervous and uncomfortable.

I felt I shouldn't be looking in, this was forbidden property.

Then I noticed a small enamel sign in red and black that had been wired to the right-hand gate. Bold serifed letters stated:

KEEP OUT
DANGER
Patrolled by
Vigilans Security PLC

This sign was echoed by another sign, identical except larger, that had been affixed to a stake on the drive by the lodge house.

I continued skirting along the wall eastwards until the property frontage ended. Here again the wall continued back at a right angle to the road. The adjoining property was one of those ugly stuccoed 1930s jobs with bright green pantiles and white walls. The lawn had stripes and the flowering beds looked tidier than Mrs Thatcher's desk top. Everything was just *so*.

Abutting the wall and between the two properties was a narrow corridor of bushes and trees, wild and overgrown. Possibly the remains of a field boundary and/or a long-forgotten footpath. If I could make my way down in the lee of the wall the greenery would hide me from anyone floating about next door. I'd be safe.

I glanced up and down the lane to see if anyone was about, but no. I pushed past a stand of elder bushes, crashed through some thorns and then found the going easier as I headed along the wall. The hawthorns and tall oaks and firs on the right kept this 'tunnel' in perpetual shadow so that about the only stuff growing here of any size was bracken.

The wall was still straight and proud. There had been no subsidence though here and there, like the front wall, areas had been rebuilt with the blue brick that didn't quite match.

In two places I noticed what must have been doors in the wall, but these had been bricked up. Years ago by the look of it.

The property was a lot deeper than it was wide. The wall seemed to go on and on, and then suddenly I looked up as the wall took another right-angled turn to the left and saw that I was standing high on the clifftops of the old railway chalk pit. The ground just fell away in front of me. There was a sheer drop of about sixty feet.

In the old chalk pit below was the small industrial estate and there beyond was the railway line and Hitchin station with a 'down' train pulling out.

The bare compressed earth of a narrow path came from the right and followed the course of the wall. I walked along it to the end of this run where the wall turned to the left and back to Shadwell Lane. It wasn't possible to follow the course along this stretch as it directly abutted the other neighbouring property. The path ran off to the right down towards the station.

A dim far off memory danced around my mind of Dick and I coming along this path in, what, the mid-1950s? We were in short trousers and carried bows and arrows (both made from bamboo) and we were whooping it up along here when a figure appeared with a large hound that gnashed its teeth. The figure wore a flat cap and had a poacher's bag slung over his shoulder. He may even have had a shotgun. He wore high leather boots. His face exuded evil.

He just stared at us. He didn't say anything. He just stood there staring. Silent. Then the dog became quiet. The two of them – silent and threatening. We dropped our bows and arrows and ran as fast as we could back to the station. I had nightmares for weeks afterwards and so did Dick and it wasn't until years later that we ever ventured along that path again (for trainspotting from the Purwell bridge).

Dick and I had been chased by angry farmers, building workers and railway employees and we had laughed about it. This figure said nothing and did nothing but he succeeded in frightening us like nothing else on earth. Is it possible that kids can pick up something instinctively about someone who means them harm?

That evil face. Those dark malevolent eyes.

The evil face ...

Evil to a child. Disfigured. Something not right about it.

It was that scar. That scar down across his eye. A scar that traversed his face like a new motorway through the countryside ... that scar ... across his face.

Could it be? No, surely not?

Was that Drax? That bogeyman of our childhood?

Was *he* Drax?

There could not have been two guys hanging around here with 'duelling' scars across their eyes. That would be more unlikely, surely, than the figure being Drax?

It must have been him!

Faint memories of memories and hazy recollections raced through my head as I tried to recall the occurrence in greater detail, with more accuracy. The scar, yes. That was what frightened us.

Had we both met Drax then? Was that figure this person who spent his last months at Sorrel House being counselled by Dick? The guy who turned Dick on to JFK?

We had met Drax? *Him*?

I headed back the way I had come. I was hot and confused.

The Leys would certainly be difficult to get inside. You'd need to bring a ladder. In fact you'd need to bring two ladders, one for each side of the wall. It wouldn't be an easy task. Then on the home run of wall I realised it would be simpler than I thought. Some of the trees on this side overhung the wall, and vice versa. All you would need was some rope to let yourself down on the other side and you'd be there. A piece of piss.

But why am I thinking this? Am I going to do a black bag job on this place? At my age? Anyway, for why?

I pushed past the elder bushes and came out on the lane. There was still nobody about and I started off and then I heard a voice. A deep voice with the broad vowels the older locals always seemed to possess.

It said, 'Interestin' place that, eh?'

The voice was unmistakably directed at me. I turned and saw a rotund old man with bright silver hair dressed in a three-piece suit of indeterminate age. He was wearing a collarless shirt and a flat cloth cap and holding a walking stick. Sitting at his feet was a Jack Russell terrier.

'Is it?' I asked him.

He smiled and replied, 'You think so. Me an' the dog were watchin' you nose 'bout.'

'I was just having a look round, that's all.'

'What's yer interest then?'

I decided it was as easy to be candid as it was to lie. 'A friend of mine committed suicide earlier this year. He was counselling the guy, the bloke who lived here. I wanted to find out something about him.'

'What was yer friend's name?'

'North. Dick North.'

The old man nodded.

'Did you know him?'

'We'd met a couple o' times. He was writing his 'istory, wasn't he?'

'Yes. What's your name?'

'Gibb.'

'Uh-huh. I'm Christopher Cornwell.'

'Mr Cornwell.' He nodded again.

'Do you know anything about this place, The Leys?'

The old man pursed his lips, looked down at the dog and looked back at me. 'Funny place, The Leys. Supposed to be a missionary school for sendin' missionaries out to the jungles an' that. But they weren't *that*! No, not *that*."

'What were they then?'

'Don't know. Weren't missionaries though. I better be on my way, Mr Cornwell.'

'Have you ever heard of a Mr Drax who lived there?'

'No. The Germans tried to bomb it during the war. Tried their damnedest, they did. The house was never the same after the Cauldwells moved out.'

'Who were the Cauldwells?'

'They was the ones who built it.'

'What happened to them?'

'Moved out during the war, they did. Might even have been before.'

'Who moved in?'

'The missionary society as they called themselves. And English soldiers. A load of Yanks too.'

'Why did the Germans try to bomb it?'

He looked at me for a moment and said again, 'Me and Duster better be on our way.'

He waved to me with his stick and then he and his dog shuffled off.

I took out Dick's bombing map. I spread it over the bonnet of a parked car and saw the clustered concentration of bombs in the area where I was standing. All those years ago Dick had said to me there was something odd about these bombs being concentrated here. Was it The Leys they were trying to destroy? And if so, why? What was going on here? And who was Mr Drax? And a missionary society?

I walked down to the station mentally exhausting myself by running unanswerable questions through my head. Unanswerable now, but would they always be so?

I sat in front of the TV that evening switching from one channel to another and quietly polishing off a half of Smirnoff. I was trying without success to empty my head of this whole matter, for a time anyway, but all I managed to do was to submerge it in an alcoholic haze.

As I staggered to bed around 11 p.m. I remembered the Centaur Security keys. I took them off my main key ring and put them at the back of the bottom right-hand drawer in my desk. They might not be that safe there but it was sure safer than carrying them around with me.

[3]

I spent the next week trying to rustle up some work. I made innumerable phone calls, had several lunches with colleagues and associates, went to Shepperton and Pinewood studios and spent a lot of time in the bars, and even bought a copy of *Screen International*, the film trade paper, to see what was happening (and buying a copy of that to find out what's happening is a sure sign that nothing is happening).

Come Friday I'd convinced myself that I would never work in the film industry again. Now what would I do?

Fuck it, I thought, I'd have an anxiety-free few days and redecorate part of the flat and put up some more bookshelves. I'd start worrying on Monday and not before.

I went down to Kentish Town early in the morning and bought some white paint and wood for the shelving and a bottle of Smirnoff Blue Label. When I got back I changed into my overalls, put *Symphonie Fantastique* on the CD player, poured myself a very large vodka and pineapple juice and started repainting the bedroom. I enjoy painting. It's like doing the washing up – not too demanding physically or mentally (you can think about something else while you're doing it) and at the end of it there is a tangible accomplishment.

I cruised through the day daubing and drinking.

That evening I got three phone calls. One after the other.

'Will you accept a reverse charges call from Darwin, Australia?'

There was only person who would put through a reverse charges call from such a God-forsaken unlikely place.

[172]

'Rupert?'

'Dad! I'm in Darwin!'

'I know. What are you doing there?'

'Working on a boat and smoking a lot of dope.'

'Speak up! It's not a very good line.'

'Darwin. On a boat. Smoking dope.'

'When are you coming back?'

'After Christmas. I've got to rush now.'

'Phone me soon!'

'Yes.'

'Promise.'

There was crackle and hiss and the line went dead. Rupert was gone.

It was so good hearing from him.

I'd no sooner picked the brush up than the phone warbled again.

'Hello?'

'It's Thom. How you doing?'

Thom Hyde was a New York producer who had worked on and off in England for the last twenty years. He had produced some big pictures over here and he was the only person I'd ever met in the film game who collected and read books. I'd done *Where the Blue Begins* for him under Roy Smart at Shepperton a couple of years ago.

'Fine. Painting my bedroom.'

'Good. Are you working or what?'

'No. Why?'

'You got anything coming up?'

'Nothing.'

'Good. We start up on 22 November, pre-production.'

'What is it?' I asked.

'*Deep Six* is the working title. It's a thriller. We're shooting here and in Northumberland.'

'Who's the art director?'

'David Ramsay.'

'Right,' I said. I'd done a couple of pictures with Ramsay. He's a bluff, pleasant guy bereft of bullshit. He'd started at the old Denham Studios after the war and had learnt his trade with Ernie Archer and Alfred Junge.

'Good, Christopher. I knew I could rely on you. I'll get back to you next week and we'll have lunch with Mark [Walker, Thom's long-time associate producer] down in town.'

'You bet.'

'Until then.'

'Good.'

So, I've suddenly got a job! Thom's pictures are never hurried so I guess I'll have nine months or a year or so. Not bad. And starting 22 November.

22 November?

The day President Kennedy was assassinated? I think it was. Yeah, it was. Now I'll have a drink to celebrate getting a job and hearing from Rupert.

The Blue Label bottle was empty already. I searched in vain for a Smirnoff half bottle. I could have sworn I had some stashed away for just such an occasion, but no. I eventually found a bottle of Odessa vodka, some cheap stuff I'd picked up in the Indian all-night shop up the road. It was half-empty.

I poured myself a large one and stuck some grenadine and ginger ale in it. A Shirley Temple with vodka, a Shirley Temple for grown-ups.

The news was on in a minute so I stretched out on the sofa and aimed the remote control at the TV. Then the phone went again.

'Hello?'

'Hi, it's Laura.'

'Hi. How's things?'

'A very busy week. How are you?'

'Good. But I wasn't good ten minutes ago.'

'Why's that?'

'Well, ten minutes ago I hadn't heard from Rupert and I hadn't a job to go to.'

'You heard from Rupert?'

'Yes.'

'Where is he?'

'In Darwin.'

'Australia?'

'Right.'

'How is he?'

'I only talked to him for a moment. He's working on a boat and smoking a lot of dope.'

'Sounds like he's enjoying himself.'

'He is. How are your *Kinder*?'

'Good. But Lucy's going through a difficult period. She's quite impossible at times. She wants to know why she can't be doing what Cathie's doing. Four years at that age is a big difference. Cathie is eighteen and *her* boyfriend stays over. Lucy's fourteen and I've put my foot down about her boyfriend staying over.'

'And quite rightly.' I doubly surprised myself by saying that. Firstly for saying it, and secondly for saying it with such animated conviction.

'They do it anyway. Lucy is on the pill.'

Jesus! There was no pussy about when I was that age! The nearest we got to it was thumbing through nudist magazines.

'Lucy is fourteen and on the pill? When I was that age I was still listening to "The Teddy Bears' Picnic" and "The Laughing Policeman" on the radio.' I skipped saying that the only sexual partner I had at that age was my right hand.

'You were?' said Laura incredulously.

'Well, almost.'

'What's the job and when are you taking me out to celebrate?'

'It's a thriller for an American producer I've known for years. It's starting up in late November. I was getting a bit worried about work, I can tell you.'

'Oh, good,' said Laura. There was a pause. I could hear her rustling through some papers. 'I thought I'd lost them.'

'What?'

'The photographs.'

'Oh. How'd you get on?'

'I've showed them to just about everyone I know. My mother has too. Nobody recognises the plump man. My mother's friend, Mr Ascham, however – he's the one who takes her out for long drives and lunch – thought Oswald was Oswald, which says something. He thought they looked very similar, though I didn't let on. But aside from that we've come up with nothing, except ...'

'Except?'

'Well, it's hardly worth mentioning.'

'Tell me.'

'My mother thought our plump guy was a chauffeur or driver because she thinks it's a peaked hat he is holding in his hand.'

'Hold on. Let me get the pictures.'

I went into the bedroom and retrieved them from a folder hidden under the rug. I took out the photographs and looked at them closely. She was right, it did look like a peaked hat come to think of it: was this the mystery object in his hand? Also the suit he's wearing and the colour. And the guy's body language. He's 'at attention' come to think of it.

'Who do we know who was driving cars in Hitchin in those days?' I asked Laura.

'The only person I know would be Briscoe's dad.'

'Right. Listen, I'll give you a shout later. I'm going to call Briscoe.'

'OK. I'll let you have the pictures back when I see you.'

'Uh-huh.'

Briscoe's dad. Right. He had a small car hire firm back in those days. Actually not so much a car hire firm as an unlicensed taxi firm that would also hire out old bangers from time to time. If somebody like my dad wanted to hire a car Briscoe's dad would be the guy he went to. He had a small lock-up garage and forecourt on Park Street (now demolished). He would know everyone working in that game in Hitchin ... assuming, of course, that the plump guy was a local man. And if he wasn't? I'd better not get my hopes up too high. This could be a dead-end.

I didn't have Briscoe's phone number in my current address book. I certainly did have it in that old red leather-bound Filofax I'd had since the mid-1970s, but where was that? It wasn't in any of the drawers in the desk and it wasn't in the filing cabinet either. Damn. I phoned Directory Enquiries and got it from them.

I dialled the number and it rang. And rang.

Then a sleepy-sounding little girl answered timorously, 'Hello?'

'Is your mum or dad there please?'

'I'll just get her.'

I heard 'Mum' being shouted in the background then after a pause a woman's voice on the line, 'Yes?'

'Hi, it's Christopher Cornwell.'

'Hello, Chris. I haven't seen you for a long time.'

'I've been pretty busy.'

'You're keeping well?'

'Yes. And you?'

'Can't grumble.'

'Good. Is Briscoe about?'

'Friday night? He's cabbing. Friday and Saturday night are the two best nights of the week.'

'Oh.'

'I can give you his mobile if you want.'

So old Briscoe's got a mobile! I guess everyone has these days except me. It's the last thing I'd ever want. I took the number down and we exchanged parting pleasantries.

I punched the mobile number.

'Draper here.'

'Briscoe?'

'Yes.'

'It's Christopher.'

'Christopher?'

'Cornwell.'

'Oh, Chris! How's tricks?'

[177]

'Pretty good.'

'You want picking up? Where are you?'

'No. I'm in London.'

'Oh, right.'

'How about us meeting for a drink tomorrow lunchtime?'

'Sounds good.'

'Where?' I asked. I didn't know what pubs were Briscoe's favourites these days and what ones he avoided.

'King's Arms? How about that?'

'Fine. What time?'

'One-ish?'

'Got ya.'

'See you then.'

'Bye.'

I hadn't seen Briscoe's parents since the late 1970s. I wasn't even sure where they lived and whether, indeed, they were both alive. I'd have to approach them through Briscoe. In fact Briscoe himself might recognise the guy in the photograph.

I called Laura back and told her I was meeting Briscoe the next day at 1 p.m. 'You joining us? You can spit from your place to the King's Arms!'

'I'm taking Lucy into London tomorrow.'

'What a pity. What time are you back?'

'Early evening. I'll leave the key on the string in case you want to come in and wait.'

'OK. Perhaps I'll see you tomorrow?'

'Yes.'

'Sleep tight.'

'You too.'

There was only about a tablespoonful of vodka left and I drank it straight from the bottle. As there's nothing else to drink, I might as well go to bed. I need an early night.

I had planned to go down to Sainsbury's at Camden Town and do the shopping before I left for Hitchin but I overslept.

Schlepping down to Camden would make it a bit tight so I decided to do the weekly shop when I got to Hitchin instead.

I walked around to the lock-up garage and then found I couldn't get the car started – the starter motor was on the blink. I eventually got it sorted out and took off up towards Archway a little after 10.30 a.m.

I hadn't given the old Merc a proper exercise in ages so just north of Hatfield on the A1(M), after I'd come out of the tunnel that goes under the shopping mall there, I slammed my foot down while I was doing 60 m.p.h. and there was a great roar as the 6.9 litre engine woke up. I was pushed back in the seat as it accelerated. The speedo climbed with increasing speed: 70 – 80 – 90 – 100. A cloud of black smoke belched out the exhaust pipes as the engine cleared its lungs and that was soon left far behind as I hurtled ahead. There was more power still to come. I looked in my rear-view mirror and ahead – no cops about. The speedo was now pointing at 120 m.p.h. and rising. I depressed the accelerator further and I was soon touching 140 m.p.h.

I once did 150 m.p.h. down a motorway in Germany in this. It was the fastest I've ever gone in a car. And the remarkable thing about this old Merc is that it hugs the road better than the new 500SELs. It sits there on the road, super-glued to the surface, even at these speeds.

I hit 140 m.p.h. This was enough. I raised my foot and the car slowed down rapidly. At 90 m.p.h. I felt I was doing about 35 m.p.h. And when I got down to 70 m.p.h. it seemed not much faster than walking.

The things about this car are that it is enormously big and difficult to park, and mightily greedy on gas. 6.9 litres need a lot of fuel. And it's becoming increasingly more expensive to maintain. I really ought to mothball it or even sell it and get a little Peugeot or a Golf. That's all I need.

I've been saying this for years and never doing anything about it, but now I must. It's crazy and extravagant carrying on like this.

I took the Hitchin turn-off and roared down that new dual carriageway that dumps you on the Stevenage Road the other side of Little Wymondley.

Parking is always a problem in the town on Saturdays but I managed to find a place in the car park behind the Sun Hotel. I picked up most of what I wanted in the market opposite the church and then treated myself to some decent ground coffee and expensive German biscuits at Halsey's in the churchyard. I walked back to the car and dumped the bags in the boot.

I sauntered over to Bucklersbury and went into the bookshop up at the top as I realised I had some time to spare. Hitchin has about five or six bookshops (including W H Smith's) which ain't bad at all for a town of this size. It says much for the inhabitants of this little corner of Hertfordshire.

I hurried down Bucklersbury to the pub.

Briscoe was already at the bar knocking back a lager. He was wearing dark slacks and a brightly patterned pullover. Around his waist was a leather money belt.

'Chris – over here. What you having?'

'No, I'll get these. What do you want?'

'I've got my lunchtime pint. No more when I'm working. Make it a mineral water. You been mugged again lately?'

'Not *lately*, thank Christ.'

I ordered a mineral water and for myself a large vodka.

There were only about a dozen or so people in the bar evenly scattered about. I hadn't been in here for years and it hadn't changed much. This was always the pub we used to come to in the 1960s if we had something to talk about and wanted some privacy. Dick and I used to come here and huddle in that corner over there planning escapades. I used to bring girlfriends here before moving on to serious drinking elsewhere.

Briscoe and I chatted about our families and work and we excavated a few mutual memories and he told me about the new Ford Scorpio he'd just acquired at some bargain price. The conversation drifted over the cost of living, the fuck-up the Tories were making of the economy and last night's TV which I had missed.

I ordered another large vodka.

'Hope you're not driving on that,' whispered Briscoe.

'Well, not right away,' I replied.

'Good.'

There was a free corner table out at the back and I suggested we move over to it. I took my second large vodka and Briscoe grabbed his mineral water and packet of crisps.

'Now what's this all about then?' asked Briscoe.

'I'll tell you. I've got a couple of photographs here and I want to see if you can identify anyone in them.' I thought it best not to lead him by saying one guy might be a chauffeur, and I certainly wasn't going to mention Oswald.

I handed him the first photo, the two figures standing outside the Hermitage.

'The old Hermitage! Had some fun in the back row there all right! Now who've we got here? Who's this? And this? Is the young geezer somebody we was at school with?'

'No.'

'Who is he then?'

'Do you know?'

'No. Don't think so.'

'What about the oldish fellow?'

'Mmmm. Let's see the other.'

I handed him the two-shot taken outside the church. I kept the portrait of Oswald in the folder.

Briscoe stared at it closely. Returned to the first picture. Stared at that again.

'Don't know the young fellow, but the old bloke is Alf Lawson all right.'

'Who's Alf Lawson?'

'Used to have a car hire firm out on the Ickleford Road. Did posh chauffeuring and that. He's dead now. My dad knew him. I used to earn a few bob polishing cars for him.'

A feeling of exhilaration swept over me like a wave. 'What else do you know about him?'

'Not much really.'

'What about your dad?'

'Oh, he'd know all about him.'

'Where is your dad?'

'At home watching the telly I'd imagine.'

'Where? In Hitchin here?'

'Yeah.'

'Good.'

'Here, what's the big interest in Alf Lawson anyway?'

'I'll tell you when I've unravelled it.'

'Like that, is it?'

'Bear with me.'

'Uh-huh.'

'Your parents are where?'

'Up on Grove Road.'

'Can we pop around and see them?'

'Why not? I'll just finish this.'

We left the pub and walked up Tilehouse Street, past Laura's house, to the top where he had parked.

'What do your parents drink these days?'

'Scotch. Why?'

'Call by an off-licence and I'll pick them up something.'

'They've always got plenty. Ain't necessary.'

'I'd like to.'

'OK then.'

Briscoe drove down to Queen Street and along and took a left into Hermitage Road and stopped near where the cinema used to be. I rushed across the road and picked up a bottle of Bell's.

We turned right on to Bancroft and down to the end and up Grove Road and we were there. The small Victorian terraced house was exactly as I remembered it, right down to the tiled path and the lupin borders and the coloured glass either side of the front door.

Briscoe rang the doorbell several times and said, 'They're

probably out in the garden. Always are about this time.'

I heard a dog barking in the hallway and then Mrs Draper opened the door. Briscoe kissed her on the cheek and she stared at me for a moment before saying, 'Christopher, I didn't recognise you at first!'

'It's been a few years,' I said.

'It has indeed. Now come in you two. We're out the back. Go straight through.'

Briscoe pointed ahead and I walked down the hall (and past the old bicycle leaning against the stairs), through the kitchen and scullery and out to the patio. Mr Draper was sitting in an old armchair reading *The Daily Mirror*.

'Hello, Dad,' said Briscoe. 'You remember Chris Cornwell, don't you?'

'Hello, Chris,' said Mr Draper. 'Haven't seen you for a while, have we?'

'That's true,' I replied.

Mr Draper got up and we shook hands. He was a thin frail man in his early seventies and completely bald. He wore old National Health spectacles that were held together with sticking plaster. There were tea or coffee stains down the front of his shirt.

Mrs Draper said, 'How is your mum keeping, Chris? We haven't seen her in a long time.'

'She's fine. Lives with her sister now down on the south coast.'

'Do remember us to her, won't you?' said Mrs Draper.

'Of course.'

'Would you two like a cup of tea?' asked Mr Draper.

'It's all right, Dad, we've been drinking. I don't, unless you do, Chris?' said Briscoe.

'No, I'm OK,' I replied.

'Something to eat then?' Mrs Draper said. 'A cheese sandwich or some ordinary cakes I've just made?'

Briscoe and I both shook our heads.

'Chris, here, has got some photographs he needs some help with. He wants you to have a look at them.'

[183]

'Photographs?' said Mr Draper.

'Where are my glasses, Ron?' inquired Mrs Draper.

I took out the picture taken in front of the Hermitage Cinema and handed it to Mr Draper who was now sitting on a rickety garden bench. He peered at it through and then over his glasses. Mrs Draper joined him and looked closely at it.

Mr Draper cleared his throat and said, 'That's Alfie Lawson there but I don't know who the young bloke is.'

Mrs Draper nodded in agreement and added, 'It's Alfie Lawson all right. Yes.'

'What can you tell me about him?' I asked.

'He ran a car hire and taxi firm ... started it just after the war ... out on the Ickleford Road. Lawson's Cars. Had a small garage there too. Then he moved to Park Street. Used to do funerals as well,' said Mr Draper.

'He was a very nice man,' added Mrs Draper.

Mr Draper thought some more and said, 'He was born in Charlton, I think. Certainly had relatives out there years ago. He's been dead a long time. Think he was killed in a car accident.'

'No, dear. It was a train accident,' said Mrs Draper correcting her husband.

'When was that?' I asked.

Mrs Draper shook her head and said, 'It was a long time ago, I can't remember when.'

Briscoe's parents were so positive in their identification that it was not necessary to show them the other photographs.

'Where could I find out more about Alf Lawson? Are there any of his friends about here still? Any family?'

'I don't know, do you, Ron?' said Mrs Draper.

Ron shook his head.

Mrs Draper continued, 'His wife is still alive, I think. She lives in an old people's home now or something, but we saw her about ten years ago when she was collecting her pension. Wasn't herself then, she wasn't. And I think he's got a daughter somewhere too. I could find out if you wanted me to?'

'If you could, Mrs Draper. It would be very helpful.'

'I'll do that. I'll certainly do that. I'll ask Mrs White around the corner. She sends Mrs Lawson a Christmas card every year.'

Mr Draper handed the picture back to me and said, 'Why are you interested in Alfie Lawson then?'

How do I answer that? I don't want to be completely candid and neither do I want to lie to them. A compromise? 'I'm doing some research on Hitchin in the 1950s and 1960s.'

'I see,' said Mr Draper.

I took their telephone number and gave them mine and then I remembered there was a bottle of Bell's in the plastic bag at my feet. I gave it to Mrs Draper.

'What's this for?' she said.

'A little present … for old times' sake and for being so helpful,' I said.

'We can't take that,' she said.

'Yes you can. You've been very helpful.'

'We'll all have a drop before you go then,' said Mr Draper.

Briscoe said, 'I've got to be getting back to work.'

I declined the drink and Briscoe said he would drop me back in town. Mr and Mrs Draper told me to come and see them whenever I was in Hitchin and I said I would.

As we were driving along Bancroft Briscoe turned to me and said, 'These photographs and that – have they got anything to do with Dick?'

'Why do you say that?'

'Just a feeling.'

'You're right.'

'What exactly?'

'I'll tell you, Briscoe, when I know a bit more. I'm just trying to put a few facts together.'

Briscoe sighed. 'A need to know basis, huh?'

'Right. Bear with me. I'll explain it to you when I can.'

'Understand. Anyway, here you are.'

I got out at the top of Hermitage Road and said goodbye to Briscoe. I walked along past the church and down in the direction of my car. I felt like another drink so I went into the Sun Hotel and got a large vodka.

I had good vibes about the Drapers and the search for Alf Lawson. I'd identified him and I felt confident that I was going to find out more, not just about him but about Oswald too.

I looked around the bar at the people drinking, laughing and chatting. Here or out there on the street somewhere there was a person or two who knew something that could help me complete this picture. They might not know the significance of what they knew, but each little fact would inch me further along the path of discovery.

I ordered another large vodka and then another. And a few more after that. The serious drinker never betrays his drunkenness, never gets refused a drink in a pub or thrown out. We're great at putting up a front.

The rest of the afternoon was a blank and the next thing I remember is waking up slouched over the steering-wheel in the Merc. It was 9 p.m. and there was vomit all over the dashboard. I was in no state to see Laura. I cleaned myself up as best I could and headed back to London.

CHAPTER SIX

I DIDN'T SHOOT
NOBODY. NO, SIR

'*Identify.*'
  '*Bellerophon … 666B.*'
  '*Location?*'
  '*Capital.*'
  '*Proceed.*'
  '*Pre-WAYSIDE contacts are still being investigated regarding LANCER grail.*'
  '*Stand by.*'

I GOT UP EARLY ON SUNDAY, showered, made myself a large Russian coffee and took it over to my desk. I sat there sipping the coffee and staring at the pile of books on Kennedy's assassination I'd taken from Dick's. A lot of books. A lot of pages.

Where to begin?

Why not the beginning?

I took a fat squat hardback volume that had horizontal lettering on its spine: *The Official Warren Commission Report on the Assassination of President John F. Kennedy*.

I went back to the front of the book and turned to the main title page. I might as well start at the beginning of the beginning, but I was not prepared for what I found there. I let out a gasp, a *Eureka!* in my mind, and nearly tipped the coffee over. This was it! There it was! Absolutely fucking amazing! There! Mute fucking evidence in the top right hand corner of the page! A thin black spidery handwriting that said:

Victor Drax
– Hitchin, 1964.

This was it! This was independent corroboration that Drax was interested in the JFK assassination. Solid rock-hard, 100% independent verification that this guy was into it! No ifs or buts. This was it!

Up to this moment Drax's interest had been supposition and inference. Now it was proven. This was *his* book and *he* had passed it on to Dick. It was Drax who had kindled Dick's interest. Drax who had turned Dick on to the assassination.

What about the other books? Would I find Drax's signature in any of those?

I quickly went through each volume checking to see if his signature was anywhere to be seen. Nothing in this one. Nothing in this one. Nothing here either.

But here on the title page of Thomas G. Buchanan's *Who Killed Kennedy*?

Victor Drax
– Hitchin, 1964.

Good. Any more?
Nothing here. Nothing here. But here

Victor Drax
– Hitchin, 1978.

on the front free endpaper of *Legend: The Secret World of Lee Harvey Oswald* by Edward Jay Epstein. Uh-huh. A continuing interest. He was still interested in the assassination fourteen years later.

And nothing in the last two, not that the absence of a signature was proof that these other books were not his.

Mmmmmm. So Drax bought two books in 1964 and then fourteen years later he was still buying them. Fourteen years of interest.

The other titles must come from him as well. I think we can take that as read.

I'll phone Laura later and tell her. She'll be knocked out by the information. Completely knocked out.

I dug out Dick's file we'd been given at the hospice and compared the handwriting on the back of the photo of The Leys with Drax's in the books. It was the same. Exactly the same.

I returned to the Warren Commission *Report* and flicked through the prelims. This was a big book and it was full of stuff I wasn't immediately interested in … pages and pages of it.

I need an account of Oswald's life. A straight biographical account. Where he was. What he was doing. That sort of thing. And here it is: Appendix XIII: Biography of Lee Harvey Oswald, page 669. Just what I wanted. Perfect. I'll read the whole thing, it only runs to some seventy pages. But first I'll top up this Russian coffee. And then I'll read it and produce a written précis:

BIOGRAPHY OF LEE HARVEY OSWALD
Marguerite Claverie, Oswald's mother, was born in New Orleans in 1907. In August 1929 she married an Edward John Pic who worked as a clerk for a stevedoring company. By 1931 she had split up from Pic and was pregnant. In 1932 she had a son, John Edward Pic.

Marguerite was then seeing a lot of a Robert Edward Lee Oswald, an insurance premium collector. He got a divorce from his wife and Marguerite got one too and they were married in 1933. In April 1934 a son, Robert, was born. Lee Harvey Oswald was born on 18 October 1939. But two months before Lee was born his father had died of a heart attack.

At various times Lee and his brothers were dumped with relatives and in children's homes. His mother held a succession of jobs and didn't seem to prosper in any of them.

Mrs Oswald got involved with another guy and moved to Dallas, then ditched him and bought a house there. It was thought that Marguerite was too close to Lee and 'spoiled him to death'.

They moved from one address to another and Lee was in and out of different schools and homes. There was precious little that was settled in his life.

Robert, Lee's older brother, joined the Marines in July 1952 and in the following month Marguerite moved with Lee to New York City and stayed with John and his young wife. There were arguments and rows and Mrs Oswald and Lee were ordered out.

Over the next eighteen months Mrs Oswald dragged Lee from one rented apartment to another while she herself flitted from job to job. Lee was a persistent truant and was hauled up before the welfare agencies and eventually found himself in court.

In early January 1954 Mrs Oswald fled back to New Orleans with Lee and moved in with relatives for a short period. The next couple of years were a repeat of the New York stay – a succession of rented apartments and one job after another for Mrs Oswald who seemed incapable of holding any job down for more than a short spell.

Mrs Oswald moved with Lee to Fort Worth in July 1956 and in the following October Lee enlisted in the Marines at San Diego, following the example of his older brother, Robert.

After boot camp at San Diego Oswald went to Camp Pendleton in California and then to the Naval Air Technical Training Center in Jacksonville, Florida. In September 1957 he arrived in Japan aboard the USS *Bexar*. He was stationed at Atsugi, about twenty miles west of Tokyo. It was here that he was court-martialled for being in possession of an unregistered privately-owned firearm. A second court-martial arose from him using 'provoking words' to a non-commissioned officer.

Oswald departed from Japan on board the USNS *Barrett* on 2 November 1958 and arrived in San Francisco on 15 November.

In December Oswald was assigned to a Marine Air Control Squadron at El Toro near Santa Ana in California.

Oswald was obligated to remain in the Marines on active duty until 7 December 1959, but on 17 August of that year he submitted a request for a dependency discharge, on the grounds that his mother needed his support. In fact he wanted to go to the Albert Schweitzer College in Switzerland and had already made an application that had been accepted.

On 11 September Oswald was released from active duty by the Marine Corps. Some seven days earlier he had applied for a passport at the Superior Court in Santa Ana. His application stated that he planned to leave the United States on 21 September and attend the Schweitzer College and also to travel, in the words of the Warren Commission *Report*, 'in Cuba, the Dominican Republic, England, France, Germany, and Russia'.

Now this was very interesting.

On 4 September 1959 Oswald included England amongst the countries he *intended* travelling in.

I poured myself another Russian coffee and then phoned Laura. No reply. I'd call her later. I returned to the Warren Commission to see what else would be revealed.

Oswald's passport was issued six days after he applied for it. He went to his mother in Fort Worth and arrived there by 14 September. He stayed there three days and then travelled to New Orleans. He booked a passage from New Orleans to Le Havre in France on board a freighter, the SS *Marion Lykes*, that was scheduled to sail on 18 September. He paid $220.75 for the ticket.

The ship was delayed and didn't sail until 20 September.

Oswald disembarked at Le Havre on October 8. He left for England the same day, and arrived on October 9. He told English customs officials in Southampton that he had $700 and planned to remain in the United Kingdom for 1 week before proceeding to school in Switzerland.

So that's it. Oswald spent a week here in 1959. He arrived on 9 October and left on 16 October. That's when he came to Hitchin, October 1959. I've dated it.

Alas, the discovery was short-lived because the next sentence stated:

But on the same day [October 9], he flew to Helsinki, Finland, where he registered at the Torni Hotel; on the following day, he moved to the Klaus Kurki Hotel.

I reread the paragraph again, thought it over, and read it one more time.

But on the same day, he flew to Helsinski …

The same day he arrived?

What the Warren Commission is saying is that he arrived in Southampton on 9 October and on that very same day flew out to Helsinki. Now that would hardly give him time to drive or get the train up to Hitchin and catch the sights, would it?

Now this is really odd.

Oswald says in Santa Ana that he intends touring through England, he tells the customs officials upon arrival that he will be spending a week here, and yet the Warren Commission says he flew out on the day he arrived.

Curious …

Anyway, on with the biography. I'll have to come back to this later.

Oswald applied for a visa at the Russian consulate in Helsinki on 12 October. It was issued two days later. The following day he crossed the Finnish-Russian border at Vainikkala and got to Moscow on 16 October. Effectively he had now defected.

The following twenty pages were concerned with Oswald's stay in Russia – how he renounced his citizenship, was given an apartment and job way down south in Minsk, and how he apparently became disillusioned with life in Russia, met and married a Russian girl and decided they should return to the United States.

So, he arrived in Moscow on 16 October 1959 and exited the USSR with his family by train at Brest on 2 June 1962. Two days later they departed from Holland on the SS *Maasdam* and arrived in the United States on 13 June at Hoboken, New Jersey.

The following day they flew down to Forth Worth and stayed with Lee's brother, Robert, while things were sorted out.

I continued reading through the Appendix and noted that aside from a trip to Mexico City in late September/early October 1962, Lee Harvey Oswald was back in the States for good.

And the rest, as they say, is history.

At 12.30 p.m. Central Standard Time on Friday, 22 November 1963, in Dealey Plaza, Dallas, President John F. Kennedy was shot. At 1 p.m. he was declared dead at Parkland Hospital.

At around 1.50 p.m. Lee Harvey Oswald was arrested at the Texas Theater on Jefferson Blvd., in another part of Dallas.

And two days later on the morning of Sunday, 24 November Lee Harvey Oswald was shot and killed in the basement of the Dallas Police Department by Jack Ruby, a local night-club owner.

We all remember *that* so well.

I made myself a not very successful chef's salad with blue cheese dressing (from a bottle) and stretched out on the sofa with a Bird and Diz CD playing quietly in the background. Then I poured myself a large vodka and orange juice and decided I needed to produce a chart of what I'd found out so far. I grabbed an A3 Goldline drawing pad and with a 0.5 Rotring went through the appendix again and produced a neat time-flow table detailing Oswald's life.

This gave me the dates of Oswald's travelling at a glance for reference. I read through it several times.

When Oswald was in the Marines he was never stationed in the United Kingdom, if he had been the Warren Commission would have mentioned it. From October 1959 to June 1962 he was living as a defector in the Soviet Union and therefore not in the position of popping over to England. The Mexican trip seemed particularly well documented and it seems unlikely that he made a secret detour and came to England then.

So what are we left with? When was he here?

We're left with this awkward 9 October visit. He arrived in Southampton and on the very same day takes a flight to Helsinki according to the Warren Commission and yet, as I'd read, he told the passport people in California he was going to travel in England and on the very day he arrives here he tells the customs officials he's going to stay for a week (and he's got $700 to do it with), but he doesn't according to the Warren Commission.

Is there anything else in the *Report* about the English visit? There is nothing mentioned in the index so I go through the detailed contents pages looking for anything that seems likely. I look in vain for any further details. There are none.

Would any of the other books add anything to Supreme Court Chief Justice Warren's findings? I searched through several. Nothing in the contents pages and nothing in the indexes.

Then I came across a fat paperback of nearly eight hundred pages entitled *The Final Assassinations Report* with a subtitle of *Report of the Select Committee on Assassinations, US House of Representatives*.

There's no date on the main title page but over on the imprint I see 1979. So, fifteen years after Earl Warren delivered his findings, the House of Representatives reinvestigated the case.

There's no index at all in this volume, just some twelve pages of contents in eye-destroying 5pt type. I go through them with a large magnifying glass and I'm just about to give up when I come across this in Part C, Section 5, Subsection (13):

Oswald's trip to Russia via Helsinki and his ability to obtain a visa in 2 days ... 267

I turn to page 267 and read the following:

Oswald's trip from London to Helsinki has been a point of controversy. His passport indicates he arrived in Finland on October 10, 1959. The Torni Hotel in Helsinki, however, had him registered as a guest on that date, although the only direct flight from London to Helsinki landed at 11:33pm that day. According to a memorandum signed in 1964 by Richard Helms, "[i]f Oswald had taken this flight, he could not normally have cleared customs and landing formalities and reached the Torni Hotel down-town by 2400 (midnight) on the same day."

The Warren Commission says he arrived in England on 9 October and left the same day for Helsinki. I open the *Report* at page 690 and check what it says:

But on the same day [9 October 1959], he flew to Helsinki, Finland, where he registered at the Torni Hotel ...

I missed it the first time around but I notice it now. The *Report* fails to say what day he registered at the Torni Hotel. It's one of those things you gloss over and can so easily miss. You assume it was the same day he flew out, but was it?

The Select Committee says his passport shows that he arrived in Finland on 10 October and yet if that were true and he touched down at 11.33 p.m. how could he get to the hotel and register within twenty-seven minutes? This is odd. Very odd indeed.

I continue reading *The Final Assassinations Report*. There's a bit about Oswald getting a Russian entry visa in only two days and then there's this sentence:

The committee was unable to determine the circumstances surrounding Oswald's trip from London to Helsinki.

That's really as class a bit of bureaucrat-speak as ever I've come across. What a mellifluous bit of nonsense! I was so angered by it that I drew a line through it with the Rotring and wrote in the margin:

> *The committee means it had no fucking idea how*
> *Oswald got from London to Helsinki!!!!*

The *Report* continued:

Louis Hopkins, the travel agent who arranged Oswald's initial transportation from the United States, stated that he did not know Oswald's ultimate destination at the time Oswald booked his passage on the freighter *Marion Lykes*. Consequently, Hopkins had nothing to do with the London-to-Helsinki leg of Oswald's trip. In fact, Hopkins stated that had he known Oswald's final destination, he would have suggested sailing on another ship that would have docked at a port more convenient to Russia. Hopkins indicated that Oswald did not appear to be particularly well-informed about travel to Europe.

Oswald was smart and no dummy. You get that impression even when studying the testimony of people who didn't like him. He read a lot and took a deep interest in current affairs. He might not have been sophisticated but he had his wits about him. Yet here is the Select Committee representing him as an idiot through the testimony of this New Orleans travel agent. Oswald was certainly bright enough to figure out on what boat he wanted to go where and if he chose Le Havre that *was* his destination, for the moment.

It's disingenuous and deceitful for the Select Committee to give the impression through Hopkins that Oswald wasn't sure where he was going and that if only he had mentioned Russia, Hopkins would have put him on another boat. Oswald didn't mention Russia (or wherever) because that wasn't where he was immediately going. He was going somewhere else.

But if one accepts the Committee's suggestion that Oswald was wandering around in a fog, just generally trucking in the direction of Russia, then one must also accept what follows as documented by the Committee itself: that is, he arrives in Le Havre and the ability to organise quickly and efficiently that was absent in New Orleans suddenly manifests itself and he's on a boat-train to England right away, arrives the following day, and then catches the only available flight to Helsinki. The Committee takes the ground from under its own feet.

This is getting fishy all right.

There's nothing more in this Sub-section, Section, or Part. Indeed there's nothing more on this in the whole *Report*.

I pick up another book: *Legend: The Secret World of Lee Harvey Oswald*. The author is Edward Jay Epstein and it was published in 1978. It's one of the books with Drax's signature. On page 93, I come across this:

On October 8, the freighter [*Marion Lykes*] finally pulled into the harbour at Le Havre, France, where Oswald and the other three passengers disembarked. (The steward remembered Oswald for not leaving the customary tip.) Neither the Churches nor Billy Joe Lord [Mr and Mrs Church and Lord were the other passengers on the boat] recall seeing Oswald on the boat train to Southampton, England, but according to British passport control records, he arrived there on Friday, October 9, declaring to customs officials that he had $700 with him and intended to spend one week in England before proceeding to college in Switzerland.

The stamps on his passport show that he left Heathrow Airport in London that same day on an international flight and landed later that evening in Helsinki, Finland. Since there was no direct flight from London to Helsinki during the time Oswald was in London, Oswald must have changed planes at some city in Europe.

Following the last word, Europe, there is a footnote reference to the notes at the back of the volume:

The CIA checked all available timetables without finding any flight between London and Helsinki that would fit Oswald's schedule. The gap led some investigators to speculate that he might have flown in a private aircraft.

None of the other three passengers on the SS *Marion Lykes* remember seeing Oswald on the boat-train from Le Havre to Southampton, but he arrived there on 9 October according to the British passport records.

The stamps on his passport show that Oswald left Heathrow Airport that same day (on an international flight?). If these stamps are genuine then he certainly didn't have time to zip up to Hitchin and the mystery becomes even greater. When was he here? When was the second trip? And how has it evaded all the researchers, including the Warren Commission and the House Select Committee?

The footnote is interesting: … some investigators have thought that he might have flown out of England in a *private* aircraft. Private or military? I guess both take off from Heathrow. What could be going on here?

If only I had some proof that it was one of those US Air Force bases in East Anglia that he flew from, then the task of placing him in Hitchin would be a lot easier. He would have stopped off here en route. The town would have been on his journey.

I get out the three photographs again, or rather the copies, and I carefully compare them with the pictures of Oswald scattered through the several books. There's no way it could not be Oswald in them. No way. But even supposing it was someone else, an incredible lookalike, what was Dick doing with them? And who was Drax and what was his interest in the assassination?

I poured myself a half-tumbler of neat vodka and went to bed. Tomorrow's another day.

OSWALD AND THE ASSASSINATION

I was up early the next morning, zoomed down to Sainsbury's in Camden, did my week's shopping and was sitting at my desk with a Russian coffee by 10.30 a.m.

Tracking Oswald's travels had increased my interest in him and the assassination and I was anxious to work my way through all of the books. In fact, tomorrow morning I'm going down to the Virgin video store to see what videos are available on the assassination. I remember seeing some on the shelves when I was last there.

I read continuously for the rest of the week and I read the books in chronological order of publication. I didn't read the whole of the Warren *Report* or the House Select Committee *Report* but I read the main sections and constantly referred back to them when checking out what the 'critics' wrote.

One of the most fascinating and unanswered questions arising from that day in November 1963 is why Oswald was arrested. Yes. *Why* Oswald was arrested. Dealey Plaza has produced many mysteries but this simple and fundamental question still remains unanswered. Neither the Warren Commission nor the House Select Committee produced a satisfactory explanation.

Fifteen minutes after Kennedy was shot, at 12.45 p.m., a description of the suspect in the assassination was broadcast over the radio by the Dallas Police Department. At 1.50 p.m. Oswald was arrested in the Texas Theater (a cinema) as a suspect in the murder of Patrolman Tippit. They questioned him for five hours and then charged him with the officer's murder. It was not until 1.30 a.m. the following day, Saturday 23 November, that Oswald was charged with the assassination of the President. (If indeed he was actually charged. Some doubt still surrounds this.)

At a press conference in the Dallas police headquarters at midnight on 22 November Oswald was asked by journalists whether he had killed the President. Oswald replied:

No, I have not been charged with that. In fact, nobody has said that to me yet. The first thing I heard about it was when the newspaper reporters in the hall asked me that question.

Henry Wade, the Dallas District Attorney, confirmed at the press conference that Oswald had been charged with Tippit's murder and not the President's.

Tippit was shot at 1.15 p.m. or thereabouts, yet the description matching Oswald was broadcast some thirty minutes earlier. Why? How?

The Warren Commission admitted that it could not answer the questions with any certainty, but it offered up a witness, Howard Brennan, as the possible source of the description.

Brennan was standing watching the motorcade across the street from the School Book Depository building, 107 feet away from the base of the building and about 120 feet away from the assassin's window on the sixth floor. It seems unlikely that Brennan could describe someone in the window as being 'white, slender, weighing about 165 pounds, about 5 feet 10 inches tall' solely on the basis of one or two uninterested glances (anyway, how could he give an estimated height of the assassin when, whoever it was, was kneeling?).

If Brennan did give this information to the police within minutes of the assassination how can the following exchange between Chief Curry of the Dallas Police Department and a journalist from KRLD-TV be explained that was broadcast on Sunday (24 November):

JOURNALIST: Chief Curry, do you have any eyewitness who saw someone shoot the President?
CURRY: No, sir. We do not.

Brennan's recollections are not to be trusted, however, because late on 22 November he was taken to a line-up at the police headquarters and failed to pick Oswald out despite seeing his picture on TV only hours earlier. Brennan would later say that he did recognise Oswald but didn't pick him out as he was afraid for his own safety. If this were so, why then did he make himself known and volunteer information to the police in the first place?

Wade the DA might be expected to know what was going on in his parish. On 24 November he held a press conference shortly after Oswald's death. He said:

A police officer [Marion L. Baker], immediately after the assassination, ran in the building [Texas School Book Depository] and saw this man [Oswald] in a corner and started to arrest him, but the manager of the building said that he was an employee and was all right. Every other employee was [subsequently] located but this defendant, of the company. A description and name of him went out by police to look for him.

A description and name …

The Warren Commission, however, denied that the name was ever broadcast.

Captain Patrick Gannaway of the police's Special Service Bureau corroborated Wade's explanation and stated that Oswald's description *was* broadcast because Oswald didn't appear in an employee roll-call taken at the Book Depository shortly after the assassination.

Gannaway said, 'He was the only one who didn't show up and couldn't be accounted for.'

The proffered explanation for why Oswald was wanted isn't borne out by the facts. First, there was no roll-call, and secondly, the manager of the Book Depository estimated there was something like a third of his staff away from the premises at the time.

Chief Curry was later to say that Oswald was wanted as a suspect after the rifle, the assassination weapon, was discovered in the 'sniper's nest' on the sixth floor. All very well, except the weapon wasn't discovered until 1.22 p.m., thirty-seven minutes *after* the police broadcast.

So, even the most fundamental question regarding Oswald remains unanswered all these years after the event.

I suppose it is inevitable in any large-scale investigation that certain inconsistencies and unanswered questions arise, but they are usually of a trifling and inconsequential nature, but here with the investigation into the assassination of the 35th President of the United States of America those inconsistencies and unanswered questions are found to be fundamental. How could this be so? Unless, of course, there was a plan to bury the truth? It can be no other way. The received history of the Warren *Report* is a spurious history. It is a false story, a concoction dished up to keep the citizens quiet. A bedtime story. There's a hidden and undiscovered reality here.

And, indeed, the House Select Committee can be seen as not so much a search for the truth as a damage limitation exercise once the Warren Commission started to sink: we think there probably was a conspiracy, but it's too late to discover anything about it and even if we did, is it really that important? Does it really matter that much now after the passage of all these years? Oh, yes, and if you want a name – how about the Mafia? A bunch of guineas in $500 suits. They've got *nothing* to do with *us*.

[2]

Laura came around on Friday evening.

We wandered up the road to a cheap and cheerful Greek restaurant in Tufnell Park. We had a moussaka each and some ice cream and then some strong coffee.

I told her how I'd spent the last week doing nothing but reading up on the Kennedy assassination and studying the evidence. I told her about Drax's signature in the books and it wasn't necessary for me to point out the significance of that.

'We ought to do something with all this,' Laura said.

'Like what?'

'Couldn't we take it to a newspaper. Get a journalist interested perhaps?'

'I've thought about that.'

'And?'

'And,' I said, 'I don't think it would be a good idea right now.'

'Why?'

'Well, because a lot of it is speculative and I think newspapers and journalists in this country like it all packaged up and complete before they run something.'

'On the better papers? The qualities?'

'Yeah, there too.'

'Come on! We've got the photos as well!'

'I know, but we stand more chance of finding out what's going on while we're still underground. The moment we go public the shit hits the fan. Right now they don't know about us, do they?'

Laura laughed and said, 'Who are *they*?'

'That's a stupid question.'

'No it's not. *Who* are they?'

'*They* are whoever it is who are behind the assassination. That's who *they* are.'

'You're getting paranoid.'

That remark irritated me and I scowled. Laura reached out and put her hand on my arm and squeezed it. She said, 'You don't really think these people are still about … here, do you?'

'Somebody is. Don't forget what Dick said to me.'

'What, specifically?'

I leant forward and in a whisper said, 'About him being fucking followed, that's what.'

'I didn't realise you meant that.'

'What do you think I meant?'

'But that could be anybody. Special Branch. The intelligence services. Who knows?'

'Could be. Could not be. Whoever did Jack Kennedy in could try anything and get away with it. That's a fact.'

Laura finished her coffee and lit another cigarette. She looked at me and winked and asked, 'How about a drink?'

'You're always telling me I drink too much. And now you're suggesting one?'

'I know, but perhaps you deserve one tonight.'

'Why?'

'All the hard work you've been doing researching.'

'I'll have an ouzo then.'

'Me too.'

Laura ordered two large ouzos and some iced water.

I told Laura what I had discovered about Oswald's trip to England.

'So he did visit England!'

'Yes. But it doesn't look very good for us.'

'Why not?' Laura asked.

'Because he arrived at Southampton on 9 October 1959 and flew out the same day for Helsinki from Heathrow, and there's a passport to prove it. *And* a hotel register.'

'Could they be forged?'

'I suppose so but it seems unlikely. I don't think even the Warren *Report* guys would do something that dangerous … though others might.'

'He must have come here some other time then.'

'It's hard to see when. The Warren Commission carefully documented all of his movements. I can't see another window of opportunity, as they say.'

Laura finished her ouzo and stared at the ceiling thinking. Then she turned quickly and stared straight at me and said, 'But there's a very *big* window of opportunity! One staring us straight in the face!'

What? What 'very big' window of opportunity? I'd spent the last week going through all this stuff. I couldn't find it and, boy, I'd looked hard enough.

I returned the stare and said, 'Laura, there isn't. Oswald's movements were put under the microscope.'

She smiled one of those big gleeful toothy smiles of hers and said, 'Russia!'

Russia? What's Russia got to do with it? I wasn't following this at all.

'Christopher, when did Oswald arrive in Russia?'

'October 1959.'

'When did he leave Russia?'

'The year before Kennedy was assassinated. 1962. June.'

'So October 1959 to June 1962 – that's, uh, two years and eight months to be exact.'

'So?' I still wasn't following Laura's drift.

'So? So! So don't you see? He had two and a half years in which he could have done anything.'

'No, he couldn't.'

'Why not?'

'Because he was in Russia. He had defected, that's why.'

'How do you know?'

'Laura, it's all documented, that's why.'

'But it isn't, don't you see? There may be a stamp in his passport saying he entered Russia on this date and another one saying he left then, but that's all you do know. The Warren Commission didn't keep an eye on him every day he was out there.'

'I know. But he was a defector and –'

Laura interrupted me. 'An *apparent* defector.'

'OK, an apparent defector, true. But the Russians were hardly likely to give him a tourist visa and allow him out whenever he wanted to go, were they?'

'You're not listening to what I'm saying. I'm not saying that. All I am saying is he was allowed in and he was allowed out. We know that for a fact, don't we?'

'Yes.'

'And we don't know if he was allowed out and in at any other time, do we?'

'No, we don't.'

'Well, then – perhaps he was. You don't know that, do you?'

'No, I don't.'

Laura ordered some more ouzo and I thought over what she had said. It's true, we all assume that Oswald was in Russia for those two years or so. It's a no-go area for research purposes. He was there and that's that. End of story. But Laura's right. We just assume he was there for all that time. Nobody I read had ever questioned it.

All sorts of other questions now begin to arise. Was Oswald a bona fide defector or was he a penetration agent for American intelligence? What did the Russians really know about him? Were they perhaps aware he was a false defector? Were they playing their own game with him? Was there something else going on that we don't know about?

There are only four things I am absolutely sure of in the Kennedy assassination: Kennedy was killed, Oswald was killed, and neither the Cubans nor the Russians were in any way responsible for either.

Beyond that, who knows?

I ordered two further ouzos and very soon Laura and I were sinking into a bout of terminal nostalgia for Hitchin and our absent but always present friend, Dick.

Well after midnight we sang our way back to the flat down the deserted streets and as soon as we arrived I crashed out on the bed in my clothes, though not without watching Laura take her dress off through half-open eyes (I told her that the dark green slip she was wearing was beautiful).

Saturday morning. Laura was gone when I woke up at noon. I was still in my clothes and I felt uncomfortable. I took a shower and dressed, made some Russian coffee and returned to my desk where Laura had left the Oswald photocopies. I was now anxious to get a better understanding of Oswald's Russian interlude.

I reread the chapters and articles on Oswald's defection with a new perspective. I wasn't just going through the material to read what happened, I was now looking for missing and unknown time. Gaps in the narrative. Holes in the broadcloth spun by the Warren Commission and its stooges.

But first I stumbled across something else that was so startling I had to go out into the backyard and take some deep breaths to make sure I wasn't imagining it. It was a serendipitous discovery indeed, and deeply disturbing too.

The Warren Commission stated that Oswald left England the day he arrived, 9 October 1959. The fact has been repeated by every writer I've read who discussed the visit. Only one critic, Sylvia Meagher, decided to go beyond what was published in the *Report* and check the supporting documentation contained in the twenty-six volumes of *Hearings*. There she found Oswald's passport stamped by the immigration officers at Heathrow Airport and it read, 'Embarked 10 Oct 1959'! As she notes, 'This is typical of the repeated misrepresentation of simple fact in the Warren Report, in spite of contradictory documentary evidence in the accompanying exhibits.'

He was here in England for a day. Now this new evidence allows Oswald time to travel up to Hitchin on the visit. He did have time to make the trip, but why? There's got to be a reason.

But, on second thoughts, it doesn't prove that he visited the town then. It just increases the odds for the date.

I returned to trawling through the discussions of the Russian defection.

In the late afternoon I came across a vanishing.

At the end of October 1959 while in Moscow Oswald visited the US Embassy there to renounce his American citizenship. That we know for a fact. The next sure date for Oswald, according to the Warren *Report*, is when Priscilla Johnson, a US journalist, interviewed him at the Hotel Metropole on 16 November. Thereafter 'for the rest of the year, Oswald seldom left his hotel room'. On or about 4 January 1960 he left for Minsk where he was given a job and an apartment by the Russian authorities.

Oswald kept an 'Historic Diary' (his title) while in Russia and it was subsequently discovered amongst his effects in Dallas. There are no daily entries for late 1959 in the diary; instead, there's merely a blanket entry of 'Nov 17 – Dec 30.' He had time to write daily entries for the busy period upon his arrival in Moscow when he was being interviewed by Russian officials on a daily basis and sightseeing, yet when shut up in his hotel room (according to the Warren *Report*) he somehow *doesn't* have the time?

The six weeks of Oswald's life commencing 16 November 1959 are a blank, a mystery. He could have been doing anything, yet the Warren Commission never addressed itself to the problem.

I looked at the photographs of Oswald and Alf Lawson at the cinema and by the church. Only one problem – they appear to have been taken in the summer, going by the light, the strong shadows and Oswald's casual dress.

Later I came across another vanishing, a bigger one that allowed more possibilities. It was in Epstein's book *Legend*:

After writing his brother a short note in 1959, Oswald disappeared from sight for more than a year. During this time he had no contact with anyone outside the Soviet Union, nor are there any available witnesses to his activities within that country.

Oswald went down to Minsk at the beginning of 1960 to work in the radio factory, but was he there the whole time? Nobody knows. Or, if they do, they're not saying.

I noticed now that my back was aching. I got up from the desk and stretched and then went into the kitchen, made a Russian coffee, took a couple of vitamin pills, had some Stilton on dry biscuits, and went back to the front room and crashed out on the sofa.

About an hour later the phone rang. I reached over to the low table and grabbed the cordless.

'Hello?'

A hesitant female voice said, 'Chris?'

'Yes.'

'It's Jean.'

'Jean?'

'Mrs Draper.'

'Oh, Mrs Draper! How are you?'

'Can't grumble.'

'Good. And how's Mr Draper?'

'Watching the telly.'

'Right.'

'I've got Mrs Lawson's address for you.'

'Oh, good. Hang on, let me grab a pen … right. Shoot.'

'St Mary's, Henlow.'

'St Mary's, Henlow?'

'Yes.'

'Is that it?'

'Yes.'

'That sounds like a church.'

'It's a Catholic nursing home.'

'Oh. Is that the village or the Camp?'

Henlow is about five miles to the north of Hitchin. That's the village. Henlow Camp is a mile or so away on the old Bedford Road and sprang up around the RAF camp there, hence its name. There's the Camp and the village, they're different.

'It's in the village, on the right.'

'Great. Thanks.'

'I'll be off now as I don't like using this thing.'

'What, the telephone?'

'Never did.'

'Thanks again, Mrs Draper.'

'We'll see you soon?'

'Sure. Bye.'

'Bye.'

She's in a Catholic nursing home is Mrs Lawson. Uh-huh. Tomorrow's Sunday. Why don't I drive up? I dialled Laura.

'Laura Sayer.'

'Hi, what's happening?'

'Ironing,' Laura replied.

'Ironing?'

'Yes, some of us still do it.'

'I gave that up years ago.'

'It notices.'

'No it doesn't,' I said. 'Well, not much.'

'What's happening with you then?'

'Not a lot, but I just got a call from Briscoe's mum. Mrs Lawson is in a nursing home out in Henlow. Fancy a drive out tomorrow? We can have lunch as well.'

'What time?'

'One-ish?'

'Fine. Have you checked with the home? Visiting hours and so on?'

'No. Everywhere has Sunday visiting.'

'If you say so.'

'Right. One-ish then.'

'See you then.'

Then I remembered what I'd been doing all day. 'You may be right about Russia, you know. I've been checking it out. There are two gaps in Oswald's stay out there.'

'I couldn't see how they'd know what he was doing all the time out there.'

'You're a smart kid.'

'I know. See you tomorrow.'

'Right.'

I lay back on the sofa, finished the Russian coffee and soon fell asleep.

CHAPTER SEVEN

CONSPIRACY OF HEARTS

'Identify.'
　'Bellerophon … 666B.'
　'Location?'
　'Capital.'
　'Proceed.'
　'Reinvestigating 1963 LANCER grail contacts with local assistance.'
　　'Stand by.'

SUDDENLY IT'S CHILL AND DAMP and the leaves are fluttering down and the days are getting shorter. Children are wearing coats, gloves and scarves. And all the pretty girls in their summer dresses have migrated for the year. Winter is setting in.

I got to Laura's a little after 1 p.m. She was wearing a long dark brown suede coat, boots and a woollen hat. Her tapered fingers culminated in long fingernails painted bright red. She wore matching lipstick. I put my arms around her and cuddled her, taking in her warm smell.

We drove north up the Bedford Road and out of town, past the Angel's Reply pub, over the River Oughton and out into the wide open fields.

I was staring across to the right to the chimney stacks of the old brickworks over Arlesey way when I felt something on my knee. I looked down and saw it was Laura's hand resting there. I said nothing and looked ahead up the road before shooting a quick glance in her direction. She was staring ahead too.

Laura said, 'Do you think we'll learn anything from Mrs Lawson?'

'I don't know. We've got to see her. There might be something.'

I'd been wondering all day what she might know and in the end I gave up. Nobody ever knows everything and nobody ever knows nothing. It would be just a further piece of the jigsaw. We'd inch this inquiry forward one sweated incremental step at a time.

I took the right at Henlow Camp to head up to the village. There were dozens of new buildings here and I scarcely recognised the place. I didn't know when I was last up here. I seemed to remember an old railway that had passed through the place but there was now no trace of it.

On either side of the road were RAF buildings – workshops, barracks, married quarters, offices and so on and these then gave way to the airfield and farmland.

Laura's hand was still on my knee. This wasn't some absent-minded gesture but a decision. I didn't know what to make of it.

'How's work going?' I asked.

Laura looked at me and said, 'I've got to get out of that firm. It's driving me crackers.'

'What are you going to do?'

'I've applied to a couple of local firms up here. There's plenty of criminal work. I might get something. I *should* get something … *if* I'm patient enough.'

'Oh.'

'I'm tired of travelling into London as well. That's also a big factor.'

Ahead was a wide sweeping road that came in from the east and disappeared to the west. It was new. I'd never seen it before. And a roundabout. Laura said it was about ten years or so old and allowed the Bedford traffic to by-pass a few villages.

We drove into Henlow, a straggling one-road village that had grown up on either side of the way north to Biggles-wade. There are some attractive older houses and cottages but the general architectural look of the place is undistin-guished. There's also an air of transience, as though people only stay here temporarily. It's a stop-over.

'Briscoe's mum said it was on the right.'

'Perhaps it's further up?' said Laura, her hand still on my knee.

'Should be here somewhere.'

I continued along at about 15 m.p.h.

'There it is,' said Laura, pointing.

Two newish brick walls curved back from the road frontage either side of a gravel drive. A peeling wooden board said, 'St Mary's Home for the Aged and Infirm.'

Laura said, 'That rubs the visitors' noses in it, doesn't it? Why not just, "St Mary's Home"?'

'Because it's Catholic?'

'Maybe.'

I pulled across the road and into the drive which led a serpentine course to a large three-storey Victorian house with modern additions. To the left of the house was a modern chapel with a ramp rather than steps leading up. There were ramps to the main house also. Wheelchairs? The aged? The infirm?

I parked the car near a water tank.

'Not much life about here, eh?' Laura observed.

'Let's find out.'

We walked over to the house and pushed open a hefty door that had recently been painted bright emerald green. We were then in a large hall bereft of furniture. Brightly coloured Margaret Tarrant-style religious prints were stuck on the walls showing Jesus performing miracles and doing good turns surrounded by flocks of open-mouthed admirers, both human and animal.

It seemed colder in here than it was outside. The walls were painted dark brown. The carpet on the stairs was threadbare. There was the sound of a TV coming from a corridor to the right.

'Anybody about?' cried Laura. Her voice echoed.

'It doesn't look like it.'

We waited. Nothing. I looked around to see if there was a bell you could push to announce your arrival. There wasn't.

I noticed that Laura was standing close to me. In fact she walked close to me as we came over from the car. Usually there was the standard human three feet between us, today we were almost touching.

'I'm going down there. There's a TV on. You hold on here.'

'OK,' replied Laura.

I headed along the corridor, my footsteps echoing, towards the sound of the TV. There was a door ajar ahead of me. The TV was in there. I stopped and listened at the door, but I could only hear some quiz programme from the set, no human sounds. I pushed the door open. It was a lounge with about a dozen armchairs and wheelchairs curved around in front of the TV. Each chair was occupied by an old person, but none of them were watching it, indeed none of them were capable of watching it, or doing much else. An old man was staring at the ceiling and listlessly punching the air, a bald woman with her eyes closed was shaking her tiny fists. A man was standing in the corner moving his legs back and forth in some obsessive pattern. The others seemed catatonic.

I closed the door and walked back to Laura.

'Any luck?'

'If Mrs Lawson is anything like the patients down there we're not going to get anything from her,' I replied in a whisper.

'Why not?'

'Because they're all completely out of it.'

A door opened and closed somewhere in the house. A woman in her fifties with bright ginger hair and dressed in overalls appeared on the other side of the hall. She was carrying a mop and bucket. She saw us and said with a heavy Irish accent, 'You're being seen to?' Her strong voice belied her frail appearance.

'No, we're not, ' I replied.

'You viz-it-ors?'

'Sort of. We've come to see Mrs Lawson.'

The woman thought for a moment and then stated, 'You'll follow me.' Which we did.

She led us to the back of the house and stopped by a closed door. I could hear a radio playing music inside. The woman looked back at us and then banged on the door with her knuckles. A voice inside said, 'Yes?'

The woman opened the door about a foot and put her head around. 'There are viz-it-ors to see you, Sister Shirley.'

'Thank you, Cathleen,' said an educated voice from within. 'Show them in.'

Cathleen pushed the door open and indicated that we should go through. Sister Shirley was a nun of small height and indeterminate age. She turned the radio off and beckoned us in before dismissing Cathleen.

The office was spartan and aside from an old desk and several chairs and filing cabinets boasted nothing more than a wall-hung crucifix, a telephone and a two-bar electric fire.

'Please sit down,' said the Sister in an unmistakably English middle-class voice. 'Can we be of help to you?'

'Yes,' I said, clearing my throat, 'we've come to see Mrs Lawson.'

'Mrs Lawson?'

'Yes.'

'Mrs Lawson?'

'Uh-huh, of Hitchin.'

'I see.'

Then there was a long silence until the Sister asked, 'You are relatives?'

'Not exactly,' answered Laura. 'We're researching something that took place in Hitchin some years ago and it is important we speak with Mrs Lawson.'

'I see. Well, I'm very sorry to tell you this, but Mrs Lawson passed away at the beginning of September.'

Fuck, I thought. She's dead. That's it. All over.

The Sister continued. 'I must also tell you that I doubt very much whether Mrs Lawson would have been able to help you prior to her death.'

'Why?' I asked. The Sister frowned at me and I said, 'I'm sorry. I didn't mean to sound so blunt.'

'I understand.'

'Thank you,' I said.

The Sister continued, 'Mrs Lawson was greatly disturbed by her husband's suicide and never quite recovered her full abilities.'

In other words, she ended up like those poor sods in the TV lounge. That's the reality behind the words of 'never quite recovered her full abilities'. So, even had we got here in time we still wouldn't have found anything out.

But what was this about suicide? Didn't Mrs Draper say he was killed in a train accident? Suicide?

'Suicide?' I said.

'Yes, suicide,' said the Sister with a confidence that would brook no assault.

Alf Lawson a suicide? The face in the photographs, that jovial moon-faced person, he committed suicide? He didn't look the type who would commit suicide, did he? And a Catholic too.

Laura looked up and said to the Sister, 'Who are Mrs Lawson's next of kin? Do you have any records?'

Sister Shirley shook her head and said, 'We are not allowed to divulge any confidential information. However, we could forward a letter for you.'

Didn't Mrs Draper say something about relatives? A

sister or something? I'd forgotten that. Good of Laura to ask.

Laura smiles and takes something from her shoulder bag. She stands, leans forward and hands it to the Sister. It's a small white card. The Sister puts her glasses on and scrutinises it.

'I am a solicitor as you'll see from my card,' says Laura in a forthright and formal voice. 'I understand that the Home has to protect confidentiality but I'm sure this is not something you'll insist upon in a legal matter. Please keep that.'

'I see, a *legal* matter,' echoed Sister Shirley.

Her attitude had changed completely. There's something about the English middle classes when confronted with authority. They wilt and buckle, even when they're brides of Christ.

The Sister smiled at Laura, an ingratiating smile, and reached for a thick indexed ledger book that was on the far side of her desk. Her finger ran down the indices and she opened it. I stole a quick smile at Laura who was still playing the part of the solicitor.

'Here we are, Mrs Lawson. She has a daughter at – do you have a pen? Oh, yes you do.'

Laura was angled over her notebook with a pen ready to write.

The Sister continued, 'At number 12 Templars' Lane, Baldock, Hertfordshire. You've got that? Yes. The daughter's name is Mrs Angela Rivers. I'm afraid I don't have a telephone number.'

'I appreciate your willingness to help,' said Laura in a brusque manner as she returned the cap to the pen. 'Very much so.'

'I'm pleased to be of help,' the Sister replied.

Sister Shirley showed us out down the corridor and we returned to the car. Laura was pleased with herself. And I was pleased with her too. I was quite certain the Sister would never have given me the information.

'Let's go and see Mrs Angela Rivers then,' said Laura.

'OK,' I agreed. 'What's the best route from here?'

'Take a left back on the road. Shouldn't take us more than twenty minutes to Baldock.'

As we drove south out of the village Laura told me to take the first left and this led us through Arlesey and the flat depressing countryside of southern Bedfordshire. Dreary bungalows and nondescript late nineteenth-century villas and terraces.

Laura hadn't returned her hand to my knee. Do I mention this to her? Should I remind her? Or just wait until she does it again? But what if she doesn't? Then what? Well, if she doesn't do it … I'll miss it. Sod it. 'I miss your hand on my knee.'

I was looking straight ahead down the road but I could see her turn towards me. Not just her head, but her whole body. Again, she was closer to me than she should have been. There was a silence and then she said, 'Do *you*?'

There was something about the way she said *you* that sent a thrill down me. A warmish thrill. A frisson even?

'Yes, I do,' I replied.

She returned her hand to my knee and then moved it about halfway up my thigh. She said nothing and I said nothing. The touch was soothing and calming.

We continued on through Stotfold (another depressing place) and on and under the A1(M) and then right down the old Great North Road towards Baldock about a mile and a half to the south.

We had no idea where Templars' Lane was and neither did the only three pedestrians who were abroad in the town that afternoon. We stumbled upon the police station quite by chance and they directed us back to the north side of town near the railway station which we had passed earlier.

Templars' Lane wasn't a lane at all but a cul-de-sac, it had never been developed further. It was a dozen 1920s semi-detached council houses on each side of the road with open fields at the end. All of the houses looked as though they could do with a bit of renovation and a lick of paint. There were more vans and transits parked in the road than saloons.

No. 12 was halfway up on the right. An old Ford Capri, wheel-less and on bricks, dominated the front garden. A disused washing machine was parked by the front door. The lights were on downstairs and as we got to the front door I could hear country and western music blaring away inside.

The electric buzzer had a loose wire coming from it so Laura went for the knocker and gave it a couple of hefty bangs.

Through the frosted glass of the door I saw someone appear. The door opened and a woman in her early fifties stared at us. She was dressed in jeans and white high heels. She wore a knitted blouse that looked like it was made of chain mail with a plunging neckline that displayed the tops of two fulsome breasts. Her hair was piled high and blond. She wore jewellery and lots of make-up. Her high cheek bones and large blue eyes accentuated a beauty that was fading fast. She didn't say anything, just waited.

Laura said, 'Mrs Rivers?'

The woman said in a husky and precise voice, 'Who are you?'

I had the strong impression that this woman was used to answering the door to people she didn't want to meet. There was a practised tone to the way she stated the question. She wasn't going to admit to anything before she found out who exactly we were.

I said, 'I'm Christopher Cornwell and this is Laura Sayer. We're friends of the Drapers in Hitchin.'

'The Drapers?' she replied.

'Yes. The Drapers.'

'Oh, the Drapers. I know.' She seemed to relax.

'We went over to see your mother at St Mary's and –'

'Mum?'

'Yes.'

'She's dead.'

'That's what we found out from the Sister.'

'I see,' said Mrs Rivers. 'Come in.'

She showed us through to the front room. The carpet was decorated with swirls of garish primary colours. There was a red cloth-and-plastic three-piece suite that was badly worn, a huge new TV, and a midi system blasting out Tammy Wynette. An old sideboard was loaded down with magazines, telephone directories and records. A mother-of-pearl table on spindly legs stood to the fore of the sofa displaying two full ashtrays, chocolates and wrappers, some beer cans and a half-consumed cup of coffee.

Laura and I sat on the sofa.

'Would you like a cup of tea or coffee?'

Laura said, 'I'm fine.'

I said, 'I'm fine too.'

Mrs Rivers sat down in the armchair facing us. A cat sprang from nowhere on to her lap. 'So why were you going to see Mum?'

I took the two photographs of her dad with Lee Harvey Oswald from my folder and handed them to her. She took out a pair of glasses from a pocket in her top and looked at both pictures closely.

'This is Dad.'

'Yes,' said Laura.

'I've never seen these pictures before. Who's this with him?'

I ignored the question and said, 'You've never seen them before?'

'No.'

'And there's no mistake, it is your father?'

'Yes.'

'Do you know when they were taken? Can you hazard a guess?'

She looked at both pictures again, holding each one about three inches from her nose.

[220]

'I don't know. Thirty years ago? Must be.'

'And you don't recognise who he's with?'

'No. Do you know?'

Laura jumped in with, 'Yes, we do.'

Jesus, I thought, you're not going to let the cat out of the bag, are you, Laura?

Mrs Rivers looked over her glasses at us and said in a voice that demanded an answer, 'Why are you interested in these pictures? What's it all about then?'

'We're trying to trace someone,' Laura said in her best solicitor's voice. 'Trace the man with your father.'

'Oh, has he come into an inheritance or something?' said Mrs Rivers.

Laura said without a trace of irony, 'Quite possibly.'

'Is there anyone else who could help us, Mrs Rivers?' I asked.

'Dad's got his suit on here so he was out on a job, driving someone about.'

'Are there any people about still who worked for him?' It was a long shot but I thought I'd ask it.

She looked at us and said before lighting a cigarette, 'Not that I can think of – they're all dead.'

So that's another dead-end. A lead leading nowhere. Still, what can one expect? This is tracking a thirty-year-old story that was faint from the kick-off. The traces and tracks have dissolved away. We're knocking on coffins here.

'I'd quite like copies of these pictures. Could you get that done for me? I'll pay,' said Mrs Rivers in a slightly plaintive voice.

'Sure,' I said. 'It won't be a problem.'

She smiled and handed the photos back to me. Then her face lit up as though she remembered something. She had. 'There is someone you could try and get in touch with.'

'Who's that?' Laura said.

'A few years before Dad died he took on a young lad to learn the business. I think Dad's idea was he'd be able to take over the running of the business from time to time so

Dad could have more time to himself, but it didn't work out that way … with what happened to Dad and …'

Mrs Rivers didn't finish the sentence, she was recalling some memory that made tears swell up in her eyes. She wiped both eyes with a white handkerchief kept in the sleeve of her top, blew her nose, relit the cigarette.

'You were saying, Mrs Rivers?' Laura whispered.

'What was I saying?'

'The young lad he took on?' said Laura.

'Oh, yes. He took this lad on. He'd probably be able to help you. He knew about the running of the business.'

'What was his name?' I asked.

'I can remember him very well,' continued Mrs Rivers. 'We had a little thing, him and I. His name is Roy Pepper.'

Laura said, 'Do you know where we can find him?'

'He sent me a Christmas card every year for years. That was the only contact we had, but the cards stopped coming when I moved here.'

'Why was that?' said Laura.

'Because he hasn't got the address and I lost his in the move. In fact, I lost a lot of things in the move,' Mrs Rivers stated with some bitterness.

She said 'the move' in such a way as to convey the impression that it was more than just a move, it was a reduction in circumstances, some trauma in her life.

'If you don't have his address, can you remember where it is he lives?' I asked.

'Yes. Great Yarmouth. He's got a car hire business there. Cabbying, weddings and that, just like Dad.'

Well, that's a lead. There can't be too many people named Roy Pepper in Great Yarmouth driving for a living. I can get all the company numbers from the local Yellow Pages in the library at Camden and just start phoning. Unless he's moved, it won't be difficult running him to ground. Perhaps he is even in the directory under his own name?

There was a silence. Mrs Rivers had popped a chocolate

into her mouth and was stroking the cat. Laura lit up a More cigarette.

I was thinking of what the Sister said about Alf Lawson committing suicide and I still couldn't square it with the jovial face in the photographs so I said, 'The Sister seemed to think your dad committed suicide.'

Mrs Rivers stared at me. 'Did she?'

'Yes.'

'Uh-huh. He did.'

She carried on stroking the cat.

'I'm sorry,' I said, not knowing what else to say.

There was another long silence and then Mrs Rivers said in almost a whisper, 'It'll soon be almost thirty years ago to the day.'

I'd thought with no basis whatsoever that the suicide was more recent, in the last ten years or so, but it was thirty years ago. Three decades ago ... almost to the day. Mrs Lawson had been in that home a lot longer than I'd thought.

'Thirty years,' Mrs Rivers continued, repeating herself, 'November 24th ... two days after President Kennedy was killed.'

What? What did she say? Two days after President Kennedy was killed? While most people can remember what they were doing the day Kennedy was shot none of them ever know the date if you ask them. Why did she mention Kennedy? Not, surely, to remind herself when her dad died?

I jumped in. 'Why did you mention Kennedy?'

'No reason. I just remember it. Everyone does,' she replied.

I was convinced there was a reason and I was convinced her reply was honest. There *was* a reason but she wasn't consciously aware of it. Something had triggered the mention.

I didn't know how to phrase this but I did it as best I could. 'I know this must be painful for you, but can you tell me something about your father's suicide?'

She stared at me. 'Like what?'

'Why do you suppose he did it?'

'He was a schizophrenic the doctors said. He was always hearing voices and saying and thinking things.'

Laura looked at me as though something wasn't quite right. She then looked at Mrs Rivers and said, 'Yet he had built up a successful business, hadn't he?'

'Yes, but he wasn't always a schizophrenic.'

'He wasn't?' said Laura.

'No, it came on suddenly.'

It came on suddenly? Does this illness come on suddenly? I thought you were born with it, but perhaps I'm wrong?

'Who told you he was schizophrenic?' asked Laura.

'The doctor.'

'What, his local GP?'

'No, a special doctor who came up from London. He had a funny name.'

'Where was he being treated?' asked Laura.

'At Fairfield,' Mrs Rivers said.

Fairfield was a big mental hospital to the north of Hitchin built a hundred or more years ago. An enormous place. High on a plateau and remote. Also, I think, known for some time as Three Counties. (Three Counties because, in the manner of the Poor Law Unions, three separate authorities got together to solve a common problem. In this case the shires of Hertford, Bedford and Huntingdon.)

Laura was warming to the cross-questioning. 'Was he a residential patient or an out-patient?'

'He just went there as an out-patient.'

'Did you consider him normal before he became schizoid?'

'Yes. He was perfectly normal until the breakdown.'

'When was the breakdown?'

'September ... late September ... or early October.'

'Of what year? Can you remember?'

'Yes. 1963.'

That seemed a devilishly short time. Laura picked up on

it. 'He had the breakdown and he was dead two months later. It came on all of a sudden?'

'The breakdown? Yes.'

'How did it show itself? How did his behaviour change?'

'He'd start shaking and sweating. He couldn't control himself, and he was always saying strange things.'

'Such as?'

'Just mad things – the world was going to end, evil people were following him, they were going to get him, they were going to get Mum and me. Nobody was safe, not even President Kennedy. Things like that. He was in an awful state.'

There it was. There was the reason she mentioned Kennedy earlier.

I went to say something but Laura put her hand on mine and said, 'Do you know what brought this on, Mrs Rivers?'

'Stress? Overwork? I don't know.'

'Did he often mention President Kennedy?'

'Yes. Dad was a Catholic and Kennedy was the first Catholic President of the United States. It meant a lot to Dad.'

'Was that the only reason he was ... concerned with Kennedy?' I asked.

Mrs Rivers looked perplexed, shrugged her shoulders and then said, 'I think so, but then when Kennedy was shot Dad felt he was responsible.'

'Responsible?' said Laura.

'Guilty somehow ... that sort of responsible,' Mrs Rivers replied.

I didn't follow her. Laura asked her why he should feel guilty and Mrs Rivers said, 'He began to feel responsible for everything bad that was happening. It was part of the illness, you see.'

'You say he committed suicide two days after Kennedy was assassinated?' Laura said.

Mrs Rivers nodded.

'Was there anything specific that prompted this that you know of?' Laura continued.

'Dad was just … going from bad to worse. The tablets he was on weren't doing any good. Then he seemed to go down very quickly when Kennedy was shot because, you know, he felt he was responsible for it … and then he started saying he knew the man who did it … and it was all too much for him … and then Dad did *it* … out at the station.'

… then he started saying he knew the man who did it. The words exploded in my head.

'How did he do it?' Laura asked.

'He threw himself under a train at Hitchin station.'

'I see,' said Laura.

'Why did he say he knew the man who killed Kennedy, Mrs Rivers?' I had to ask her that question.

'It was part of the illness. The doctor said people like Dad latch on to things. They don't know what they're doing.'

'Yes,' I said. 'Let me ask you a couple more things. Did your dad ever mention a man named Drax or a house called The Leys … in Shadwell Lane?'

'I can't remember. They don't mean anything to me,' she replied after several moments of silence.

What had happened to Alf Lawson? The photographs were proof that he did know Lee Harvey Oswald, but what of the breakdown and all of the associated delusions and strange behaviour? Could he have been got at in some way?

And the suicide? Just like Dick's – at Hitchin station. Two bodies there now. No, three, if you include Reginald Hine.

Mrs Rivers began to sob. Laura went over and put her arm around her.

Should I tell her that her father did indeed know Lee Harvey Oswald? Or would that confuse her still further? I would tell her, but today wasn't the best time.

Mrs Rivers said, 'I haven't thought about Dad in such a long time … for years. You put it out of your mind, don't you?'

'It's difficult,' said Laura comfortingly.

I thought it was significant that Alf Lawson deteriorated rapidly after Kennedy's assassination. It must have arisen from his recognition of Lee Harvey Oswald on TV and in the papers. The US President is killed and then he sees the guy he's been photographed with and, one can reasonably suppose, chauffeured about too. He knows him.

Mrs Rivers said something about her dad being fearful for Kennedy's life, so does that mean he had wind of something while Kennedy was still alive? But how? What?

Something had leaked. But from where? How?

There was one other question I had to ask Mrs Rivers now that she was regaining her composure. 'Did your dad ever warn anyone or go to the police about what he thought was going to happen to Kennedy?'

'He knew everyone in Hitchin and they all thought how sad it was, his illness. They understood that he didn't know what he was saying.'

Uh-huh. But what about after – after the assassination? Did anyone connect what had happened with what he was saying? Or were his Kennedy allegations just buried amidst the other claims and nonsense of his illness? Did the ostensible sheer unlikelihood of what he was saying blind people to the possibility that he was talking the truth? I guess so. There's no mention of Alf Lawson in any of the books on the assassination I've read.

Mrs Rivers wipes her eyes, stands up, and says 'We'll have a cup of tea.'

'Let me help you,' says Laura as she follows Mrs Rivers to the kitchen.

I take Laura's packet of More cigarettes from the cluttered coffee table and light one of them up. My head is racing around with what Mrs Rivers has said. But what does it all add up to?

Later, after a couple of cups of tea and hesitant small talk, Mrs Rivers says, 'I always knew someone would ask me one day about Dad's death.'

It was dark as we drove out of Baldock on the road to Letchworth and Hitchin. There was a light rain and gusting wind.

Laura had taken my hand from the automatic gear shift when I was pulling out of Templars' Lane and had been holding it firmly ever since.

We had been going over and over what Mrs Rivers had told us, trying to make sense of it, trying to understand what was going on behind it. It was important for us but as Laura said, 'I don't think it would mean an awful lot to a sceptical outsider. We've got hearsay that a schizoid claimed thirty years ago that he knew Kennedy's assassin, and not much else.'

'We've got the photos too. And, by the way, Oswald wasn't Kennedy's assassin. He was the patsy. He was set up for it.'

'Uh-huh. Kennedy's alleged assassin. Anyway, an able QC would make mincemeat of a photographic resemblance or any anthropologist expert you'd get to bat for you.'

'I know, but this is not a court of law yet, this is a citizen's committee of inquiry!'

'So where do the citizens go now?'

'I think we should track this guy Pepper down in Great Yarmouth. He might have something interesting to tell us.'

'Yes, that sounds a good lead.'

The light rain was now becoming a heavy downpour as we drove through Letchworth.

'We've now got three bodies at Hitchin station,' I said.

'Three?' replied Laura.

'Uh-huh. Alf Lawson, Dick, and Reginald Hine.'

'Hine? What's he got to do with it?'

'Nothing, I don't think, but that's where he committed suicide, isn't it?'

'Yes. So?'

'It's just that I thought of him when I first heard about Dick. I thought there might be some connection. You know, that Dick emulated him, copied him, if Dick's mind was unbalanced.'

'What, that Dick chose to go the same way as Hine?'

'Yes. Two Hitchin historians ... and don't forget the rule of three.'

'What's that?' said Laura.

'Wasn't it a World War One thing? Once is an accident, twice is coincidence, three is enemy action?'

The rain eased as we passed under the railway bridge and into Hitchin. There were church bells far off – Sunday evening in Hitchin. The town seemed deserted. Everything was well with the world.

I parked up at the top of Tilehouse Street and we walked arm in arm down to the house.

There was a note on the kitchen table from the girls saying that they had gone over to a party in Stevenage. Laura filled the percolator and put it on the stove and then disappeared upstairs. I poured myself a large vodka and sat back in the rocking chair looking at the three pictures: two men, or rather a man and a young guy, a bright summer's (?) day in Hitchin, late 1950s, early 1960s. Smiles and sunshine. Within a few years one would have gone 'mad' and committed suicide, the other would have been arrested for shooting the 35th President of the United States and then, two days later, would be shot dead himself, by a night-club owner with Mafia connections.

Did I expect to see something on their faces that would foretell their fortunes? Did I hope to see something here that would provide a key to what would subsequently happen?

What did I expect to find?

I poured myself another large vodka and returned to the chair.

Laura appeared wearing an ankle-length black kimono

with a bright red dragon embroidered on it. She looked startling, if not stunning too. She noticed my amusement and said, 'I needed to put something loose on … and you're going to get done for drink-driving some time, you know that?'

'Don't remind me.'

'I will.'

Laura stood over me and looked at the photographs. I said, 'It's strange looking at these, isn't it? We know what was going to happen, but they didn't … *then* … did they?'

'Mmmm – what's going to happen to us that we don't know about?' said Laura as she gazed at the photo of Alf and Lee outside the Hermitage Cinema.

'Nothing I hope,' I said. 'I want to live to a ripe old age in a surprise-free zone.'

I finished the vodka and wondered if the coffee was ready yet. The percolator was spluttering away. 'You want a coffee, Laura?'

'Uh-huh. Black.'

I took two mugs from the cupboard and poured the coffee. It didn't look that strong yet, but it would do. I put the mugs on the table and sat down to look at today's *Observer*. Laura was still standing at the other end of the kitchen looking at the photograph. I checked whether there was anything worth watching on TV tonight – *nada*. Nothing at all.

'You can date this photo, you know,' said Laura.

'What?' I replied not really taking any notice as I scanned the review section's book pages.

'You can date this exactly … or within a few days.'

What was Laura talking about? Some neutron-activation process or whatever they called it for dating artefacts? It would cost a million dollars and wouldn't be that accurate anyway. I wasn't really paying attention.

Laura came over and put the photograph down in front of me and pointed to it and said, 'You can date it from that!'

I looked at the picture. 'From what?'

'From that. See! The hoarding there! It says LILLI PALMER and then the beginning of the title, but it's partially obscured by Oswald's head.'

Yes, indeed, the display board said Lilli Palmer and there was the title of the film, obscured largely by Oswald. The first three letters were C – O – N.

'All you do,' said Laura, 'is find out what film she was in that had a title of which the first three letters were C – O – N. And then find out when it was released, when it was playing at the Hermitage. It's that easy.'

I was dumbstruck. I'd looked at this photo a thousand times and I'd seen Lilli Palmer's name and, I guess, the beginning of the title, yet this had never registered, least of all as a means of dating the picture. Never registered, period. I'd noticed it but never realised its significance. Jesus.

Looking at this picture is like looking at the Zapruder film, the famous 'home movie' that shows Kennedy being assassinated. Despite your most strenuous efforts your eyes always focus in on the President himself, and stay there. You don't notice what else is going on.

So that's it. Find out what the film was and find when it was released! A doddle as they say. I could kick myself for not recognising that. I really could.

I stood up and pulled Laura to me. I could smell her hair and the perfume she was wearing and I could feel her body underneath the kimono. I don't think she was wearing anything else.

'Laura!' I said, 'you're a genius!' It sounded corny but it was the first thing that came into my mind.

I held her tight and she put her arms around me. We stood there for what seemed like several minutes and then Laura moved her hands up to my head and put her lips to mine and we kissed. Not a kiss of friends, but a kiss of lovers. My hands moved up and down her body and over her breasts and I wanted her there and then. She was yielding to me, but then she froze and whispered in my ear, 'Later, not tonight.'

That was a sage thing to say and I was immediately glad she said it and saved the evening. I was feeling like Carl Solomon, the poet, after he attended a preview of a Stanley Kubrick film in the 1950s. Kubrick went up to him after and asked him what he thought of the picture? Solomon said, 'I'm sorry, Stanley. I didn't notice it. There's too much going on in my head.' There was too much going on in my head aside from the sudden gear change in our relationship, there was the afternoon with Mrs Rivers and what she had said and not said, and there was the possibility now of dating the photographs. My head was a riot of whats and ifs.

Laura kissed me lightly on the lips and said, 'We've both had a long day.'

'You're right. I'd better be moving.'

I finished my coffee and Laura hugged me on the doorstep and we kissed goodnight.

I drove down Tilehouse Street and up Hitchin hill at a fast clip. The rain had abated but the roads were still wet. I put a Charlie Parker tape on the cassette at full blast and roared down the Stevenage road. I was soon on the motorway and heading south.

The first thing I did when I got home after pouring a very large vodka and mango juice (all that was left in the fridge, and only four days past its sell-by date) was go to the bookshelves and find my copy of Ephraim Katz's massive film encyclopaedia. I looked up PALMER, LILLI.

When I started at MGM Studios back in the 1960s the white front office building there with the tower had large framed photographic portraits of films stars lining the walls of the lobby. Next to the one of David Niven was Lilli Palmer's. I'd never heard of her then and I remember asking one of the production staff who she was. 'Used to be Rex Harrison's old lady,' was the reply. I found out later that there was a little more to her career than that.

PALMER, LILLI. Actress. Born Lillie Marie Peiser, on May 24, 1914, in Posen, Germany. Biographical details. Screen debut in London in 1935. More bio. And here a list of films. Quite a few of them. I'm looking for something from the 1950s or early 1960s that begins with the letters C – O – N. Concerto? Concubine? Concrete? Confess? Contract? Nothing so far. Nothing here? But what's this? *Conspiracy of Hearts*, made in the United Kingdom in 1960. That looks like it. Now, it couldn't be anything else, could it? I run down the remaining titles. There's something called *The Counterfeit Traitor* made in the US in 1962. But that's C – O – U, and it has the definite article preceding it. I'd better check the photo again.

I took the photo and looked at the hoarding closely under the linen tester by the Anglepoise. There was no definite article to be seen and the first three letters were decidedly C – O – N. Then *Conspiracy of Hearts* it had to be. It couldn't be anything else. It was made in the UK and released in 1960. The Hermitage was a first-run cinema and therefore it would have been shown there the year of its release. 1960. The Hermitage never screened re-runs.

So, if I go to the British Library's newspaper division at Colindale tomorrow I can now save myself a lot of work by starting at the beginning of 1960. It shouldn't be too hard to find the reference.

I undressed and got into bed. It was 9.45 p.m. Too late to phone Laura? I dialled her number and she answered on the second ring.

'Hello?' she said, sounding sleepy.

'I didn't wake you, did I?'

'No, I was just reading. I always do before I go to sleep.'

'What are you reading?'

'*Casanova's Chinese Restaurant* ... by Anthony Powell.'

'Intriguing title. I've never read any of him.'

'You should.'

'OK, I will. This is just a quick call. I just wanted to say how nice it was seeing you today ... being with you.'

'It was nice seeing you too. It always is.'

'We'll talk later.'

'Yes. Goodnight, Christopher.'

'Goodnight, Laura.'

I hung up the phone and put the light out.

[2]

It was late morning when I finally woke up. I had a quick shower, some coffee and muesli and then I was out on a bus and down at Camden and in the public library.

The reference section had a complete set of UK telephone directories and Yellow Pages. I took the Norwich area directory down that covered Great Yarmouth and looked up the name Pepper. There were about fifty of them listed for this part of East Anglia, and nowhere was a Pepper Car Hire or Taxi Service to be seen.

Fifty of them. I guess Pepper is one of those uncommon common names.

There was no Roy Pepper but there were several R. Peppers and none of them were listed for Great Yarmouth.

She said Roy Pepper, but Roy might be his nickname. I can't afford to take down only the Rs.

Mrs Rivers said Great Yarmouth, but by that did she mean specifically Great Yarmouth or a nearby village or hamlet? My eyes ran down the addresses. There were Peppers in Hemsby, Salthouse and Acle for instance. Were these places anywhere near Yarmouth or were they the other side of Norwich? I didn't know.

I had no choice but to transcribe every number except those that couldn't possibly be Yarmouth numbers, those with addresses in Norwich, Lowestoft, Cromer and other places I recognised. This left me with some thirty numbers on my pad.

I now went through the Yellow Pages for the area. I started with CAR HIRE and took down all the Great Yarmouth numbers. Then I moved on to MINI CABS, then TAXI & PRIVATE

HIRE VEHICLES and finally, WEDDING SERVICES, for good measure – Rollers and big Mercs for weddings might be his thing. I ended up with about forty numbers. That plus the thirty or so of private subscribers gave me a total of approximately seventy numbers to call.

This was going to be a bigger job than I'd realised … and for what I thought was a rare name in a small town. Still, it could have been worse – Smith in Birmingham or Brown in Manchester.

It was raining lightly as I left the library and walked up to the underground station. I was a bit under the weather, but a quick drink would probably improve matters an appreciable degree. I didn't really have time to go to a pub as I wanted to get up to Colindale so I picked up a half bottle in an off-licence and made for the station.

I got a day return ticket and went down the escalator and along to the Edgware line platform. There was nobody else about so I managed to have a couple of quick unselfconscious slugs before the train pulled in. I got in the head carriage and the only other occupants got out at Belsize Park so I managed to get another taste or two in before a party of au pair girls flooded the carriage at Golders Green.

When the train arrived at Colindale I felt a lot more human. I walked out of the station and across the road to the newspaper library.

I applied for a day ticket, not being a member, and wrote on the application that I was doing 'social research', whatever that means.

It was a few years since I'd last been here but the place hadn't changed any aside from the introduction of a few computers and terminals. I took a request slip and after dumping my folder on a seat went over to the card index to make sure they did actually have what I wanted, then I filled it out:

DATE: *25 October 1993*

SURNAME AND INITIALS IN BLOCK CAPITALS: *CORNWELL, C. E.*

SEAT NO: *38*
NEWSPAPER TITLE: *Hitchin and District Pictorial*
PLACE OF PUBLICATION: *Hitchin, Herts*
SHELFMARK: *1114*
MONTHS AND YEARS REQUIRED: *Jan to Dec 1960*

I put down the whole year as the old *Pictorial* was a weekly and the fifty-two issues were not likely to run to more than two volumes.

I returned to the desk and waited. Sometimes I've had what I wanted in a few minutes, other times I've waited an hour. The place was only about half full today so I didn't anticipate waiting too long.

Depending on how long it took to track this film down I could also check out the reports on Alf Lawson's suicide, see if there was anything of interest there. And why not Reginald Hine's too while I was at it?

Everybody in Hitchin knew about Hine's suicide but nobody ever seemed to have any details about it. I remember once years ago checking in the museum and they couldn't even tell me the day in 1949 it happened. A museum with thousands of his papers and they didn't even have the exact date. Staggering. I'd always meant to ask Dick about it and find out what he knew, but now that was too late.

The *Hitchin Pictorial* hadn't arrived so I went over to the reference section and found *Palmer's Index to The Times* for 1949. Hine had a reputation beyond Hitchin and *The Times* was sure to have reported it. I looked Hine, Reginald up and there was the reference to the report: April 16, 1949. I now had the date for the Hitchin paper.

I went back and checked the card index and found the *Hitchin Pictorial* was then known as the *Herts Pictorial*. I filled out request slips for the paper for March and April 1949. Alf Lawson was covered by another request for the *Hitchin Pictorial* for November and December 1963, and while I was at it I also put in a request for *The Times* for April 1949.

When I got back to my seat the two large quarter-leather bound volumes were resting against the table. I took the JAN-JUN volume and placed it on the lectern. I checked the cinema adverts in each issue. There was nothing in January, nothing in February, nothing in March, nothing in April, nothing in May, and nothing in June.

I picked up the JUL-DEC volume. My eyes were swimming a little and my fingertips were jet black from the newsprint. I stretched and yawned.

Right, July 1960. Nothing in that month.

The little boxed ads for the Hermitage raced by with the titles of early 1960s cinema.

... and there, finally, Thursday, 11 August [1960], for three days:

> *Lilli Palmer – Sylvia Syms*
> CONSPIRACY OF HEARTS

So the photographs were taken on one of three days in the summer of 1960. The August of that year. I've dated them! I felt like throwing my arms in the air and shouting Yippee!, but then a single stark fact hit me like a shit monsoon. That was when Oswald was supposedly in Russia. This couldn't be right.

I took my notes out of the folder and found the Oswald time-line I had put together. Right. He was in Russia. He'd arrived there in October 1959 and he would stay there until June 1962.

The Epstein quote I'd pencilled in the margin caught my eye:

After writing his brother a short note in 1959, Oswald disappeared from sight for more than a year. During this time he had no contact with anyone outside the Soviet Union, nor are there any available witnesses to his activities within that country.

This was also what was said in the Warren *Report* and

this was what Epstein had checked out for himself, yet here was Oswald in Hitchin in August 1960.

I looked at the *Hitchin Pictorial* again, at the copies of the photographs I had in the folder, at the Oswald time-line, at the Epstein quote. There was something going on here that sent a shiver through me.

I felt like some character in a Philip K. Dick short story who suddenly discovers that everything he reads in the newspapers is a lie told just for his benefit. It was as though a conspiracy was imploding in upon me.

This simple fact shattered the whole Warren *Report* into a thousand pieces.

Could this Oswald be a double? But then how to explain the same name and what Mrs Rivers told us? No, it was Lee Harvey Oswald himself all right. He was here in Hitchin when he should have been in Russia.

I needed a drink.

I walked down to the loos and went into a cubicle, sat down, took a couple of deep breaths and hit the white spirit. I closed my eyes and told myself that I was calm and tranquil and that everything could be explained (though I couldn't see how).

I went back in and up the steps to the reading room. The other volumes I had ordered were now leaning against the chair.

The first volume I picked up was the *Hitchin Pictorial* covering Alf Lawson's suicide. I soon found the coverage. It was a front page story:

THREW HIMSELF IN FRONT OF A TRAIN
Sad Death of Alf Lawson – Much Loved Local Figure

There was a photo of Alf taken 'on a recent outing he organised for Hitchin handicapped children to Great Yarmouth' and below that the story. But it was surprisingly scant on detail about the suicide itself. His body was found just to the south of the station at around 8.30 p.m. on Sunday,

24 November 1963. A passenger waiting at the station had noticed something on the tracks and had reported it to a Mr Wooley, a railway employee, who had investigated and found Lawson. The inquest was not told the name of the passenger. His local GP said something 'traumatic' had resulted in Mr Lawson having a physical and mental breakdown earlier that year, but details of the trauma were absent. Dr Edwin Goodyers-Hamilton, a 'Government [?] neurological specialist', said Lawson suffered from an acute 'persecution complex' and was 'deeply schizophrenic' though he admitted to the coroner that there was no history of this illness in Lawson's family. Verdict: suicide.

The rest of the article was taken up with quotes from friends, neighbours and local worthies expressing their shock and saying what a kind man he was, and a list of local charities that had benefited from his good works.

Nothing else.

The following week there was a report of the funeral and that was it. I hadn't known what I'd find, but I'd thought I'd find something. Some little detail or tell-tale clue. But there was nothing.

Nothing.

Exit Alf Lawson.

And now for *The Times*. 16 April 1949. The front page in those days never had any news on it. Just small ads, nothing else. I checked my notes and saw that *Palmer* had said page 3.

Page 3, here we are. Boy – just seven columns of nothing but news items aside from a couple of display ads in the bottom right hand corner – for Bourn-Vita and for Braithwaite's Screwcrete Piles ('for carrying Heavy Concentrated Loads in Deep Water'). News, news and more news.

There was more news on that one page than there is in the whole of *The Times* now (and no 'lifestyle' features either!). And that was just this page. The other pages were equally full. Acres of stuff.

I was beginning to give up the search, believing that *Palmer* had got it wrong, when I found a single paragraph at the very bottom of column 2. There was a small headline set in bold italic caps that were not much larger than the body-type:

KILLED BY TRAIN

and underneath:

Mr. Reginald L. Hine, 64, of Willianbury, near Hitchin, Hertfordshire, was killed when he fell in front of a train at Hitchin railway station on Thursday. He was the author of the "History of Hitchin" and "Hitchin Worthies," and also wrote "Confessions of an Uncommon Attorney." He was a partner in the Hitchin firm of Messrs. Hartley and Hine, solicitors. He leaves a widow and one married daughter.

And that was that.

What would the local paper reveal?

I put *The Times* down and picked up the broadsheet bound volume of the *Pictorial*. I leafed through the pages and found the Wednesday, 20 April 1949 issue. In the top right-hand corner of the front page were two headlines, one presaging what was to appear over the piece about Alf Lawson fourteen years later:

FLUNG HIMSELF IN FRONT OF TRAIN
REGINALD HINE'S TRAGIC DEATH

The article said Hine's death was 'unexpectedly sensational' and that he threw himself in front of a train at Hitchin station the previous Thursday. That would have been 14 April.

The inquest recorded a verdict of suicide.

Hine had driven to the station intending to board the 11.12 a.m. train to King's Cross and had purchased a ticket. He'd arrived early and sat talking to a friend on a bench by the refreshment room. As the slow train from Cambridge pulled in Hine raced across the platform and threw himself in front of it. The event was witnessed by many holiday-makers off for their Easter holiday.

The body was carried across the tracks and taken to the mortuary at Hitchin hospital where an inquest was held on Saturday under Mr F. G. Shillitoe, the coroner.

Reginald Hartley, Hine's former partner in the legal firm, identified the body. Hine had apparently left the partnership at the end of March.

Dr Howard Dimmere who had been his GP for the last thirteen years told the coroner he had treated Hine several times for 'threatened nervous breakdown', and that Hine had been depressed for some weeks past and was under treatment. It was on Dr Dimmere's advice that Hine had retired as a solicitor.

The last person to speak to Hine was Matthew Owen Bevan of Little Bury, Stotfold. He'd arrived at the station to meet some relatives and saw the 'deceased' leave his car. They had met on the platform and were 'talking normally' when Hine suddenly rushed across the platform and threw himself in front of the train.

Before recording his verdict Shillitoe said, 'A note was left for the coroner, which I do not propose to read because I do not see it could serve any useful purpose, but it does not leave me in any doubt as to the situation.'

I reread this last paragraph. Hine left a note for the coroner? Was that correct or did the paper get it wrong? The coroner? Admittedly, Hine probably knew Shillitoe, but why would he leave a note for him? Don't suicides usually leave notes for their wives, children, parents or other next of kin? No, the paper must have got that wrong. And, anyway, where was the note left? Or did Hine have it on him?

The note left the coroner in no doubt 'as to the situation'? Presumably Hine's intention to commit suicide. I wondered. But why did he not read it out? Surely it would have served the useful purpose of publicly establishing Hine's intention to commit suicide, if indeed that was the case? Coroners have considerable power and I think it is next to impossible to challenge their decisions unless, of course, one gets the verdict overturned, but this happened over forty years ago and there was a fat chance of doing anything about it now.

Would the note still be in existence somewhere? Possibly, but whoever had custody of it would probably not give it up.

The actual physical facts of Hine's suicide, unlike Lawson's or Dick's, seemed established beyond any doubt according to the paper.

And according to the GP he had been treating him for *thirteen* years for threatened nervous breakdowns, yet Hine had carried on work as a professional man in that time, written several books and innumerable essays and continued to be a family man and a well-respected Hitchin 'worthy'.

Something had triggered Hine to commit suicide, but what could that be? What was in the note?

A promising lead had again proved inconclusive and had spawned yet more questions.

This was like chasing will-o'-the-wisps.

CHAPTER EIGHT

FINDING AND SORTING PEPPER

'Identify.'
  'Bellerophon … 666B.'
  'Location?'
  'Capital.'
  'Proceed.'
  'A Previous Contact has been identified …'

I WAS UP EARLY and I decided to do something I hadn't done for ages – go jogging. So I dug out my old running suit and puffed and wheezed my way up to Parliament Hill and back. It's a great way of clearing your head.

Then I had a ten-minute snooze on the bed, got showered and made myself some coffee and toast.

It was time for Mr Pepper.

I took the list of telephone numbers out of the folder and decided to start with the residential numbers.

'Hello? Do I have the right number? I'm looking for a Mr Roy Pepper who used to live in Hitchin?'

'I think you've got the wrong number.'

And again.

'No Roy here. Sorry.'

And again.

'No, squire. Not here.'

Then it's a dozen calls and still no joy whatsoever. I

poured a large Russian coffee and thought for a moment if Mrs Rivers had got Great Yarmouth in Norfolk confused with Yarmouth on the Isle of Wight?

I resumed dialling.

More numbers.

More *No*s.

This is getting mind-shrinkingly boring and I'm beginning to give up all hope of finding him, and I'm only halfway through this list. Mmmm. I'll switch to the car hire and taxi firms in Great Yarmouth, see if my luck's any better there.

The best way to handle this I thought was just to say, 'Roy Pepper please,' and then hang up if I didn't get the right response. It was quicker and saved on the telephone bill. Here goes.

'You got the wrong number.'

'Who?'

'Sorry, never heard of him.'

'We got a Roy *Burroughs*.'

'Nobody here called that.'

'Never heard of him.'

'You misdialled.'

'Nothing to do with this firm.'

'Not here there ain't.'

And then: 'Hold on, he's in the garage. I'll call him.'

Pegasus Car Hire!

'Hello? Roy Pepper.'

'Mr Pepper, my name's Christopher Cornwell. You don't know me.'

'Yes?'

'You used to live in Hitchin, didn't you?'

'Yes, few years ago.'

'You used to work for Alf Lawson?'

There was a pause then, 'That's right. I started with him, in 1958, the August.'

Pepper sounded friendly, jovial and relaxed. He had a gentle voice with a faint trace of some rural inflexion.

'I saw Angela Rivers the other day and she said you were in Great Yarmouth somewhere. I tracked you down by calling all the local hire firms.'

Mentioning Mrs Rivers would, I hoped, give me some credibility and show that this was a 'friendly' approach.

'Angela, how is she these days? I haven't heard from her for ages.'

'She's fine. She's living in Baldock.'

'I'd heard she moved.'

'I'm doing some research on Hitchin in the 1950s and I was wondering if I could come up and have a chat with you some time? Perhaps we could go for a drink or something?'

'Fine. When were you thinking of?'

'This weekend some time? How are you fixed?'

'Hold on, let me just check the diary.'

I wondered what if anything he could tell us. He was friendly, apparently had a good memory, and he was semi-running the company with Alf Lawson. Would he remember anything about Oswald? About Drax? The Leys?

'Saturday's out, got a lot on. But how about Sunday?'

'That would be fine.'

'After lunch?'

'Sure. Give me your address.'

'It's "Casa Loma", Nevada Avenue. We've just moved. On the north side of Yarmouth, off the A149, the Caister road. On the right. A few minutes out.'

'Casa Loma', Nevada Avenue, Great Yarmouth, didn't strike me as the sort of house the hackettes at *The Observer* would be rushing to feature in the colour section. It sounded expensive bad taste, but Roy was happy there and sounded proud of it too.

'Great. We'll see you then.'

'Uh-huh. And your name again?'

'Christopher Cornwell.'

'Right, Christopher. Until Sunday. And bring Angela's address with you, I'd like to get in touch with her again.'

'I will. Bye.'

'Bye.'

This looked promising.

I spent the afternoon cleaning and tidying up the backyard and garden. I hadn't been out there for about six months or so and the place was a tip. I ended up with six black refuse sacks full of rubbish that I dumped out the front for collection the next day. Then I grilled a steak and sat down and watched *Seven Samurai* on the video and dozed off afterwards on the sofa.

When I awoke it was just after 9 p.m. and after making a Russian coffee I called Laura.

'How you doing, Laura?'

'Surviving. And you?'

'I was up early, went for a jog, cleared up the backyard, watched *Seven Samurai* and contacted Roy Pepper.'

'What an achiever! I got up, went to work, and came back. And now I'm going to bed.'

'Not bad.'

'You should try it some time.'

'I'm back on the treadmill on 22 November,' I said. 'Kennedy's anniversary.'

'Good.'

'Want to come on a day trip up to Great Yarmouth this Sunday?'

Laura thought for a moment. 'Why?'

'To see this guy Pepper. That's where he lives.'

'Oh, yes. I forgot. I haven't been there for years, since I was a child. That's where Mr Peggotty lived in a boat on the beach, isn't it?'

'Was it?' I couldn't remember.

'I think it is. Yes, sure – a day out at the seaside.'

'In October, yet!' I said.

'I like resorts off-season. You have them all to yourself.'

'Listen, I went up to the newspaper library yesterday and checked out that Lilli Palmer film at the Hermitage.'

'What did you find out?'

[246]

'The film's called *Conspiracy of Hearts* and it was on at the Hermitage … hold on … it was on there for … here it is – Thursday, 11 August, 1960, for three days. That was when Oswald was supposed to be in Russia. It was his "missing year" there. His first year out there.'

'Have you checked the Warren Commission on this?'

'Laura, I've checked everything. I had my notes. The official story was that he entered Russia in October 1959 and was there until June 1962 – the whole time. It's impossible he was in Hitchin, but he was.'

'I don't understand this.'

'Neither do I. It makes you think there's something really going on out there none of us know about.'

'Shouldn't we go to the papers with this?'

'I think we should, but after we've seen Roy Pepper. He might be able to help us.'

'I hope so.'

'What did he sound like?'

'Friendly, willing, helpful.'

'Good.'

'When I was at the library I also checked out Alf Lawson and Reginald Hine.'

'Anything of interest?'

'Nothing really on Lawson. Nothing beyond what his daughter told us really. Hine was a bit more intriguing.'

'They never talk about the suicide here,' said Laura.

'I know. He was sitting on the station talking normally to this guy, after he'd bought a ticket to London, then he suddenly got up, raced across the platform and threw himself in front of this train. There were lots of holiday-makers there who saw it.'

'How awful!'

'Yes. He'd apparently been treated by this doctor for thirteen years or so for "threatened nervous breakdowns". The doctor was at the inquest.'

'Thirteen years? A *threatened* nervous breakdown?' asked Laura.

'Yeah, threatened. Anyway, the paper said he left a note for the coroner, but they must have got that wrong. The coroner said the note left him in no doubt as to what happened yet he refused to read it out.'

Laura said, 'Coroners can do what they like.'

'I know. So that's that with Hine. I guess it is too late to reopen the case now?'

'It might be. Do you suppose Dick copied him?'

'I'm sure Dick didn't. I thought at one time maybe he did, but not any longer.'

'Why?'

I thought for a moment and realised I had no real reasons so I said, 'I don't know.'

'Are you coming up Saturday or Sunday?' Laura asked.

'It'll have to be Sunday morning, bright and early. The car is in for a service and a new starter motor Friday and Saturday.'

'Right. See you then.'

'Yes,' I said. 'About seven-thirtyish?'

'Yes. But we'll speak before then.'

'Of course. Goodnight.'

'Goodnight Christopher.'

I hung up, poured myself a large brandy and went to bed. I slept like a log.

[2]

It was a bright Sunday morning tempered by a cold inter-mittent wind. Winter was upon us. I had a clear run up to Hitchin and got there a little before 7.30 a.m. (The old Merc was running like new.)

Laura gave me a big long kiss on the lips and we stood in her doorway clasping each other over shouts from her daughters inside of 'Leave it out!' and 'How gross – at *your* age!' and giggles from assorted boyfriends. The young see love as their prerogative.

'How come the *Kinder* are up so early?' I said.

'They're not up early,' Laura replied, 'they're up *late*. They just came back from a party.'

'Oh.'

Laura was wearing an Aquascutum mac over a black top and leggings. Her lips were pinkish in colour and matched her painted nails. Her hair was pulled back severely and was held by a clasp that matched her lips and nails in colour.

She cuddled up to me in the car and at the top of Tilehouse Street as I finished turning around we necked some more (necking, as Laura explained, being her daughters' current buzz word).

We drove in silence holding hands out of the town and through Letchworth and on through and out of Baldock too.

The moment you leave Baldock on the Royston road the country opens wide. The land is now that gentle undulating chalkland that stretches as far as the eye can see. The sky is immense. It's at this point I've always felt East Anglia begins.

'I did a little investigating of my own,' said Laura as she put on her dark glasses.

'Oh, yeah. Find out anything?'

'My mother has a friend who knew Reginald Hine.'

'Really? I didn't know that.'

'Yes. She worked for him in the 1940s. His name is Geoffrey Hasler. He was a solicitor too.'

'With Hine?'

'No, he was with another firm, in London.'

'So there's still someone about who knew him?'

'Yes. There must be others too,' said Laura as she lit one of her More cigarettes.

'What did he tell you?'

'Well, a lot. Starting with – did you know that the day Hine died was the same day President Lincoln was shot? I've got it here.' Laura took out a notebook. '14 April? Did you know that? It was also the same day Handel died? It's Cuckoo Day too.'

'Is Hasler cuckoo?'

'That's what I was beginning to think,' laughed Laura. 'I was then expecting him to say that there was some occult connection between all these events. You know, the Masons or the Rosicrucians were behind them all. That sort of thing.'

'But he didn't?' I asked.

'No, thank God.'

There was a light rain now as we swept around Royston on the bypass that skirts an industrial estate that looks like the food production plant in *Soylent Green*.

'Hasler lives in this big house on the London Road,' Laura continued, 'and I told him he should will it to the National Trust.'

'Why?'

'Because the house is still in the mid-1930s. Nothing has ever changed in it since then – the furniture, the wallpaper, the Bakelite radios, the phonograph, the standard lamps and antimacassars. Time has stood still there. He doesn't even have a TV, or central heating. You could go in there tomorrow and shoot a period film. It's perfect.'

'What's he do now?'

'Not much, he's retired. He lives alone, aside from an elderly housekeeper. He's wealthy, I think.'

'So he knew Hine?'

'Yes. He met him before the war and they used to go on walks together around Hitchin. He was interested in local archaeology then and Hine, of course, knew a lot about that.'

'So he got to know him quite well?'

'Yes. He said Hine was always a bit manic-depressive but only mildly so and he often suffered from migraines too, but he'd learnt to live with it. He'd made accommodations with his condition and seemed to live a normal and full life in spite of them.'

'Did you mention this thing about being treated for threatened nervous breakdowns for thirteen years? The stuff in the paper?'

'Yes. He remembered reading about it at the time and it came as a shock to him. He said he wasn't that intimate with Hine but they did talk about personal matters from time to time. And Hine never ever said anything about being treated like that. As he said himself, you're not *threatened* with a breakdown for thirteen years, are you? You either have it or you don't.'

'Right.'

'He said there was a rumour going around the town after the suicide that Hine had done it because he had got involved with another woman.'

I'd never heard that before. 'Any truth in it?'

Laura said, 'Hasler didn't think so. You couldn't keep secrets like that in Hitchin. He said, however, that Hine confided to him that he was being followed shortly before he committed suicide.'

'Followed? Hine! By who?' I couldn't believe this.

'Hine thought it had something to do with a break-in at his offices when some papers relating to the Cauldwells were stolen.'

'Who are the Cauldwells?'

'Hold the steering-wheel tight and brace yourself.'

'Yeah.'

'The Cauldwells were the family who lived at The Leys.'

'Where Drax lived? The guy Dick knew?'

'Yes. The Leys.'

The Cauldwells, yes. I remembered it now. That old man with the dog had mentioned the name when I was mooching around up Shadwell Lane.

I was almost trembling. There were two suicides in Hitchin that had some connection with The Leys – Dick's and Hine's. I was sure Alf Lawson's had too, but we had yet to discover what that was. 'You didn't tell him what we knew about The Leys, did you?'

'No, I didn't, but I asked him what he knew about the place. He didn't seem to know much. The Cauldwells had built it in the 1870s or 1880s and had lived there for a couple of generations. They were bankers or something in the City of London. They built it there near the station so they could travel to and fro from London. The place was requisitioned during the war by the government and it should have been returned to the Cauldwells after the war. They wanted to pull it down and redevelop, but they never got it back. Hasler said the reason they didn't get it back was because of the papers that went missing. This break-in got Hine into a state and he thought he had let the Cauldwells down, said Hasler, and that was the reason, ultimately, he thought he committed suicide.'

'Do you believe that?'

'It's possible. There was obviously something going on.'

'Does Hasler?'

'Yes, he does. It's his way of making sense of it,' said Laura.

'Did Hasler know anything about what was going on there during the war?'

Laura replied, 'He said it was some secret planning project or something. He said nobody knew – the war was going on and people had other things to worry about.'

'Mmmmm. Did Hasler say what papers went missing?'

'No. He didn't know exactly, but amongst them would have been a contract between the Cauldwells and the government or whoever.'

'How could missing papers prevent the house being returned to the Cauldwells?'

'Very easily. A contract goes missing. That's all you've got to do. It isn't difficult. You could face years of litigation in order to get back what is rightfully yours.'

'Who ended up owning The Leys?'

'Hasler didn't know but he said if we were to write to the Land Registry they'd tell us.'

'Did you ask him about Drax?'

'He'd never heard of him.'

'What does this all mean?'

'It's tantalising and, ultimately, like everything else, inconclusive, isn't it?'

[252]

'Yes, and a long way from Dick's suicide.'

'Or nearer,' Laura whispered, 'and there's a connection, isn't there?'

We drove on, past the war museum at Duxford and out on to the A11 and then northwards, skirting Newmarket and its gloriously open heaths and then into Suffolk at Red Lodge.

We continued on up through the fir trees and sandy heaths of Breckland, through and not around Thetford (once the capital of the whole of East Anglia and now rather sad and overlooked, and also Tom Paine's birthplace), and up to the Norwich ring-road and then east along that on to the Yarmouth road which, after Acle, is virtually dead straight and level as it races across the partially reclaimed marshes to that jewel at the end of the East Anglian rainbow – Great Yarmouth.

The rain clouds were massing ominously and as we had a little time to spare I drove down to the front and parked facing the sea.

The sea air was salty and invigorating and we walked hand in hand down across the sand to the sea. Standing off the coast and shrouded in mist and spray were several North Sea oil rigs or platforms, looming up out of the waves like mechanised leviathans. We took a couple of photographs of each other (Laura had brought her camera) and then Laura stopped some elderly couple and got them to take pictures of us as we kissed, skipped and embraced on the beach.

We drove along the front which was surprisingly busy, though none of the fairgrounds, arcades or attractions seemed to be open, down to the southern tip of the spit and the Nelson monument which once arose triumphantly alone from the sand dunes but is now surrounded by an industrial estate. We took some more photos there and then drove back and out on to the Caister road. Beyond several caravan parks, now mothballed for winter, we eventually came to Nevada Avenue, a name that was a misnomer twice over. Nevada it wasn't, and neither was it an avenue. It was a treeless cul-de-sac of pricey modern one-storey ranchhouses as I think they are called (no, they're *not* bungalows!), built for people who think that when they switch *Dallas* on they're going to get a mega-dose of good taste. Laura said I was a hopeless snob. She may be right.

We pulled into the drive of 'Casa Loma', quite the largest house in the development. The wide pink forecourt to the house had enough room for a dozen or so cars. There was a garage with three up-and-over doors to it, street lamps hither and thither and partially hidden sod lamps at various angles to illuminate the place at night. The ranch-style fencing seemed to have been bought as a job lot and was placed everywhere.

'I particularly like the wishing well,' I said.

'It's the illuminated windmill on the rockery for me,' cooed Laura.

We got out of the car and walked across to the recessed front door that was situated beneath a curved stucco-effect entrance. There were Spanish tiles set into the floor.

The cold winds were coming straight off the North Sea and straight down Nevada Avenue. Leaves were being blown around in spirals. It was very chill.

There was a brass door pull. Laura pulled it out and it shot back in with a thud. There was a pause and then a whole peal of chimes sounded within the house. A poodle or some such dog yapped and then the door was opened by Roy Pepper himself.

'Come in. It's really nippy today. I'm Roy. You're Christopher.'

'And this is Laura.'

'Hello, Laura.'

'Mr Pepper ... Roy, hi.'

'Let me take your coats.'

Roy Pepper must have been in his mid- to late-fifties but he looked younger. He had a shock of white hair and a

[254]

chubby face though the rest of him was slim. He was wearing an open-necked Hawaiian shirt and a pair of light-coloured slacks. He had that bright, clean and well-scrubbed look that new-born babies have. His movements were fast and jerky, fussy almost.

We followed him through to a lounge that had large curved panoramic windows looking across to the dunes and the North Sea. The floors were tiled and littered with small rugs thrown here and there. There were several large sofas and wickerwork chairs and cushions. A thick slate at one end mounted on bricks painted white was the bar. There were dozens of bottles and glasses. The walls were covered with elaborately framed colour photographs of him and his wife and of weddings featuring his sons or daughters or whoever they were.

'Now be seated and I'll get you a drink. What would you like?'

Roy wasn't talking tea or coffee. He was poised at the bar.

Laura said, 'A lager for me, please.'

'And you, Christopher?'

'Vodka and whatever you've got.'

'Coming up,' said Roy as his dextrous fingers went to work mixing the drinks. I noticed he already had a Scotch on the go.

I could tell he was proud of this place so I said, 'Pretty smart place, Roy. Business been good?'

Laura whispered to me out of the corner of her mouth, 'You phoney.'

'Very good,' said Roy. 'The car hire's always been a good dependable little bread-and-butter business, but it's the bodyshops that have paid for all this.'

He waved his hand in the air in a theatrical gesture.

'I do mainly crash repairs and insurance work like that,' he continued. 'That's where the money is. I've got two shops here in Yarmouth and one in Gorleston and I'm just about to open another in Lowestoft. I'm turning work away. There's yours, Laura. And yours, Christopher.'

'Thanks,' said Laura.'

'Cheers,' I said.

Roy deposited himself in a wicker rocking chair opposite Laura and me on the sofa. He was a voluble character and this was always a great advantage when you needed information.

'You probably think this is all a bit loud,' he said as he waved his hand about again, 'but you'll have to take that up with the wife. I run the business and she runs it here. She doesn't have a say in how I run the company and I don't have a say in running here. It's a good recipe for a good marriage, I can tell you. Cheers.'

'Cheers.'

'Cheers.'

Laura put her glass down and asked Roy why he was in Great Yarmouth. One question to our Roy and he was off and running.

'Well, because this was where I was born and this was where I grew up. Pepper's an old East Anglian name. Plenty of them in Suffolk and Norfolk and we're all related!

'My dad was a trawlerman and he got washed overboard when I was two. My mum took me to live in Rutland during the war and we came back here in 1945. She was killed in a car crash in 1953 and I went to live with her sister who was a widow on a pension and lived in Hitchin, in Tristram Road. So I spent the next ten years there.

'Then when I decided to set up on my own, in car hire and chauffeuring and that, I thought there was only so much trade in Hitchin and I wanted to go where there was a growing market. So Yarmouth seemed the answer. I knew the place well and I had plenty of friends and contacts here so I came back. The wife and I were at school here together just after the war.'

'How long did you know Alf Lawson?' I asked.

'Alf? Let me see, I worked for him for about four years but I knew him long before that. I first met him when I was working at that little garage on Park Street that was run by

Henry Russell. I was a trainee mechanic and I often used to work on his cars when he couldn't do them himself. He was a good tipper, was Alf. Then I was a delivery van driver for a while and then I worked as a driver for a firm in Stevenage that did weddings and things. I used to see Alf in town from time to time and we always stayed in touch. Anyway, Alf didn't have any sons and he wanted someone to run the business for him so he could have more time to himself, so he asked me to go and work for him. That was the beginning of 1959. And I was with him right up until the end. Same again? I'm out.'

'Please,' I said, handing over my glass.

'I've still got some,' said Laura.

'He was a good bloke to work for, old Alf. And don't forget to give me Angela's address before you go, will you?'

'I won't,' I said.

'Good,' said Roy as he finished mixing the drinks and returning with them. 'Here you go.'

'Thanks,' I said. 'Cheers.'

'Cheers again,' echoed Roy.

Roy wasn't sparing on the vodka. I couldn't have mixed a more generous vodka and orange myself.

'Tell me,' I said, 'about Alf's suicide.'

'First of all,' Roy said, 'you tell me why you've driven all the way up here to see me. How's that for a fair exchange?'

'Fine,' I replied. 'It all starts with a friend of ours who allegedly committed suicide at Hitchin station.'

'Like Alf?' Roy suggested.

'Just like Alf. This friend sent me some photographs and a note just before he died and the note didn't explain anything. We eventually established that one of the people in the photos was Alf Lawson, and we thought you might know who the other person is … was.'

Roy thought for a moment and then said, 'Who are you two? What do you do?'

Laura replied. 'I'm a solicitor and Christopher works in the film industry as an art director. We grew up on Whinbush Road with Dick, our friend who committed suicide.'

'You're nothing to do with the police or the government are you?' responded Roy.

It was a strange question.

'Nothing whatsoever,' said Laura. 'Why?'

'Nothing at all,' I added. 'You could ask Mr and Mrs Draper. We grew up with their son, Briscoe. I mean Leonard.'

'I remember old man Draper. He was always getting involved in scraps,' said Roy.

'I think he's a bit too old for that now,' I replied.

'Probably is. So you've got some photographs you want me to look at?'

'Yes.' I took the photos out of the folder and passed them across to him. He looked at each one carefully, occasionally looking up at Laura and me. He went through them a second time and then said, 'I need another drink.'

He walked across to the bar and poured himself a large malt whisky and then returned to the rocking chair. He stared at the two of us and then after a lengthy pause said, 'That's Alf Lawson all right.'

'But who's the young man with him?' Laura asked.

Roy stared straight at Laura and said nothing for a few moments. Then he said, 'Who do *you* think he is?' His eyes switched to me and he repeated the question. Roy certainly knew something about the figure of Oswald. He knew this wasn't Joe Six-pack, but who did he think it was? What did he know?

I didn't know what to say. I didn't want to tell him a lie and I didn't want to lead him by telling the truth. I wanted Roy to tell us something independently.

Laura jumped into the silence. 'We think he's someone very important.'

'Very important?' said Roy.

'Internationally important,' Laura replied.

Roy and Laura stared at each other.

Laura outstared him and he lowered his eyes and said, 'What country would he be from then?'

'We know. Do you?' snapped Laura.

'America,' whispered Roy.

'We're talking about the same person then, aren't we Roy?' Laura said.

We were.

Roy looked through the photographs again, dwelling on each one, before saying slowly and quietly, 'He had a different name then.' The *then* seemed to resonate and linger. *Then*.

'What was that?' asked Laura.

'Alec Hidell. I always remember that because my wife's maiden name is Bidell and it rhymes with that. We were just courting then … long distance.'

Hidell …

When Oswald was arrested in Dallas he was carrying a forged identity card that bore the name 'Alek J. Hidell,' yet the attached photo was of Oswald himself. This was also the name Oswald allegedly used to order the Mannlicher-Carcano rifle, the assassination weapon, from Klein's Sporting Goods in Chicago, a mail order firearms outfit. There were other references to this name as well …

I thought it best not to mention any of this to Pepper as I didn't want to distract him from what he was telling us.

'So you met him then?' I said.

'Yes, I did. Several times over a couple of months while he was here. We were about the same age. We had the same interests. We went to a couple of dances, the cinema.'

'How many times did you meet him?' Laura asked.

'Four or five times, about that. Not any more I wouldn't have thought. The college didn't like their students mixing with the town at all so it was a bit difficult for him, you know?'

'What college?' said Laura.

'The place up on Shadwell Lane.'

'What place was that?' Laura asked.

'In the big old house up there on the left with the wall around it. *That* place. You'd soon find it. They put it about that it was this missionary college that sent missionaries all over the world but we all knew that was a load of guff. It was something to do with the government … it was.'

Roy was talking about The Leys. Laura and I exchanged glances.

'Yeah, so this was what they put about, that it was sending missionaries all over the place. There were always people coming and going and we never knew what was going on there. You used to get a lot of septics there though.'

'Septics?' said Laura.

'You know, septic *tanks* – Yanks. Rhyming slang. You had all those American bases up the road in those days in Norfolk and that and I suppose they had something to do with them. Lots of Yanks here then. The place was American, but you used to get a few snooty officer-type English there too.'

'You have no idea what was going on at the college?' Laura asked insistently.

'No idea. It was all hush-hush and we used to drive them about but nobody would ever talk about what went on. Alf probably knew a lot because he did all the driving for them. He only used me when we were double-booked. I didn't do that much.'

'Was that how you met Oswald?' I said.

'Yes. I had to drive him up to the American Embassy one day and that big PX around the corner, just off Grosvenor Square. We got chatting. It was a Saturday and I said I was going to a dance in Henlow and he asked if he could come.'

Laura asked him what Oswald revealed about himself.

'Well, not a lot. He was a friendly enough bloke and quite funny and always had plenty of money. He always stood his rounds, he did. Said he was an ex-Marine and he was studying or training for something. I never took much notice. Why should I? He was going to do some travelling as well. He'd been about quite a bit, all over the place. He'd been to more places than I'd read about.'

'Tell us about the college again,' I said.

'There's not much more to tell you than I have already. We didn't pay it any attention as long as they paid their bills regularly, which they did. You got different people booking cars all the time, but there was some bloke out there who was like an operations manager that Alf was matey with. A bloke with a military bearing who'd come by the office sometimes. Not at all friendly. Had a big scar down one side of his face.'

'Drax?' volunteered Laura.

'That's him. Yes. Drax. I've always had a block about his name. Very odd character. Kept himself to himself, though he had the odd drink with Alf.'

Laura said she wanted to know about the jobs they did for the college. Who did they take where?

'All over the place. You might take somebody up to the theatre in London and wait and bring them back. You'd even go down to London Airport or Southampton and meet someone off a plane or a boat, or they'd go to offices in London. It was pretty varied. Up to the bases in East Anglia and that. As I said, Alf did most of them ... but I've still got all the accounts books in the basement down at the garage. I could tell you every job Alf did and how much he charged. I keep everything. I never throw anything away. I brought all the books with me when I came back up here.'

'Could we see them?' Laura asked eagerly.

'This would really help us,' I added.

'You're welcome to look at them but you'll have to give me some time to sort them out. I've got about forty tea-chests and boxes full of stuff down there ... but one thing.'

'What's that?' said Laura.

'You leave me out of this. You don't mention me at all anywhere to anyone. OK? I want your word on that.'

Pepper said this with great seriousness.

We both agreed to his request.

'Now, I'll tell you for why. I never thought of Hidell again. Had no reason to. And Alf never spoke hardly at all about the place. He said it was hush-hush and the account there was too valuable to jeopardise. Then in the autumn of 1963 Alf starts going a bit loopy. A bit mental. But by then I'm virtually running the company by myself anyway. I had six full-time drivers and about ten part-timers and Alf only put his head in the door a couple of times a week. So he starts going a bit funny but the business is running smoothly.

'Oh, yeah, I forgot to tell you this. We stopped doing the work for the college at the end of 1962 because they decided to use their own people to do the work, though Alf went up there now and again to do private work for that bloke – what's his name?'

'Drax,' said Laura.

'Yes, Drax. So anyway, President Kennedy gets shot. I was sitting in the office, it was a Friday afternoon wasn't it, or the evening? I'm sitting there and I hear he's been shot on the radio and we all talk about it. Nobody can believe it. The next day I'm watching the telly at home – I was renting a little first floor flat then all by myself above a shop in Sun Street – and I'm watching the news on the telly and it's all about Kennedy and the police bring this bloke out they've arrested and I say to myself, Roy, old son, he looks familiar. But I couldn't place him. Then later that night when I saw some more news they were also showing these photos of Oswald and I said to myself – that ain't Lee Oswald, that's Alec Hidell. I know him!

'Well, I didn't think any more of it. They'd arrested him and he was guilty and that was that. The police and the FBI and all those people would investigate him and they'd know everything about him there was to know. What could I tell them? He never told me he was going to shoot anyone or do anyone any harm. So I forgot all about it.

[262]

'What I did think was odd was all this business about him being a communist and defecting to Russia. He never struck me as a communist. He was like, you know, a typical ex-Marine. All for Uncle Sam and that.

'Then he got shot himself! It was as hard to believe that as it was that Kennedy got shot.

'Anyway, I came up to Yarmouth to see Alice, the wife, though we were only engaged then, and I told her all about this and how I'd met Oswald and everything and she said I had to go to the police and tell them what I knew. I said I didn't know anything but she said I had to go anyway. So I did when I got back to Hitchin just to get her off my back.

'I went around the old nick and the copper at the desk showed me to a room out back and then Sidney Falks arrived. He was one of the inspectors, just about to retire. A big fat man from Yorkshire who'd come down south in the early 1930s. He liked a drink and a flutter on the horses. Nice chap. So I tell him what I know and he's really interested and then we do a statement and I sign it. It didn't say anything more than what I've told you. Sid was very interested and said he'd pass it on "upstairs" to the right people.

'I didn't think anything more about it. I'd forgotten all about it. Gone right out of mind. Then about a week or so later I'm in bed and it's about six in the morning. There's this heavy banging on the front door at the bottom of the stairs. Bang! Bang! I get out of bed and open the door and these four hefty guys in suits rush into the place and start tearing everything apart. They're looking for something. These two governors then come in and they're well-dressed and very smart and one of them flashes some card at me. I don't know what it said because you can imagine I was a bit confused by all this happening. They said they had a search warrant and I could be in serious trouble. Well, they didn't find anything of course! And God knows what they were looking for. They were just putting the frighteners on me. Then this elderly bloke comes in with a carnation in his overcoat and all the rest of them are Yes, Sir, No, Sir, to him. He's holding my statement in his hand, the one I gave to Sid Falks. And he says to me "Are you a communist, Mr Pepper?"

'Me, a communist? I just laughed, but it wasn't a real laugh. Just a nervous one.

'And he says he wants to know why I'm going around stirring up trouble, asking questions, saying things and telling lies?

'What lies? I wanted to know.

'He says that I'm stirring up trouble by saying that Lee Harvey Oswald was here in Hitchin when they all know he was in Russia then. He wants to know if I'm a secret communist agent or something trying to stir up trouble with the Yanks?

'I tell him I was just telling the truth and I'm not a communist.

'I get bundled in this car and driven up to London. They say they're from some security organisation and I'm in dead trouble for stirring up shit.

'I get taken in this room like a padded cell and left there for a couple of hours all by myself to stew. They told me I might spend years in this cell. Years. And nobody would ever know I was there.

'Then these two youngish guys come in and talk to me about my statement and wouldn't I agree I was mistaken? You know, it's really easy to make a mistake and I was free to go as soon as I signed this other statement saying the first statement was all a big joke and that and I didn't know what I was doing when I made it.

'I was scared out of my wits by then and signed it right away and they got a car to take me back to Hitchin.

'I was scared shitless by this and I've never spoken about it since, until now. It was, I suppose, one of the reasons I decided to leave Hitchin.'

Laura and I were both speechless. I finished the vodka

and sank back in the chair. Laura fumbled with one of her More cigarettes.

I gazed at the ceiling as I tried to take in all of what Roy had told us. I didn't know where to begin.

Laura puffed on her More and then said, 'Could you not get anyone to corroborate what you said about Oswald. Someone from a dance you went to or something?'

Roy looked up from his empty glass and then said after a pause, 'I don't think anyone I knew met him more than once. And don't forget it was a few years earlier. Nobody had any reason to think about him again during that time and when you see the assassin of the President of the United States on the telly you don't connect him with your own little town.'

He was right.

We would have to come back and talk to Roy again quite aside from having a look at Alf Lawson's books, but I had one further question for him now. 'Was there anything odd about Alf Lawson and his death?'

'I think there was but I don't think we'll ever find out. He went really loopy that year and was saying all sorts of mad things.'

'One of them was that President Kennedy was going to be killed,' I said.

'I know. He must have found out something. Something leaked out somehow. I don't know. But I'll tell you this, anything is possible. I wouldn't put anything past them. There are some really evil people in the world. They are capable of anything. Alf recognised Oswald all right on telly and that was when he finally snapped. He was a devout Catholic and if he felt in any way he was responsible ... or even the fact that he was associated with what had happened, I don't think he would have been able to live with himself. Well, he couldn't, could he?'

Laura said, 'Do you think he was pushed in front of the train?'

'I don't know. I think you can put people in a position

where they'll jump for you. Someone knows all about Alf but they'll never tell. I think you have to look in the direction of that bloke – what's his name?'

'Drax,' Laura said.

'Yeah, Drax. I've got some funny block about his name. Drax. And you've got the question too of who took your photographs of Alf and Alec, or Oswald. I'd put my money on Drax … I wonder what happened to him?'

'He died of cancer of the face in a hospice in Hitchin about a year ago,' Laura whispered.

'He did, did he? He stayed on, didn't he?'

'Stayed on? What do you mean?' I asked.

'The college was sort of shut down in early 1964 and I think they moved up to Cambridge somewhere, so I heard. It was a rumour. Drax and a couple of others stayed on. I think Drax was too old then to do much. I bumped into him once walking down Sun Street after all this happened. I was married then and we'd gone back to Hitchin for the weekend. Must have been about 1965. He stared straight through me. But he knew it was me. He knew it was me all right. No mistake.'

By now I was virtually catatonic. I was running through my mind everything that Roy had told us, trying to analyse it, weigh it up, fit it in with what I knew. Trying to see what the big picture was and how it related back to Oswald and who and what he was. And there, ultimately, was the question that hung over Dick's death. My friend, Dick North. My and Laura's friend, Dick North.

I was also trying to figure out where we were to go from here. What the next move should be. And where, finally, this would lead to. I was confused and, perhaps, frightened too.

[3]

I was in no state to sit behind the wheel of a vehicle and I asked Laura to take over. We drove in silence back to the front and then found a restaurant in a side street that was open and had a promising menu tacked up on the window. The place was empty apart from us. Laura ordered the lasagne and I settled for a double cheeseburger with French fries. I also ordered a bottle of Pellegrino.

'It's been an interesting day so far,' quipped Laura in a coy matter-of-fact manner.

'Quite enough for me,' I replied. 'I couldn't handle any more. This burger's really good.'

'I don't know how you can eat that.'

'It's good beef. It's delicious. Much better than you'd think, for a little place like this.'

Laura had some sorbet and I had a cassata and then the Italian waiter brought two espressos.

Laura offered me one of her Mores and I lit up and said, 'So what's the next step? What's your counsel?'

Laura drew on her cigarette and exhaled and then said, 'Well, we've got a good witness with a great story who'd impress a jury with his honesty and candour, but he won't testify. So that's a problem. A very big problem.'

'What do we do then?'

'We've got to play it by ear for the time being. If we want to find out more about the college we'll have to bear with him until he digs the books out, but I'm not sure what they'll tell us.'

'A lot, I think. They'll tell us who they picked up and where they took them. We'll be able to build up a picture of what was going on there … to a degree anyway.'

'Then what?' said Laura.

'I don't know. Go to the papers perhaps? We'll have to see.'

Laura sighed and wistfully said, 'It's a pity life isn't like a Jeffrey Archer novel.'

'What, you mean preposterous?'

'No, I mean all the answers are delivered at the end, like in *Perry Mason* on TV. It ends with all the questions being answered. All the loose ends tied up. I'm not very sanguine

about our chances of coming up with *all* the answers ...
with any answers.'

'But we've got to try,' I said. 'We might come up with
some.'

'I know that, but we're working in a narrow field. We're
burrowing away at a footnote in a much larger mystery –
the Kennedy assassination. You're not going to answer *this*
until you answer *that*, and the truth of it all is receding at
an ever faster rate. It's like that thing cosmologists talk
about.'

'What thing?'

'The Red Shift is it? No, that's to do with wavelengths or
something. Some term they use to talk about the expand-
ing universe.'

I looked into the remaining froth of my espresso and I
reluctantly agreed. The big mystery hadn't been solved
and this little mystery wouldn't be until that was.

'Who do you suppose turned Roy over at his flat?' I
said.

'Could have been any one of a dozen outfits. MI5, MI6,
military intelligence, some super-secret Whitehall operation.
Take your pick. Exactly who they were doesn't really
matter, the fact that this happened is the important thing.
Who it was comes later.'

'You're right,' I said. 'Shall we go?'

'Let's.'

I got the bill and settled it with my VISA whilst Laura
left some change for the tip. We walked out and into a
seriously cold wind that was fresh off the North Sea.

'Are you driving or am I?' asked Laura.

'You mind if I drive now?'

'No,' replied Laura.

I backed down the street and out on to the front. I drove
along and took a left at what I thought would lead us out
of town but I soon found we were going down a one-way
system in a part of town that didn't look familiar. I continued and took a couple more lefts in what I hoped was the

right direction for the Norwich road. It wasn't. It led south.

I was just about to swing another left when Laura said, 'You've already been down there.'

I took a right instead and continued. Then ahead of me I saw that massive Yarmouth parish church and I knew where I was.

'We're being followed,' Laura said quietly.

I looked in the rear-view mirror. There was a car behind us all right, but wasn't there always when you were in a town?

I shot a glance at Laura who was staring into the wing mirror. I continued up the dual carriageway towards the main road out of town.

'They've been following us since the seafront.'

Since the seafront?

'How do you know?' I said.

'Because I've been watching them in the mirror here.'

'The police? None of my lights are defective or anything.'

'I shouldn't think so. It's a BMW.'

I looked in the rear-view mirror again. It was still light enough to see that Laura was right. A black BMW.

'Following us, eh?' I echoed.

'Uh-huh,' said Laura.

'It figures, but we're not absolutely sure, are we?'

'Test it out then.'

'Test it out? What do you mean?'

'Keep going around this roundabout and go back down the road we just came up.'

The idea of being followed was scary and to disprove Laura's contention and put my mind at ease I did as she said. I kept going around the roundabout and then took the turning we had just come up. The BMW stuck behind us like glue.

I accelerated down to the next roundabout, circled around it and came back up the way I had just come. The BMW was still there.

'They may not know we know we're being followed,' said Laura. 'Particularly after all that messing about earlier in the centre of town.'

I continued on and the BMW stayed dutifully behind me.

I looked in the mirror again and saw the car cornering out of a junction to follow me. It wasn't a big BMW, just a mid-range model.

I was now heading down the long flat and straight A47 towards Norwich. The marshes fell away to the left and right and were criss-crossed with ditches, dykes and pools. Mist was gathering in pockets some distance off. The light was now beginning to fade. I turned my side-lights on.

'Why don't you pull into that lay-by there?' suggested Laura. 'Let's see what they do.'

I wasn't sure I wanted to see what they'd do but at the same time I was getting irritated and uptight, and paranoid.

I indicated left and slowed down and then pulled off the road, coming to a gentle halt at the end of the lay-by. The BMW had stopped some distance back, short of the lay-by. None of its lights were on. We waited.

'Doesn't look like anything's going to happen … does it, Laura?'

'No. Let's get going.'

I took my foot off the brake, gently depressed the accelerator and indicated right as I pulled out and re-joined the road. I was doing a comfortable 50 m.p.h. now. I looked in the mirror and there was the BMW keeping up with me.

Some distance ahead of us, perhaps a mile or more, I could see one or two oncoming cars, or the lights may have been a wayside house or even a barge on the waterways. It was hard to tell through the gathering mist. There was nothing behind me after the BMW. The road was deserted.

The BMW seemed to be slowly gaining on me so I increased my speed accordingly and I was soon doing an easy 70 m.p.h. Then, while I was looking in the mirror, it shot forward to overtake me. At least I thought it was going to overtake, but it didn't. It came up alongside and stayed there, not much more than three feet away.

'God, what are they doing?' shrieked Laura.

I glanced quickly across at the car and saw that there were two guys in the front. They were both in their mid- to late twenties, with short hair and brightly coloured shirts. Neither of them appeared to be wearing seat-belts.

I upped my speed gently to 90 m.p.h. They increased their speed accordingly so they still remained abreast.

What were they going to do? Was their front passenger window going to roll down and a shotgun appear, just as they do in the movies? Or what?

We could only wait.

I dropped back down to 70 m.p.h.

They followed.

I went down to 60 m.p.h.

So did they.

I looked across again. The passenger in the front seat was grinning and shaking his index finger back and forth as if to say, you naughty boy. He looked an evil bastard all right. A thug.

Was all this just to put the frighteners on us or was there something more serious intended? I wanted them to make a move and they did, right there and then.

The BMW edged over until there wasn't much more than a dozen inches between us, then it edged closer still, then it hit me broadsides and there was a metallic scraping sound. It hit me and immediately pulled off. Then it hit me again. It was trying to force us off the road and down the embankment into the dank ditches of the marsh.

It hit again and the Merc shuddered but kept straight on. I was gripping the steering-wheel and correcting each slam which sent scary judders down each of my tensioned arms.

These two spivs had made one very serious under-estimation. Their mid-range BMW was no match for this Merc. The Merc wasn't only a lot bigger, it was a lot more solid. The thing was built like a Panzer tank. Its momentum kept it on track.

Laura was clutching my arm, terrified. I told her we'd soon be out of this. That no harm was going to come to us. But I wasn't so sure.

What options were open to me?

The 6.9 litre engine could soon get me up to 150 m.p.h. but this wasn't the sort of road you'd want to do those speeds on. It wasn't a motorway and when you're going that fast anything can happen.

What about ramming them?

I looked at the speedo. I was now doing 75 m.p.h. I fell back to 60 m.p.h. and they followed. Then they went into me again. It was the biggest whack so far and there was a God-almighty crashing sound of metal against metal. They were getting impatient. The Merc shuddered and seemed to crab slightly to the left. I glanced to my right and saw that the BMW had come off worse. It was wobbling to the left and right. The driver appeared to have some temporary difficulty correcting the steering.

'Laura – you got your seat-belt on?'

'Yes.'

'Hold tight.'

I edged our speed up incrementally. 70 m.p.h. 80 m.p.h. They followed. I wanted them to think that I was frightened and panicking. 90 m.p.h. And now 100 m.p.h. They kept up with me but increased the distance between us. This speed had made even them cautious about ramming.

I took my foot off the accelerator now and pushed it down on the brake so we rapidly dropped in speed down to about 30 m.p.h. The BMW shot ahead of us and only started to slow when the driver realised we had fallen back. I came to a rapid halt. The BMW came to a halt a few seconds later, and then I kicked down the accelerator the full whack and now there was a mighty roar as the 6.9 litre engine powered-up. The power sped through the transmission and hit the wheels which screamed over the road's surface. We were pushed back in the seats as the vehicle shot forward.

There was the BMW ahead of us, stationary on the right-hand side of the road at an angle, the back projecting slightly into the road.

The two guys had no time to wonder what we were doing before the Merc battered into the angled inside rear of their vehicle at a little over 50 m.p.h. The Merc's momentum carried it forward without so much as a blink and the BMW shot forward and then off to the side amid a din of collapsing metal.

Laura was looking back as we sped ahead. 'It's gone off the road! Off the road!'

I sped ahead with my foot down. We were now doing 90 m.p.h. I wanted to get out of there fast.

Neither of us said anything until we got to Acle, the first village at the end of the marshes.

Laura was shaking but she still had her wits about her. 'We've got to report this.'

I'd been thinking that I'd race back to London and get Dennis the Greek and his bodyshop mates in Camden Town to do a quick repair job on the Merc and nobody would ever know anything about it. It would never have happened. But I guess she was right.

We found the tiny police station in the village and I made a statement that fudged slightly what happened at the end. Laura made one too and they seemed mightily impressed she was a solicitor. A patrol car radioed in that they had found the BMW half-submerged in a ditch but there were no signs of the 'kids' who had been driving it, the joy-riders. There had been an attempt to torch the vehicle but only the interior was burnt.

We learnt that the vehicle had been stolen from Lowestoft earlier in the day.

We drove down to Norwich and checked into a small hotel near the cathedral. Neither one of us could face the journey back. We went straight to bed and sleep, in each other's arms. Not even the possibilities arising from the incident on the A47 would conspire to keep us awake. I awoke just after 8 a.m. Laura was still asleep in my arms. The sky was bright blue and cloudless. A shaft of sunlight penetrated the room through the gap in the heavy curtains.

Yesterday.

It didn't seem like yesterday. It seemed like some mythic day only half-remembered from a distant age. There was an unreality about it. Dreamtime.

Laura slowly awoke some time later, saw me looking at her and then she kissed me on the lips and smiled. She stretched and yawned and said, 'What a beautiful day!'

It was.

I pulled Laura closer towards me and kissed her. She arched her body forward and put her arms around me. I ran my hands down her back and over her hips and down her legs. There was a warm firmness to her body that excited me. She was whispering my name into my ear. We both wanted each other there and then. I parted her legs and touched her wetness and entered her.

'I've entered you, Laura. Entered you.'

I was looking into her eyes as I said that.

'You haven't entered me. I've *engulfed* you!'

We made love, we fucked, and we screwed and afterwards, as we lay in each other's arms, Laura said, 'I always knew that would happen one day, I really did.'

'But it took a long time.'

'You always have to wait for good things.'

Good things.

There was a warmth and completeness within me now that I hadn't felt for fifteen years or so.

We got down for breakfast just as the last orders were being taken. Laura had croissant and muesli and fruit juice. I had croissant, bacon, mushrooms, tomatoes, fried bread and coffee. Afterwards we checked out and wandered down the street to the Merc. Every panel on the driver's side would have to be replaced. The horizontal scoring and dents ran the whole length of the vehicle. It looked as though the car had brushed up against a First World War tank with a flail attachment. Surprisingly, the twin chrome bumpers at the front had taken most of the impact when I had rammed the BMW and the headlamps and indicator assembly were untouched. But there was a buckle in the bonnet.

We walked around Norwich cathedral and looked at the statue of Sir Thomas Browne and then drove leisurely back to Hitchin holding hands.

When you're in love the rest of life becomes incidental. I got back to Tufnell Park a little after 10 p.m. There was a message on the answering machine from Thom Hyde asking me to call him – urgently. First I dialled Laura.

'Laura, hi. I just got in.'

'Good. Thanks for calling me. You're all right?'

'Fine. And you?'

'Fine. I did enjoy today so much.'

'I did too.'

'And remember what I said. Think about it.'

'I will. I'll call you tomorrow.'

'Goodnight.'

'Goodnight, my sweet.'

I did remember what Laura had said. She said I should move in with her. And what did I say? Give me some time to think. I want to, but give me some time. I must have sounded like some coy virgin. Laura said you've had enough time. You've had over thirty years! What do I need time for? Don't I know what I want to do? Why the hesitancy? I dialled her again.

'Laura? It's me again.'

'Chris.'

'Put my shyness down to not being used to such fabulous offers. Give me a couple of weeks or so to sort down here out and I'll be with you.'

'We'll be happy. You'll see.'

'I know. I never doubted that. I'll talk to you tomorrow.'

'Good.'

'Till then.'

'All my love.'

I phoned Thom at home. It sounded like there was a party going on in the background. We exchanged politenesses.

'You were going to start on 22 November. Right, Chris?'

'Right.'

'Can you do a few days this week and next week before that commencement date? Out at Pinewood?'

'Sure. No problem.'

22 November.

The day Kennedy was shot.

CHAPTER NINE

IN AN UNDERGROUND DARKLY

'Identify.'
   'Bellerophon … 666B.'
   'Location?'
   'Capital.'
   'Proceed.'
   'LANCER grail secured and safe. SUSURRUS shut-down anticipated within forty-eight hours.'
   'Stand by.'

I HAD HOPED TO GET AWAY from Pinewood early but it was just after 9 p.m. when the meeting ended. Thom and the director wandered off to the bar and I stayed behind in the office filing my sketches in the plan chest and keyboarding some notes on my laptop. Thom seemed surprised that I didn't want a drink and, with a shit-eating grin on my face, I told him that I was on the wagon and hadn't touched a drop in over a week. He looked at me incredulously.

Just before I was about to leave I phoned Laura. I was looking forward to the weekend with her.

   'Hi!'

   'Hi, Christopher.'

   'I'm just leaving. It went on later than I thought. Sorry.'

   'That's OK. What time do you think you'll get here?'

'M25 shouldn't be too bad at this time. Little over an hour, say.'

'Good. I've cooked lasagne.'

'I can't wait.'

'Did you get hold of Roy Pepper?'

'I tried him a couple of times at the office this morning, but he was out. I didn't get a chance this afternoon.'

'Call him over the weekend.'

'I'll do that.'

'See you soon. A big kiss.'

'A big kiss to you too.'

My address book was open in front of me on the desk. I turned to the end of the P section and found Pepper's name and home address and two phone numbers, office and home. I'd give him a quick shot now before I left.

I dialled the ten digits on the push-button phone. There was a silence and then a click before the number started ringing.

It rang for about forty-five seconds before a voice said, 'Hello?' It was Roy Pepper.

'Hello, Roy. It's Chris Cornwell.'

'Mr Pepper here. Can I help you?'

'It's Chris Cornwell, Roy.'

'Mr Pepper here. Can I help you?' The voice wasn't that of the buoyant and matey Roy we'd met that Sunday afternoon a couple of weeks ago. No, this was cold and formal.

'Roy, it's Chris Cornwell. Can you hear me?'

'Chris who?'

'Chris Cornwell.'

'How can I help you, Mr Cornwell?'

How can I help you, Mr Cornwell? What's this jerk playing at?

'We came and saw you a couple of Sundays ago. We spoke about Hitchin. Remember?'

'I'm sorry, Mr Cornwell. But I think you must be mistaking me for someone else.'

[278]

'I'm not fucking mistaking you for anyone!'

And with that he hung up.

I immediately pressed the recall button on the phone. It rang again. And it kept ringing for what seemed like well over a minute. Then it answered. Pepper's voice again: 'Hello?'

I said, 'Now listen to me very carefully, pal. I came up and saw you the other day and we talked about Alf Lawson and certain other things. Now I don't know why you're denying this, but let me tell you something – you're not going to get out of this that easily. You're not going to fob me off, OK?'

There was a pause and then he said, 'I'm sorry, but I think there's been a mistake.'

'There's been no fucking mistake at all! You were going to dig out those account books of Alf Lawson's and *those* are what I want. Got that? Do you understand me?'

Pepper's voice now had a slight tremor in it. 'I'm going to hang up now ... and I'd advise you not to call me again.'

I was losing my patience and I didn't want him to think I was going to go doggo on this. 'I want those books and I'm going to be on your ass till I get them, understand? Somebody might have got at you, but I'm going to get at you even more!'

He hung up.

Pepper had been got at all right.

I strode out to the Audi Thom had loaned me (while the Merc was being repaired by Dennis the Greek) and shot out of the studios at some speed. I was angry and uptight. I wanted to have it out with Pepper there and then. I'd drive all the way up to fucking Great Yarmouth now and show him I meant business if I had to.

By the time I got on to the M25 I'd calmed down and regained my equilibrium. Pepper had been leant upon, that's for sure. But by who? I kept returning to that question and the question of the two yobs who tried to force us off the road. Was there a connection? It seemed to me there had to be.

Pepper didn't strike me as the type of guy who would do a volte-face on his own. He seemed somebody who knew his own mind and would keep to any decision he made. There were outside influences at work all right. Somebody had leant on him in no uncertain way and done a pretty good job. Pepper wasn't going to do any more talking, much less let me have Alf Lawson's account books if, indeed, they were still in existence now. This avenue of research had come to a halt in a cul-de-sac as real as fucking Nevada Avenue. No way out except back the way you came.

Now, let me get this straight. Some time in the last two weeks since we were up in Yarmouth, Pepper had been got at. How did they know he had to be leant upon? How did they know he had to be talked to?

I knew we were going up to see Pepper and so did Laura, but neither one of us discussed this with anyone else. Who else knew about the trip? Yeah, Angela Rivers knew we'd contact him, and by extension Mr and Mrs Draper and Briscoe, possibly, would know too. But can I see any of those snitching on us? I can't. And who to?

Who does that leave?

That's the wrong question. The question is: what does that leave?

The telephone.

Could my phone really be tapped?

I can't see any other logical explanation. I'd said to Laura at the beginning of the year, after I received the photos, that we shouldn't say anything on the phone just in case someone was listening, and we hadn't – for a few days. But custom reasserts itself. We were soon talking freely again down the lines.

OK, if the phone is being tapped and that's how they got on to us visiting Pepper, why wasn't he visited before we got up there so we didn't learn anything from him? Surely that would be the logical thing to do? Why visit him *after* we'd seen him?

That question vexed me as I drove up Ridge Hill and

down to the turn-off from the M25 to the A1(M). As I was going northwards through the Hatfield Tunnel a possible explanation suddenly erupted in my mind. Could it be that they, whoever they are, didn't know, either generally or exactly, what Pepper was going to say to us? It was only afterwards that they did?

But, if that's true, how did they find out? Laura and I haven't discussed it on the phone and Pepper wasn't going to talk about it to anyone. That's for sure. How did they know?

Another thing. If what I'm thinking is true, then the people who visited Pepper now are not the people who visited him then, after the assassination.

And that's even more chilling.

And where do the yobs in the BMW fit in? What was that all about?

No matter how I looked at this jigsaw puzzle I couldn't get all the pieces to fit. There was always something left over.

I took the Hitchin turn-off and belted down the dual carriageway at a solid 80 m.p.h. I drove down Hitchin hill, Park Street, and parked the Audi on the left just short of the old London Transport bus garage at the foot of the hill.

I got my bags out the back, locked it with the remote, and walked up Bridge Street into Tilehouse Street and to Laura's.

'Mum's in the loo,' said Lucy after she opened the front door and before she rushed back upstairs. I put my bags down in the hall, took out the presents I'd got for Laura, and went through to the kitchen.

Laura walked in and threw her arms around me and we kissed and hugged. I held her waist and pulled her towards me and ran my hands down over her buttocks. She was wearing that black kimono again with the dragon em-broidered upon it and nothing underneath. Her body felt warm and yielding.

'I want you, Christopher,' Laura whispered.

'I want you too, like I've never ever wanted anyone else!'

'And you shall have me ... however you want. But first you've got to eat your lasagne!'

'You got a deal, beautiful.'

'Sit down then.'

I went back to the table and took the two wrapped gifts and said, 'Here you are – for you.'

'It isn't my birthday or anything!'

I'd bought Laura a couple of Carmen McRae CDs and one of those large gift baskets from the Body Shop that contained emollients, unguents, soap, lip salve and God-knows what else, everything in fact except a spermicide. It was the biggest basket I could find.

'Fabulous!' said Laura.

'The Body Shop thing was a bit of a soft option. I never really know what to get women.'

'It's great. And Carmen McRae too!'

We kissed and hugged again and then Laura sat me down as she prepared the lasagne from the oven.

She sat opposite me and we started eating while playing footsie under the table.

'Would you like some wine?' asked Laura.

'No, I'm fine. Thanks,' I said. Then I remembered. 'In fact I haven't had a drink of any kind for over a week.'

Laura looked at me sceptically.

'No, really,' I said. 'Not a drop of anything. I absolutely promise you. Truly.'

'Truly?'

'Really.'

'Good, but you're permitted a glass of white wine with a meal when you're here.'

'I'll pass.'

'OK, but I'm going to have one.'

The lasagne was perfect and I asked for seconds. I also asked for seconds of the garlic and cheese bread.

I told Laura about the phone call to Pepper and what

had been going through my mind on the drive up. What did she think about it? How could she explain it?

'When something odd like this happens – you don't mind if I have a cigarette while you're still eating? Thanks. When something odd like this happens there's either a really mundane and ordinary reason, or something's gone on you'd never be able to fathom in a million years given what you know.'

'So what's the mundane reason?' I asked.

'There are several. He did have second thoughts. He awoke in a sweat in the middle of the night and thought of his family and everything he'd built up, that's one. His wife could have had a go at him and laid the law down. That's two.'

'And three?'

'You've already arrived at three. That's him being visited,' said Laura as she drew on her cigarette.

'You call that mundane and ordinary?'

'It's a reason that's mundane and ordinary, though the event itself may not have been.'

'What about the unfathomable?'

'We don't know. That's why it's unfathomable.'

'OK. Pepper didn't strike me as the sort of guy who'd go back on his word once his mind was made up.'

'He didn't me either,' said Laura, 'but we're basing our assessment of him on a meeting that didn't last much longer than an hour or so. We could both be wrong.'

'I don't think we are.'

'But we could be. The man could be a joker, a con man, for all we know.'

'I don't think so. He was visited.'

'Who by?'

'If we knew the answer to that we'd almost be home and dry, wouldn't we?'

'Or dead,' said Laura.

'Don't say things like that, Laura.' It's one thing for me to think things like that but it's another for Laura to say it.

SIXTY-THREE CLOSURE

I'm paranoid and I'm entitled to think like that, but when Laura voices it the thing takes on an objective existence. And that makes me nervous.

Laura laughed. 'You get so serious at times!'

'I'm not getting serious. It's just that I think there are some things one shouldn't say. Talk of war breeds war, you know?'

'If you say so. Would you like some sorbet or some cheese or both?'

'Sorbet would be OK, thanks.'

Laura took the dishes away and I said, 'Leave them in the sink. I'll do them in the morning.' Laura was going with the girls to Cambridge tomorrow. I was going to stay here and sketch out some more set designs. The washing up wouldn't take long. As my grandmother always used to say – A little help is worth a lot of sympathy.

I asked Laura how she thought they had got on to Pepper and whether my phone, our phones, were tapped.

Laura lit another cigarette. 'We should assume they are.'

'I was hoping you wouldn't say that.'

'I'm not saying they are, I'm just saying we should *assume* they are. That's all. We don't even have facts to speculate on. We don't know what's going on.'

'You can say that again.'

'Let's go to bed,' said Laura.

'A good idea.'

I followed her up the stairs and into the bedroom.

Laura put one of the Carmen McRae CDs on the player by her bed and turned the volume low. The lights were low too.

We made love slowly and deeply and we were one. And after, as exhaustion and fulfilment gradually gave away to sleep, I felt tears in my eyes.

I was being shaken. My head was going from side to side. Somebody was saying something. Sleep was coming to an end abruptly.

I opened my eyes and focused on a figure. It was Laura

leaning over me. She was dressed in her suede coat with a scarf and a woollen hat.

Lucy was standing beside her and saying, 'Let's throw some water over him!'

'We're off now, Christopher,' Laura whispered.

'Off?'

'Yes. It's 9.30. You wanted waking.'

'Oh, yeah. Thanks.'

I sat up in bed and rubbed my eyes. Laura bent towards me and kissed me on the lips.

'Erhhhh! How can you kiss him when he hasn't cleaned his teeth!' shrieked Lucy.

Laura stared into my eyes and said, 'I'll see you this evening.'

'Right. Have a good day and drive carefully,' I said.

'I will.'

I squeezed her hand and she left the room waving goodbye to me. I got down under the duvet and heard the thud of the closing front door.

It was warm and secure and I could still smell Laura under the bedclothes. I dozed fitfully for twenty minutes or so and then sprang from the bed. I grabbed my bathrobe and went down to the kitchen. The TV was on, showing a rerun of *Sesame Street* or something similar. I put the kettle on and made a cup of strong decaffeinated instant coffee. I sat down at the table and took a More cigarette from a half-empty packet that was next to the white wine Laura was drinking last night. I lit it and gazed out of the window. Though there was a cloudless sky and bright sunshine it was a cold day outside. It was coldish in the house too.

I thought of my life as an hourglass and how when you're young there's so much sand in the top you never worry about it being exhausted. You've got a million years ahead of you. Life will last for ever. Then you get to your fortieth birthday and there are intimations of mortality. You know you're not a permanent fixture in the cosmos.

At my age there is more sand in the lower chamber than in the upper. It stands to reason, unless I'm going to live to my mid-nineties or so.

All this time and where am I?

I've come home to Hitchin, finally.

And I'm happy.

I thought of Laura and a couple of tears appeared in the corner of my eyes and ran down my cheeks.

What I was looking for all that time was here in Hitchin … and I knew her all the time.

Laura.

Even her name had become something that enthralled me. Laur-ra. Laur-ra. A feminine form of the Latin name Laurus, meaning 'Laurel'. I'd looked it up in my Oxford *Dictionary of First Names.*

I tore a sheet from the kitchen roll, wiped my eyes and blew my nose. I mustn't sit here getting maudlin, getting sentimental. I finished the cigarette and the coffee and gathered the washing up together and did it all in about twenty minutes. I tidied the rest of the kitchen up and mopped the floor. The room looked neat. In fact, I'd do my work in here.

While I was in the shower I started thinking about the conversation last night with Pepper. It made me angry and frustrated again. I thought of phoning him now but I sensed this would serve no useful purpose. It would be bad timing. Don't make a move when you're angry – it'll invariably be the wrong one.

I got dressed and went downstairs. Boy, the house was quiet when everyone was out. I took my work bag and portfolio into the kitchen and unpacked the pads and pens. I read through my notes and started to think about ideas for the night-club scenes.

I didn't think for long before I decided I needed another cup of coffee before I really got started. Then I decided I needed a cigarette before I actually got started, so I took one of Laura's Mores and lit up. I remembered that famous reply some American writer gave an interviewer who asked him how he began work on a new novel. The writer was silent for a moment and then said, 'First I defrost the fridge.'

Perhaps that's what I should do.

I tried to concentrate on the night-club set, but I couldn't. I was restless and I couldn't do it right now. What I needed was some fresh air, a stroll.

I'd walk up to Market Square and get the paper. I'll be OK then. Yes. A stroll. Some fresh air.

I grabbed the dark green Berghaus anorak I'd found earlier that week in the office at Pinewood (Thom said I could keep it), made sure I'd got my keys, and stepped out on to the street, making sure the door was closed behind me.

[2]

It was cold all right and when I looked up I could see gathering rain clouds. I zipped up the anorak and crossed the road diagonally, arriving on the corner of Bucklersbury.

Tilehouse Street was virtually deserted but Bucklersbury was crowded with people coming and going and spilling on to the road to the irritation of the motorists who were reduced to a crawl.

Heavy metal music was blasting out of the music shop on the right and a knot of metallers in decorated black leather jackets were on the pavement animatedly talking about gigs past and future. I continued on, past the bookshop (making a note to call in on the way back), and to the square. I picked up a copy of the *Indie* and the current *Private Eye* from Martin's there and then crossed the square in the direction of Sun Street to walk back that way, but then I changed my mind and decided to wander down by St Mary's to the market stalls and have a look around. There used to be a guy there who always had a fabulous selection of cheeses. I'd see if he was still there, see what else was going on.

I was thinking and cursing Roy Pepper as I walked by Halsey's shop in Church Passage, trying to figure out what I could do now, when it occurred to me that there was something I could do and I could do right now, though it wasn't directly related to Pepper, just incidentally related. Why didn't I go up and check out The Leys properly? Sure, I'd walked around the place but I hadn't been inside. There might be something I could discover. Who knows what was in there? I could scale up one of those trees and drop down the other side of the wall, no problem. A piece of cake.

Then an inner voice said, you're not prepared, you're not psyched-up for it.

That little inner negative voice that always rains on my parade.

OK, then. What do I need to check the place out? A full SAS assault kit? Huh? No. All I need is a torch, some adhesive tape should I have to break a window, and a good solid screwdriver or crowbar in case I have to force anything. That's all.

I found all three items in the market on a stall that sold stuff for motorists (they didn't have any crowbars so I went with a beefy second-hand screwdriver). I was ready. I didn't even need a drink.

Let's do it.

It began to rain as I emerged from the market and walked up the steps and across St Mary's Square. I turned the collar of the anorak up and continued down the Walsworth Road. The light rain had become heavier by the time I got to the Baptist church and far off there was the sound of thunder.

I turned into Shadwell Lane and told myself there was no going back now. The adrenalin was being pumped through my body and my heart was racing. I was both apprehensive and exhilarated at the same time.

On I continued. This is it. I'm going to do it.

Last time I walked up here I was totally unselfconscious. Today I feel like I've got a placard around my neck saying

ABOUT TO COMMIT AN ILLICIT ACT! and that everyone's eyes are upon me. Crazy, I know, but I'll overcome it.

Like most things in life, confidence is what it's all about.

As it's Saturday there's quite a bit of traffic coming and going up the lane.

I'm abreast of the first run of the wall that leads to the gates of The Leys. Everything OK so far. A couple of people doing things with their cars in front of their garages on the opposite side but they're not paying me any attention. The traffic has thinned out. The rain is abating. Good auguries perhaps. Keep going.

Here are the gates ahead of me. I steal a glance as I walk by and see a small Portakabin inside, just past the lodge, that wasn't there before. What's that for? A security guy or something? What's been going on since I was last here?

I continue walking. The road is deserted now. This looks good. Perfect. Just up there the wall ends and there's the strip of bushes and trees that separate the house from the adjoining property. Duck down there and I'm home and dry.

Anyone looking? Any traffic about? I look over my shoulder back down the lane. All OK there. Nothing ahead either. A few more steps and I'm gone. Keep going. Almost there. Almost.

Then I see a woman on the opposite side of the road. She's standing in front of a laurel hedge holding a pair of shears staring at me. Not doing anything else but staring at me. She's a plump woman, in her sixties I'd guess. Grey hair beneath a headscarf. Looking like she owns the whole bloody road. Why hadn't I noticed her before?

She looks like the sort of woman who peers out behind her curtains whenever a car passes or whenever there's a noise on the street. That sort of behaviour. The behaviour legitimised by these Neighbourhood Watch schemes.

She's still staring at me. Waiting to see what I do.

I guess this neck of the woods resembles Los Angeles. The most suspicious character is a pedestrian. The guy who's walking. He's the one to keep your eye on.

[289]

There's no chance of me slipping off the road and into the undergrowth now. She'd be on the phone to the police in no time at all. Fuck it.

I've no other choice.

'I say there!' I exclaim in an exaggerated upper middle-class voice as I stride across the road towards the woman. 'I say! Can't seem to find the railway station here!'

The woman visibly relaxes upon hearing the intonation of her own class and realising that I am not a threat to Property. Her arms fall to her side. Her shoulder muscles become unknotted. She quits biting her lower lip.

She starts pointing. 'Not up here. Down there. Turn right at the end. Straight ahead.'

'Jolly good. Thanks awfully!' And I turn and go back the way I came. I can hear her snipping at the hedge as I stride purposefully away.

Now if I'd really thought about this the best approach to The Leys isn't on the lane here but along the footpath from the station that leads up through the trees and around the chalk pit. A much better bet.

I turned right on the Walsworth Road and continued briskly up to the station. I strolled into the station yard and then took the narrow footpath that leads up to the back of The Leys. I felt much better in every way now. There was none of that anxiety and apprehension I'd felt on Shadwell Lane. There's always a right way of doing everything. This was decidedly it.

The footpath rose sharply and led a serpentine course through the trees and bushes to the clifftops of the pit. And there ahead of me now was the high wall that girdled the house. I continued on until I found a suitable tree, an ancient oak that wouldn't be too difficult to climb, with several mighty limbs that overshot the wall and connected with the trees growing on the other side.

I stopped and waited. There was nobody about. And it was silent except for the noise of light traffic far off and a train pulling out of the station.

I checked the pockets of the anorak to see I still had the tape, the torch and the screwdriver and then I zipped the front further up. Right, here goes.

I grabbed the first branch in my right hand, put my left foot against a lower branch and with some considerable effort raised myself up. My right foot was now on that branch and my left hand had grasped this branch. Up some more and over to the left here and then up again and I was in the main fork of the tree a foot or two above the top of the wall.

I was sweating now and I paused to get my breath back. Tree climbing is most certainly a young man's endeavour. It's quite amazing how out of practice you become in a mere thirty-odd years. Quite amazing.

I could see the back of The Leys itself now. An odd Gothic building with ranges on either side and rising to three storeys in the middle. A big place all right. It looked empty and deserted, but not neglected. There was a raised area immediately behind the house, a sort of promenade, and then a parapet with steps at either end that led down to the lawn. This must have been the scene of some fine summer parties when Queen Victoria ruled the waves and the pink bits of the globe.

I looked down to the footpath some fifteen feet below me. It looked a long way. What seemed a good idea at ground level now seemed a little iffy at this altitude. But this was the easy part. Scrambling up that limb there and making the crossover was going to be rather difficult.

Now, there's only one crossover I can make and that's going to take me to the beech tree there on the inside. I can manoeuvre myself down to its fork but that's some ten feet above the ground. How do I get down then? There are no branches at all. I suppose I could lower myself down and drop the last few feet, but how am I going to get back up on the outward journey? Christ, this is getting difficult. There's no way, even if I were to find a box or something to step on, that I'm going to pull myself up to that height.

Perhaps I could find a ladder? Perhaps there's another tree that would be easier? Come out another way? Screw it – I'll worry about that when I get to it.

I edged myself along the oak's limb with my legs straddling it. It was slow-going and I daren't look down. A foot at a time. Slowly. I reached the top of the wall and found that it was easier to stand on the brick and make the crossover here than further on. I crawled down the beech limb and stopped. So far so good (as the man who threw himself off the top of the Empire State Building said as he passed the third floor).

I could now get a better and fuller view of the back of the house and decide where I'd break in. The ground floor windows and doors were out of the question. I hadn't seen any guard patrol the grounds yet but I couldn't take the chance on a smashed pane or a forced door being discovered. The left of the house descended to a one-storey range that was probably the scullery and laundry rooms. There was a massive drainpipe that wouldn't be too hard to clamber up and that would take me to the roof and from there I could easily get up to the first floor and get in through one of the windows, and no foot soldier is going to notice that from ground level.

There was the possibility, of course, that the whole place was wired-up with some sophisticated sensing alarm system, but it didn't look like it (what did I expect to see, a notice to that effect?). Anyway, that was a chance I'd have to take.

I eased myself out of the fork and grabbed a thickish branch just below it. Here goes, I swung down and hung there. My feet were about five feet from the ground. Pray to Christ I don't break an ankle.

I let go, fell, and tumbled down on to the wet grass. I looked around. All clear. I got up and scrambled across the lawn to the safety of a row of rhododendron bushes that led towards the side of the house.

I crouched in the undergrowth and waited. Better to be

cautious now that I've got this far. I peered out across the lawn and waited. The place was empty, quiet and still.

I was getting a high from this. Some actual thrills. The sort of thrills you think you only get when you're a kid. You feel good. A buzz.

If only Dick was here to share it with me. That would be perfect. He'd enjoy this. It would be a rerun of that night we broke into the Buffer Depot. The two of us taking on this place.

This time last year Dick was alive. A living entity. And now as a result of him dying I'm crouching in the bushes waiting to break into a place that might reveal something about the circumstances of his death. It's been a long winding path. Who would have believed it? Dick perhaps. He'd have appreciated the sour irony all right.

Still no movement out there. I guess I can assume it's safe to proceed … but hold on a moment, when agents are doing black-bag jobs like this, don't they have a cover story? What's mine? What bit of hokum have I got to spin? How do I explain away my presence here? That would be difficult.

Fuck it. Let's go.

I moved up through the bushes towards the house. I reached the end of the rhododendrons and crouched down, peering along the back of the house. This could be the trickier bit. Once I broke cover I had a thirty-foot dash in the open across to the scullery, then I had to clamber up the drainpipe. Once I was on the roof there I would be unseen by anyone walking below.

To the left of the drainpipe were several wooden garden chairs neatly stacked against the wall. They had high backs and would be just the thing to help me scale the beech tree on my way out, I think. Good. That's a real break.

There's the torch, there's the tape, there's the screwdriver. Everything set. Right. Give it a couple more minutes and then make a dash for it.

No movement. All quiet. Wait. Be patient.

Five, four, three, two, one. Go!

I ran out of the bushes, across the grass, up the steps, over the gravel and to the drainpipe. The brackets holding it to the wall were beefy and staggered at three-foot intervals. I was up it in a flash and on the roof. Easy.

I scampered along the valley at the foot of the slate roof until I was behind a parapet that hid me from view. There was no sign of anyone below.

In front of me was a sash window about four feet wide and some six feet high comprising an upper and lower pane. I stood up and saw that there was a single catch on the inside halfway up.

I knelt down and took the tape from my pocket. If I stick this across the bottom of the upper pane I need only knock out a small area in order to be able to put my hand through and throw the catch. There's no need to smash the whole window.

I placed three strips of the two-inch tape across the glass horizontally and then held the business end of the screwdriver on the tape directly in front of the catch. Then I banged the palm of my hand hard against the handle of the screwdriver. There was a high-pitched truncated piercing sound as the screwdriver moved forward through the glass. I immediately yanked it back so as not to cause any more damage than was necessary.

There were several diagonal cracks reaching to the upper corners of the pane and the area where the screwdriver had pierced was shattered. I carefully pulled off the tape with the glass shards adhering to it and then tapped a small area of cracked glass that fell inwards. I put the tape through the hole and then put my hand in and turned the catch.

I looked around and paused. I couldn't see anything or hear anything and no alarm was sounding. In I went.

I pushed against the frame of the lower pane and it went up surprisingly easily with only a few scrapes and groans. The loose fit of the casement was in my favour.

After a quick glance over my shoulder I climbed in and shut the window behind me. I doubted that even the most eagle-eyed security patrolman would notice the small hole and the cracks in the glass from ground level.

I sat down on the floor to catch my breath.

The room was of a generous size and empty except for a large single bed with wooden head and tailboards, a dark wooden bedside cabinet and a Lloyd loom chair by the door on the far side. Two carpets had been positioned on the brown linoleum at the side and at the foot of the bed. An embossed wallpaper with floral motifs extended up to a picture rail that ran around the room. There were no pictures hanging from it. The room hadn't changed any since the late 1940s.

What do I do now?

I'm on the first floor. I'll go down to the ground floor and methodically search the place from top to bottom. Right. That's what I'll do.

I got up and went over to the door. I turned the ornate brass handle and opened it. There was a corridor ahead, carpeted with framed engravings of biblical scenes hanging from the walls. I peeked into the rooms off the corridor – all bedrooms like the one at the end. The corridor opened on to a large room with a much higher ceiling. There were about eight rows of military-style bunks, each row about three bunks deep. Lockers faced the bunks on the opposite side. These were unlocked and empty. Above them was a clock mounted on the wall: hours 1 to 12 in large black figures and then, within them, hours 13 to 24 in smaller red figures. The place looked a little like a barracks but it wasn't. Something else went on here.

A grand staircase led down to the ground floor. It was nearly twelve feet wide and made of some exotic hardwood. A thick-piled red carpet ran down the centre of it. The sides of the staircase were panelled with the same wood. In two recessed alcoves high above the stairs, facing each other, were two busts. One looked like Homer and the other could have been anyone from Marcus Aurelius through to Julius Caesar, certainly a Roman, but just who was anyone's guess.

There was a smell of mustiness and decay to the house. An air of some past decade. The show had moved on. I was exploring the past.

I could hear a soft rain against the coloured skylights high above me. A gentle and persistent drumming.

The main hall was vast, both horizontally and vertically (reaching up through all three floors). Extending out from under the carpets was a dark green marble flooring that met the panelled walls. There were various massive and solid Victorian sofas and tables. Standard lamps were placed in the far corners where the light from the vast chandelier didn't quite reach. Nobody had skimped on kitting out this place.

But I wasn't interested in the domestic and architectural niceties of The Leys. Another day I might be. Today I was here in a functional capacity. I wanted to know what went on here. Fuck everything else.

Ahead of me was the main entrance to the house, high double doors with brass fittings. The surrounding glazing was of coloured glass depicting, like the engravings upstairs, scenes from the Bible.

At eye level on the right-hand door was a small rectangular slide made of same wood as the door itself. A spy-hole I guess. I slid it back and there was a view, through a small aperture, no doubt disguised within some decoration on the front, out of the house and up the pink drive that came down from the gates. I could see the lodge house at the far end of the lawn and the Portakabin I'd seen from the road. There was nobody about. I slid the cover back.

I took the corridor off to the left. The first couple of rooms had been interconnecting reception rooms when the house was built. They were now empty and covered in dust and plaster that had fallen from the decorative ceilings.

Both had the 24-hour electric clocks displayed in prominent positions. Large bay windows looked over the grounds. The third room had originally been a library, all four walls were shelves but they were now bare. All I found was a copy of *US News and World Report* on the floor with a December 1965 date.

A large room that took up the whole width of the house and which may have been a ballroom to begin with now looked like a lecture theatre. There were rows of tubular steel chairs and a podium. A small pull-down film screen was hung behind the podium but there was no sign of any projection equipment. To one side of the room was a free-standing flag pole, but there was no flag around to give some of the game away.

This was getting frustrating. I didn't know what I was looking for but I sure as hell wasn't finding it. I retraced my steps down the corridor and then crossed the hall to the other side of the house. More large rooms with tubular chairs, rooms with desks, and in all of them the 24-hour clocks.

I went up a small winding servants' staircase to the first floor that brought me out on the corridor just down from where I got in. I walked past the bunk beds to the other side of the house and found much the same thing: individual bedrooms and then, at the end, another bunk room.

What was Lee Harvey Oswald doing here? There had to be some clue. Some clue that suggested something of what went on here. But then I suppose the people who run places like this (whatever they are) are professionals and when they quit they take everything with them. That's their game ... but then nobody is infallible, are they? There are oversights and mistakes. And that's what I'm looking for – oversights and mistakes.

I climbed the main staircase to the second floor, the top floor. Several bedrooms and bathrooms, a couple of spare rooms crammed with tables and chairs, 24-hour clocks everywhere and that was it.

A steep narrow staircase led up from the landing here. To the roof? I went up it to find that it led to an observation tower, a roof-top belvedere. There was a roof above it but the sides were open from waist height up. It was windy and raining and cold. I knelt and peered over the top. I looked down upon the front lawn of the house and the driveway leading up past the lodge and the Portakabin to the front gates. There was no sign of movement.

I went back down and sat at the top of the main staircase. I lit a cigarette and thought about what to do next. I'd done all three floors and found nothing. No clue, no suggestion, nothing.

The only sounds I could hear now were my breathing and the wind and the rain above me. The smell of mustiness and damp was more noticeable up here. It seemed to rise up the staircase.

Too late. I got here too late. It's all gone. The evidence has disappeared.

I descended the steps to the ground floor hall. I stubbed the cigarette out on the sole of my boot and then slid the butt under the carpet so there was no evidence of my visit.

There is one last place to check out, but that's just a formality. The basement, or cellar. I'll see what's down there. All houses like this have basements and the entrance was invariably to be found in the kitchen area. It was usually only ever the servants who needed to go down there and fetch regularly.

I went down the corridor to the kitchen and began looking for the cellar door. It wasn't anywhere to be found there, nor in the scullery or the other adjoining rooms. I methodically checked each room. No cellar door. This was odd. I continued looking and extended my search back up the corridor.

Next to a pantry was a solid door that I opened. It opened on to a brick wall. An old brick wall but not as old as the house itself. I checked the pantry and the room to the other side and deduced that the bricked-up entrance would have led to a void between the two rooms. There was definitely a space there, but what? There was no way I could find out save demolishing the bricks, and that was out of the question.

I walked back to the hall. This whole venture had become a complete waste of fucking time. I've turned up nothing. Nada. Zip. Fuck all!

[3]

There was a film location down in Dorset ... It was a contemporary thriller called *Dark Deception* produced by that jerk from the BBC whose name now escapes me. It was a small budget affair with a cast of unknowns. We were shooting in this big house just outside Dorchester. I remember being shown around the basement. There was a poky stairway leading down from just off the kitchen for the servants and then in the hall there was a grander descent disguised behind panelling for the master of the house whenever he wanted to inspect his wine cellar.

Perhaps it's worth having a final scout around the hall here to see if there's a disguised entrance?

I hadn't noticed anything on my first look around here. There's certainly nothing down that corridor there, so what does that leave? A hidden entrance in the hall right here?

I checked each wall and under the staircase. There's no disguised door here. I looked around. If it is here, where could it be? I retraced my steps. It couldn't be either side of the door. It's not down this wall, it's not under the stairs, nor this wall, nor at the back here.

There are two further possibilities. The library down there and that other room further on which was once a billiard room (the table had gone but the marker board and cabinet were still in place on the wall). Those are two likely ingresses for a master with a wine cellar.

I entered the library and looked about. Just solid shelves down that wall. The fireplace there and what's that to the side? Shelves only the width of a door and a brass door handle at waist height? That looks likely.

I strode across the bare floorboards. This was a disguised door all right. I turned the handle and there was a raw scraping sound. I pulled on the handle to open the door. It moved a few inches and stopped. I pulled again with more force. It wouldn't move. I shone the torch down the back and I could see steps going down. This was it.

I pulled on the handle again with all the force I could gather. My knuckles went white and the door shifted not a tad. Mmmmm. I now grabbed the inside of the door with both hands and put my right foot against the side of the legitimate bookcase. I pulled and pushed at the same time. It moved a fraction. I tried it again. Another fraction. Rather than sustaining the push-and-pull I started doing it rhythmically with quick jerks. This was less taxing and more effective. I soon had it open about twelve inches or so, certainly enough to get through.

There was an overpowering smell of damp and decay. I stood at the top of the stairs waiting for the stale air to evacuate. From somewhere in the darkness below I could hear a gentle dripping sound echoing. Further off and perhaps deeper down there was a muffled whirring sound.

I took a couple of steps down and shone the torch ahead of me. I could see nothing except the steps disappearing into the darkness, the black void. This had obviously been the route down for the boss to his wine cellar (or whatever). But why was the servants' entrance back near the kitchen bricked up?

A few more steps. Still black ahead. More steps. Still black. More steps. More darkness. The beam of light still showed the steps descending with no end in sight. There was something strange about this.

This was no ordinary cellar, it was far too deep for that. I shone the light down at the steps and looked at them more closely. The steps were concrete and not the same date as the house. More recent. The risers were reinforced with horizontal metal strips. The nosings on the treads were made of some light coloured alloy. This was a high-spec staircase. This wasn't some local builder's job. And it wasn't the master's ingress. No, sir.

The steps continued. The whirring sound got louder.

I noticed that there was now a rope banister on either side of the stair. I grabbed it for support. You'd only have to fall down these stairs once and you'd tumble into eternity.

I turned and looked back up to the door I had come through. I could see the light. It was way back and high up, small. I'd come down a long, long way.

I continued down and now the steps curved around to the right and then there was a level stretch which led on to what seemed to be a balcony on which other flights of steps terminated. I took out my Swiss army knife and marked a cross on the wall of the passage down which I had come. You wouldn't want to get lost here.

There was a metal railing and then what appeared to be a deep drop beyond it. The whirring sound was coming from the depths down there. Could the sound be pumps, pumping out water? They certainly weren't circulating air. I took a two-pence coin from my pocket, tossed it over and counted. One – one hundred. Two – one hundred. Three – one hundred. Four – one hundred. Five – one hundred. And then a distant resonant sound as metal hit metal. A muffled sound, almost lost in the vastness of the depths.

Five seconds down. What's the rate of fall per second? Roughly seventy-five feet. That times five gives a depth of around 375 feet. Can that be so? Can this place be that deep? Jesus.

This cellar definitely wasn't an original feature of the house. Somebody had added it. Probably soon after it was taken out of private hands. During the war or perhaps a little later.

Chalk is one of the easiest and cheapest rocks to tunnel through. It's also one of the safest. God knows how many thousands (millions?) of cubic yards had been excavated, but how? This wouldn't have been carried up through the house and out the main gate. There must have been some other way.

That other way must have been the chalk pit behind the house, over by the railway. Nobody would have remarked on chalk being removed from a chalk pit. It would have been put straight on the railway trucks and ended up as some back-fill or spoilbank someplace, or even at a cement works. There would be a secret entrance out into the face of the pit.

That was the importance of having this place. That was why they wanted it! They could excavate this and nobody would be any the wiser. That was why they had to have it.

But why here? And who were they?

I continued along the balcony. More steps led down on to it. There must have been a lot of people coming and going when this was operational and they didn't all sleep upstairs in the house. The balcony now narrowed and there were several corridors leading off in different directions. I went straight ahead. The corridor opened on what appeared to be a large room with a vast circular table in the centre. The torch's beam was not strong enough to see the far side. The table just curved off on either side and disappeared into the darkness.

The surface of the table was covered with a large map. Here was Ireland, there England, and there stretching into the void was the beginning of continental Europe. Scattered about on the surface were long billiard-like cues, presumably for moving objects about the surface of the map. This was some planning room, but planning for what? There were no model ships or aeroplanes or model anythings to betray what the map was used for. On the wall behind me I found a 24-hour clock, much larger than the others. The centre had drop-down plates that spelt out the day, the month and the year. This clock had stopped at 13.35 on Saturday, 10 February 1968. Had there been people here until then? Didn't Pepper say it closed in 1964?

I headed back out of the room and along the corridor. I peered around a couple of doors. Offices with desks and filing cabinets. In the second office I went over to a filing cabinet, one in a bank of ten or so and opened a drawer at random. It was stuffed full of files. I took out a bulky file and opened it. On onion-skin paper was a carbon copy of a telegram, or was it a letter? Certainly some communication:

AIRTEL: BUFA 448/HA TO USDA/DC
      7/7/58
Circulate: N/A

BELLEROPHON IN COMMUNICATION AS OF
1500HRS GMT YESTERDAY.
REGRET FURTHER AMPLIFICATION OF RA/456
REQUEST NOT POSSIBLE AS OF 1200HRS TODAY.
POTENTIAL PARTICIPANTS ON ALERT.
STAND READY FOR COLLATERAL INTERCEPTS.

GX-PZ/448/HA
1615hrs
6789 via 4223ec

What did that mean? Who was Bellerophon? *What* was Bellerophon? This was meaningless to anyone who wasn't on the inside. What was BUFA 448/HA and USDA?

This was a carbon copy so, presumably, this place was BUFA #48/HA. But what was that? It was an AIRTEL being sent to USDA/DC. United States something? Defense Agency? Was there such a thing? Department of A-something? What could that stand for? Department of the Army? Did that exist? DC was obviously Washington, DC. Headquarters, in other words.

So this place was something to do with American intelligence. But what?

And what exactly was Lee Harvey Oswald doing here? He must have been working for US intelligence, but doing what? Somewhere here were the answers to these questions. Well, if not the answers, certainly indications.

I rifled through the rest of the file: several hundred similarly meaningless coded AIRTELS utilising names from classical mythology. There's no way you would ever discover what the actuality was behind them.

I carefully put the file back from where I'd taken it. I randomly searched several of the other filing cabinets. All full of the same nonsense. The AIRTELS went back to the early 1940s on the left and continued up until 1968 on the right. They told me nothing.

Nothing at all … except that this was an American intelligence post of some kind. And that single piece of information was important enough. The clincher, however, was above the desk. There at the end of the torch beam was a framed photograph of Ike, Dwight D. Eisenhower sitting behind his desk in the White House.

This was some American operation, but what?

And how did it exist all of these years in Hitchin without anyone getting a whiff of what was going on? Well, Dick got a whiff all those years ago when he showed me that map with all the German bomb plots on it. Pepper and Alf Lawson had a whiff, but they had no idea what they were really dealing with. Some of the residents in the nearby houses on Shadwell Lane probably had a suspicion or two, but what would they have known beyond thinking it was some hush-hush government project? Nothing, that's what.

Was the secret and obscured knowledge of this place a contributing factor to those tales Dick and I heard as kids about secret tunnels in the chalk pit, secret tunnels under Hitchin? Had those stories arisen with the building of this place?

And another question: why had these papers been left here? Had they been overlooked or just forgotten?

And what else was still here?

I left the room and continued back up the corridor to the

landing area and the whirring sound coming from far below.

This isn't a place I can explore alone with a small pocket torch. I need some help. I need a couple of big lamps as well. Then I could really start nosing about. I'll have to come back.

I walked up another corridor and discovered a number of small rooms that resembled padded cells. There was no furniture in them. They were empty except for the padding that covered all four walls, the ceiling and the floor. The heavy doors had grilles on them. These were for shutting people up.

But who?

The last of the cells had several leather straps fixed into the wall about six feet up. There were ancient stains below them on the wall and on the floor. I couldn't tell whether it was blood, urine or excrement.

I didn't want to hang around here.

Another corridor, wider than the previous ones, led to an open landing from which descended two escalators, both silent and motionless. What was down there? This place was even bigger than I imagined. It seemed to go on for ever.

I wanted to get out now. I wanted to leave this place. The atmosphere was oppressive. The vibes were bad. I'd had enough of it. And I could do with a really large vodka.

I followed my steps back to the main landing and found the entrance with the cross on the wall. I went down the corridor, the level stretch, and then up the steps as fast as I could go. There, far ahead of me, was the tiny crack of light from the door. It seemed a mile away. I climbed the stairs quickly. I had to get out of here now.

By the time I reached the door I was out of breath and panting hard. I paused and then peered through the gap. Everything was as it was before. The room was empty and silent. I squeezed through and then pushed the door shut with my shoulder. I'd have to come back, and come back soon. This place was too important to let any time go by –

circumstances could change, things could be moved out. Anything could happen.

I quickly left the room and went up the corridor to the main hall. I now had to make my getaway, as swiftly and invisibly as my arrival.

In the hall I went up to the front door and slid back the spy-hole. I wanted a last look out to see the coast was clear. There was the drive, there was … there was a brand new black Volvo estate parked up there, this side of the Portakabin. It wasn't there before. There was no one inside it and I couldn't see anyone moving about around it. I waited, hoping to see something, but nothing. Where had *that* come from?

It's time to move. I slid the cover back and went up the main staircase to the first floor. I checked the front and the back of the house through the windows in the bunk room and could see nothing. The coast was clear. I'm on my way out.

Down the corridor I went and opened the door of the bedroom through which I had gained entry. I went in and walked over to the window.

A voice said, 'Christopher, dear boy. How are you?'

CHAPTER TEN

STAY IN YOUR OWN MOVIE

'Identify.'
'Bellerophon … 666B.'
'Location?'
'North Hertfordshire.'
'Proceed.'
'Confirming SUSURRUS shut-down within forty-eight hours.'

A VOICE.

I imagined it, didn't I?

There's no one here … is there?

I stood motionless in front of the window, the words ricocheting through my head – *Christopher, dear boy. How are you?*

Where did they come from? Where?

I heard the noise of a creaking floorboard. I turned. There was a figure standing in the doorway. A figure enveloped in black and red with a large hat and long hair. He had a beard and was resting both hands on a silver-capped walking cane. Several of his fingers displayed large silver rings. His age was unfathomable, it could have been anything from fifty to seventy.

'You mustn't be so surprised,' said the figure.

This was a figure I'd seen before. This was a figure, indeed, I'd met before. It was this Georges character who'd approached me by the church when I came up for Dick's funeral. The guy I'd seen at the funeral, outside Dick's house and at the station when I was done over.

He was standing there looking straight at me. He was wearing his three-piece black corduroy suit with a matching cape. His black hair curled down over his shoulders from beneath a wide-brimmed fedora. His Vandyke beard gave him a saturnalian air that was abetted by his small and piercing eyes.

I was silent. I stood staring at him.

He took something from his pocket. It was a pack of cigars.

'Would you like one? They're Cuban,' he said, offering them to me.

I shook my head. No.

He lit one of the cigars and puffed upon it.

'You've led us a bit of a song and dance, Christopher, I must say. Still, that's all in the past now, isn't it?'

What did he mean? I remained silent.

He continued puffing away on the cigar. The blue smoke was curling up to the ceiling in lazy spirals. He took several steps into the room.

'How did you know I was here?' I said. 'Nobody saw me arrive.'

'You are making an illogical jump in your reasoning. You're saying that because you saw nobody, nobody therefore saw you, aren't you?'

'Yes,' I agreed.

'Illogical and wrong, as you've probably gathered.' There was a faint American accent in his voice. Educated.

'I didn't see any security guards,' I protested.

'The security guard over there in his little cabin and the notices at the front are merely set dressing for the locals who would expect such precautions to be taken. There are sensing and surveillance systems here that will signal an earthworm raising his head above the lawn.'

'Why was I allowed to go as far as I did then?'

'I think we should discuss this over a spot of lunch. Are you in agreement?'

I nodded. 'What's your name? Georges what?'

'Kurzian. I'm sorry, I should have introduced myself again. Georges Kurzian.'

'And who do you work for?'

Georges smiled. 'Well, you've heard of a soldier of fortune. You might say I'm a projects manager of fortune.'

'That doesn't answer my question, does it?'

'No, it doesn't. I apologise. It partly answers your question however.'

'How?'

'I'm freelance. I work for whoever needs my services.'

'And who are you working for now?'

'I believe I'm working for an American intelligence agency, but I'm not altogether sure.'

'Why are you giving me the run-around? You know who you're working for,' I protested.

'I'm being perfectly truthful and candid with you, Christopher. I do not know for sure who I am working for. This is the nature of the business.'

'You said you're working for an American intelligence agency. Which one? The CIA? The NSA?'

'I said, Christopher, I *believed* I was working for an American intelligence agency. And I added that I was not altogether sure. They may want me to think they are American, but they may not be. On the other hand, they may be American yet they present themselves in such a way as to make me think they are not American. This game gets very complicated sometimes. It gets to be like some short story written by Borges. Nothing is what it appears to be.'

'Are you what you appear to be?'

Georges smiled again and said, 'That depends on what your perceptions of me are.'

'Are you American?'

'Yes. I was born in Vermont.'

'Uh-huh. What's your current job? What are you up to?'

'We can discuss this more fully over lunch, but you've probably realised it is not unconnected with the photographs of Lee Harvey Oswald. These, I'm told, could give some of the game away were they to fall into hands that shouldn't have them.'

That answered that question, but not fully. I wanted more details. 'Who are you working for then? You must know.'

'I've told you I don't know. If I did, I wouldn't be in a position to tell you, but I don't. So I cannot say any more.'

'Do you care who you work for?'

He drew on the cigar and slowly exhaled the smoke. 'I care that I do my job properly and to the best of my ability.'

I had so many questions to put to him I wasn't sure where to start. While he was talking I'd get in as many as I could.

'These photographs of Oswald. Who took them?'

'Mr Drax took them, as I think you've gathered. He was a trusted custodian of this little place here, but as his years advanced he became a little gaga and less trustworthy than had been envisaged. He may even have been responsible for the Cambridge phone call. We don't know. Anyway, he handed them to your friend, Dick, together with a file that was safely recovered some time back.'

'Why did he?' I demanded.

Georges exhaled on the cigar again and said, 'I think the enormity of Kennedy's assassination may have preyed on his mind as he got older and more isolated. Perhaps he needed to confess … and purge himself before he met his Maker.'

'Confess what?' I asked.

'Your friend Dick may have been able to answer that. I'm afraid I really don't know.'

'What do you know about Dick?'

'Not a great deal, beyond him being the next link in the chain of possession. I've been trying to establish what happened to the photographs after his tragic death.'

Did Kurzian know anything about the circumstances surrounding Dick's death? I had to ask him that question. This was the question that started everything. This was the alpha, and the omega, of this odyssey.

Kurzian was now looking out of the window through which I had come. Then he turned and faced me. 'Do you like Chinese food?'

'Yes.'

'Good. We shall go to the Chinese restaurant on Sun Street. The food is quite good.'

'I must ask you one question before we go.'

'And what's that?'

'My friend, Dick. Did he commit suicide or was he murdered?'

Kurzian stared at me silently for several moments and then scratched his beard.

'I have to know the answer to that,' I said. 'I've got to know.'

Kurzian raised his cigar to his lips and then paused. 'I would like to know the answer to that myself. It was his death that made me suspect that there were other players in this field. Until then I believed I had the game to myself. That made me wonder. I do not know for sure one way or the other, but the balance of probability is that he was murdered.'

'You had nothing to do with it?'

'Nothing at all. I give you my word.'

'Who did then? Who could have been involved?'

'I have no idea. If I did I would tell you.'

He must have some idea, some suspicion. 'Was it the CIA? The NSA? You must know.'

'I don't,' said Kurzian. 'And don't keep mentioning the CIA and the NSA. These are low-level operations. The organisations we are dealing with are as hidden from the CIA and the NSA as they are from the man in the street. Do you understand?'

'No, I don't,' I said.

'Didn't Benjamin Disraeli once write that the people who really govern and run things are very different from the ones we think govern? That's what I'm talking about.'

'What, some super-secret global conspiracy?'

'Super-secret certainly,' said Georges.

'And powerful? How powerful?'

'Conspiracies more powerful than you could imagine … and more inept at times than you would believe.'

'That sounds like a quote,' I said.

'It is now that I've said it,' he replied.

'And you work for them and yet you don't know who they are?'

'I'm one of many disownable freelance agents. There is nothing to connect me with them or anyone else. I'm only told what I need to know in order to complete an assignment. That's all. Nothing more.'

I lit a Marlboro. The first cigarette I'd had in an hour or so. 'Are people murdered by this organisation? These organisations?'

'Undoubtedly. Others are compromised. It depends on the circumstances.'

'Have you ever murdered anyone?'

'No, I'm an investigator.'

'Who does the murdering?'

'Geeks, psychos and the dispossessed usually. There is no connection between them and the organisations. They don't know why they're doing a murder. They don't need to. Others, those that require some skill or finesse, are handled by professionals. They wouldn't know why either. They may be fed some bullshit, but it wouldn't be the true reason … you see?'

'I guess so.'

'I am getting cold here. Shall we go to lunch?'

Kurzian indicated the door. I walked out and he followed me. We walked down the corridor and past the bunk beds. I was curious what he knew about this place and I asked him.

'I don't know much about it. Originally some sort of bunker was built underground here by the British government at the beginning of the Second World War when it was feared the Germans would successfully invade England. I think the idea was that as the German army swept up through England this would be a secret redoubt behind the lines in the occupied zone. There were many like this built, I understand. The struggle would be continued clandestinely from here.'

'And what happened after the war was over?'

'The USAF had it for a short while as a command centre, for a year or two, then after that I do not know.'

We descended the main staircase and went out through the main doors. The rain had stopped and the clouds were clearing. There was the faint possibility of some sun.

Our feet crunched on the gravel drive as we walked up towards the parked black Volvo.

I stopped and faced Kurzian. 'Why are you telling me all this?'

Kurzian stopped and smiled. He straightened his hat and said, 'There are two reasons. The first is that I believe we should be honest with each other, and the second is that what I'm telling you is not repeatable.'

'Not repeatable!' I laughed.

'This is true. You may repeat it but I do not think anyone will believe you, not that you've got that much to tell anyway. The governments of the world are very adroit at creating a certain climate, one that quickly marginalises anyone who is not in agreement with consensual truths. If you were to go around saying some of the things you could say, you'd quickly be categorised with the paranoid and the discredited. You'd be classed with those who believe that Robert Maxwell is still alive, that Abraham Lincoln was murdered by the Jesuits, that Elvis is alive and working undercover for the FBI, that the US government allows extra-terrestrials to abduct American citizens, that … well, the list is endless. You would be writing your own one-way ticket to the lunatic fringe. No mistake about that.'

Kurzian stopped walking and started prodding the gravel with his cane absent-mindedly. Then he looked up and said, 'We shall come to an accord today. I believe you have these photographs, the ones I was talking about. They need to be returned to their rightful owners. I've been told that I can offer you up to a certain figure for them and that this deal would also include your silence on the matter ever after.' He paused, smiled at me and then continued. 'It appears, I think, that it isn't the photos of Oswald that matter so much, rather it is where questions about them would lead. The questions that would be asked.'

So, he knows I've got the photographs ... no, he doesn't know I've got them. He thinks I've got them. And he wants them back. I'm in a stronger position than I thought.

We continued in silence to the Volvo estate. Kurzian took a pair of black kid gloves from the pocket of his jacket and put them on in what seemed a ritualised manner, carefully pulling and pushing down each finger, flexing the hand, and smoothing out the wrinkles. He noticed that I was looking at him do this and smiled before saying, 'I have a small fetish about driving gloves. I could not drive without them. These are a pair I picked up in Spain recently.' Then he laughed.

The Volvo had a black leather interior and a sun roof. It looked like it was only a couple of weeks old. About fifty or so medium-sized Jiffy bags were stacked in the very back of the vehicle while numerous box files and folders had been thrown on the rear seats.

Kurzian climbed into the driving seat and indicated to me to get in. I opened the door and sat in the large passenger seat. There was a sweet smell of new leather.

Kurzian leant across me and opened the glove compartment. He took out several small packages and papers. He sorted through them and then asked me to hold them. He looked around in the glove compartment again and said, 'I seem to have lost my RAC card. Damn.' Then, nodding at the papers and packages I was holding, he added, 'You can put those back in there. Thanks.'

He started the engine up, pulled back the gear selector and eased the handbrake. We pulled forward towards the gate. Kurzian then gave the horn a burst and a slim grey-haired elderly guy in a blue security guard uniform came out of the Portakabin and waved before opening the front gates.

'How much does he know?' I said to Kurzian, indicating the security guard.

'Dear Eric?' Kurzian replied, 'Oh, nothing really. Like all of us, he only knows what he needs to know. He thinks I'm an American property developer interested in buying this place.'

Kurzian stopped halfway out of the gate and wound the window down. The security guy came over and Kurzian said, 'We're just going out for lunch, Eric. I'll be back in a couple of hours. OK?'

'Certainly, Mr Schlesinger. Yes.' The accent was English, from somewhere in the Midlands.

As we pulled out on to Shadwell Lane I turned to Georges and said, 'Why did he call you Mr Schlesinger?'

Kurzian said nonchalantly, 'Because that's who he thinks I am – Schlesinger, a property developer.'

I sensed a discrepancy in what Kurzian was saying. If Eric doesn't know from shit, who then was monitoring the sophisticated sensing devices Kurzian said were installed all over The Leys? Were there, indeed, sensing devices? Or was Kurzian spinning me a yarn? This Eric couldn't be stuck out here without picking up on what was special about the place, or could he? I wondered. Were there still operatives below ground somewhere? I'd tackle Kurzian about this over lunch. Pin him down and get some answers.

Kurzian came to a halt at the end of the lane and waited for a break in the traffic.

'What do you know about the assassination of Kennedy?'
I said.

'A very interesting subject,' said Kurzian as he pulled
forward on to the Walsworth Road. 'Very interesting
indeed, the death of Lancer.'

'Lancer?'

'I'm sorry. Lancer was the US Secret Service's code-
name for the President in 1963. Lace was the First Lady.
Caroline and John Jr were Lyric and Lark respectively. The
family's code-names all began with Ls.'

'Why do you call him that?' I asked.

'Habit, I guess,' said Georges.

'Do you have any inside track on it? The assassination?'

'Why should I?'

'Why should you? Because your paymasters also had
Oswald on the payroll out here in Hitchin when he should
have been in Russia! That's why.'

'Hold on,' said Kurzian. 'First of all, you are again making
an assumption that may be illogical. You're assuming that
the people behind The Leys are also the people who are
currently employing me. That isn't necessarily so.'

'How come you're out at The Leys then strolling
around?' I demanded.

'The Leys may not belong any longer to the people who
were there earlier. It may have changed hands.'

'Listen,' I shouted, 'if you want some help with these
photographs, I want some answers from you. Some real
answers. Not all of this nebulous shit. Do you understand?'

'We'll talk over lunch. OK?'

'OK!' I reluctantly agreed.

Georges took a right down Hermitage Road after the
traffic lights changed and then, at the end, a left into
Bancroft. He pulled up just short of a bus-stop.

'You can't park here,' I said, 'there are yellow lines.
You'll get done.'

'I won't be a moment. I've just got a couple of things to
pick up from the shop here.'

If he wanted to get a parking ticket that was his affair.

Kurzian got out, reached back for his walking cane, slammed the door shut and walked around the front of the car and headed towards W H Smith's. He was halfway there when he turned back and came over to me. I pressed the button and the window wound down.

'You're right,' he said. 'I may be a few minutes. Why don't you park the car and meet me in the restaurant? The keys are in the ignition.'

'Park it where?' I said.

'There's usually places free even on Saturday in the car park behind the Sun pub. Do you know it?'

I did. It was behind the Sun and access was from Queen Street down a narrow lane that wound past the Biggin.

'Where's this restaurant then?' I asked.

'Going down Sun Street from here it's on the right. Nearly opposite the Sun Hotel itself.'

I knew where he meant though I hadn't ever noticed the restaurant. If I park behind the Sun all I need do is walk through the courtyard of the pub and I'd be there at the place.

'OK,' I said. 'I am insured, aren't I?'

'Of course. And do make sure the car's locked.'

'I will.'

Kurzian strode off back to Smith's with his walking cane swinging rhythmically in the air. I got out of the car and walked around to the driver's side.

I climbed in, switched the ignition on, snapped the seat-belt shut, took the handbrake off and put it into gear. I looked in the rear-view mirror and over my shoulder. It was all clear. I indicated right and pulled out and drove up to the traffic lights at the foot of Brand Street which were showing red. I waited for them to change.

After a moment or two they changed and I pulled forward on to the semi-pedestrianised High Street and then left at the end into Market Square and down and around into Sun Street. I saw the Chinese restaurant on the right

[317]

that Kurzian had mentioned. I continued along to the end and paused at the junction with Bridge Street.

I had a lot of questions for Kurzian and I wasn't going to let him wriggle out of answering them. After all, I had the trump hand. I was arguing from a position of strength and he wasn't going to fob me off with any of this fuzzy shit. He certainly knew more than he was saying, but how much more I wasn't sure. I may have to tell him to go back to his people and tell them I want to see them. I want to talk with the organ grinder, not the monkey.

I want answers about my duffing up at the station, the break-in at my flat and the one at Dick's. I want answers about those yobs who nearly killed us coming back from Yarmouth. And more. I want the full story. And I'm going to get to the bottom of Dick's death too. I'll make sure they won't get away with that.

I accelerated out into Bridge Street and down and over the bridge over the River Hiz to take a left at the mini-roundabout into Queen Street.

It was a pity Laura wasn't with me now. She'd be a lot of use with this guy. She'd really know how to handle him. She'd extract every last drop of information from him and no mistake. In fact I'm not going to make any decision about anything until I've spoken to her later. I'll tell Kurzian that. I've got to speak to my lawyer. She'll decide what I'm going to do. But I won't tell him that until the end.

After the traffic lights I turned left into the narrow Biggin Lane and passed the eponymous Biggin on the left, the ancient half-timbered almshouse built for old and needy Hitchin women by some long-forgotten monastic order (forgotten by me, that is).

Whenever I go by the Biggin I always think of what Herbert Tompkins wrote in his book on Hertfordshire at the turn of the century. He was talking about Hitchin generally when he said he'd like to see a painting of the town from Windmill Hill by Turner, a scene in Market

Square by Millet, a Purwell Mill by Claude Lorraine, and a portrait of one of the old ladies in the Biggin by Rembrandt. Perhaps in some alternate universe these actually exist? Perhaps Dick has discovered them?

Over the Hiz again and now to the left past some bleak hideous back of a supermarket, a high expanse of cold brick, alienating and completely out of scale.

The car park was half-empty. I'd park up the top near the low wall that delimited the yard of the Sun. Two minutes' walk and I'd be at the restaurant.

I edged the car into a space next to an old rusty red Ford Escort. I turned the ignition off and then there was a knock on the window. I looked up. There was a young police officer indicating that I should wind down the window. He didn't look any older than my son. What did he want?

I pressed the button and an electric motor whirred into action, lowering the window. 'Hi,' I said.

'I just noticed you drive in, sir.'

'Uh-huh.'

'Is this your vehicle?'

'No. I've driven it here for a friend. We're going to have lunch now, over in Sun Street.'

'I see, sir. Do you have your driving licence with you?'

'Yes, of course.' I took my wallet out and handed the licence to the officer. He took several steps away from the vehicle and scrutinised the licence. He turned his back on me and said something into his radio. I couldn't make out what it was. He listened as someone replied.

Returning to me, the fresh, clean-shaven, red-blotched face of the young constable was bereft of emotion as he stated, 'This vehicle was reported stolen earlier this week, sir. You're under arrest on suspicion of being in possession of a stolen car.'

'What? What are you talking about?'

'Please step out of the car, sir.'

'This is crazy!'

'Please step out of the car, sir. *Now.*'

I got out and slammed the door shut. 'I'm meeting a friend across the way there in Sun Street. It's his car. He can explain. It's his car. It's not stolen.'

The constable ignored what I was saying. 'I've radioed for assistance. A car will be here shortly.'

'You've made a big mistake, you really have,' I said. The officer said nothing.

I lit a cigarette and leant against the bonnet. This is fucking amazing, it really is.

When I was halfway through the cigarette a new white Rover shot into the car park and screeched to a halt behind the Volvo. Four men got out and walked towards us. They looked like plainclothes CID officers and, indeed, they were. The older and more senior of them said to me, 'You're coming with us.' Then he pointed to a younger officer and added, 'Stay here with the PC until the pick-up truck arrives.'

'Yes, sir,' he replied.

'This way, please. And into the car,' the officer said to me. One of his officers held my arm. I was put into the back of the vehicle with an officer sitting either side of me.

The car sped forward through the car park and up Biggin Lane.

'There's been a dreadful mistake,' I said. 'I didn't steal the car. It belongs to an American called Georges Kurzian, I mean Schlesinger. That's his other name. I was parking it for him. We're going to have lunch in the Chinese restaurant on Sun Street. It's his car.'

None of the officers said a thing. All of them just stared ahead. No flicker of emotion passed over their faces.

'If you send someone to the Chinese restaurant he'll be there any moment now. He'll explain this to you. There's been a dreadful misunderstanding. I didn't steal the car.'

They said nothing.

I cannot fucking believe this! Just as I was getting to the bottom of this whole Dick-Oswald business this has to happen. Some dumb, stupid misunderstanding. Some dumb stupid cock-up. Some accident. A hand dealt by chance. Jesus fucking Christ.

'Look, what do I have to tell you guys to get you to understand me? Eh? What do I have to tell you? Answer me that!'

The officer on my left said coldly over a yawn, 'We've heard all these stories before. You'll have plenty of opportunity to make a statement later.'

'What statement? I don't have to make a statement. I've just been telling you the truth!'

Fuck this. I can't believe it!

Now, my best bet is that Kurzian turns up at the restaurant and waits for me and when I don't turn up he'll get suspicious and think I've made off with the Volvo, that I've stolen it. Then he'll get on to the police and they'll realise the mistake they've made and then I'll be released. Yeah, that's it. Right.

No, there's an easier way.

'What I'm telling you can be corroborated, and corroborated right now. This guy Kurzian owns ... no, he has an interest or something in The Leys on Shadwell Lane. The big place. He's got a security guy called Eric there keeping an eye on the place. He wears a blue uniform. If you go up there or call him he'll confirm to you what I'm saying. I left there about half an hour ago with him, Kurzian. Go up there. You'll find it's all true.'

The three monkeys said nothing.

Christ almighty! What a fucking disaster. What a total fucking disaster.

We now passed under the railway bridge towards Walsworth. This wasn't the way to Hitchin police station.

'The local nick's back there. Not up here! Where are we going?'

The driver cleared his throat and said, 'We're going to the Area Crime Squad in Letchworth.'

'What are we going there for?' I demanded.

Nobody said anything.

What was going on? Why would I be taken there just for stealing a fucking car? Area Crime Squads deal in serious crimes, not stupid bloody motoring nonsense.

There's been a million-dollar misunderstanding here all right. A real misunderstanding. But I'll get it cleared up, this misunderstanding. That's for sure.

[2]

I was interviewed by a couple of officers who seemed uninterested in what I had to say. I was charged with being in possession of a stolen vehicle and then sent down to the cells.

I just sat in that cell waiting for some officer to come in at any moment and say, 'Sorry, sir, there's been a complete misunderstanding! You're free to go. Can we offer you a lift back to Hitchin?' I really did. But that didn't happen.

I couldn't get hold of Laura but they allowed me access to a duty solicitor, a young guy, not very smart, suspicious and peering out from behind pebble glasses. I told him about Kurzian and the lift into Hitchin. Nothing else. None of the background. Nothing else. I just told him to contact Laura and tell her where I was. I'd leave the rest to her.

Just after 11 p.m. the cell door was opened and I was taken back up to the interview room. There were three officers present, the detective constable and detective sergeant from the earlier interview and a more senior officer called Abberline who was dressed in an expensive suit and a striped shirt with what looked like a regimental tie. His hair was grey and well cut. He had a pronounced suntan and looked a youngish mid-fifties.

I sat at the table opposite Abberline. The other two officers stood to Abberline's right near the tape recorder that was recording the interview.

'You are Christopher Cornwell of Fortess Road, Tufnell Park, London?' asked Abberline.

'Yes.'

'And you were arrested at 2.35 p.m. this afternoon, Saturday, 20 November 1993 in the car park at Biggin Lane, Hitchin, for being in possession of a stolen car, a Volvo Estate, registration number K942 EYN?'

'Yes, but I hadn't stolen it,' I replied.

Abberline wrote something in the yellow notepad he had on the table in front of him. I couldn't read what it was but the rest of the page was already filled with writing. I noticed he was wearing large gold cufflinks. He then looked up at me and said, 'What is your explanation for being in possession of this vehicle?'

'I've already told you … and the other officers. You know.'

Abberline said nothing, just looked at me. The silence was uncomfortable and, I realised, I'd have to repeat the story again.

'I met a friend, Georges Kurzian, early this afternoon at The Leys on Shadwell Lane. He's also known as Schlesinger, that's his other name. We drove into Hitchin to have lunch. Kurzian drove the car. He stopped by W H Smith's, on Bancroft, and said he had to pick up some things. We were going to have lunch and being as parking was difficult there he asked me to drive the Volvo round and park it behind the Sun, in the car park there. And then we'd meet in the Chinese restaurant on Sun Street. That's it.'

Abberline said nothing. He was just looking at me again, waiting for me to fill in the silence.

'I told your officers,' I continued, 'that if they went to the Chinese restaurant they'd meet Kurzian and he'd be able to explain this all to them. I also told them that if they went to The Leys on Shadwell Lane which Kurzian sort of owns they'd get confirmation there. From Kurzian himself or Eric, the security guard. Did they do that? And, anyway, I think you've got your wires crossed. Kurzian has got enough money not to need to steal cars. He wouldn't do that.'

'The vehicle was stolen from Lady Margaret Road, Tufnell Park, on the morning of Wednesday, 17 November

1993. Lady Margaret Road is only a couple of minutes' walk from your home. That is correct?'

'Yes,' I replied, 'but what's that to do with me? This is some bizarre coincidence or something.' I just began to think of the import of this 'coincidence' when Abberline hit me with another question.

'What was your reason for stealing the vehicle?'

'My reason? *My* reason? There wasn't one. I didn't steal it. I keep telling you that.'

Abberline stared at me and said slowly, 'Your fingerprints were found all over the vehicle.'

'Didn't you find any others?' I asked.

Abberline said nothing.

I then remembered Georges putting on those leather gloves. That's why they didn't find his dabs anywhere. 'Kurzian was wearing gloves – that's why you didn't find his.'

Abberline made some more notes and then said, 'Who is Mr Kurzian?'

'A friend … well, more an acquaintance actually.'

'Can you tell me something about him? How long have you known him?'

I had to keep quiet about Georges. I couldn't say anything more about him than I had to. If I dropped him in it now the chances of getting further information from him would vanish.

'Do you mind if I have a cigarette?' I asked.

Abberline shook his head. He didn't mind.

I lit a Marlboro.

'How long have you known Mr Kurzian?' Abberline said again.

'Not very long.'

'How well do you know him?'

'Not terribly well.'

'And you were going to have lunch together?'

'Yes.'

'Why?'

'We had some things to talk about.'

'Such as?'

'Areas of mutual interest you might say.'

Abberline scribbled something down again and then said, 'You stated that Mr Kurzian has property on Shadwell Lane?'

'Well, he's got an interest or something in The Leys. Yes.'

'How do you know this?'

'He told me.'

'What were you doing at The Leys?'

'I walked out there this morning.'

'Why? To see Mr Kurzian?'

'No … uh … yes.'

'You had an appointment with Mr Kurzian?'

'No.'

'But you went out there to see him?'

'Yes.'

'Knowing he would be there?'

'No.'

'Had you been there before?'

'No.'

'But you knew he would be there?'

'Yes … no.'

I looked across at the two officers leaning against the desk. One had his arms folded, the other had his hands in his pockets. They both had a smirky look of disbelief about them. They weren't buying anything I was saying. Abberline had made a note and was staring at me again. I couldn't read his face, but I was aware that my answers weren't coming up kosher in his reckoning.

'I know this all sounds a bit odd, but I'm telling you the truth,' I said.

Abberline tapped his fountain pen against his upper teeth and said, 'You say you walked up to The Leys. Where did you walk from?'

'From Tilehouse Street. I was staying with a friend. She's a solicitor.'

Abberline was waiting for me to say something more, but this time I thought that's it. Let him do the talking.

After what seemed a few minutes but in fact was only a few seconds Abberline asked another question. 'When did you arrive in Hitchin?'

'Last night.'

'Had you driven up from London?'

'No, Pinewood Studios, Iver Heath. I'd been working there all day … and I drove up in my car which is parked at the bottom of Park Street. Well, it's not my car. It's an Audi that was loaned to me by Thom, the producer I'm working for. Get your officers to check that out. They'll see it if they go down there.'

Abberline placed his fountain pen down on the table and made a motion to the two officers. One of them took from the table a large Jiffy envelope and handed it to him. Abberline gave it to me and said, 'Do you recognise this padded envelope? It was found on the back seat of the Volvo when you were arrested.'

I took it from him and said, 'I've never seen this before.'

'Very well,' said Abberline, 'I would now like you to take out the contents of this envelope.'

I reached in the Jiffy bag and withdrew a gusseted American legal folder with a flap and a ribbon tied in a bow securing it closed. I recognised it right away. It was the folder I carried around with my notes on the investigation into Dick and Oswald. The folder also contained the copies of the Oswald photographs taken in Hitchin. My name, address and phone number were in my handwriting on the front.

What was this file doing here? I'd put it under my bed at home about a week ago. I sat motionless as a chill wave of fear and anxiety swept over me. I was afraid to continue.

Abberline waited for me to do or say something. I couldn't. I was transfixed.

'Do you recognise the folder within the padded envelope?'

said Abberline. This time there was a menacing demand in his voice that had been absent before.

'Yes, I do,' I said. 'It's mine.'

'Would you now untie the folder and take out what you find inside?'

I pulled the pink ribbon and the bow disappeared. I opened the flap and took out the contents. Gone were my papers and notes. Instead there were photographs. 10 x 8 black-and-white glossies. Dozens and dozens of them.

'Do you recognise these photographs?' asked Abberline. His voice was cold and insistent.

The top photograph showed two girls aged about twelve or thirteen in school uniforms. They were kneeling in front of a naked man in a mask sitting on a sofa. His penis was large and erect. He looked like he was in his late thirties, tall and slim with a beard and neatly coiffured long hair. One of the girls was holding his balls. The other had the end of his penis in her mouth.

There were several copies of that photograph.

The next photograph showed the girls naked with the man entering one of them while she licked the other. There were several copies of that too.

A second man, again masked, appeared in subsequent photographs for foursome shots and the locale was switched from the sofa to a bedroom. The final pictures were taken in a bathroom – 'golden showers' and come shots.

There were six or so copies of each photograph.

This wasn't some amateur photographer but a professional who knew what he was doing. Each shot was properly lit and the framing was perfect.

The two young girls looked dazed and drugged. In some of the shots their faces were grimaced in pain.

There would never be anything sexually new for them to discover with boys their own age. They had it all, and some, in this single photographic session. A crash course in defilement.

Abberline carefully described each photograph and asked me whether I knew anything about it. Each time I answered No.

The subject of the photographs blinded me to something that now hit me like a 100 m.p.h. steam locomotive. My eyes had centred on the two young girls and the men and I hadn't realised that each and every one of the photographs had been taken in my flat. There was *my* sofa, there was *my* bedroom, there was *my* bathroom. Someone had broken in and taken these pictures there.

'Do you recognise these photographs?' Abberline asked again. His voice was harsh and unforgiving. He was coming in for the kill.

'No, I don't,' I said. 'I've never seen these before in my life.' And with that I pushed them back across the table.

Abberline continued staring at me as did the two officers.

'Is there anything else you would like to say about these photographs?'

I realised now that I'd been set up. Georges had plucked, parcelled and trussed me up like a Christmas turkey for the police. I'd been given to them on a plate. Georges' planning and preparation were faultless.

'I've been set up,' I said.

Abberline made a further note and asked, almost desultorily, 'And who would have done that, sir?'

'By Kurzian. Georges Kurzian. He's set me up.'

'A man who, on your own admittance, you hardly know. He wants to set you up?'

'Yes. I know it sounds crazy, but it's true.'

'Why?'

'Because I discovered something about Lee Harvey Oswald, that's why!'

Abberline, I could tell, recognised the name but didn't seem to be able to place it.

'Oswald,' I said, 'was the man who was supposed to have assassinated President Kennedy. In 1963.'

A smile broke over Abberline's face. He'd known all along who Oswald was. He'd just wanted me to say it.

'Look,' I continued, 'Kurzian is some sort of freelance for some intelligence agency. Probably American. This agency had a place here in Hitchin right after the war and up until the late 1960s. Oswald was here, in Hitchin, when he was supposed to be in Russia. He was here for some of the time anyway. My friend Dick North found out about this and they killed him. I started investigating Dick's death and I got these photographs showing Oswald here, in Hitchin, when he should have been in Russia. He was in Russia but not all the time the Warren Commission said he was. Kurzian seems to have been employed to get these photographs back. He or somebody connected with him murdered my friend and he's set me up. Don't you see?'

There was silence. Abberline and the two officers betrayed not a trace of emotion.

'Listen, I'm not bullshitting you. This is the truth. And I've got the photographs to prove it. They're in a security deposit box in London. I can get them and prove this to you.'

Abberline looked at me and pointed to the photographs on the table. 'Do you recognise where these photographs were taken?'

'Yes. They were taken in my flat in Tufnell Park.'

'You did not mention that before. Why was that?'

'There didn't seem any point then,' I said, and even before the words were out of my mouth I regretted phrasing it that way.

Abberline jumped on my remark, 'There didn't seem any point *then*?'

'I didn't mean to say that. I was confused. I was going to mention it.' I was in a hole and I was digging myself deeper.

'Can you explain how these photographs came to be taken in your flat?'

'No, I can't. Someone broke in and took them there. That's what happened.'

'So your flat was broken into for these photographs? Did you report the break-in to the local police?'

'No, because I didn't know the place was broken into. Until *now*.'

'So,' said Abberline in a quieter voice as he gazed at the ceiling, 'someone broke into your flat without leaving any evidence whatsoever that they had done so. There were no broken windows or forced doors. No sign whatsoever?'

'Well, there was a break-in and they ransacked the place and I did report it to the local police.'

'You just said you didn't know your place was broken into, did you not?'

'Look,' I said, 'there was a break-in when they ransacked the place but they were looking for something then. This is obviously another break-in ... just to take the photos ... I think ... I don't know.'

'Mmmmm,' murmured Abberline with a look of disbelief.

I wasn't explaining things too well.

Abberline wanted to know if I thought it was the same people both times. I said I didn't know but they were probably connected in some way.

The detective filled half a page with notes.

'How then,' Abberline mused (and mused was the right word) as he looked up, 'do you suppose they gained admittance?'

'For Chrissakes, I don't know. A key? Perhaps they had a key?'

'And how would they have obtained that?'

'I don't know.'

'So, to sum up: what you are saying, Mr Cornwell, is that the photographs were taken in your flat but without your knowledge? That someone illegally obtained entry, took the photographs, and left without leaving any trace that they were there? And that the first you knew of this was now? Is that correct?'

It sounded unbelievable but I had to say 'Yes.'

'Right.'

Abberline pointed to a folder on the desk behind the two officers. The officer nearest Abberline passed it to him. Abberline took out several A4 sheets that were stapled together in the corner and handed them to me. 'Do you recognise this list of names and addresses?'

There were about six or seven names and addresses on each sheet. None of the names did I recognise. The bulk of the addresses were in London and the south-east but there were others from all over England: Norwich, Birmingham, Manchester, Carlisle, and even several in Scotland.

'These mean nothing to me,' I said. 'Nothing at all. Who are they?'

'Members of a paedophile ring, sir. And I suppose you were not aware of that?'

'No, I wasn't. I'm not a paedophile and I've never had anything to do with child porn.'

'Uh-huh. Do you own a manual Adler typewriter?' Abberline said.

'Yes. How do you know?'

'We believe these names and addresses were typed on that Adler machine and we're asking the forensic lab to check that.'

'How do you know I own an Adler?' I demanded.

'Because,' said Abberline, 'a search warrant was executed on your flat this evening, and that's where this list of names and addresses was found.'

They'd turned over my flat without telling me! They'd gone down to Tufnell Park and gone through all my stuff! 'What gives you the right to do that without telling me!'

Abberline smiled and said quietly, 'A search warrant from a magistrate, sir. That's what gives us the right.'

'The tapes, Michael, please,' said Abberline to one of the officers.

The officer on the right said, 'Yes, sir,' and left the room. The other officer just stared at me while Abberline continued making notes. I lit another cigarette.

A few moments later the officer returned with a large

cardboard box. 'On the table, please,' said Abberline.

The officer placed the box on the floor and started taking video cassettes from it which he placed on the table. I recognised them as the cassettes from the shelf behind my TV. They were the video cassettes that I used for recording TV programmes and films. On the edge of each, on labels, I had written in black spirit marker whatever it was I'd recorded.

Abberline said, 'These video cassettes were taken from your apartment this evening. Do you recognise them?'

'Yes,' I said.

'Is that your handwriting on each of them?'

'Yes, it is.'

'Good. Now do you recognise these two?'

Abberline reached into the box and took out two cassettes that were each in one of those clear polythene evidence bags with zippers. I looked at them. They were mine.

'Those are mine too.'

'What does it say on the label of each?'

'This one says *Throne of Blood* and that says *The Blue Lamp*.'

'What do these tapes contain?' Abberline said, still dangling them in the air in front of me.

'Well, I'd have thought that would be obvious. One's got the Kurosawa film, *Throne of Blood*, and the other's got Jack Warner in *The Blue Lamp*.'

'They contain nothing else?'

'No. That's it.'

'Mr Cornwell, both tapes contain the opening ten minutes of the two films you mention, but after that there are a couple of hours of child porn on each. Can you explain how they got there?'

'No, I can't. Well, yes I can. If what you say is true, that there's child porn on them, then the same people who got into my flat, Kurzian and whoever, also did this to my tapes. I don't know anything about them. I've had a couple of adult porno tapes over the years, but never child stuff.'

'Is there any child porn on the tapes we haven't yet examined, Mr Cornwell?'

'I don't know. They're just tapes with films and TV programmes on them as far as I am concerned. Nothing else. I promise you. What do you think I'm doing with all this stuff, eh?'

'The evidence seems to point to you producing and distributing child pornography, but we have yet to prove that. At the very least, mere possession of child pornography carries a maximum sentence of five years. It is in your own interests to co-operate with us.'

'I am co-operating with you. I don't know anything about it. I've told you, this is a set-up. I'm innocent. Totally. Absolutely.'

Abberline was about to say something when there was a knock on the interview room door. Michael opened it and exchanged a few words with a plainclothes officer. He then went over to Abberline and whispered something in his ear. Abberline listened and then announced for the benefit of the tape recorder, 'It is now 11.45 p.m. and the interview with Christopher Cornwell will be resumed after a short break.' The other officer switched the machine off and Abberline left the room without saying a word to me or the other officers. He pulled the door shut with some force. Then there was silence. I lit another cigarette. The two officers were saying nothing.

'Any chance of a cup of coffee?' I asked.

The two officers looked at each other and Michael said, 'I could do with one myself. What about you, Ron?' Ron nodded in agreement.

Michael picked up the telephone on the desk behind him and it was answered without him dialling. 'Herbert? Yeah. What are the chances of three coffees? Good. Thanks.'

I continued smoking and saying nothing. There had to be a way out of this set-up, but what it was God alone knows. The evidence, on the face of it, looks overwhelming, but surely somebody must see that it is too overwhelming? It's all too neat and tied-up.

What's going to happen next? Should I ask the two officers who are still staring at me? Or what?

I'll just have to sweat this out for the time being.

I stubbed the cigarette out and closed my eyes. I heard Mike's voice say, 'You're only making it more difficult for yourself, you know?'

I opened my eyes. Michael was staring at me. And Ron was too.

'How do you work that out?' I said.

'By not co-operating with the old man. By denying it all,' Michael replied in a sneery voice.

'Do you expect me to admit to something I'm not guilty of, eh? Do you expect me to say Yes when the answer is No?'

Michael shifted his position against the desk. 'We've got a strong case against you for possession. In fact, it's open and shut. You'll be charged with that and held on remand pending our inquiries. There could be more serious charges … depending on what we uncover. *And* we mustn't forget the stolen car.'

I was trying to think what could be more serious than possession if that carries a maximum of five years? A couple more years for alleged producing and distributing? Shit, I wouldn't get a sentence like that for murder, would I? Certainly not for manslaughter.

And what are they going to uncover? At this rate they could uncover anything. What else has been set up out there for them to find? Jesus, I'm going to be lucky ever to get out of prison alive.

'We checked out The Leys, you know.'

They checked out The Leys! And what about Eric? 'What did you find out then? Did you speak to Eric?'

'It's owned by a property company in Mayfair. They've never heard of your friend Kurzian and they don't have a resident security guard. You sent us on a wild goose chase, you did.'

[334]

'You're just saying that. I'll get my solicitor to check it out. She'll come up with something, don't you worry. And the place isn't owned by a property company, some intelligence service owns it. OK?'

'Be our guest.'

'I will.'

'The more you deny it the deeper you'll get yourself in. I'm telling you.'

I ignored what he said and lit another cigarette. My last one.

An elderly officer brought in three coffees on a tray. I took my cup, thanked him, and sipped it. I wouldn't have known it was coffee had I not been told. It was the sort of coffee you got in a railway buffet back in the 1950s – milk with some ersatz flavouring. It was awful.

There was a question I wanted to put to the police again. I'd already asked several of them earlier but I'd been brushed off with noncommittal or evasive answers. I thought I'd try it on these two. 'How come I was arrested?'

'What do you mean?' said Ron.

'Let me put it another way. The officer who arrested me in the car park was there waiting for me, wasn't he?'

Michael and Ron looked at each other and then back at me. Michael said, 'It was an anonymous tip-off.'

'Anonymous, eh?' I said sceptically.

'Yeah, it was actually,' said Ron. 'We didn't know the strength of it so a young PC with nothing else to do was sent down there. *If* we'd known the strength of it, *if* it had come from a known informant, we'd have gone down there mob-handed.'

I felt he was telling me the truth. 'Thanks,' I said, 'but don't you realise that this was the guy who set me up?'

They said nothing.

'You've no idea who it might have been?' I said.

'Somebody in your circle you've fallen out with?' suggested Ron.

'I'm not in any circle,' I snapped back.

[335]

Michael sneered and said, 'Crooks are always falling out with each other. We get our best tip-offs that way, don't we Ron?' Ron nodded in agreement.

A few minutes later Abberline walked back in and sat down. Michael turned the tape recorder on and Abberline spoke in to the microphone again. '11.58 p.m. Saturday, 20 November 1993. Resumption of interview with Christopher Cornwell of Fortess Road, Tufnell Park, London.'

Abberline placed a large black plastic folder on the table and tapped it with his pen as he looked at me. 'When your flat was searched this evening my officers discovered keys to a security deposit box.'

These were the keys to Centaur Security in St James' where I stored the originals of the Oswald photos. Had they gone down there and retrieved the pictures?

'Do you recognise these keys?' said Abberline as he held the keys in front of me in another of those zippered evidence bags. This one was not much bigger than the keys themselves.

'Yes, I do.'

'What do these keys relate to?' asked Abberline.

I thought that was an odd way to phrase it. I said, 'They are for a security deposit box at Centaur Security in London.'

'Which you started to rent earlier this year?'

'Correct.'

'When exactly?'

'August.'

'What does the security box contain?'

'Photographs that will prove that I was set up. There are photographs there of Lee Harvey Oswald in Hitchin when he should have been in Russia. The originals. Originals which my friend Dick was killed for.'

Abberline opened the black folder and produced from it the 10 x 8 stiff-backed manilla envelope I had placed in the box some three months ago. He handed it to me.

'Do you recognise this envelope?'

'Yes, I do. It is the envelope from the deposit box.'

I looked at the envelope carefully: the 3M Magic Mending Tape over the flap, along the sides and along the end. My signature here and there written across the tape with a black spirit marker. There on the front in my handwriting was:

Christopher Cornwell
LEGAL TRUST DOCUMENTS/August 1993

Nobody had touched or tampered with the envelope. The tape and my signatures were undisturbed. This was my 'Get Out of Jail Free' card.

'And you placed this envelope yourself in the deposit box?'

'Yes, I did.'

'And not someone else?'

'No.'

'And nobody else has had access to this box?'

'Right.'

'Has the envelope been opened since you placed it there?' said Abberline, who was now staring at the envelope and not at me.

'No, it hasn't.'

'You are quite satisfied as to that?'

'Yes,' I said confidently. 'If I can open this now I'll prove to you that what I've been saying is true.'

'Please open it then,' said Abberline.

[3]

I'm alone in the cell now and I can't sleep. I'm tired and aching and exhausted, yet sleep eludes me. There's too much running through my mind. Unanswered questions, what-ifs, anxieties. And when I close my eyes it gets worse. Goblins, sprites and devils leap out of the darkness and taunt me. The whole JFK demonology is waiting for me in there.

[337]

I keep thinking of all those deaths associated with the Kennedy assassination, all those mysterious deaths that have taken place in the wake of what happened in Dealey Plaza exactly thirty years ago tomorrow. Those convenient deaths of witnesses, of those on the periphery, and of those with some inside track. There have been gunshot victims, those who have had their throat cut or been killed by an unknown karate assailant while taking a shower, those who have died as a result of hit-and-run car accidents, in plane crashes, from drug overdoses, axe wounds to the head, electrocution, and so on. Others too have been shot at and intimidated in other ways. Others have simply disappeared.

But what about those who have been compromised and discredited? How many more have gone before me? Who is going to prepare a roster of *us*?

What was that headline and article I read in *The Independent* at the beginning of the year on my way up to Hitchin? Something about a cocaine dealer claiming he was fitted up because he had proof that Thatcher's government was involved in some corrupt overseas aid deal? Yeah. Perhaps he did? But who is going to believe the word of a coke dealer facing a heavy sentence?

I didn't.

And who is going to believe me when this is over, even in the unlikely event that I am found innocent? Who? No one, that's who. I'll just be another con with a story to tell, that's all. And at the same time Laura's translated to being a kiddie-porn dealer's moll. It's that simple.

While I was opening the 10 x 8 manilla envelope in front of Abberline I still believed that the Oswald photographs would be there. I really did. But, of course, they were long gone. Somehow the envelope had been opened, the photos taken out, the negatives of those photos taken in my flat put in, and the envelope sealed without me being able to detect it. I guess that's an easy enough task for the people who murdered Kennedy. The sort of trick they can do before breakfast. Easy. No sweat.

The negs were the clincher to the police. I wasn't just a consumer of kiddie porn, I was also a producer and a distributor. I'd gone into business doing it. I wasn't just corrupting juveniles, I was also making money out of it. That's the sort of guy I am. I made the mistake of thinking that the Kennedy assassination was a one-off event. Some never-to-be-repeated aberrant incident. It wasn't. It was just another day in the life of a secret system none of us know anything about: a system that can assassinate the President of the United States and get away with it and continue getting away with it, and follow it up years later in another country too. It's that powerful. And if someone says I'm talking nonsense, I'll ask them this fuse-blowing question: if the legal government of the United States is so strong and powerful, how come they've never ever found out who murdered Jack Kennedy, their 35th President? Why are the men responsible for it still walking free?

If you can't answer that – keep your mouth shut.

It's already Sunday, 21 November 1993. And tomorrow will be the thirtieth anniversary of the assassination of President John F. Kennedy.

Soon the sun will be rising and I'll be taken from the cell and questioned again and again and again.

How did I end up here without doing anything other than asking a few questions? I should have followed Ken Kesey's advice to Paul Krassner: Always stay in your own movie. Not even Laura is going to be able to get me out of this mess.

I can't think of a way out, of what to do, but I'm sure if I had a bottle of Smirnoff Blue Label in front of me I'd come up with something. I'm sure I would. Really … I would. *You* know that.

A MYSTERY TO US

'Identify.'
   'Bellerophon … 666B.'
   'Location?'
   'North Hertfordshire.'
   'Proceed.'
   'SUSURRUS completed. Full shut-down.'
   'Recorded.'
   'I am ready to come in now.'
   'Proceed to railway station for 2100 Zulu rendez-vous.'

FROM: *The Hitchin Free Mercury*, Thursday, 25 November, 1993:

MYSTERY STATION DEATH: POLICE BAFFLED

Local police are baffled as to the identity of a man whose body was found on the tracks at Hitchin station last Saturday. The body appears to have been run over by a train.

The man was well dressed and was probably in his early sixties. He had longish dark hair and a Vandyke beard. He was wearing a black suit and a matching cape. His wallet contained over £1500 in cash and several forged documents in the name of 'George Hidell'.

The body was discovered a little after 9 p.m. by Network South East employee Roy Pilgrim (32) of Willian Road, Hitchin, who was inspecting the track.

Said Roy, 'I first thought it was some bags or something that had been blown on the track, but when I realised what it was I was gob-smacked.'

Roy was later treated for shock at Hitchin hospital.

Det-Insp. Stiles of Hitchin who is leading the investigation said the police have not ruled out foul play, but they have little to go on. He is appealing for any witnesses to come forward.

Det-Insp. Stiles said, 'We have drawn a blank on this man's identification, including fingerprints. None of his clothes had any labels either. He is a mystery to us.'

DID YOU SEE THIS MAN? See artist's impression and call the MERCURY HOT LINE now.

APPENDIX

THE CAMBRIDGE CALL

He may even have been responsible for the Cambridge phone call.
Thus says Georges when talking about Drax to Christopher
in the upstairs room at The Leys.

Christopher did not appear to pick up the reference, but
if he did, subsequent events would prevent him from ever
quizzing Georges about it.

The first public knowledge of the 'Cambridge phone call'
came when a CIA telegram sent from London to Washington
on 23 November 1963 was released under the Freedom of
Information Act in 1976.

The telegram as declassified by the CIA reads, with con-
jectural restoration of deleted matter in brackets, as follows:

1. [DELETED]
2. EXPRESSIONS OF SORROW AND SYMPATHY RECEIVED FROM
TOP COMMAND [BRITISH GOVERNMENT] AS WELL AS WORKING
LEVEL. EFFECT IN U.K. IS ONE OF PROFOUND SHOCK AND PUBLIC
REACTION HERE SIMILAR TO DEATH FRANKLIN ROOSEVELT.
3. DUE TO BACKGROUND MAN CHARGED WITH ASSASSINATION,
[BRITISH] REPORTED MORNING 23 NOV FOLLOWING DUE SOME
SIMILAR PHONE CALLS OF STRANGELY COINCIDENTAL NATURE
PERSONS RECEIVED IN THIS COUNTRY OVER PAST YEAR,
PARTICULARLY IN CONNECTION WITH DR WARD CASE.
[BRITISH] REPORTED THAT AT 1805GMT 22 NOV AN ANONYMOUS
CALL WAS MADE IN CAMBRIDGE, ENGLAND TO THE SENIOR
REPORTER OF THE CAMBRIDGE NEWS RPT CAMBRIDGE NEWS.
THE CALLER SAID ONLY THAT THE REPORTER SHOULD CALL
THE AMERICAN EMBASSY IN LONDON FOR SOME BIG NEWS AND

THEN RANG OFF. LAST NIGHT AFTER WORD OF THE PRESIDENT'S DEATH WAS RECEIVED THE REPORTER INFORMED THE CAMBRIDGE POLICE OF THE ABOVE CALL AND THE POLICE INFORMED [SECURITY SERVICES]. IMPORTANT THING IS THAT CALL WAS MADE ACCORDING [BRITISH] CALCULATIONS ABOUT TWENTY FIVE MINUTES BEFORE PRESIDENT WAS SHOT. CAMBRIDGE REPORTER HAD NEVER RECEIVED CALL OF THIS KIND BEFORE AND [SECURITY SERVICES] SAY HE IS KNOWN TO THEM AS SOUND AND LOYAL PERSON WITH NO SECURITY RECORD. [SECURITY SERVICES] WANTED ABOVE REPORTED PARTICULARLY IN VIEW REPORTED SOV[IET] BACKGROUND OSWALD. DEPENDING ON CIRCUMSTANCES, HQS MAY WISH PASS ABOVE TO [FBI] AS [BRITISH] COULD NOT REACH [FBI] THIS MORNING. [BRITISH] STAND READY ASSIST IN ANY WAY POSSIBLE ON INVESTIGATIONS HERE.

Several writers have claimed they know who made the call but no evidence has been adduced to support their nominations. Drax was cleared of making the call by his agency and it seems highly unlikely that Alfie Lawson was responsible. So who does that leave? Who else is out there?

[NOTE: The telegram was first reproduced in Michael Eddowes' *The Oswald File* (New York: Clarkson N. Potter, 1977), p. 228. Eddowes notes the reference to Dr (Stephen) Ward, the osteopath at the heart of the Profumo Affair, who had committed suicide some four months prior to JFK's assassination. Several writers have suggested that there was a connection between Ward and JFK, as did Eddowes, and who can yet say?]

A NOTE ON THE TYPEFACE

This book was composed in PALATINO *– a face designed originally by Herman Zapf for the German typefounders Stempel in 1950. The roman has broad letters and strong, inclined serifs. The italic has a lightness and grace that reflects its calligraphic origins.*